THE
HEART
OF A CHILD

A Novel

By Patti Brady

Patti Brady

WWW.GRACENOVELS.COM

PERIDOT PUBLISHING LLC

Peridot Publishing LLC
12195 Highway 92
Suite 114 – 218
Woodstock, Georgia 30188

REDEEMER
Nicole C. Mullen
© 2000 Lil' Jas' Music (Admin. by Wordspring Music, LLC), Wordspring Music, LLC.
All rights reserved. Used By Permission.

This book is a work of fiction. The events in this novel are imaginary. All characters and dialogue are entirely fictional and not intended to represent any person living or dead.

ISBN-13: 978-0-9790669-0-0
ISBN-10: 0-9790669-0-5

Dedication

This book is dedicated to the real citizens of Woodstock, Georgia, past and present, an array of intelligent, hard-working folks, among which, so many are competent, caring, and kind. They are a big reason more than a few newcomers, myself included although no longer new, have been drawn to live among them in the last two and a half decades of extraordinary regional growth.

Acknowledgments

From you, I gained a harvest of knowledge. Your encouragement and support were a treasure. You made a big difference in my work. Thank you.

Manuscript medical consultant - Gayle Brackin

Writing advisor - Juanita Hughes, columnist for *The Cherokee Tribune*, author, *But What Do I Know?*, hostess for Woodstock Visitors Center at Dean's Store, former head librarian at Woodstock Library

Website consultant - Samantha Hunnius, web and print design

Writing consultant - Bobbie Christmas, author, *Write in Style* and *Purge Your Prose of Problems* (Zebra Communications)

Self-publishing consultant - Carolyn Porter (Empower Productions)

Cover design - Matt Pramschufer (e-moxie.com)

Book designer - Jonathan Gullery (selfpublishing.com)

Printing - Ron Pramschufer (selfpublishing.com)

Most importantly, I thank my family. You listened, you guided me, and you gave me time.

CHAPTER ONE

H E WAS A YOUNG man, too young to be so well acquainted with sorrow. According to the world, his background afforded him everything. In his own estimation, he possessed nothing of value. His future stood on shifting sand, ready to topple like the mighty, metal horse on the beachfront estate he knew in childhood. Meanwhile, a single factor kept him alive—a job of backbreaking labor held off his demise.

His boss flung the door open and tromped inside the empty construction office. Hank followed. The door smacked shut. At the desk, they stood opposite one another, almost toe to toe, their thick soles encrusted with clay. The tan face of his boss heightened in color and spilled a torrent of words.

"I've had it up to here, Hank. You've been missing for days, and it's one in the afternoon. Why bother to show up, now?" said Phil Arnett.

Hank took a step back from the blast and said nothing.

"Did you take off or have you been somewhere in a drunken stupor?"

Hank shook his head.

"Screwy, plain screwy," said Arnett. "When you're here, you do the work of three men, but what good is it if I'm never certain you'll get out of bed on any given morning?"

Hank shrugged, and his eyelids came down briefly.

"And that unexpected temper of yours. It'll get you in trouble one of these days." Arnett took off a baseball cap and tossed it next to a grimy, black phone. Dust and rumpled documents blanketed the desk. He plopped in his office chair and picked up a walkie-talkie, ready to give another order to one of the supervisors outside. He hesitated, still focused on Hank. "Back in March, you swore you'd go insane without this job."

"I meant it."

"Well, this is your *last warning*," Arnett said, reaching over, swiping the keys to the front-end loader from Hank's hand. "An absence of five minutes or a single mess up, and you're out of here."

Another pause ensued as Hank looked down at the pale green linoleum scratched and dull from dirt tracked in each day. His fingers made two passes through his sun-streaked hair.

"*Typical*," said Arnett, who flipped a pencil across the room, swatting the master plans that sat on a tall easel. "Not one word to reassure me. Well, let's see if you can pick up the spec changes from Bennington at the Douglasville site. The fax is on the blink, and I've got to have them by four thirty. *So hustle.*"

Hank eyed the distinct hands of the office clock and took off.

Nearing the end of his trip, he zipped along I-575, heading north. The burning sun had trekked far across the afternoon sky. Bright with summer intensity, the flat canvas above brandished a blue so shrill it was almost white. Truck windows down, hot air swirled around the cab, buffeting his face.

Traffic had been rough. His boss waited. Hank looked up from the interstate into the rearview mirror of his Ford 150. Half a mile behind, the patrol car he'd been keeping tabs on moved up the line of cars, toward him.

His stomach churned. Getting pulled over—an event almost as unwelcome as his father on the phone, debonair and disgusting. Like early that morning. A phone could be slammed down, though. Dodging the cops was altogether different.

Hank re-checked the reflection. No change. The speedometer bobbed at sixty. Of all the drivers, why him?

Irritation traveled down his arms and into his strong hands tightening around the steering wheel. An urge to give the accelerator full pressure fluttered by. A wry chuckle came from his throat. Why not obliterate himself with the next concrete pylon? An amazing mixture—water, sand, gravel, and Portland cement—he spent his days framing and pouring or sometimes breaking and hauling that heartless substance capable of exerting a will of its own. Years ago, hadn't Carl's overbearing boss been crushed on the job? The "rogue" wall flattened the skinny guy to ten times as wide. Well, that was Carl's story.

Hank shook off the bizarre image. Up ahead, the first Woodstock exit drew his old truck like one of those huge junkyard magnets. He just might slip away from his pursuer in the nick of time.

His sight went back to the mirror. The patrol car gunned its engine, closing the gap. The vehicle swerved masterfully from the fast lane to take its place behind the truck. The flashing, blue light came on. Hank's brows drew together and locked downward. A word exploded from his mouth. He pressed the clutch and ruthlessly jammed the stick down into third, making the truck shudder. The golf putter serving as a paperweight tumbled forward. The documents that had been his mission flew up and around the cab. With one hand, he made desperate grabs. Air streams sucked sheets out the window where they did riotous somersaults and rained on dashing automobiles. A few pages, plastered to windshields of faster cars, moved past his hanging mouth. He downshifted twice more, yanked the wheel to the right, and stomped on the brake. The truck lurched to a stop in the northbound emergency lane, just short of the exit.

He grappled with the remaining papers, trying to return order, until he gave up and slapped the putter on top. Sick with fury, the muscles in his thighs and calves quivered. The sweltering sun forced his blood to race, and his teeth ground each other like unmeshed gears. Wasn't he supposed to remain in the truck? Well, he'd rather be blasted to hell than roasted in the cab. He jerked the door open and stepped out, silently demanding a breeze. The truck gave a little as he leaned his hefty frame against it. His breaths came fast, and a deep frown presented itself. The officer sat in the patrol car doing a license plate check.

Minutes passed. Hank opened and closed his right hand, slow and unceasing, imagining the pleasure of squeezing someone's features until their flesh ran. The humidity and droning cicadas increased the pounding in his head, so he scanned the area for distraction. Fifty yards ahead, a young woman on the southbound side, stood too close to the interstate. A little boy, arms flailing, struggled in her hold.

The surly look around Hank's eyes and mouth faded. He moved off the truck and stood tall. The girl's head turned slowly as though she surveyed her surroundings. Her movements were unsteady. Menacing forms of steel and glass rose over the horizon and tore by. The wakes of exhaust-filled air whipped around the girl, wringing her clothes and hair. The child batted her collarbones. The boy's head, topped with black hair, shook back and forth with turbulent negativity. Hank's eyes narrowed with tension as the child wiggled downward and slipped to the ground. The boy ran in a circle around the woman. She grabbed him and dashed from the roadway.

Their unseen observer leaned back against his truck and its chipping, powder-blue paint. His observations of the woman continued, despite the distance. Delicate proportions. Lightly tanned skin. Dark brown hair like a ruffled satin curtain played around her shoulders. A white blouse covered her frame and a navy gathered skirt ended at the bottom of her knees—a look vaguely old-fashioned.

Like an annoying commercial, the patrolman approached. Hank served up his license and papers. The officer took the items and backtracked to his patrol car. Hank's gaze returned to the unusual vignette.

Rush hour had begun. An overpass and its wide opening below intersected the space between him and the young mother trying to calm her child. Traffic noise drowned the furious cries of the toddler. Hank saw the little boy's legs thrash and kick off sneakers. The woman sought their landing places and strained to gather each shoe while she clung to her squirming bundle. She succeeded, and Hank's face softened. Farther away from the road, she sat down with the boy in her lap and returned the shoes to his feet. His crying tapered. It appeared she spoke to him, lightly kissing his face and wiping away the path of his tears.

The southbound cars and trucks slowed. Coming to a standstill, they crowded end to end. Hank walked a short distance, looking to the left and right. A collision up ahead, he figured. The mother and child were hidden from his sight. He turned back, his goal to check the time on the cheap clock attached to the truck dash with Velcro.

His steps hastened; the officer strolled around the vehicle. Hank reached the spot at the same time a wasp swooped in wearing its burnt orange color like a banner of intent to put a few drops of fire into something. Waving it away, Hank bent toward his human adversary who crouched and examined the bald tread of a rear tire.

"Hey, could you speed it up? If you have to give me a ticket, that's fine, but I've got to get back to work or the boss will have my head." The officer turned his attention toward Hank. Other than adamant, unblinking eyes, he gave no regard to the question and went back to work, moving in slow, procedural style. Hank mumbled and glanced at the muffler held up with a coat hanger. He rose.

A zealously hot sensation seized the skin on Hank's forearm. Harsh words charged from his mouth.

The officer glanced up and stood. "Got somethin' to say to me?"

"*No, sir.*" Exhaled air shot from his nostrils. His hand curled into a fist and released. He broke off the movement and shoved the hand into his jeans pocket.

The officer wrote on his pad and moved to the front tires. The wasp still hung around. When it seemed ready to fly merrily away, one of Hank's firm limbs drew back and knocked the insect maybe all the way to Marietta.

The heat dried out his throat and encouraged the sweat trickling down his chest. He rubbed his hurting flesh and remembered. An open beer lay hidden in a compartment under the seat.

Imbibing was useful on those days when the debates he had with himself weren't successful in quelling the thoughts trying to crack open his skull. Lately, his low condition had grown worse, except for those rare moments of release when Earth's beauty hit his brain like a stiff drink.

He knew the song of summer that year; he could have written the lyrics. Dried out grasses and random roadkill lined the roads, but regal blue herons, searching the creek waters, slow and graceful like dancers on pointe, elevated the scenery from common to sublime. That August, the sidewalks were so hot the surface could singe a child's bare feet on the way to the mailbox, but the scent of phlox and gardenia, emanating from the yards of the older homes on and near Main Street, drifted in luxurious, meandering paths as dusk pirouetted in, scattering the heat.

Full of contradiction and mystery, the season was like no other he had known. Despite the natural elegance that called from every direction, he had reached the limit of his strength, and despair often flooded his thinking. With August, a familiar impasse returned. The first day of the month, platinum cufflinks and Hank's twenty-fourth birthday arrived. One week of bitter hours drained since then.

On his better days, he killed every ounce of wrath while on his job. Yet at the end of the day when he returned to his darkened rooms, he was certain of only one thing—utter defeat held seductive power.

The patrolman continued his stem-to-stern inspection. Hank fidgeted until the waves of heat from the roadway coaxed his vision to the scenery beyond the traffic corridor. Tulip poplars and sycamores reached upward. Leaves of the sweet gums fluttered and shimmered in the heat-driven updrafts. With that image softening the stinging on his arm, he leaned against the truck and let his eyes glaze over.

The interstate drivers, who might have contemplated the roughened man and his battered transportation, would be shocked to know of his wildly opulent heritage. Most people dismissed Henry Hartford Averill as simply another laborer in the building boom north of Atlanta. Work clothes, a three-day growth of beard, and a tad too much girth hid noble features and a powerful frame.

As it was, his appearance also disguised his tender conscience and immense intellect so thoroughly he was like the rusted out Chevy lying upside down in Little River ravine, near the Highway 140 bridge and county line. Only heaven knew the unsightly wreckage concealed Confederate gold, beneath a thick layer of silt.

The officer finished another round of communications on his car radio and returned to the truck. Hank answered his questions in a cooperative manner, but the arteries still surged in his neck, and the muscles in his upper back pulled taut as he waited for the officer's request to search the cab. Instead, Hank watched him write down infractions—burned out taillight, expired tag.

Traffic in the opposite lanes moved again. The officer droned on about vehicle safety while Hank's line of sight drifted to the spot where the two travelers had been. The woman carried the child as she climbed straight up the grassy slope to reach the exit ramp. Normally, pedestrians along the interstate grabbed the authorities' attention—like Uncle Rakey had, on the Sixes overpass where he tried to catch fish that swam in the empty space below.

Lucky lady. Maybe this patrolman was blind.

The patrolman wound up his lecture. Hank's eyebrows jumped with alarm. He thrust his head in the cab, zeroed on the clock, and winced. Lest he forget, his sight shifted to the jumble of decimated papers on the seat. All the refinement of his past evaporated. His lips pulled tight against his teeth. He backed out of the cab and released a growl. Like a pile driver, his broad palm butted the door frame, sending that side of the truck inches off the ground.

CHAPTER TWO

EARLIER, THE MORNING OF the same day, the young woman and her child traveled down from Knoxville with ten other Mexicans in a weathered van. She had traded their suitcase and the clothes inside for fare. The man also took her tooled leather shoulder purse but let her keep the hairbrush, soap, toothbrushes, and a few other items that she tied in the center of a kerchief. He tossed the nametag labeled Elizabeth Gutierrez into her hand.

The trip ended in Dalton, Georgia, leaving the mother and son, half an hour past one, at a diner near the freeway. Patrons of the roadside haven quickened their step in that direction. The smells of hickory smoked bacon, buttery fried eggs, and sizzling burgers greeted everyone. Elizabeth let the other people pass. The boy stood beside her. She pulled a small money purse from the kerchief. Her fingers sifted inside the leather bag. A dollar bill and eight cents.

In the restroom of the diner, the child positioned his toy, a stuffed lion, on the sink counter. They lavished their faces and hands under the cool faucet. The boy laughed as his mother cranked out a paper towel. They exited and found a booth with a view toward town.

The middle-aged waitress, on whom nothing was ever lost, brought them water and took the brief order. She returned with the glass of milk and offered a large handful of cellophane-wrapped crackers normally intended for purchasers of the Chicken Velvet Soup. The shoulders of the mother lifted, and her voice carried a lilt when she spoke her appreciation.

Cool air poured from the vent above. Elizabeth looked through the plate glass window at Dalton and the blazing hot outdoors. Her stomach growled. She spied the corner of a cracker still in the package, emptied the cellophane on her fingertips, and put the salty crumb on her tongue. A bank of clouds slid by. She placed her elbows on the smooth tabletop and rested her chin in the palms of her finely formed hands. In the country of *Norte Americanos* only three days, mother and child had moved quietly and unaccosted through public places and alien settings.

The clouds moved on, letting the sun appear full force again. It streamed through the tinted glass, highlighting the young woman's presence as she stared at the rooflines of the industrial area just beyond the rise. The people in the van had told her about this town and its carpet mills straddling the hillsides like modern, steel-covered, castles.

Inside the eatery, a dozen conversations rambled onward. The cooks, wanting some limelight, clanged their metal spatulas as they worked at the grill. A baby fussed. His older brother held the jingle jangle of car keys just out of reach. Elizabeth angled her position away from the activity and rubbed her temples in slow circles. Taking out a folded map from her kerchief, she looked at her son seated next to her. His hunger fended off for a while, he sat happily, taking in the people and the place, and the cars outside.

A young couple lounged in a booth nearby. The male slouched in the hard, molded seat. His girlfriend chattered incessantly. His attention strayed. She began another anecdote.

Bold gestures punctuated the girl's story. She shifted constantly and swung a leg to some frantic, internal beat. Except for the young mother, immune while lost in her map, everyone's ears were forcibly chained to the girl's broadcast. The tale centered on the successful return of a piece of clothing, its front stained, a button missing. "I confused that geezer dame's mind so bad she was willing to give me a refund just to get rid of me. Then I figured, after all my effort, the least they owed me was a tube of Maximum Mauve. So-o-o on my way out, I bopped right by the cosmetic counter and *swish*. It was mine."

As one story ended, another began nonstop except for bursts of the girl's laughter. The patrons, ears shriveled by her grating voice rounded out with the clatter of dishes, unconsciously pulled their shoulders upward or covered an ear and tried to concentrate on the merits of their lunch.

A cigarette haze lingered above the couple. The remains of their meal littered the table. The young man leisurely tore napkins into short strips, silent and brooding. Then his college-age face, listless like a stagnant basin of sewer runoff, took on some animation. He was drinking in the sight of the Hispanic girl bathed in sunlight as she considered the tracery of highways on paper. To his overused senses, she was fresh and renewing, like an unexplored perfume or some long-forgotten glade dressed in the mystical colors of celadon, emerald, and jade. He fixated on her smooth brow then her short, clean nails with healthy, pink beds. He pulled his gaze away and whispered to his girlfriend. They caught the eye of the young woman and floated smiles her way.

The waitress stood near the cash register. Minutes had passed without a new customer. It was a rare let-up. Her sturdy arms under her ample bosom, she scanned the wide spectrum of humanity—tested families returning to the north from DisneyWorld, a few overfed curmudgeons coffee-happy and pontificating, and the usual, small army of wilted salesmen. But the aberrant couple and the point of their interest made the waitress pause. Her eyebrows arching sharply, she telegraphed curt messages more terminating than a stop sign. It wasn't the first time she had seen the flies attracted to the honey. The couple left some money and drifted out.

Elizabeth, head bent and eyes unfocused toward her lap, still sought a solution. The racket in the place had dropped a notch. She turned to her son, combed the locks of his hair with her fingers and wiped the line of milk from his lip. His tilted back his head and let a few last drops slide down the glass into his waiting mouth. He asked for more, but she pointed to the buildings on the hill and the train tracks nearby, telling him to watch for the next engine ready to load its cars. He got on his knees and placed his hands on the window. She went back to the paper before her.

According to the map, Vidalia was 350 miles away. Her aunt and uncle left Mexico before their niece was born. The last letter to reach Santolo told of a house of painted concrete block and white metal awnings. Since then, five years followed without a word.

Elizabeth's son, peering out, pulled to stand on the seat. One of her arms encircled his legs. She let her eyelids close. She sank back against the seat. Ringing like a cymbal, an iron pan hit the floor and her eyelids flew open. The boy sat down. She let out a long, soft breath. Fingering the money purse, she turned her vision toward the town again. She crushed her paper napkin into a tight ball and rose from the table. Her slender arms picked up the child, his toy, and their small bundle.

With the child situated on her hip, she reached for the door. "Take care out there, Hon'," the waitress called. Elizabeth nodded and thanked her. One of the cooks requested canned tomatoes from storage, and the waitress responded. Elizabeth went out with her son.

The ninety-nine degree air swallowed them. At first, she did not advance but kept her look fastened on the road leading to the gargantuan manufacturing plant and warehouses. Like the onion farms due south, the carpet industry had been granted special waivers concerning the hiring of undocumented workers.

She went forward through the diner parking lot. Blinding-white gravel. Glaring windshields. Her normally strong legs relayed messages of fatigue, but she continued over the sharp rocks pressing indentions into her thin soles and making her feet throb with soreness. Anything alive had fled to cooler environs. Weaving her way around automobiles too hot to touch, she glanced up. The clouds had thinned to a scarce few, making her squint to keep out the strong light. Quick as the strike of a North Georgia copperhead, a hand grabbed her wrist. She jumped back, clutching her son. The hold on her wrist released.

"Sorry," said the young man sitting in a parked car. "Didn't mean to frighten you. We thought you might speed right by."

Her hand went over her heart. "Oh, I see," she said.

"We're headed to Florida. Need a ride?"

She stumbled over a few sentences, telling the couple from the diner her destination, trying to make up her mind. His eyes had darkened but his smile was imploring.

"Vidalia is hardly out of our way," he added. "Hop in. But make it quick."

Elizabeth hitched her son higher on her hip. The late model car shone under the sun, matching the gleam of the couple's perfectly straight teeth. Without a pause to listen inwardly, she reached for the handle.

She rode up front, the child in her lap. The male drove. Ranting lyrics and jarring sounds pulsed from the CD player. "Where is your husband? How old are you?" he probed, and "Aren't you weighted down with the kid?"

From the back, the girlfriend thrust her face and hands over the front seat. "I'll hold him. Otherwise, straight-jacketed by this car, I might leap out the window." Her mouth spilled laughter, but her face now sagged.

Elizabeth turned halfway around to speak. Her refusal was cordial but firm. She thought the girl reached into her handbag for candy or a stick of gum, but a pill shot into her down-turned mouth.

"Pump it up, Sean. Let's get this car *moving*," screeched the girl. She collapsed lengthwise on the back seat. Her never-still hands patted her stomach while her feet tapped against a side window in sync with the strobe-like clamor storming their ears.

Elizabeth turned back and faced the windshield. From the corner of her eye, she observed the driver. She tried to loosen her knotted back by scrunching her shoulders. Time trudged by. The child hid in sleep across miles taxed with cigarette smoke and coarse language. An hour into the trip, the driver left the interstate for a two-lane highway. From the position of the sun, she knew they headed east a while. They came through a place called Canton. They headed south again, this time on I-575.

Ultimately, they neared the town of Woodstock. He turned the player down. The boy was sleeping, he said, and wouldn't even know they stopped to party. The side panel hid prime stuff. There was a friend's place where they could crash, only thirty minutes away, once they traveled east, past the podunk town they were about to enter.

"Stop the car," said Elizabeth.

Mocking words hit her, and then a brief period of silence moved in. The young man pulled a .38 from his pants pocket as if he had forgotten and was checking to see what he had placed there. Equally blasé, it was returned. Watching the road ahead, he joked and supplied reasons for her to conform to his suggestion. Meanwhile, the girl lying in the backseat jabbered mindlessly at the sky passing in the rear window.

Elizabeth's hand slipped into her cloth parcel. With the sharp tip of her nail scissors, she pressed his side. "Let us free," she ordered with a jab. His body flinched. Scowling, he slowed the car and veered toward the outer emergency lane.

The few cars, ahead, raced away. To the rear, the lanes were deserted.

"Get out!" he yelled, while the car still rolled. His girlfriend came out of some other world and sprang to sitting.

Elizabeth opened the door, tightened her other arm about the child, and turned, ready to jump. A foot slammed her backside. Her head jerked back. Her body flew. Turning to spare her son, her right side hit the burning asphalt.

The couple's shouted insults came first. The gray smoke of their churning tires followed and the car took off. She struggled to rise with her son from the roadway but dropped again. Gravel cut into her shin and forearm. Her perception spun. She looked at her son catapulted from slumber, his face contorted with fright. With another strong effort, she stood, holding the child.

Trembling, she looked back. The lull in traffic would soon end. Her child's arms thrashed the air. His little hands pelted her shoulders. Cars topped the low hill and sped by as she contended with her son. Arching backward, he pushed with his arms against her and stopped. His body straightened, and he wiggled downward, free. She gasped. Not seeing, not hearing, he ran around her. She grabbed him and fled away from cars roaring past, over to the buffer.

Her son still hollered. His legs kicked. Navy blue sneakers sailed in rebellious arcs and landed in the tall grass.

From a fair distance, a young man, unaware of their rough ride, had begun watching.

CHAPTER THREE

RANKLED MORE CRIMSON THAN redline on a pressure gauge, Hank rubbed his palm and rotated his painful wrist. He pocketed the ticket, without even a cursory look at the fine. Then he hauled himself into the truck cab that was a poor fit, cramping his long legs and causing the top of his head to skim the roof absent of lining. His features plunged into blankness. His body sat motionless.

The lowering sun entered his pupils, slicing into his consciousness. He thought of Arnett again. Hank clamped his jaws shut. Without options, about to have the last bit of stability disappear from his life, he started the engine and sent the truck forward.

He exited the freeway and took a left across the overpass onto Highway 92, the east-west thoroughfare through town. The year before, Woodstock had celebrated its Centennial, reaching back one hundred years to 1897. It wouldn't be long before the town coasted into a new century and another rush of astounding development.

With traffic slow as sludge, Hank crept toward the western sun. Only halfway over the bridge, his truck came to a halt on a road clogged by too many vehicles wanting their own way. Happy, talkative people in an open air Jeep preceded him. His head leaned forward, loaded with animosity. He made his eyes turn away from the annoying content-ment. As he waited, his sight rose. With the changing grade, the torn and severed earth of the work site, on the left, a quarter mile away, dominated the view. Comforted by the wounded landscape, he let all anger seep from his body. His focus moved back to the foreground. Ahead, on the side of the road, the girl with dark hair walked. In her arms the child rested, his face still flushed with spent tears. Hank's curiosity got the best of him, and he squeezed into the right lane.

Traffic hummed again and Hank's truck passed the pair as a toy lion dropped from the boy's hand. The toy bounced and rolled down into the deep culvert adjacent to the road. The planning stage to convert a portion of 92 into six lanes had only recently begun. Eventually those changes would cover the water sluicing over rocks and through the huge concrete cylinders.

The red light down by IHOP caught Hank's truck and held it still once again. He regarded the pair in his rearview mirror. The child broke out with new wails of crying. Holding him, the girl crumpled into a sitting position at the edge of the ditch.

The light turned green. Traffic moved. The truck took a right past the pancake place and went down the side street. Hank pulled right again, onto the massive parking lot of Home Depot. To complete the large loop, he turned back and aimed his vehicle in the direction of the two pedestrians holding his interest. Cutting on the diagonal, across the few empty parking spaces, the truck narrowly missed a van whose driver followed the rules but lobbed comments like missiles. Hank shot back a look.

After parking as close as possible, he trotted toward the front vehicle entrance that bridged the culvert, and crossed. He strode toward the two people. The child stopped crying. The young woman, her expression wary, stood.

"Need help?" he asked, reaching them.

"My child dropped his toy in the ditch."

The swirling, muddy water released the lion from the rocks. The observers scurried along the top of the slope as the toy floated out of sight, into a long drainpipe. Hank raced down the boulder-filled bank.

"No! It may not be safe," she called. He stopped, not eager to search a man-made snake den.

He climbed back up. "Ma'am, I'm so sorry," he said and looked at the child, fearing a strong reaction. Nothing. Only staring.

The adults let out relieved sighs and smiled at one another.

She lowered the boy from her hip to the ground where he scanned Hank up and down. The girl brushed away strands of her hair that had fallen forward.

"Your arm is bleeding," he said, taking out a handkerchief exceedingly white, monogrammed in pearl gray floss.

She pulled her arm down and edged back one step.

"It's okay." He moved closer and pressed the soft cloth to her forearm. "Now hold here. With some pressure." He gave her some space and searched his pockets, aware she self-consciously shifted her good leg in front of the scraped one. At least her shin had fared better than the arm.

"It is not within my means to pay for such a fine bandage," she said.

He grinned at the formality of her speech. "It's nothing," he replied, pulling out a wad of shoelaces. "The guys on the job give me a hard time about my preference. In my judgment, that useless worker's handkerchief they recommend is invisible. Keep holding."

"I will."

He held the tips of the strings and let them unwind. "I don't go to work without a spare set of these. On the job, shoes are my best friend."

"Yes?"

He wrapped the strings around the cloth and tied knots.

"There, that should hold it," he said. His smile brought out the best in his features. "My name's Henry, but I like Hank better."

"Your kindness is commendable," she said. "I am called Elizabeth," then motioning to the child, "and this is my son, Manuel."

He looked down at the boy then once again into her brown eyes. "Yes, I can see that. Same eyes." The child stared. Hank chuckled. "He seems fascinated by my shoes. Or maybe their size."

They moved away from the culvert.

She began telling him of the unfamiliar things in the United States that captured the boy's attention—escalators at the airport, a businessman's laptop, and on the plane, his first video.

Hank wasn't listening fully. He puzzled over the pleasure filling him.

The boy also slipped away, pulling free of his mother's hand as she spoke. He squatted to study a field cricket resting under scant shadows made by the scrawny arms of spurge weed.

The girl's voice broke through Hank's pondering. "I see you like mangos." Her arm pointed to the truck dashboard where a line-up of three luscious fruits sat, their skins ripened to rose.

"Oh. Yeah. Wedging them between the windshield and dash ensures they don't roll around like ostrich eggs." His words elicited her light laughter.

"When I was a child, pork with mango salsa was my father's favorite dish. We had our own tree."

"So that's why they caught your eye. Where are you from?"

"Mexico."

"Mangos need water. You must not be from one of the dry regions."

"I come from a small area of tropical clime, northeast of Puerto Vallarta. We often have a light rain shower blown in by the Pacific winds. Usually in the afternoon. Just long enough for everyone to run from the plaza to wait under the market awnings, eat a piece of guava bread, and come out again." She paused, keeping a watch on her son who tried to make fluttering yellow wings land on his open palms. "Manuel, let the butterfly remain free."

"Actually, the mangos aren't for me," Hank said. The girl stopped tracking the boy and seemed to pay close attention to his words. "They're for my neighbor. She left Florida in '46, and to this day, her greatest regret is not having tree-ripened mangos straight from her yard. A vendor at the Farmer's Market, south of Atlanta, sells prize specimens. He gets them for a few chefs in downtown Atlanta, and me, but I'm afraid I've let those sit on my dash too long. I've been … very tired lately."

He watched as the girl went to reclaim her son who wandered toward the culvert. The child insisted she look at a rock with shiny flecks. She bent down. Hank heard her tell the boy his find was probably igneous granite, formed under molten temperature, and that it glistened with mica. It appeared the child did not understand, and Spanish commenced for the first time. Her tone, feminine, nurturing, was light as a bird song.

The conversation grew distant. Troubling thoughts made Hank spellbound. He recalled a recent evening.

He had been sitting in the den with the false fellowship of a babbling television. A loaded pistol lay on the arm of the frayed and sunken easy chair. He told himself earlier, he'd just see how long it took the cold steel to warm in his hand. Almost reclining, legs outstretched, and head resting on the upholstered back, he fixed his eyes on the ceiling. He faced the fact there was nothing worth heading toward as he knocked back two double shots of his favorite bourbon, one of his few concessions to quality and expense. With doubts eroding his resolve, with the immobilizing effect of the whiskey, he fell into agitated sleep where he sat.

Hank slipped back into the present. The woman and child were returning. The boy put the stone in the pocket of his miniature jeans. Hank massaged his stung forearm to keep the last remaining flares in check, but his emotions had already tumbled. The clearness in his eyes became shrouded by doubt, and he snapped out a terse offer. "Look, it's late. I've got to get back to work. You want a ride home?"

The child's head snapped up. So did the mother's. "I apologize. We have taken too much of your time." She lifted the child and turned away.

Hank watched them leave. She moved in one direction then switched to another while surveying the stores and businesses along the road. A sinking feeling knocked around inside Hank's chest, and he trooped over. "You don't have anywhere to go, do you?"

"We have made it through other difficulties. Thank you, again, and good day," she said calmly and left him behind.

He had no idea of the depth of her understatement or the fact that she would never rely on an earthly person to be her hero. But he was aware she had fortified herself from deep within. Her features were untroubled, her voice steady and assured. She held herself like the daughter of a king.

Having learned of his purpose for the mangos, she discarded her plan of asking him to trade one fruit for the barrettes in her cloth bundle. The treasured hair ornaments, carved from tortoise shell to resemble seagulls in glide, had been a gift from her friend Yolanda.

Hank saw that her departure did not slow. The boy's face, looking back, became smaller. Hank's head cocked a little to one side, and his palms turned outward in puzzled reaction. Condemning thoughts swept in. He had been the dashing Sir Drake, on the docks, laying down his cape to protect the queen's shoes from the slurry of water and fish guts. Without warning, he changed into a different person, giving the cape a jerk the moment she took a trusting step. Yes. Jerk. What a new and justifiable name.

His legs started moving. He spotted Heckle Timmons creeping by in his car, down Highway 92. Self-appointed reporter for the Soapbox column, the man craned his neck searching for the latest town oddity. Hank muttered an epithet and increased his speed.

Twenty yards separated him from the travelers. Visually, the boy had not released Hank. "Wait!" Hank called and ran. "I have a screened porch you and your child can sleep on."

"Thank you, but we must be on our way." She moved on, letting her words flow back.

Hank stood still, thinking. After a moment, he trotted ahead until he caught up and walked briskly behind the girl. "If you're worried about your safety, you can keep my handgun out there, on the jacket hook, away from the child." She continued her pace. "Besides, my neighbor brought over a pot of stew last night. And I can't eat it all," he ended with a lie.

The boy looked at his mother. She slowed her determined march and halted.

As she turned to face Hank, he was amazed again by her self-possession. She studied his face. She looked at the ground as though, unhurried, she consulted someone in her head. Her features angled up again.

"I accept your offer. We will be on our way in the morning." She wore a guarded look.

Hank's notice was drawn to the boy. Still held by his mother, the child's gaze was locked on Hank's shirt pocket. Hank looked down. About an inch of his sunglasses showed. He smiled and put them on the laughing boy.

Hank led them to the truck, with the promise of another toy. The replacement for the lost lion was a blue, metal Slinky. Sometimes, he spent the remaining minutes of his lunch break sitting in his truck, pondering the likeness between the rhythmic, unchanging movement of the coiled wire and the dull, purposeless days of his meaningless life.

They drove away. Down in the darkening waters of the culvert, the stuffed animal washed through the lengthy concrete pipe, lodging among the boulders where the lion remained tight and secure.

CHAPTER FOUR

WITH HIS PASSENGERS NEXT to him in the truck, Hank pulled in front of the office trailer for Chandler Construction. Dusty vehicles roared off the site and jumped in with homebound traffic. Under a locust tree, a workman wet a towel with the last ounces of water from a cooler that sustained the men each day. He pressed the cloth to his face and then the back of his leathery neck. On the way to their vehicles, two other men, empty lunch boxes tugging at their lean, ropey arms, scuffed the dirt with their leaden feet.

Chandler Construction was one of the many companies involved in the skyrocketing growth north of Atlanta. On the spot where Hank's division graded earth and built foundations, a Target, Kohl's, and other stores would eventually open their doors for business, and the modest town would continue to amaze everyone with leaping changes. Phil Arnett, head superintendent, leaned over a makeshift, plywood table. Two men flanked him. His head turned from side to side as he conversed about an area on the blueprints spread before them.

The men at the table looked up from their subject to the truck cab where Hank sat with a woman and child. The mouth of one man fell ajar. After three years, the workmen knew little about Hank. They had not particularly liked him. They understood him even less.

Earlier that spring, with deadlines looming, even the boss had reached the height of frustration. Hank showed up at noon that day, causing Arnett to vent his anger while old Minnie calculated payroll. Arnett slammed a file drawer closed and looked at Minnie. "That Hank, he's an enigma as far as I'm concerned." Minnie shook her head sadly.

A gangly worker named Gil took his paycheck from Minnie and ran from the trailer, tripping over his own feet in a rush to reach his coworkers. Outside, Gil gave way to laughter.

Carl, their supervisor and a riddle himself, looked up from his clipboard. "Man, the way your ribs are knocking against each other, it must sound like a drum solo inside. What's got you in such a state?"

Gil's mouth swung open, ready to broadcast. "I just heard the boss call Hank an enema!" With that, a round of jokes was launched, each more crude than the last.

Carl frowned. "I love a joke better than anyone, but can y'all skip the cornball humor and get back to work?" He turned his back to them and used hand signals to direct a driver moving a dump truck in reverse. All the while, Carl recited Shakespeare for his own pleasure.

The men ignored Carl's familiar idiosyncrasy, and they continued their creative characterizations of Hank, causing more guffaws to break out. The butt of their jokes was busy commanding a roaring bulldozer thirty yards away.

Carl signaled the truck to stop. He went for his supply list and spoke with his casual, sidelong delivery, "Watch out, Gil. If he gets wind of your joking, he's liable to forgo roasting you with a wisecrack and, instead, scrape you across the red clay."

They corked their jesting; they had seen his physical strength steadily compound over the seasons.

Out of earshot, at the trailer's small window, Arnett watched Hank work and mulled over the incongruity of the man—precision and thoroughness coupled with absenteeism bordering on indifference.

Hank's peculiarities had made themselves known to everyone. The first day, he showed up wearing khakis, tennis shoes, and a fancy designer shirt. They clued him in about where to buy heavy-duty jeans and work boots.

"Hey, man," said Carl, "if you don't have some steel over your 'piggies,' one falling piece of rebar, and your speared toe will swell up like a cantaloupe. Lost four that way." Carl let loose with a toothy grin and limped away.

Making matters worse, the dreamlike sounds of Debussy or a stirring Verdi opera occasionally came from Hank's beat-up truck. Sometimes, his coworkers found him at break, poring over the latest theories of physics when he wasn't sitting there in a dumb fog. Then there was the time they watched him spend his lunch hour lying on his stomach, photographing the mad rebuilding of an ant mound leveled by the tire of a front-end loader.

Keeping their lampooning in check was Hank's uncanny ability to diagnose and repair a pneumatic drill, a delivery truck that wouldn't start, and the broken air conditioner in the boss's trailer. Each time as Hank worked in a state of focused frenzy, he was deaf to Arnett and content to endeavor past quitting time.

At the current moment, Hank shut the truck door and leaned in the window, noting that Elizabeth's line of sight was on the goggle-eyed men at the plywood table. She pulled the visor down and moved back into the created shadow. He told his passengers he'd only be a minute. He headed to his boss, hoping the executioner's axe would be swift. Standing before Arnett, he gave the news of company documents making an untidy checkerboard on the interstate. He was sorry about the long absence, he said, and handed over what was left of the papers.

Silence stilled the scene until it was harder than cured concrete. Finally, Arnett came to life. "No matter," he said. "The fax is working again. The spec changes came over the line an hour ago."

Hank blinked in response to his good luck, and his face began to reflect the good news. One of the men taking it all in turned his head and spat.

On the way to his truck, Hank hollered back that, come morning, he'd make up for lost time by arriving early. As he drove away with the girl and her son, he checked the rearview mirror. The men's attention had not reverted to their work.

The truck got back on 92, cut through at Bascomb-Carmel, and reached Bells Ferry Road. Air streams flowed through the cab windows. At the floorboard, the asphalt flashed by a rusted-out hole the size of a quarter. They turned onto Kellogg Creek Road, and it wasn't long before the pickup followed another road and then climbed the long, unpaved route cutting through Hank's property.

The lush woods had a peaceful quality in the changing light of a sinking sun. Shafts of golden light broke through the shade here and there. A spring bubbled from within a small outcropping of mossy rock, to form a branch of crystal water.

Elizabeth's gaze went from one scenic spot to another as they wended through the living sanctuary, and she was reminded of home. As a child in Mexico, she had often scampered among the tropical vegetation, playing with friends. Together they climbed into the tree branches, bringing their cloth dolls to see the view. Careful to smother their giggles, the girls dropped large seedpods on startled siblings walking on the path below.

Her favorite memory of those early years was the afternoon spent alone, underneath the limbs of a papaya tree. With a clump of grass as her pillow, she lay, looking into the changing collage of green above. Her light brown legs showed remnants of the rich earth and leaf matter carpeting her playground. Placid, melded with the jungle as she was, an unexpected thing happened. Overhead, a scarlet macaw flew by and landed in the tree limbs. The bird's striking primary colors made the lively weavings of the village women pale in comparison. Elusive in habit, it was not often that a macaw, once near the town, came down from the high canopy. Frozen with pleasure, the child sent little whistles and affectionate phrases upward. Occasional bold squawks from the bird failed to frighten her. She stayed with the macaw until the afternoon shadows stretched across the ground, and the bird flew away.

Elizabeth was only eight at the time of the visitation, and her grandmother chastened her for the lengthy disappearance. "Little one, do not scare your old grandmother so, even if most of us see the macaw only a few times through the span of our years. And what of the famed quetzal? If you should spy that matchless bird, will you take a week to return? If so, I will be quite dead from fear for you." The grandmother's strong reaction could be forgiven; it had only been two months since the child's family was gone. But Elizabeth held fast to those hours when it seemed the bird had wanted to soften her pain.

On the Georgia hillside, the truck slowly continued its way up the narrow path. Tires ground over gravel, and the chipmunks, moles, and white-footed mice took cover. Through the periphery of Hank's vision, he saw the girl lift her sable hair off her neck to feel the evaporating moisture cool her skin. His mind was captivated by the way a few brief curls caressed her damp nape. He ordered his focus away, to the winding path he knew by heart.

The engine groaned up the slope. A few washouts jostled them like popping corn as they rode along. The boy jumped up to stand on the seat, unfettered by seatbelts that were non-existent in a decrepit vehicle and the last thing on Hank's mind. The girl made her son sit. He pointed to things outside, smiling and chattering.

Farther up the trail, the road split. Thick summer growth made it impossible to see deep in the woods. They took the left fork where overhanging hickory branches sheltered them from the frenetic pace of a modern world. They came to the crest of a small rise where a large clearing and a white, painted-brick cottage waited. That portion of property along the shoreline of the big lake was obtained in 1950 as a one-hundred-year lease by Hank's grandfather. Two years later, the lease transferred to Hank's grandmother. She divided the acreage and subleased to the Eversons and Harold Barner. Homes so close to the water would remain an anomaly for decades to come.

The house, built in '53, wore classic lines more befitting an old-line suburb. The civility of the design made a pleasing counterpoint to the wild abandon of the countryside. To most people, the structure seemed ill-suited to the rugged man. The formal boxwood plantings around a circular cobblestone drive had been lovely at a former time but now were overgrown and lumpy. A beveled glass fanlight softened the front door. A small covered porch, architecturally detailed with two columns and a short railing around the roofline, shielded the entrance. Two courtyards had been symmetrically placed on either side. A tall, black shutter hanging askew, as well as worn, painted surfaces, shouted neglect.

Hank parked the truck on the right side of the house near the feathery branches of Leyland Cypress making a high wall of thick green lace. He forgot to point out the close proximity of his neighbor's home hidden behind that long row of trees, leaving it to the girl to shore up her confidence.

Elizabeth quelled her curiosity to see the rest of the grounds. Once again her back stiffened, and her face lost all casualness. Her child went complacently along as they got out of the truck. She looked forward as they walked toward a side entrance with a small stoop.

The man opened the door to an unpretentious kitchen having the warm glow of pine walls. In the center of the room was a gray Formica table. Some of the vinyl seats and a back had split open, but after so many years, the chrome legs still gleamed.

"Come on in. Put your things down," he told her.

She stepped inside with Manuel. Dirty dishes filled the sink. The open trashcan held fast-food wrappers. A gas range grabbed her notice. She came near but held herself back from running her fingers along the smooth baked-enamel surface. Under the glass covering of the stove clock, the hands had fallen to lie together at the bottom. The knob that had held them at center was missing. Her mind did not mark the dated design of the white appliance or the brand name written in that once-modern script. All that registered was the luxury of four burners rather than one. Only the Carteña family stove had been as large, but the appliance was old and made of heavy black iron.

Her attention was drawn to a scarred picture frame secured to the opposite wall where it couldn't be missed at mealtime. She stepped closer. The frame held a marriage license, signatures missing. The man walked to the item, took it from the wall, and tossed it in the trash.

From the refrigerator, he took a pitcher of cold water, enabling Elizabeth to catch a glimpse of a covered pot that probably held the neighbor's gift, a jar of pickles, a bottle of ketchup, and a nearly empty gallon of milk. Someone must think much of him, she thought considering the stew. Her carriage relaxed, and she took the glass handed her.

In the cool interior, tiny beads of sweat created by the high temp outside still rested along the ridge of Manuel's cheeks. He gulped water from a frosty glass and beamed at Hank. Acting on strange inspiration, Hank stuck his fingers inside the pitcher and flicked water down onto Manuel's overheated skin. The child's eyes squeezed shut, and his mouth dropped open. Carried further by impromptu, Hank crouched, resting on his haunches, and dipped Manuel's hand so the boy could have revenge. Manuel's grin broke out. Droplets splattered Hank's face. He made huge blinks, his expression aghast. Like a dog twisting water from its coat, Hank shook his head, bounced, and wiggled. The child went wild and Hank released his own bursts of laughter that stalled suddenly in his throat. He got up and stood as massive as the ancient Frigidaire next to him. With a "clank," he placed the pitcher a little too hard on the counter.

Child's play. His earliest memories were of his caregiver telling him to occupy himself outdoors but to stay within the walls. His enclosure was the ornamental, eight-foot-tall barrier surrounding the grounds of the Palm Beach mansion at the edge of the ocean. At a very young age, he wandered the neatly clipped zoysia, between the hibiscus and palms. After a time, his small feet always led him to the gate where he peered through to the beach. On the sparkling white sand, a proud horse stood, two dimensional, highly stylized, larger than life. Iron oxidizing in the salt air, the steed designated the Averill property. Only the child could perceive the minute degree the sculpture leaned to one side, destined for a fall.

A landscape firm was paid a huge sum by his father to tend the estate grounds filled with sultry plant specimens, elaborate walkways, and Chippendale outdoor seating. A jungle gym or swing set had never been part of the plan. The child would not own a ball, a trike, a dog, yet a corner of his room overflowed with expensive preschool toys designed for learning. And each night, he crawled into his English antique bed and enveloped himself in luxurious Belgian linens, hoping to hear voices rise from somewhere in that labyrinth of a home. Human noise was the only thing capable of driving away the impassive sound of the sea.

"May we use your bathroom?" the girl asked.

"Sure," he said flatly.

Blank faced, he led them without a word through the den to the bathroom centered on the hall. On the left, the passage led to the bedroom situated at the front of the house, and to the right, the laundry room stationed at the rear.

Despite the shift in mood, the child went where his mother led. When she saw the tub, she hesitated.

"Do you mind if I wash my son before dinner? Our travels have left him quite dirty."

"Yeah, me dirty. Can Slinky wash, too?"

"Go right ahead," said Hank.

Manuel had never stopped playing with the toy once the man showed him how to make it come alive. Already, in the boy's eyes, Hank was a magician, a clown, and a friendly giant.

The child's father and uncle were not equated so favorably. To Manuel, they were devouring jaguars, those golden, black-spotted animals scouring the perilous hills of home, as the two liked to tell him, closing with their chortles. It was then that Manuel learned to hide.

CHAPTER FIVE

S ET WITH DISHES AND silverware, the table was a peculiar sight to Hank's mind. He turned to the cupboard. Taking a jar of drink mix off the shelf, he muttered a fiery phrase meant to show his indifference then hoped the child hadn't heard him. He filled the pitcher with water and measured out the powder. The kid would probably like it. On the label, a smiling lemon waved and clicked its feet in the air. The caption read, "When life hands you lemons, make lemonade with Jumpin' For Joy Mix." A sarcastic grin popped on Hank's face; it was the drink he sometimes got a craving for.

His cynicism shortly gave way to something more orthodox. Splashing sounds and a child's laughter came from behind the bathroom door. The atmosphere was enough to pull a skeptic out of his brooding.

They gathered again and sat down before servings of savory beef stew. He watched as the woman and child dropped their heads to whisper gentle Spanish words in prayer. Of all the meals he had eaten in the fabulous homes of his social sphere, the practice of thanks before a meal was rare. Except for the Annendale's. That family's spiritual assurance was their proud heritage and carefully purchased places in heaven. When Hank had been seated at their dining table, Judge Annendale laced the blessing of the meal with references to God in deep, drawn out tones. The effect was the impressive, doom-like sound of "Ga-a-a-a-awd," which failed to capture Hank in its net.

He pushed the memory aside and considered his guests. "Please take more stew. That's a small serving."

"No, thank you," she said. "You must be fed well to do your work." She turned away and tidied her son's chin with a napkin. She returned to her meal. The attitude of his guests was quiet and unobtrusive as though they did not want to disturb his dining. Maybe he could get the child to talk.

"How old are you, Manuel?"

"Me *dos*," the child replied while using a spoon to stuff small bits of meat into his mouth. His small hands and arms were absent of baby fat. Definition was already replacing fleshy cheeks.

"No, Manuel, you are three years old, *tres*," his mother reminded. "He persists in saying he is two, I think because three is the number of pats he receives when he has disobeyed. His birthday was in February."

Hank stared at his stew. He looked up again. "Where is his father?"

She lowered her eyes. "In Mexico."

They returned to their meal. Hank continued to observe the toddler who interrupted his chewing with a dimpled grin, showing almost all his tiny teeth. Dark bangs reached just above the brows of his inquisitive eyes. Once in a while, he turned to question his mother in Spanish, but she gently shushed his chatter.

"What is he saying?" asked Hank.

She hesitated. "He wonders if you are the mayor."

"Why in the world?"

"Only three people in our village own a vehicle. One of them is the mayor, and his honored car is not as modern as yours."

"That junk heap of mine is twenty years old." His wide smile brought a twinkle to his eye.

"The mayor's Studebaker was bought in 1958, I believe. By his father, Luis Mercado."

"And its honorable status?"

"Luis was in Mexico City at the time, serving in government office. Alejandro, our mayor, loves to tell how his father performed a favor for an elderly couple from the United States. It concerned the release of a relative detained for questioning. Afterward, the couple sold Señor Mercado the car for a handful of pesos."

"They gave it away."

"It was the first vehicle to be a part of our village."

"Isn't your mayor embarrassed to drive something so anti-quated?"

"Oh, no. Some say the car is what finally convinced Ana Lopez to marry him." She studied him as he struggled to contain his amuse-ment. "It is in fine condition. It is taken out only for a very special occasion."

"And what is that?"

"Festival of the Virgin of the Waterfall. It is the most important day for our town. Alejandro brings the car out of its shed and the older boys beg to be the ones who will wash it until it gleams. Afterward, he gives some of the young children a ride. Next, they are sent out, and a large group of ladies crowd in wearing their best dresses. Alejandro does not like the stones and mud of the roads, so he circles in the soccer field until the band stops playing." Hank's torso was shaking. Pink rose in her cheeks. "You must understand; my village is very small. In the mountains. Time moves slowly for us."

"Pardon me," he said as laughter slipped out. "It's a funny picture. All those ladies."

An understanding look came across her face. "It is worse than you realize. Those women who vie for the places of distinction are not very graceful in the rush. With some planning and overlapping, eight can squeeze in, even though a few have grown broad with the years. Two others, Juliana and Maria, are close to ninety in age. For them it is 1958 again. They powder their faces and paint their lips rose red. Wearing old dresses and crumpled crinolines that hang on them now, they carry the same hats and white gloves of their youth." She brought a hand to her mouth, covering her smile. "And poor Alejandro. He only wants to get the tradition speedily accomplished, but first it is necessary to deal with his pouting wife. Ana demands she must sit next to her husband, so he must use his most ardent diplomacy to displace one of his passengers before he proceeds. By the end of the ceremonial drive, everyone waiting in the plaza can hear the sharp tongues of the women arguing. Finally, the car slides to a halt next to the podium. As always, our weary mayor jumps out of the car, wiping his brow and yelling, 'The cologne and fussing have given me a migraine!' And so, no one objects as he gives the same speech every year."

Hank was laughing, but he caught sight of the puzzled look on the boy's face.

Over most of his shyness, the child spoke, "Where your children?"

"Well, Manuel, I have none."

"No?"

"No. You see, I am not a father because none of the girls will marry me. They say I am *loco*," Hank added with a grin.

"Ha, ha, you *no loco*," exclaimed the child.

Hank glanced at Elizabeth. She got up quietly and began to clear the table.

"Please forget about that," he said with double meaning as he took the dishes from her hands. "Let me get some blankets for your sleeping pallets. I'll take care of the other." He left to gather the bedding.

The girl took her son, who faded in energy, to the bathroom for a final visit. After their preparations, they walked back into the small den that was dressed in golden, varnished pine like the kitchen. Hank pulled aside the drapes, which covered glass sliding doors, revealing the screened porch.

"Very pretty," said Elizabeth, looking out into the last moments of the day's light to see the long vista of a lake cove spread out below.

How many months since he'd seen the view, he wondered. He slid the door aside. Manuel was first, making a series of short hops through the entryway. Elizabeth followed but stood on the threshold and handed the pillows to Manuel. She took the remaining bundle from Hank and moved just inside the porch.

"Thank you for your hospitality tonight. We will leave at daybreak. May God's favor be with you always." Without a moment's waste, she slid the door firmly closed and busied herself making their pallets.

He was startled into brief paralysis. They did not look back at him.

The predictability of the dishes drew him away. He hurried through the kitchen tasks, silently berating himself. After taking a shower and putting some clothes in the dryer, he used the bedroom phone to call his neighbor.

"Hello, Hank. How was work today?" said Abby

"Another hot one."

"Yes, like it's been said, even the grasshoppers are dragging themselves along."

"Exactly."

Abby Everson was tiny with age and topped with pale blond hair. He thanked her for the stew but did not mention his company. With more patience than usual, he listened to her talk about the Japanese beetles in her yard and the state of her husband's leg.

Abby's mouth pulled to one side as she put down the phone. Her husband, Trent, looked up from the book he was reading. Crutches waited near the sofa. A hassock supported his cast-bound leg. As she sat down next to him, he put an arm around her, drawing her near, and tickled her cheek with the white mustache of his tidy beard.

"What's the matter?" he asked.

"He wasn't very open, as usual."

"He's allowed some privacy, I think."

"Trent, he's growing even more reclusive."

"Now, Abby, you know you are long past child rearing. It's not fair to start over again on Hank."

She chuckled softly and put her head on his shoulder. Then her head popped up again. "Remember his father, all concerned? It's been over a year since his last call. And things have only gotten worse."

"You're ignoring my advice, aren't you?" he said.

"Some girl knocks him for a loop. Now, that strange mother of his passes, sending him on a downward spiral since January."

"Has he ever been headed in an upward direction?"

"Those two summers with Kate. He was happy then."

"He'll be okay. Give it time," said Trent.

"It's been three years. I'm not certain his father told us the full extent of Hank's troubles."

"That may be, but you know there are things over which we don't have control. Probably a good thing."

"But, one more heartbreak, one more loss... I wish there was something I could do"

"Let's keep trusting God, Abby." Trent hugged her shoulder lightly and returned his attention to a collection of essays. Abby got up and dusted the books on the shelves.

Hiding a sigh, Trent closed his book. He took Abby by the hand and walked her outside to admire the deepening sky before they sought their bed.

Hank stepped softly into the darkened den. Looking toward the porch, his eyes were rewarded with the sight of the child sleeping contentedly and Elizabeth sitting on her pallet with her face inclined over a book that fit easily in one hand. The light of the kerosene lamp illuminated her. Her legs were curled next to her and her toes peeked from under her skirt. The dark shimmer of her hair contrasted with the white blouse she wore. It was a scene of simple, elegant beauty. He walked over and knocked softly on the glass. He motioned to the shoulder holster and gun he held extended in offering. She shook her head in refusal and returned to her little volume. A long, rickety table from the side of the porch had been moved to block the spot where the glass doors opened for entry. A wind chime made by Carl's wife, a craftswoman, graced that very table. Hank had given in to Diana's nagging to share a meal with them. Now, the table ornament was ready to ring out if anyone should try to enter. He stepped back from the glass.

Retreating through the den, he glanced into the opening that led to the more formal décor of the living room, a place seldom entered. In the laundry room, he turned off the last light. A blade of disappointment cut a swath through the positive thoughts in his mind, and he turned down the dark, featureless hall to his bedroom.

The heavy warmth of the summer night held him to his bed. Only his mind could move, and he thought about the way she treated her son—as though the boy was precious and full of worth. Other faces flipped through his memory. Unpleasant thoughts trailed along. A light sweat formed on his arms and chest, burning, like he'd taken a slide down rough-textured concrete.

Elizabeth extinguished the lantern light. She was about to be carried into rest when her senses held her back briefly. Floating over her like a dream was the smell of the lake's piney woods, the soft hooting of an owl, and a cool evening zephyr whispering through the screens.

CHAPTER SIX

EARLY THE NEXT MORNING, he pulled on fresh jeans and a clean work shirt. Buttoning from his neck downward, he recalled the graceful scene of the night before as she read in a circle of light. When he reached the last buttonhole, he found himself shy one button. His effort had begun too fast out of the blocks. He'd just start over. He was a model of patience; the answer he was seeking had come effortlessly, falling into his mind like a loblolly pinecone silently breaking free to land on a carpet of brown straw.

Elizabeth awoke as the sun, full of glory, was just beginning to rise above the mist across the lake. She sat up and looked at her sleeping child. Through the side screen, she could see the truck was gone. She lowered her head in prayer. Waiting and listening, she felt the urge to turn around. She dismissed the prompting and released the praise building in her heart. " 'The morning brings me word of Your unfailing love, for I have put my trust in You,' " she whispered. The impression returned. Her eyes opened and her head lifted. She turned around from where she sat facing the lake. Taped to the glass doors was a large piece of white paper with a message—"Please stay longer! From your friend and helper, the Slinky Man." Underneath the words, a caricature of Hank showed the toy moving with carefree energy from his head to his hand. "P.S. - Please feel free to come inside. All I have is cereal and a can of soup, but help yourselves to anything you discover. When I get home, we'll go find something for dinner."

Elizabeth was weighing each word when she heard the laughter of her son. Puffy-eyed, he pointed at the drawing. "Han! Han!"

At work, Hank's agitation caused him to make mistakes; his work-mates had nothing better to do than closely observe him all morning. *For what,* he wondered. With the scrutiny he was receiving, a liquid lunch began to have amazing appeal.

Wiping the sweat from the back of his neck, he came down from the scaffolding next to the foundation form he was assembling. His head ached. His eyes felt grainy. He rubbed their sockets, then the muscles of his face. Sleep hadn't come easy. Tonight might be the same. He unloaded more of the heavy frame components from the truck hoping to drive away a strong compulsion to race home. The metal lengths dug into the thick muscle from his neck to his shoulder. Dust billowed up, sticking to the oil and moisture coating his arms.

He laid the metal in the dirt near the scaffolding and paused. Had the sign worked? He returned for the next load. Could she even read his words? Her book might be only drawings or maps. Gloom fell around Hank's head, tightening his chest as easily as exhaust from the heavy machinery they sometimes manned. Later, when the whistle blew, he couldn't leave fast enough. Who cared if Arnett prohibited his men from a couple of drinks at noon?

After lunch, Hank continued preparations for a partial foundation of the mega-store complex that would occupy them for many months. Everything had to be perfect for the trucks coming in the morning. Once the operation began, there was no backing out. He had never been on a job where the pour had gone wrong, but he knew with certainty it meant large financial losses and long delays.

Six feet up, with his arms stretched above his head, he secured part of the foundation frame while his face, angled upward, received the full brunt of the sun. Drops of sweat made their way into his eyes. Roger and Gil walked by, letting little snickers travel up.

Roger stopped moving. "Hey, Hank. Wanna hear about the curva-ceous lady I met at the bowling alley?"

Hank flung out his response. "Careful, Roger, that lascivious brain of yours could turn to mush in this heat. Then we'd no longer be forced to hear of your pernicious proclivities."

Gil, inferring the point only through Hank's tone, let his shoulders bounce as he chuckled.

Roger, a slow grin filling his entire face, spoke at the rate of a lazy shuffle. "I do believe I get your meaning, Hank. So I suggest a change. How about givin' us the highlights of your night with that lovely mamacita?"

Hank climbed down. Three long strides. His knuckles planted into Roger's obnoxious grin with such force that Roger was knocked off his feet and blood poured from his nose.

"Yes she's a mother, *and she's somebody's wife,*" Hank shouted. "I'm surprised you haven't had the slime blasted out of your head a long time ago." His victim was almost beyond hearing.

Crazed with pain, Roger rose like a mad dog lunging wildly. Hank took some hits to the face. Linchpin skinny Gil, hoping to strangle their adversary in an arm lock, jumped on Hank's back. But, Gil, no more troublesome than a tick waiting for removal, barely held on, and Roger, blinded by his own blood, missed with several swings.

Warding off Roger, Hank reached to the rear to take hold of the mild nuisance pummeling his kidney from behind. With a firm grasp of Gil's shirt, Hank swung the man around and held him suspended in the air. Hank's right fist slammed into Gil's chin.

"What a slobber-knocker!" screamed one of the onlookers.

Arnett stormed out of his office. It was a good thing he did. Five more minutes and Hank's whole life could have ended that afternoon with a charge of manslaughter.

"Knock it off, you dimwits!" Arnett bellowed, pulling Roger and Hank apart. Gil lay on the ground moaning and cradling his face. "Have you guys gone mad? Fifteen trucks from Thornton arrive in the morning. Another work halt and we won't be ready." Disgust was written on his face. "I ought to fire you all, but they'll just send me three more like you!"

Hank and Roger, still standing, breathed heavily from their exertion. Between glares, they checked their injured parts and straightened their blood-spattered clothes. Arnett ordered everyone back to work and called for an ambulance.

Hank traveled toward home, not allowing himself to imagine the continued presence of his visitors. The day had been rotten, his work had suffered, and his eye and cheekbone ached. He couldn't understand it; the men were jubilant, almost friendly. His consternation extended to Carl who had rewarded him with slaps on the back and congratulations as soon as Arnett was gone. It was the first time Hank had ever hit anyone.

When the truck pulled up, the house looked as lifeless as before until the screen door off the kitchen flew open. Manuel was on the stoop before his mother could stop him. Having had no experience with steps in Mexico, he turned around and backed down using his hands to aid in the descent, then he scrambled over. Manuel's words came out, alternately in Spanish and English, so rapidly and with such childish tones that Hank didn't have a hope of understanding. Elizabeth watched from the door. Like a happy possum, Manuel giggled and threw his arms around Hank's leg. Little, bare feet accidentally came to rest on one of the man's work shoes, and the child didn't back up from his hug. Hank was at a loss, so he strode toward the house, causing Manuel's laughter to increase. At the steps, Hank's instincts took over, and he reached down and pulled Manuel into his arms.

He opened the door. Abby and Trent were seated at his table. Elizabeth moved to the stove where lake trout fried in a pan. The aroma of a home-cooked meal was almost as pleasant as the vision of the young woman.

"Hope you don't mind us inviting ourselves for dinner, especially since Manuel and I are responsible for the main dish," said Trent.

"Not at all. I'm always glad to see you and Abby." He rallied a smile. "If you'll excuse me, I'll go take a shower before we eat."

Elizabeth stared. "Were you in an accident?"

The boy, perched on Hank's forearm, enjoyed a prime view.

"What? Oh, my face. It's nothing. Manuel and I wrestled a bit in the yard before I came in. But then this brute, here, hit me a good lick." He mimicked punches using Manuel's fist to box Hank's battered jaw. He finished with a comical look of pain. The child was charged for play, but Hank lowered him to the floor.

"Okay, how about the real story?" asked Trent.

"Um. It wasn't anything, really. Just two of the guys at work."

"Uh huh?"

Hank said nothing, but his eyes accidentally deviated toward Elizabeth and then back to his neighbor.

"Oh, I get your drift," Trent replied.

Hank turned away before Trent could see Hank's mouth tighten and pull askance. "I'll be back shortly," he mumbled, leaving the room.

Trent looked at Elizabeth who took up her tasks again. Abby rose from her chair to help. Ever the philosopher, Trent spoke an aside to whoever might gather his meaning. "Oh it is so true. In a town of blind men, the one-eyed man is king."

"Trent, you've lost us," said Abby as she turned to more practical matters. The salad needed tossing, and the rice was just about perfect.

CHAPTER SEVEN

EARLIER, ON THAT DAY of flying fists, with the question of Hank's guests deciding to go or stay, events helped shape the outcome.

Elizabeth, invigorated by the coolness of the morning, moved efficiently, returning the porch to its normal state. She came out of a cloud of thought. Manuel had slipped from her watch. The sliding door was still pushed aside from their visit to the bathroom. She called within, thinking he had returned. No answer came. Turning, she glanced past the screens and saw him below, starting across the second flagstone terrace, which led to the final level and the lake beyond. She threw open the screen door. He was almost halfway there. Calling his name, telling him to stop, she flew down the porch steps, beginning the chase. An overlooked piece of flagstone, raised a few millimeters, snared the front of her shoe. Down she went. From the ground, she looked again to the terrace. Her child had stopped, his focus riveted. Something powerful was overriding her calls, and he moved forward again.

The sounds of distress reached Abby working in her garden next door. A ten-foot- tall hedge of viburnum separated the two lower yards. Those thick plants, along with the upper row of enormous Leyland Cypress, hid evidence of Hank's close neighbors. An arched opening, seven feet tall, had been cut into the viburnum long ago, making the two backyards accessible. It was through that green doorway that seventy-six-year-old Abby came running. Her heart pumped harder when she saw the toddler scurrying down toward the dock and deep water. She ran harder. The child's progress was slowed by steps dividing the second and third terrace levels. Her instincts told her the lure was the blue and white skiff tied to the dock's far end. The boat bobbed sprightly, with all the appeal of a bathtub toy. Abby raced along the well-worn path which angled across the slope, enabling her to meet him. Catching him in her arms, she swayed for a second or two with the momentum of his little body against her petite form. Her grave but gentle look gave the boy pause. At that moment, the young woman arrived, and the child spoke to her in rapid Spanish. At the speed of laser light, Abby catalogued different scenarios that might account for the presence of people on Hank's property.

Elizabeth knelt down and held Manuel lightly by the shoulders. His chin tilted down but his eyes looked up at her. She spoke her admonishment in a firm, soft voice. Then she stood.

The women introduced themselves.

"I am so grateful for your quickness. Thank you for your help," said Elizabeth.

"You're welcome. Once, our family almost had a terrible mishap with water. Is Hank at home?"

"He is at work." Elizabeth looked away from the woman's eyes.

"Your son seemed to understand my English."

Elizabeth faced the older woman's gaze. "I made an effort to speak English to him from the time he was an infant. I knew we would be traveling to this country some day."

"He's a handful like my boys were."

Elizabeth perceived an opportunity to divert the attention. "Do you have daughters, as well, to take care of you?"

"Oh, they live some distance away, but they know I won't be fussed over. Listen, I very much doubt that Hank has any food in the house. Why don't you and Manuel come have breakfast on the deck with me and my husband?"

Elizabeth was hesitant, but the woman's gentle smile had a calming effect like the loving hand of a mother against a feverish brow. So she did not resist when Abby took her gently by the elbow and led her toward the break in the tall hedge.

"I knew you wouldn't deny us old folks the excitement of some company," Abby said. Manuel ran ahead as though it was a place well known.

Coming through the archway, Elizabeth spotted an older man with crutches on the deck of a log house. They approached and Abby introduced her husband. He invited them to have a seat under the table umbrella and jumped right in with light conversation while Abby put breakfast together. After learning where the woman and child were from, Trent practiced his Spanish with Elizabeth until the boy pointed to the sky. An ultralight cruising above the lake launched Trent's tales of flying. The child took a seat on the man's knees, facing the water, and Trent began takeoffs and landings, adjusting flaps, checking instruments, banking left and right.

Abby came outside carrying plated omelets filled with ham, cheese, and asparagus. Elizabeth assisted by moving Abby's Bible and journal aside. Flossie, the Everson's orange cat, sat on the deck rail watching birds land on the feeder. Held aloft by a metal pole, the feeder was out of reach. Intermittently, the cat's tail flicked a tense sweep. Manuel hardly took his eyes off the frustrated hunter who gave up and entered the house through a pet door.

Trent turned to Elizabeth. "I'm usually the breakfast chef," he said, "but my leg is going to keep me out of the kitchen. Soon as I'm well, you must come over for milk and the best cinnamon rolls for twenty miles around. And I'm talking scratch."

Elizabeth puzzled a bit over the "scratch" part but tried to show delight at his offer.

"Now, Trent, it's going to be many weeks before you're out of your cast. We don't know if Hank's company will be staying that long."

Elizabeth continued eating.

Manuel put down his cup. "We sleep in a room wif no walls."

"He means the screened porch," his mother quickly inserted. "Hank was kind enough to let us use it for the night. Mrs. Everson, may I help you clear the table?" she asked, rising from her seat.

"Oh, no. I can manage. But, please, call me Abby."

"Why don't you bring my tackle out?" said Trent. "I can show Manuel where the fish hide in the lake. Of course, because of this cast, I'll need you ladies to join us." The gentleman sent a questioning look toward Elizabeth. Manuel gazed at his mother with pure, expectant hope.

Abby and Elizabeth carried a tote bag, fishing rods, and tackle box. Behind them, Manuel walked alongside Trent who struggled over the terrain with the aid of his crutches. Ignoring instructions to stay off his leg, he could no longer ignore the call of the lake. When they reached the dock, a tiny life vest was taken out of storage. The dock had always been absent of railing. Manuel's arms were guided through the armholes, and Abby secured the bindings snug. They walked farther down the gray boards. At the end, Adirondack chairs waited, painted in high-gloss enamel red so brilliant, so happy-looking, people smiled when they first saw them. Two of the chairs were at dock end. Two others sat behind and faced one side of the cove. Trent threaded a rope through the life vest and tied the other end to the dock. The fishermen took their seats. Abby turned over an empty bait bucket and rested Trent's cast leg on top. He handed a cane pole to the child and then tossed his own line into deeper water.

Grade at the cove edge dropped quickly, and, so being, the appearance of the shoreline in winter was minimally affected by the seasonal level changes determined by the Corps of Engineers at Allatoona Dam. That summer held a high water mark and, the day, not quite the scorching heat of the previous morning. The old man and the child by his side looked longingly, as, every now and then, a fish propelled itself out of the water, then fell, slapping the surface with a playful clap. Northward, outside the cove, small, white sails, launched from the almost fifty-year-old Atlanta Yacht Club around the bend, slid through the dark green luster of the deep channel.

Abby put on a hat and smoothed sunblock on her legs and arms. After the women settled back in their seats under the blue topaz sky, an occasional dragonfly hovered nearby, studied them, and moved on. No one spoke. The only sounds were those of nature. The water lapped lazily against the stanchions of the dock and buoyed the skiff to make it tap against its mooring. A red-winged black bird, clasping one of the reeds at the edge of the water past Hank's property, sent calls of contentment skipping across the lake. Mild breezes rocked the bird gently up and down on the long, curved leaf forming its throne. The water beneath reflected the image of the bird and the clean-white clouds that lazed along. Elizabeth could smell the warmth of the sun on her skin and in the safety of the moment became drowsy. Rousing herself, she resisted the idyllic scene. With confidential tones, she was ready to talk.

"Abby?"

"Mm-hm."

"Earlier, when I removed your things from the table, I discovered you are a woman who listens to God."

"Well I hope so, but all my life I've had to fight being more like Martha than Mary."

Elizabeth smiled. "It is the same for many of us."

"Only in my latter years have I learned to sit at His feet. I was raised with a strong work ethic," said Abby.

"I am sure He is pleased with the way people like you get things done when others are still talking and fretting. Perhaps you are like Joshua?"

"What a compliment; but if I'm not careful, I tend to rely on my own strength. Joshua was a man of faith." Abby took out the colander from the bag beside her and snapped beans.

"Would you give me your counsel?"

"Certainly." Abby paused at her task. She noticed the girl's glance in Trent's direction. "Don't worry. From the back, his hearing isn't good, although he doesn't believe me. How can I help you?"

"I must find employment, and I have not known Hank long," she said, still overstating their acquaintance. "Can you tell me of his character?"

"Oh, Hank Averill is one of the kindest young men I know. It doesn't surprise me that he offered you a place to stay. I always knew his heart matched his size. I guess that's why it bothers me he's been sad of late."

"Yes. His moods are quickly changeable."

"Hank's mother passed away in January. The event has made him... a little morose."

"As it would anyone."

"Well, yes, but..." Abby lightly stroked her bottom lip with her finger. "He's also had... disappointments."

"Would it be prudent to offer my services as maid and cook? I need money to travel to my aunt, and I cannot keep depending on your neighbor's generosity."

"Of course it would be okay. Besides, Trent and I are right next door if you need anything. But you can't continue sleeping on the porch. In late September, the night temperatures will start dropping.... Trent?"

"Did you call, Abby?"

"Please stop your fishing for a moment," He turned with a quizzical look. "Remember Kate's old garden shed?" she began.

Hopefully, Trent would forgive her meddling. In Abby's judgment, the girl was graceful as the swirling lace of a *mantilla*. A little of her Indian blood showed through, combining with her Spanish features to create an interesting mix. She appeared to have schooling. And there was something else about her—tranquil, hidden, and strangely attractive. Abby's orchestrations could be excused.

At the time, it was not apparent that the Mexican girl might be married. Elizabeth's ring finger did not wear a band of gold, but she was owned by a man named Javier as thoroughly as the sword-like agave plants possess the arid soil of Mexico.

CHAPTER EIGHT

ALMOST TWO THOUSAND MILES away, in a village set high amid the rising grade where the angles of the Occidental Mountain range of Mexico begin, a young man walked into his two-room hovel after his absence of three months to discover a change in his carefully constructed world. A late day meal was not waiting. She was not there to greet him. He walked through the main room into the sleeping chamber. The few clothes she owned and the child's things were absent. They would be hiding somewhere in town. A pitiful plan.

The sneer on his face dissolved and his stride hardened to a standstill. She was the only person who knew under which floorboard he kept the money from his nefarious comings and goings. When adding to his cache, he liked to frighten her with his words, her slim neck in one of his hands and the other hand holding his knife against the soft skin of her throat.

More assured, he walked to the wooden slat in the corner of the main room. Lifting it, he saw blackness instead of the clear plastic bags of green American dollars. A roar blasted from his lungs. Fury sent him about the place, destroying any remnants of her domesticity—the curtains she had embroidered, the mismatched dishes she washed with such care, and the child's bed she made from discarded wood. Next, he went to the shelf. Her books remained, along with the picture of a strange garden with a building she called a pagoda. Next to the cardboard illustration was a ceramic dog with shaggy, white hair falling around its black eyes. Had the little statue come from Eduardo? It was an extravagant thing. He knocked it to the floor and went back to the place of his stash.

Ten thousand dollars gone, but Javier Gutierrez still had many thousands more, buried deep in the mountains. After three years in the business, he was a wealthy man. Even now, he had just returned from two months travel on the circuit with more earnings inside the backpack he flung down when he entered the house. His dream was not improbable, that he could someday fill the place of Julio Santiago, leader of the newly-formed cartel in Puerto Vallarta. Javier's earlier years of low-level thievery had come to an end when he met the man.

From his view out the window, he could see weeds had sprouted in the plot. There would be worms on the cassava plants, too. He walked through the room and stood in the doorway of his house, arms braced against the opening while he considered where she might be. He fought off darts of rejection. Where was his ungrateful woman? Valentina would have the answers.

Walking up the hill through the village, swelling his chest as though the surroundings were his domain, he thought of an earlier visit. On the way in from his trip, he had stopped at Felipe's house, bestowing on the man a superior gift of Don Julio Banquez Tequila. Santolo was Felipe's jurisdiction as police chief, and Javier had learned years before that the man would turn his head for money.

The grade leveled out. He sauntered through the plaza. With narrowed eyes, he viewed each person who passed. The villagers, glancing away, knew to avoid him, the surest method of evading his cruel impulses. He was a man ruled by fiery passions and an absence of mercy.

Forty yards from Valentina's hut, he saw Carlotta's brood of yard hens. He began his favorite game of trying to reach the birds at a silent, surreptitious trot before they scattered and flew. When he succeeded, an unsuspecting bird would become the ball for his soccer-style kick. On that late afternoon, it was a meaty fowl, delayed in finding its evening roost in a *jacaranda* tree, tempted by a tasty beetle. A rain of loose feathers and Javier's guffaws at the sailing bird let Carlotta know what would be her family's meal on the morrow as the hens seldom lived a full night after the ordeal.

Two banana trees flanked Valentina's open doorway. Javier paused at the threshold, letting his eyes adjust to the dim light. He spied the woman's back as she leaned over the stove, stirring the contents of her pot.

"Good afternoon, *Abuela*," he called in meaningful tones.

Valentina, a quiet, gentle creature, turned around to see the only person in the world she hated. All her life, she had served others with love, and she had eliminated all negative emotion, except concerning this person. Now she felt triumphant, even vindicated, forgetting the *dicho* learned as a child—"Be vigilant after victory; then the wolf comes." So the woman, who never said an unkind word to anyone, was primed to spew her long-held vehemence as she watched him enter without invitation. She presented her back and let the wooden spoon spear the broth and come to rest on the side of the pot. Returning to face him, her chin trembled with emotion as she smoothed the fine, silver-white hairs at her temple, back toward the darker ones of her bun. The room was warm. She wiped the perspiration from her face and boldly looked in his direction.

"So the dirty dogs from the street must enter our houses now? No, I was blinded by the light. It is the vermin, instead." Her overloaded nervous system made her head shake imperceptibly and her mouth fill with too much spittle. Her eyes became wide, open pits of anger.

Aggression escalated in Javier's fists as her words tumbled out, but he recognized the emotion that drove her, and for a few heartbeats, he enjoyed watching someone else under its thrall and he smiled.

"So you are back again," she continued as he moved closer. "I was hoping you had received some bullets in your chest on this trip."

"Shut up old woman and tell me where she has gone," he threatened, with an upraised arm.

"To the United States. Where you can never reach her again."

"Ha! She is not sly enough to sneak through the border with the child. And strength? I hope the insects are eating her flesh right now in the jungle where she has fallen."

"You are sickening. Do you not even care for your son?"

He did not answer, and his look was impatient.

Valentina let out a breath. "She has taken him to a children's hospital in Knoxville, Tennessee."

"What a waste to spend effort on that puny invalid. The child doesn't have the toughness to live much past his third birthday. Perhaps it was not my loins from which he came."

"I wish it were so. But Manuel has others who care about him. There is a kind doctor. He does not ask for a fee."

"Aha! That is how she got a visa. She is probably seducing the old Gringo right now in order to get pretty dresses and a fine car," he said with amusement. "But it does not matter. There is another I would share my house with." He paused. "To what city has she gone?" Calmness oiled the question. "I would like to send any funds she might need for the boy."

"She bought their plane tickets with money that Yolanda gave her, and Dr. Weston is-"

"Who?"

"Dr. Weston. He is sponsoring their stay. They will not need any of your filthy money." Javier smiled at her ignorance.

The grandmother knew a lot, but Elizabeth had kept some of the details to herself. When Javier left months before, Elizabeth spent a day traveling to Puerto Vallarta to place large funds in a Mexican account, confirming to U.S. authorities that she planned to return to Mexico. The concern of the INS was always to stop the enormous flood of illegal aliens and the resulting drain on U.S. taxpayer services. Elizabeth decided she must do anything to attain the visas. So for that day, she relied only on human reasoning. Even Yolanda would have disapproved. The decision would have its ramifications.

Elizabeth also considered the consequences in coming back to Santolo. She purchased return tickets, another positive sign to the authorities, but those plane tickets were destined for another region of Mexico where she would travel by bus to Carmella and relatives from her father's side. Javier would always be her husband, but how could it benefit her son to have a healthy body if he must live under an attitude of death?

A dog barked outside. Javier's urge to punish the old woman for Elizabeth's offenses was waiting to break through. Valentina could not resist inflicting more pain.

"I am sorry that Elizabeth will not be here to see your lifeless body on the day God has had enough of your black heart." Her words flew out of her mouth like ravens while Javier stood grinning.

Valentina wiped her hands vigorously on her apron as though she wished she could wipe him as easily off the earth. She tromped to her stove and whipped the spoon around the pot. Hoping to send him away with a new fear, she concocted her weapon while tasting the broth. She called over her shoulder, "Now get out of here. I know nothing more except that I hear Eduardo has also left our town for a stay in El Norte. Perhaps they are together."

Javier's eyes sparked. In the heat of this new knowledge, his vision went from blazing silver to a red hue. He rushed toward the back of the heedless grandmother. Valentina felt no pain, was not even sure what caused the feeling of pressure beside her left shoulder blade. Dropping to the earthen floor, she only sensed a deep peace. Her eyelids closed, and she murmured the word, *"Cristos."* Then in the quiet, life left her body and her spirit rose.

Javier ran out of the hut. Darkness was coming. He did not tire as he ran down the roads and paths leading to his house. As he entered his doorway, stomach pains harassed him like crab pincers. He sat down at the rough-hewn table. His hands pressed against a century of ridges and crevasses in the worn grain of the wood. He looked at the cloth napkins lying in the center of the table. Her pretensions made him sick. What could be simpler than the sleeve of one's shirt? She must think she is still one of the Carteñas. He kneaded the flesh of his flat, muscular belly.

Eduardo Carteña, refined and unremarkable, was the source of his acidic envy. Disequilibrium manifested itself in Javier's mind, a by-product of the knowledge that Eduardo might have the *machismo* to steal Elizabeth from him like a valuable horse or a bag of gold coins. It was out of character for the soft-spoken Eduardo, but perhaps, he had wanted her that badly. Javier's teeth clenched and his brow furrowed. Shaking himself out of confusion, he grabbed an old metal coffee pot sitting in front of him like the lone spectator of his mortification. He used all his strength and slung the tin object at the wall, and he screamed, *"Doesn't he know who I am?"*

CHAPTER NINE

HANK HURRIED TO THE kitchen where everyone waited. His eyes scanned the array of vegetables dishes and the salad from Abby's garden. Large fish fillets, garnished with lemon and parsley, lolled across one of Kate's old platters. A lump of butter melted over corn bread in an iron skillet.

"You look mighty happy," said Trent. "Must be true that hunger's the best sauce."

"I haven't eaten this well in a long time," he said. "Thanks, everyone."

As they ate, the two men talked about the progress being made on the new construction. Elizabeth said little while Abby engaged Manuel.

"Are there any foods you don't like?" she asked and took a taste of slaw.

The child was puzzled, having lived among people who were thankful for each meal. His mother clarified in Spanish. Manuel smiled. "Me likes everything."

"I can see you will grow big and strong. My children didn't always appreciate their meal. When Roy, my son, was little, I sometimes served liver with onions, making him so unhappy. But one occasion was different. I came back to the table from the kitchen, and most of the liver on his plate was gone. So I gave him a big slice of cake as reward.

Well, it was an awful hot summer. No air conditioning back then. By the end of the week, I could not figure out what was making the awful stink in my house. Letting my nose be my guide, I looked in the vase on the sideboard and got the surprise of my life."

"You think *mofeta* in your house?" Manuel asked.

"What?"

"A skunk," said Elizabeth.

"Oh. You know, that might have been better than rotten liver."

Hank put down his glass. "I didn't think skunks were indigenous to Mexico."

"They can be found in certain parts," said Elizabeth. "Manuel has not seen one, but I read to him a great deal. My friend, Yolanda, brings him books."

"She bring me *Jorge el Curioso*," said Manuel.

Abby's fork paused mid-air. "Brings what?"

"Curious George," said Elizabeth.

"Oh, of course, the monkey," said Abby laughing.

"A Spanish version?" asked Hank.

"Yes. Fifty times, we have read that book."

"There's a whole series," said Hank. "When I was little, I thought he was the bravest monkey in the world."

"*Es verdad*," said Manuel with all seriousness.

Finished with the meal, they pushed back their chairs. Elizabeth poured coffee. Everyone relaxed except for something they sensed lingering and unsaid.

Abby told Hank how she became acquainted with his guests. She played down her important role, only saying they had met outside. Even Trent wasn't aware she prevented Manuel from going headlong into the drink. Elizabeth grew quiet, distracted with motherly ministrations. Trent kept glancing her way. Finally, he tossed his napkin on the table and cleared his throat.

"So tell us more about Santolo, Elizabeth. You mentioned it's near Puerto Vallarta."

"Yes, near but far. The steep terrain and the *Rio Ameca* keep the villages apart and separated from Puerto Vallarta, and then there are the difficult roads. It is a bus ride of four hours although Yolanda can make it in one hour with her jeep."

"How is that?" asked Trent.

"The bus trundles slowly along and there are many stops. If it does not break down at least once, the passengers consider themselves lucky."

"Any industry?"

"Only farming now. For a century, the silver mine provided work until it closed in 1936. Things have slowed ever since. The haciendas are long gone and we have shrunk to a small village. Some would judge us quite backward now." She glanced at Hank.

"Your village is *mestizo*?" asked Trent.

"Yes. There are few *indigenas* left in our locality. From the early 1800s, there was much intermarriage when Santolo was an important town filled with Spaniards and other Europeans who came to prosper from the silver. There is also the tale of a small group of people who came even earlier, across the Pacific from a distant island, before the conquistadors arrived. No one is certain of the truth."

"Well, whatever the case, you are an intriguing result," said Trent.

"Thank you," she said, adjusting her tone toward formality. Her eyes were hidden as she looked down at the porcelain bowl that had held her ice cream. A fingertip absentmindedly skimmed the curve of the rim decorated with a thin, silver line.

Manuel sat atop an old unabridged dictionary, watching the affable gathering.

"By the way," Trent said, clearing his voice, "isn't there something you wanted to ask Hank?"

"Yes." Elizabeth's eyes rose from the bowl. Her line of sight met Hank's. "I was wondering if you would consider hiring me as your housekeeper. For a season or two. I am also proficient at cooking." His lips parted. She put up her hand. "Before you answer, I must inform you of my reason for being in this country." He gave a small nod. "I came here to get help for my child." Everyone's eyes switched to the boy who climbed down from his chair. He made a straight path to the den and the toy plane Hank had scrounged from the attic. "Our plan to get aid has been halted, and now we are in unfortunate circumstances." The adults turned their attention back to Elizabeth. She hesitated, evaluating Hank's face to see whether it signaled indifference or caring.

"What kind of help does Manuel need?" asked Hank.

"He has a heart condition. Care would be free in Mexico, but I was advised it could mean a delay of years. Perhaps, too late. Also, I would have to move to Mexico City. I have no money, and I have no family there. My cousin, Elidia, was warning enough."

"What happened to her?" asked Hank.

"She and her husband left Santolo and went to Mexico City to find work. Later, high wages in the U.S. drew him away after the baby was born. For a while he sent money. Then it ceased. He never returned after he chanced upon a woman here. Elidia and the baby moved far out to find lower rent. The bus ride into Mexico City, where she cleaned residences, was two hours each way. Sleep would sometimes overcome her on the long bus ride home. When she woke up, the money she had earned would be gone. When the bus was full, her only choice was to take the long journey standing up. She is no longer well. She gave her child to the nuns."

"I see. No, that wouldn't be good," said Hank.

"Three days ago, Manuel and I flew from Mexico. In Knoxville, we expected to meet Dr. Richard Weston, our sponsor."

By now, her audience strained to keep from blurting out their questions.

Hank spoke first. "Exactly what is wrong with Manuel?" The child ceased moving where he sat on the braided rug. The toy in his hand was held still.

"Manuel has a heart defect and some other abnormalities. His liver and stomach are not in the right locations. Without heart surgery, the lifespan is often no more than a dozen years."

"You've got to be kidding. He looks perfectly healthy to me," said Hank.

"Yolanda, the nurse in our village, suspected his problems at birth but thought it best not to tell me right away."

Elizabeth paused and Hank grappled with the fact that the beautiful boy was a jumble inside.

"When did you detect his situation?" said Abby.

"Soon after delivery. He had difficulty nursing. When he cried, I noticed that his skin and nails had a bluish tinge. My grandmother has seen many newborns over her lifetime. She came to my house very sad one day. Conchita, her friend, believed his condition signified a bad heart."

"Did Yolanda reveal Manuel's situation to you then?" said Hank.

"Yes. She returned after a month of her duties elsewhere. She said that often with the misplacement of organs there are heart problems as well, but they don't always make themselves known for a month or longer. Again she listened to Manuel's heart. She heard a soft murmur.

"Yolanda assured me he would be fine for a while, but he would need surgery as a young child. She knew of a doctor who might help us. Years ago, she received training in operating room procedures when she was in the United States. Miguel, her husband, was a guest lecturer in international government studies at the University of Tennessee. Dr. Weston became Yolanda's mentor."

"She didn't want to work in Guadalajara or Mexico City?" asked Trent.

"Yolanda's heart is for the forgotten villages."

Elizabeth stopped the narrative. Manuel yawned, but a trio anxious faces pointed toward her.

Hank put his forearms on the table and leaned forward. "So, this doctor in Tennessee agreed to help?"

"Yes. Yolanda knew Dr. Weston sometimes operated on children of other countries as an act of charity. She contacted him, and he suggested we come to him when Manuel turned three. When the time came, I had to fight my fears. I had never been far."

"Didn't your husband want to come with you?" asked Hank.

Trent and Abby glanced at one another with surprise.

"No. He does not care for me or the child," she replied, matter of fact.

Hank heard ambiguity in what she said. Was that financially, emotionally, or both? "What happened when you arrived in the U.S?" he asked.

"Dr. Weston was supposed to meet us at the airport. We waited three hours and then took a taxi to the doctor's office. It was five in the afternoon. The office was full of people. At first, I didn't know whom to approach. Everyone seemed preoccupied or talked with one another, their faces serious. A young woman was in charge. I explained I was there to see Dr. Weston. She was assisting a man seeking some documents. I was not sure she even heard me. Demands were all around her. Manuel and I sat down to wait. I listened. I could detect sadness, making the situation clearer to me. The young woman broke free and walked over. I would not be able to see the doctor, she said. The news had reached the hospital that morning—he died, a day earlier."

CHAPTER TEN

FOR A FEW MINUTES, they sat around the table, processing the knowledge that Elizabeth and Manuel had come all that way for nothing. Hank recalled the child's exertion riding to the house, wrapped around Hank's leg. A hint of consternation moved across Trent's face as he stroked his beard. Abby went to the stove for more coffee, shaking her head and making a few female clucking sounds.

Manuel was lying on his back, playing with the old model plane left at the cottage a thousand summers ago. Mimicking engine sounds, he flew the B-17 in lazy figure eights, but after another lengthy day, fatigue wore him down. The child turned to his side and brought the plane in for landing. He grew still, and Elizabeth started to get up.

"I'll check on him," said Hank rising. The house held the warmth of the day. He slipped one of the sofa's quilted pillows under the boy's head. Manuel opened his eyes a small degree. "Need anything, Manuel?"

"No... bueno."

Hank returned to the table. "Elizabeth, what happened to Dr. Weston?"

"He was in Japan for a medical conference when his heart failed."

"My goodness," said Abby. "I am so sorry."

"Thank you, but I would be ashamed to feel self-pity when I think about Dr. Weston and, now, the people of that country. They are suffering from a terrible tremor."

"Yes. Trent and I saw the news reports last night."

Hank pushed past the side topic by catching her eye. "Elizabeth, didn't you say the doctor planned to be in the U.S. for your arrival?"

"Dr. Weston was on the way to the airport, about to take his flight home, when he collapsed."

"What a turnabout," said Abby. "What'd you do?"

"For a while, nothing. I was confused. In the office, I took a seat again and listened to everything going on. Eventually, things settled down, and I was able to explain our situation to the temp."

"Temp?" asked Hank.

"Yes, everyone referred to her in that manner. Am I in error?"

"No. Not at all. Whom was she standing in for?"

"Mrs. Yardley, Dr. Weston's secretary. She had left for Japan, to bring the body home."

"Why her?" said Hank.

"I learned the doctor never married. His sister is elderly, and Dr. Sandholm, his associate, was required in New Zealand. So the duty was left to Mrs. Yardley."

"Couldn't someone have let you know about the doctor before you left Mexico?"

"It was too late, and such a grave shock must have caused Mrs. Yardley to forget we would be arriving. Dr. Sandholm called her deep in the night with the news. Her instructions were to inform the hospital of the doctor's death and leave immediately for Japan."

A vexed note in his voice, Trent asked, "Didn't anyone offer to take you in?"

She shook her head. "The day was late. The office was empty of everyone except the girl. She offered to make overnight arrangements. I consented, knowing I had to form a plan quickly." Her eyes traveled from face to face. "But, no matter, Manuel and I are here now. I should get back to my question."

"Please. What happened next?" asked Hank.

She looked down at the table, remembering. "A taxi dropped us off at an inn. We had been sent to a fine place with air-conditioning, even a television. I did not have abundant funds. Yet I thought it might be unwise to walk about so late in the day, looking for an alternative."

"Did you phone Yolanda?" said Trent.

"Not then. I had only enough money for the room."

Abby patted her hand. "You are strong."

"I have a source of strength outside myself." The women exchanged a knowing look.

"What happened in the morning?" Hank asked.

"Dr. Sandholm was going to call the office at ten o'clock. Yolanda had mentioned his competency as well. So Manuel and I set off. I made one wrong turn, but we were there in time."

"You walked?" asked Hank.

"Yes."

"How far?"

"About four kilometers."

"In this heat? What about Manuel?" said Hank.

"I carried him. It was not difficult on walkways smooth and white like cream. However, problems soon developed. The doctor's call did not come in. I tried to reach Yolanda at the clinic, but the phone is out of service. It must be due to one of our tropical storms."

Trent sighed. *"Could anything else go wrong?"*

Elizabeth chuckled. "I was not the only one with trials. Poor Jilly. She was most overwhelmed."

"Who?" asked Trent.

"The temp. We spent the day together. When she cried, I felt like a big sister. I answered the phone, so she could get her work done."

An annoyed look marched over Hank's face. "What did she have to be stressed about?"

"She felt she might not last on the job until Mrs. Yardley returned from the funeral in North Carolina." Elizabeth was quiet for a moment, thinking; then she broke into light laughter.

"What is it?" asked Hank.

"My new friend left me doubting my English proficiency."

"Your English is impeccable," said Abby.

"Thank you, but she used many phrases of which I am unfamiliar."

"Like what?" said Abby.

"She was distressed about missing her lunch break and a sale at her favorite store. She described it as a place with skirts to 'knock her boyfriend's eyes out.' I took her words to be an idiom." Trent and Abby nodded with wry looks. "Jilly was kind. She ordered sandwiches and invited us to share them. It was a fortunate thing. Until Hank's stew last night, Manuel and I had little to eat."

"Oh, I hope it wasn't too heavy on seasoning," said Abby.

"It was delicious. We were most grateful to Hank, and now we thank you as well."

Hank glanced away. Did they have to know his every move? And couldn't they skip the digression? He broke in. "So, did you ever talk with the other doctor?"

"Yes. The call came in at five o'clock that afternoon. I thought my turn would never come. First, there was the accountant, the hospital director, and then another doctor. Over an hour passed before the phone was handed to me. No one had prepared the way."

"Was there a problem?" asked Hank.

"The doctor was not receptive."

"What do you mean?"

"His voice was tired and impatient. My courage was slipping. I clarified that our situation had been predicated on Dr. Weston's promise. Dr. Sandholm was affronted that I would bother him after what he had been through. He said my request was ridiculous. That I should not expect the medical community to be worrying about every sick child around the world. I found myself silenced and I began to cry. Then he shouted his last response and hung up."

"And just what were the good doctor's parting words?" asked Hank.

"'I am not like Dr. Weston. Go back from where you came.'" Her words had come out in understated fashion.

Hank sat back.

Elizabeth looked into Abby's pale blue eyes brimming with water. The young mother took hold of the old woman's hands and spoke softly, saying, "Do not be sad. Dr. Sandholm is going to do the surgery. I will convince him. By December, he will be back from New Zealand. When that time comes, I believe he will agree to help." She turned to Hank. "I must have work until then. If I am asking too much, you have already given us the rest we needed."

Hank looked at Manuel still sleeping. "You must stay as long as necessary."

"Would room and board plus thirty dollars a week be acceptable?" she asked.

"Let's settle on three hundred a week until we can figure out what to do about that doctor," he added with a ring of finality.

She uncrossed her legs and sat up straight. "*Oh no.* The sum would not be appropriate."

"Then we'll go with your suggestion."

She smiled sweetly.

Trent brought up the garden shed. They woke Manuel, and the group went to inspect it with flashlights. Hank sealed a few holes in the structure and added a wooden swivel to secure the door from the inside. He swept the wooden planks and brought the rollaway bed from next door. Abby put simple curtains on the two small windows. A chest of drawers, an easy chair, and a floor lamp were squeezed into the tight space.

It was not long after, that everyone lay in their own beds with cool white sheets beneath them. Earlier, a brief shower tempered the evening.

It had not occurred to the others to ask how the travelers spent their last night in Knoxville. While in a back room of the medical office, waiting to speak to Dr. Sandholm on the phone, Elizabeth was kept from seeking early-out-the-door Jilly for aid. After Elizabeth hung up, it was the custodian who closed and locked the office behind her and her son.

The Tennessee evening promised summer light until eight thirty. By asking questions of the women Elizabeth passed on the street, she was directed to a downtown shelter. A Guatemalan woman told her of the transportation system that would take mother and child south. The old woman, gray hair wisping around a sun-burnished face, gave the girl a worn map and a small cluster of grapes for the boy. "The van will come by in the morning." The hunched woman spoke from lips etched with many lines. "They might be willing to barter for your things," she added.

In addition to that night among thirty cots and drifting odors, Elizabeth spared her newest hosts knowledge of the wild ride from Dalton, an event she was earnestly trying to forget.

CHAPTER ELEVEN

HOLDING HANDS, TRENT AND Abby finally drifted off to slumber while Flossie sat sphinx-like, eyes shut, near their feet. Next door, the new Samaritan lay wide-awake. His gray matter worked hard like the giant cement mixers that showed up at the work site, ever turning, no matter how heavy the load.

Over-warm, he pulled one of his feet from under the sheet. The foot jutted over the bed, twitching back and forth at the ankle with pent up energy. His mind stayed on the girl and her son. Perhaps the ancient Greeks were right, he thought. All-powerful beings entertained themselves by disrupting the plans of earth's creatures. For humans, no amount of diligence or good will could ever guarantee a satisfactory outcome with fickle, arbitrary gods watching from above. At least the knowledge saved a person from more futile effort. Turning his head on the pillow, he sought the phosphorescent green digits of the clock. It read almost one.

He threw the sheet back, slung his muscular legs over the side of the bed, and sat up. The rain had stopped an hour ago. The house was quiet. His head hung down, weighted with questions as moonbeams streamed through the French doors onto his tousled hair, thick torso, and feet strong in sculptural detail. He rose and walked to the double doors. He leaned against the doorframe to look out into the celestial illumination pooling in the open courtyard. His grandmother's untended roses had dropped most of their leaves, exhausted from the summer heat. His attention shifted to the patio's brick pavers—consistent, lasting, purposeful—and his mind was eased.

The search for order and permanence had been the returning theme of his existence. He continued to ruminate, standing there, taking pleasure in the woods past the drive veiled in midnight blue. No, the Greeks were wrong, he reminded himself. There could be only one God. The world would have flown into chaos just the other side of its beginning with separate wills and whims having their way. In nature, there was a mind-boggling unity of purpose, a complexity and cooperation so startling it was beyond human comprehension. Exactly who reigned from that high place, Hank was not sure, but he considered it took tremendously greater faith not to believe in God. He held a love for science but was fearless and honest in his search. Truth he valued above all things, whatever the cost. Carefully, he allowed his thoughts to drift into the past.

After the family's earliest years at the Palm Beach estate, their other primary residence, a classic Georgian near posh West Paces Ferry Road in Atlanta, became little Hank's permanent station and the parents' designated stop over as they blew in and out like loose leaves. It wasn't long before the child discovered that contemplation of mechanical things had the power to relax him when his sense of security remained in flux. His penchant began one ordinary morning. His parents were absent as another caregiver resigned her position. He was sent to find a companion until another nanny was hired.

Four-year-old Henry found the upstairs maid lounging in the chintz, overstuffed chair in his mother's room. The girl reclined sideways, her slim legs dangling over one of the round arms of the chair. She drank purple fruit punch and turned the pages of a celebrity magazine. She didn't look up. Henry stepped close and tried to cover the glossy faces with his small hands. He spoke softly, "Miss Allen just left. Connie says you're supposed to watch me."

Her eyes glowered. "Shoot. Why's all the dirty work shoved on me? Did you act bad again?" He gave a nod and a regretful look. She dropped her glass into an empty tuna can. Her face screwed up like a crumpled brown bag. Henry's expression became unnaturally grave for a child, and he turned to leave, but the girl with the cute nose and unwashed hair sat up. "Hold on," she said. Her appearance mellowed. She brushed her lap free of cracker crumbs, and leaned toward him. "Little Henry Averill, always so serious. Lighten up, okay? We'll go play."

He followed the girl in search of scissors and paper, into his father's library, a room richly masculine and paneled in Honduras mahogany, a room to which he had never been invited. At the big desk, she cut out daisies, rabbits, and cowboy hats. What thrilled Henry more were three mechanical banks sitting nearby. A large crystal ashtray brimmed with pennies inviting his fingers to touch. Being under the care of the girl would help.

"Why does my father have all these pennies here?"

"Those are to make his banks spin, and twirl, and pop. Sorta like when Denny takes me to the dance club." She gave a pretty grin and pointed to the slots which Henry had been keenly aware of seconds after entering the room. Disco tunes hummed from her throat while she cut with the zeal of a second grader who'd been given scissors and free rein of the paper supply room.

The girl's lively music suddenly stopped.

"*No rowboats,*" Henry repeated. "I want a corsair."

"A *whut*?" Her eyebrows drew together. Her mouth was slightly open, and her lower lip protruded.

"A three-masted corsair."

"How old are you?"

"A sailing vessel. With crow's nest, weaponry, and sails—lateen and square."

She sighed, eyeballing him with resentment.

Henry did not look away. She pulled the paper close. Her eyes almost crossed as the snipping resumed, slow and careful. His hand slunk toward the ashtray. Two fingers like small forceps grasped a piece of copper. His hand slid to the bank, and he deposited the first coin. A British soldier silently fired his tiny musket. Henry's sight flew to the girl. She bore down on her task as though she attacked a blemish. With the next coin, two angry cats facing one another circled their arms and claws in a feline melee. On the third bank, a Boy Scout camper raised the flag, a rooster flapped its wings, and the hidden sun jumped to its spot above the mountain. Penny after penny was fed as his mind pondered the mechanisms inside. Every movement was unfailing, each action reliable. One hundred and four pennies later, the girl's hand was cramping, and Henry was summoned for lunch.

The next morning a wild search commenced for the banks that disappeared during the night. They were found under Henry's bed. Tools, secreted away, had helped him peek inside. He succeeded in refastening the soldier and the cats. The interwoven network of the camp scene, however, fell so completely apart it was beyond Henry's ken to close it again. Lawrence Averill cruised in from the Caribbean and laughed when told of the incident. Finding another caregiver was not as amusing but he succeeded.

One month later Lawrence took off again. Each time Lawrence left on one of his flings, the servants with less integrity knew they had months to dally with each other or spend in indolence as their paychecks were deposited with unfailing regularity.

Among the bunch, however, were two trustworthy employees— Constance, the head cook, well-rounded and ruddy cheeked, and Davis, the elderly butler, tall and as thin as an ironing board. They monitored the state of the art security system and made sure that none of Lawrence's Oriental porcelain or silver *repoussé* was carted away. A lifted painting would set off alarms at the monitoring station, but the sculpture, artifacts, and decorative ornaments lying about were a constant worry with Mr. and Mrs. Averill spending so little time in residence.

Two years remained until a pension would ripen for Davis. Constance was dependent on the health benefits. Their good working relationship and generous compensation made them value their positions all the more. Out of loyalty, they periodically risked waking the boss's ire.

Mundane details of daily living annoyed Lawrence. Minutiae, boredom, and conflict he despised. Smooth sailing was his preference.

Why worry, his mind-set. So, he attributed their stories and warnings to the anxieties of old age.

There in those cold rooms filled with priceless antiques, Scalamandré textiles in lifeless shades of ecru, and a collection of art works that rivaled a small museum, Henry sometimes wandered, searching for something to lessen his undefined fears.

Constance, steeling herself against back pain, had her hands full feeding six servants and the Averills when in residence. Davis, restricted by heart palpitations and joints locked up like cement, could do little to entertain Henry other than card games and renderings of Mickey Mouse.

After the bank escapade, Davis went on a quest in the basement. Soon Henry discovered the inner workings of an old radio and typewriter. For a little while, with a toaster or a clock, the child found distraction from the solitude of his very privileged life.

His mother, Charmaine Andersen, was not intentionally cruel, but totally blind to the uncertainty she created in her son. She had been taught by her parents to think of herself as the product of exceptional DNA and millions of years of evolution. Mother and father lived for the blossoming of the daughter, their opus and obsession.

Wealthy intellectuals, the Andersens were Danish natives living in Britain. Their manor house overlooked the Windrush River. They escaped the oppressive taxation through special British tax laws for non-national residents with offshore accounts.

Lars Andersen, Cambridge professor, dedicated the remainder of his life to his writings on psychology and education. A latecomer to parenthood, his home became his laboratory, with the birth of a child.

In the remote surroundings of the Cotswolds, Charmaine was raised with the primary goal to seek her full, human potential. "The mind is all" was her parents' frequent rejoinder. Starting at three months, trained technicians worked with the infant and continued throughout her childhood with a progressive immersion in knowledge and the arts. During the Sixties, when Charmaine entered her teens, the household was filled with the revered minds of the day. In their salon gatherings, the newest ideas were deposited in a weak mind. Further into the evening, over glasses of sherry, the latest accomplishments of the girl were assessed as Charmaine entertained on cello.

Until she went off to the university in Paris, her education and social life had been totally within the closed circle of her home's erudite chambers. Her only friends had been adults whose hidden motive lay in scrutinizing The Experiment. The Godless philosophies she studied left her with an unfeeling, self-centered heart. She entered the world attractive and brilliant but crippled by the invisible cord tying her to the two people at the center of her dependency. Growing up in a hothouse of narcissism, Charmaine naturally became oblivious to the needs of others, even her own child.

Shortly after Henry's fifth birthday, Lawrence received Charmaine's call from an ashram in Oregon. Her tone was calm and convinced. She was returning to England, alone, and the move would be permanent. Lawrence didn't argue. In a note, he left the job of informing the child of Charmaine's plans in the capable hands of the current nanny, Miss Schwartz, and he quickly departed for the enticements of the Far East.

For his son's care, Lawrence had always hired the best. He had finally gotten it.

Miss Schwartz, the final caregiver in a line of five, read the news and reached her limit with the unstable household. The father was gone again, and the mother wasn't coming back. Miss Schwartz, more competent and caring than the other women before her, would last most briefly. How it would hurt her to leave the child after such a short time. She knew how capable of reasoning Henry was for his age, and so she refused to be the bearer of such news. He would easily understand that his mother did not want him.

Charmaine would have denied such words, even been surprised to hear them. It was only that her investigations could be carried out so much better in the quiet of her elderly parents' supportive home. Henry would always be her son.

Within two years, the mental techniques Charmaine hoped would heal her mother of myasthenia gravis failed. A year later, when Lars Andersen was diagnosed with brain cancer, he died after giving himself a lethal injection. He was ready. The remarkable strides for humanity that his daughter was to have made never came about. There had been no peace prize, no ambassadorship, no landmark essays, and he knew there never would be.

Miss Schwartz, finally locating Lawrence Averill in the Philippines, gave her notice by phone. He offered a large raise, but she did not wish to silence the scruples that would scream like the alarm on a baby gate each time the only remaining parent disappeared.

To Lawrence's thinking, the situation was becoming hopeless, but he would not use flirtation. In this sole area of self-government, the women working in his household were left alone.

"Look, Miss Schwartz, I know we've gone over these problems before, but I promise you things are going to change. I'm depending on you. My son needs proper care."

"He will never have proper care unless one of his parents is involved in his life. I could have been starving him, and you wouldn't have known. A child is not a plant that can be plopped into the ground and left to grow on its own."

"That's why I hired you. I trust anyone Hadenholdt and Linden sends me. Miss Schwartz, I love my son, but I am extremely busy."

"Sir, your home is a sham. Your son could not sleep Saturday evening because of the party going on in the maintenance man's apartment. Last week, a woman from Brazil was staying in the gardener's house, and I found what looked like packets of cocaine by the pool. What if Henry had gotten into them?"

"You would never let that happen, I'm sure. Why didn't you call me? I would have taken care of that right away."

"You know perfectly well the reason. I am very lucky to have found you, *now*. Mr. Averill, the thing that bothers me most is that it has taken me months to develop any affect with your child. He is a wonderful, bright little boy, but the first few weeks he spoke only a dozen words to me. And now that we've begun to bond, I'm just another person exiting his life."

"Yes, I see. He needs more company. I think Mr. Richardson, my secretary, has children. I'll hire the people from one of those play-gym places to entertain twice a week. Will that make you stay?"

She took a deep breath. "Mr. Averill, your son needs you, and you'd better make room for him, because I'm calling child protective services."

The sound of the phone being slammed down was like the blast of ceremonial cannons across Manila Bay. He moved back and forth through the living room of his hotel suite. The serenity of the room done in seafoam and alabaster hues did nothing to modulate his apprehension. The breezes on the balcony failed to curtail the tightness around his collar. That hungry-looking boy on the street, the one who begged to shine his shoes or get him a cab, wasn't he only three or four years older than Henry? So who was taking care of the street urchin?

Lawrence called the agency demanding a stand-in until he arrived at the end of the week, but the Averill name was no longer inducement for the agency to risk being liable for support of parental neglect.

After some soul-searching, Lawrence's plan was to be a real father, and for a season he made a valiant effort. The first night of his return, with the largest bed sheets they could find, a desert tent was made of the early 18th century dining room table. The points of two umbrellas would save them if wild beasts approached. They played with flashlights inside their make-believe fort and drank Kool-Aid from paper cups, leaving red stains on the valuable Kilim. For the first few days they did everything together. By the end of the week, Lawrence's mind was elsewhere. Habits of a lifetime, the annoying restriction of his pleasures, it all became too much. The efforts he made dwindled until he rationalized his engagements and distractions once more.

Davis, slow moving and taciturn, and Constance, cross with recurring bouts of pain, took care of the child during the day. Medication put the cook under too deep to give proper nighttime supervision when Lawrence was gone in the evenings, so Henry was allowed to sleep on a cot in Davis's room. The snores of the worn out man did not bother the child. He even grew to like it. But once in a while, the boy shivered as his eyes locked on the man's bony chest. Henry wondered what it meant when the rumble sometimes stopped, and Davis, his cheeks and eyelids sunken, lay still and pale in the dim light.

When child protective services came for their appointed visit, Davis led the way into the library. They encountered Henry's father—sedate, thoughtful, wearing gold reading glasses and poring over the words of John Quincy Adams. He was dressed in gray wool slacks and a navy blazer displaying the family crest. Lawrence did not offer any of the superb aperitifs sitting on the French blackamoor console that was hastily hidden under a piece of tapestry to prevent misinterpretation of his sophisticated decorative taste. Instead, he offered perfectly brewed Ceylon tea poured from a silver tea service into Sèvres porcelain while Mozart played softly in the background.

The social workers and Lawrence hadn't spoken long when a call, timed to coincide with the interview, came in from his secretary. Lawrence was sure to speak within earshot of his guests. *Would Mr. Richardson please see that Lawrence's trip to take Henry to the Guggenheim was arranged for the twenty-first of the month? And yes, Lawrence and the boy would be stopping by Mercy Hospital for Children on their way through Baltimore, so please have the check ready for their charitable donation.*

Lawrence's inquisitors, shamed before they had hardly begun, apologized profusely as he gracefully led them out.

Lawrence did not leave town through winter, spring, or summer. Then, by Hank's sixth birthday, Lawrence was free; his son was ensconced year-round in boarding school. In his luggage, Hank carried the finest children's clothes and a nagging thought tucked in among them—as his father had come to know him, the son was found wanting.

Back on that day when Miss Schwartz left, the relocation of Hank's mother was presented by the butler and head cook. They were both a little more stooped that day. Davis rubbed his hands together while Constance struggled with a croaking impulse in her throat. Finally, they delivered the facts and made it clear they would be caring for him until his father arrived. Henry took the news with quiet resignation; he had never learned to have expectations of maternal care.

Constance and Davis did not protest when Henry's arm reached above his head and sought the assorted tools from the butler's drawer. Sitting down in the middle of the kitchen floor, he proceeded to disassemble and reassemble the Deluxe Wonder-Baker Master Mixer, and at least for the length of the afternoon his fears were chased away.

Feeling the pressure of the coming workday, Hank looked at the clock and returned to bed. His eyelids drooped to a close, but he told himself before he let go of the tugging rope holding onto his consciousness, he would find a way to help Manuel, even if Hank had to find a way to come up with the money himself.

CHAPTER TWELVE

CATASTROPHE RATTLES THE EARTH like a toy. Destruction roams where he pleases. Stomping. Grinding his boot. He surveys and sees the hedges of protection, meager when compared to the enormity remaining for his consumption and delight. And he laughs. Deep, deep belly laughs. Knowing the Giver of every good and perfect gift gets the blame. Knowing the Giver is long-suffering, dispensing his cleansing judgment rarely and only to protect life. Knowing, despite man's saving grace—a leftover, divine conscience—his ignorance, his dearth of trust sometimes fosters the wrong association. The destroyer squats and takes his ease on the earth, reclining, grinding out a wallow with his stinking backside, thinking he knows all he needs to know. But the Giver is wiser, by a universe more. . . .

On the other side of the world from Georgia, a man was lying, not in repose but in a twisted heap. His left shoulder throbbed with distress. The dust clogging his nostrils and mouth made him gag. His tongue swabbed weakly around his dry mouth as he battled the rising terror. Dr. James Sandholm lay on his back, his head forced to the right, his left knee bent at an improbably tight angle, joint and tendon crying out as though bludgeoned. Just over twenty-four hours had passed with his head delicately sandwiched between the rough surfaces of twin concrete slabs. The rest of his body was held firm by all manner of things.

The doctor had been hitting golf balls in blissful ignorance at a driving range in Japan where a dozen sportsmen executed smooth swings. They stood within a three-tiered structure designed to hold thirty golfers and maximize land usage. Businessmen and foreigners happily paid the large fee, unprepared for the behemoth that would soon shake the city.

Sandholm's early morning hours were spent with Mrs. Yardley, finalizing details with Japanese authorities. Her return flight, a few hours later, included a casket in cargo. Sandholm was elated, finally free from the snarl of details that had occupied him. Though not disposed to grieving, he considered the end of his partnership a great loss; Weston had amazing instinct and surgical expertise.

Bordering on self-hatred, Sandholm remembered he talked himself into hitting balls before his flight to New Zealand. He had walked the two blocks from his hotel to the golf range where his drives traveled straight and far from his position on the bottom level tier.

The quake's massive energy had released, knocking him to the ground. He scrambled up and fled the weaving platforms. His mouth fell open, and he fought for balance as the grass rolled under his feet in waves. A sickening feeling registered in his throat. Shards of glass plummeted from the windows of a nearby office building. He raced back to the careening structure. In a moment of deepening confusion and thunderous noise, the groaning building twisted, crashing down on its occupants.

He woke, held motionless, in a gut-wrenching panic. Heavy pressure. Mind-shattering confinement. His cheek lay in a pool of regurgitated breakfast. The moans of the dying greeted his ears. As a surgeon, his sense of smell told him there was blood among the ruins. Close by, the remains of two steel coolers, now only eighteen inches tall, protected him from the immense weight above. Would he be squashed with a sudden shift above, or would his death be slow asphyxiation?

Between the battles for control of his mind, periods of unconsciousness slipped by. Coming to, again, he tried to open his eyes wider as if that would enable him to see through the few inches of thick black space between his orbits and the rubble. Not one photon of light met his retinas to help drive away the fear. The fingers of his right hand wiggled, the only thing free to move within his full body cast.

Hours passed. He screamed for aid. Reasoning became distorted. He lost track of time. Soon, delirium began. Strange sights from the past came forward and receded. Like his hailed academic paper. Modifications of Surgical Technique for Infants with Oncocytic Cardiomyopathy. He was there, again, at the banquet, ready to receive another ubiquitous plaque on surgical innovation but embarrassed by his gushing parents. A family of eight. A hot dog stand in Queens at the end of WWII. Sheer commitment and humble labor. Finally, a modest neighborhood restaurant. Sandholm received his commendation with annoyance creeping in. He looked into the audience, gauging his mother who wore a dress far from stylish and who talked a lot, proud of their simple eatery. And there was his dad, trying to strike up a conversation with the hospital CEO, probably anxious to share the merits of his new cordless drill. After the ceremony, James Sandholm carefully circuited the gathering, avoiding family until he could slip away.

Concrete dust worked its way into Sandholm's eyes and stayed there, but the burning was mild compared to the self-reproach making his soul cringe.

Hours later, the doctor viewed another short play from the archives of his mind. An incident. Three decades earlier. He lost his best friend that day.

Jimmy Sandholm, stellar student, received his teachers' extravagant praise. Brandon, best friend, struggled through each term, his learning disabilities undiagnosed. In the final months of senior year, Sandholm's mushrooming sense of superiority drove friends away, while Brandon was loved for a good nature full of spontaneity and wit. To Sandholm, it seemed every good-looking girl longed to be transported to domestic heaven with the guy at her side. Then, trouble bombed Sandholm's paradise. The girlfriend making his head spin, said goodbye, tired of his cocky self-importance.

The last school dance was almost over. A slew of balloons and confetti fell from above. The class president prepared to announce the awards. Who would be Senior King? Sandholm knew. First, he wanted to pop that balloon.

"Brandon, how come you got here late?" he said.

"The Jetta wouldn't start after I got to Julie's."

"That's bull. She was busy writing your history paper, so you could come to the dance." Brandon started to object, but Sandholm was still on a mission. "You know, your Dad's going to be really proud at graduation."

"Yeah, that's pretty standard," Brandon replied with one of his isn't-life-the-greatest-grins.

"A sixth grade drop out, wasn't he?" He paused, no longer hiding a smirk. "Well, that's why an orthodontist's favorite patient is a young man with very crooked teeth and an expectant wife."

"What are you saying?"

"Imperfection is usually passed on, especially a muddled brain. So watch out for finals. Graduation isn't guaranteed." The young people nearby turned away or looked at the floor.

Squirming in the dark of his prison, Sandholm could still recall the anguished look on Brandon's face as he stormed off.

It was an odd selection of events that came to him as he shuddered with cold in that coffin-like space. It was difficult to get enough oxygen, and his body was growing numb. He was left to think more. About his prestigious college and how it had hammered some humility into him. He wondered, hadn't he made some positive changes in his life? His temper, for one. He'd certainly been working on it. And he wasn't the same guy as back then, young and full of himself. Surely, he wasn't as self-centered. Then, he remembered a Mexican boy.

Falling into jagged sleep again, the strangest specter of all materialized in Sandholm's subconscious. It was Dr. Weston's face, as real as any former day when they discussed a patient or a new procedure. Weston . . .The Teddybear, they called him. Eyes filled with optimism. A head of curling brown hair and a beard dotted with gray. His young patients responded with trust to that ready smile below apple cheeks. Naturally, it bothered Sandholm when he secretly learned staff referred to someone as Polar Bear.

He woke, still hemmed in, berserk with desire to explode from the place. The sound of creaking metal and a few shifting noises pierced his eardrums and made his torso register vibration. Quiet again. His respiration increased. His blood pressure went wild. His nose stopped up. No air came through. His jaws, held closed by debris surrounding his chin, strained until his teeth opened a quarter inch. He took quick intakes, through mucus collecting at the back of his throat. In. Out. The fiery, raw skin on the side of his congested nose rubbed more against the rough stone slabs encasing his face. In. Out. In. Out. The mucus crackled. A chest so compressed, he could hardly cough. In. Out. In. Out. His eyelids squeezed tight, holding back the emotions that could literally drown him.

Unseen, light and life entered that hopeless place. Somewhere, someone who did not even know of him prayed.

His nose cleared. His desperate heartbeats slowed. Calm came and he had air.

Then his mind froze. As real as if the man were there with him, he heard Weston say, "The children are waiting."

CHAPTER THIRTEEN

DR. SANDHOLM WAS UNCOVERED to join the living, again. As they rushed him to the emergency room, he kept thinking that during those hours when concrete squeezed the audacity right out of him, he would have gladly given all his assets for a glass of water to drink and one last brockwurst with slaw at a certain counter in Queens.

At the moment they pulled the doctor from his tomb, Hank was waking in Georgia at an early hour. He turned off the alarm and rose from bed. He dressed and left the cottage. Driving along in the burgeoning light, everything came up before his eyes, clean and new. All the negativity had been wiped away, and it was as if everyone, unafraid of another failure, had been given a fresh start. The donut shop was open and serving coffee. School bus drivers did practice runs of their routes that would be in full swing by the end of the month. The bus headlights moved confidently like beacons showing the way. People were already out taking their morning exercise, waving warm hellos through the dawn mist. Cars, headed toward jobs in and near Atlanta, filed into the streets.

Four hours of sleep. He wasn't the least bit tired. First at the site, he paced back and forth in the foggy air when he looked up to see Phil Arnett's truck pull in.

"What are you doing here so early? You're usually a quarter hour late."

"I've got to talk to you. I need more work."

"Huh? Does this have something to do with that girl?"

"Look, all you need to know is that you can count on me. Have you got any overtime or not?"

Arnett promised to let Hank know by the end of the day. Then he turned toward the construction trailer. A grin slid over his face, crinkling the lines across his tan cheeks and at the corners of his discerning eyes.

The morning lengthened, and the haze burned off the streets and low-lying fields. Despite the torturous sun, Hank stormed through his work. He thought of the boy and his upturned face animated at the sight of the old plane with decals peeling and pieces loosening. Hank labored on. Moisture drenched his shirt and stuck to his skin, but he hardly noticed.

Earlier, in the garden shed, Elizabeth waited for the truck to leave before she woke Manuel and dressed him. They entered the house. She read his note and pondered the large sum he left for her to stock the kitchen. She was to request a ride from Abby. By eight o'clock, the house was straightened, and she attacked the bathroom with cleanser. At nine, Abby stormed the kitchen, her arms loaded with summer harvest. Elizabeth handed her neighbor the note.

"I need to go shopping, too," said Abby. "Let me get my purse, and we'll be off."

Abby handled the large Explorer with ease in Woodstock's mid-morning traffic. "Things have changed here, very quickly," she said. "Some say there used to be at least one cow or goat on every corner."

"Yes? I see there are many stores and business establishments, now," said Elizabeth.

"Oh, and traffic during rush hour? You'd think you were in Atlanta."

They pulled in front of Ingles Grocery and before they could reach the sidewalk, three locals greeted Abby. They entered. Abby put Manuel in a cart. The market had what he called "beautiful everywhere music."

Except for his eyes scanning the shelves and freezers, Manuel sat in the cart, almost afraid to move. The smells of cleanliness, the order, and the vast selection of food and household items put a smile on Elizabeth.

"I know," said Abby sensing her thrill. "It's shameful to think of the times I've put off the grocery shopping."

A teenage boy bounded toward Abby. "How's life, Mrs. Everson?" He took the hefty watermelon from her arms and put it in the cart.

"Sometimes, hard to handle. Thanks, Lee."

"Yes. I heard about Trent."

She stepped back and looked at the top of his head. "You've grown."

"I'm close to six feet."

"When does practice start?"

"Monday. But I'm in intimidating shape. I've been eating five meals a day, taking twelve supplements, running morning and night, lifting weights, and trying to do some lengthening magic hanging by my knees. You don't suppose my vertebrae will let go of their disks?"

"I don't think so. But no matter how scary looking you become, you'll always be one of the nicest young men I know."

"*Mrs. Everson. Please.* I won't be welcoming visitors at the ticket table. Besides, you know Coach Ramm." A few shoppers cocked their ears as they pretended to study the melons and squash.

"Known him since he was a child. So cute. Jeffrey had more curls than a girl. Leanne Avens used to say Shirley Temple must've been his mother."

"Who must'a been?" said Lee, but Abby went right on.

"Yes, I remember. Jeffrey was our paper boy back when we lived on Dobbs. Couldn't have been more than ten."

"Well, he's fifty, now, Mrs. Everson, and he hardly resembles anything cute. Maybe we're not talking about the same guy. You know, nostrils flaring, eyes bulging, tongue lashing. And you should see him when he's mad. No, if you ask me, he's more like a drill sergeant who eats a side of beef for breakfast and downs it with a steaming cup of Tabasco just to give himself an edge. Matter of fact, he's so tough he makes our water boy dig a well first."

"Lee, we don't believe you one bit," said Abby between her laughter. The rest of his audience no longer hid their eavesdropping. He was making their sides hurt.

Not long after, Abby leaned over a meat case, explaining to Elizabeth the American names for the different cuts of beef when a confident voice summoned from behind.

"Well, hello, Abby." The words were spoken by a sleek woman wearing a sleeveless linen dress the color of tangerines.

"Hello, Marissa."

"I'm sorry to hear about Trent's leg." The woman's perfectly made-up eyes shifted back and forth between Abby, Elizabeth, and the child.

"Thank you. He's doing well." Abby knew to make it brief. "This is my friend, Elizabeth, and her son, Manuel."

Marissa stared. Elizabeth stood straighter and adjusted her blouse.

"It's nice to meet you," Marissa said, looking at the watch on one of her tan arms toned from tennis and golf.

The lady epitomized North American women to Elizabeth who was reminded of the elegant women dressed and posed like artwork in the glossy magazine she enjoyed on the plane. The pictures of stylish clothing and expensive jewelry were so stunning to her provincial eyes that she was certain the magazine must be of value in itself.

Marissa hastily continued, "Well, I've got to get back to business, but first let me give you a flash memo. I expect to see you and Trent at the gala for this year's drive of the John T. Manning Charitable Foundation." Her head flicked. "Come to think of it, you haven't been in a few years. You know my father would be disappointed if he were alive." Finally, she allowed Abby to get a word in.

"Trent and I apologize. We're getting somewhat on in years. I'm sure we won't be missed."

"Now, Abby, I've gotten the impression some people think an evening is not complete unless the community's most popular couple is present." A flicker of hurt played for an instant around the sharply defined line of Marissa's mouth.

"Oh, we're just easy to please," Abby replied as Marissa backed away with her cart.

"Well, have a nice day." The lady transitioned into high gear on shapely legs revealed by her brief dress.

"Thank you. We wi-" Abby's voice died out, spoken to the back of the woman scooting away.

Elizabeth's last sight was of Marissa's smart leather sandals, each studded with a tiny gold ornament. They held Marissa's expertly groomed feet with nails polished in a milder shade to compliment the dress. Elizabeth had heard about such beautiful women, like the wives of dignitaries and businessmen in Mexico City.

Abby sighed and pushed the cart ahead. Manuel, looking down from his perch in the cart, spotted red, white, and blue frozen treats. Quiet until now, he begged his mother to put them in the basket, but she refused. The budget cuts of meat, staples, and dried goods would total sixty dollars. Abby declared she was making a gift of the flavored icicles, and they moved to the next aisle.

Their shopping was coming to a finish. At the end of an aisle, twenty feet from the crowded fast-lane checkout, they parked the basket to the side and made a final survey of their lists.

The commotion began when Manuel, still seated in the basket, was inspired to lift a jar of mayonnaise off the shelf. The item was just within reach, and that very morning he had seen a lady on Hank's TV spread the creamy stuff on bread as her happy family waited in the background. Just as Manuel offered the quart jar to his mother, his strength failed, and the jar crashed onto linoleum. Most of the glass and glistening white spread lay in a greasy mass below the child's hands, but a fist-size glob had flown into the center of the lane.

"Lee Wyatt. Open register four," the intercom blared.

The hardworking teenager came loping around the aisle's far end, with the irrepressible spirit of a colt let out of its stall to play. He didn't comprehend Abby's alarmed features until his foot hit squarely in the oily mess. His three observers could only watch with mouths gaping, eyes wide. "Whoa-o-o-o-o!" he cried, sliding by, arms circling wildly. In the next millisecond, he gave way, skimming flat and feet first across the slick floor. One hundred and eighty pounds of momentum hurled toward the line of unwary shoppers, and then impact. One, two, three, four, five! People landed like live pins in startled disarray. "Strike," yelled a laughing spectator. Everyone came running. Flabbergasted, but unhurt, the victims tried to gather their dignity and rise from splayed positions. Manuel was ready to bawl, but Abby began with powerful, grandmotherly utterances until he understood he would not be taken to jail. Safe from the fray and watching, Marissa Manning should have been focusing on her good fortune. Instead, the woman, who had never raised a child, walked toward Elizabeth with poorly hidden disdain. "You'll need to monitor your child more closely." Then she returned to her shopping with dedicated movements and concentration on the selections at hand.

Finally, the laughter died down. The victims of youthful exuberance forgave Lee while he apologized with all his might. Then movement among the people began to slow. A strange quiet made its way through the store. One by one, the shoppers stopped what they were doing to look up. A visitor paused at the entrance closest to the drugstore. Standing there in his silent, inquiring way was sixty-two-year-old Uncle Rakey, as naked and skinny as a hatchling.

Abby told Elizabeth to wait with the cart and headed toward those sad eyes and that wobbly body.

Marissa met Abby half way. "You're not going to take him home in your vehicle, are you?"

"Yes, I am," replied Abby who continued toward the man. She put one arm around his shoulders, steadying him, and with gentle words led him out to her car as though nothing was amiss in Woodstock. No one could handle a disaster like Abby.

CHAPTER FOURTEEN

ABBY WRAPPED UNCLE RAKEY, waist down, with a picnic blanket and situated him in the back seat of the SUV. Elizabeth and Manuel stayed in the store while the cashier scanned the groceries. After the bags were loaded in the vehicle, Abby tore open the package of frozen treats and handed one to Manuel and one to Uncle Rakey, reminding him to stay covered. Then she calmly backed out of the parking space and headed away from town.

Manuel looked at Rakey in that unabashed way children do and smiled. Their cardiac difficulties, one congenital, and the other pathology related, coupled with their cognitive development, put them on planes of existence not so far apart.

"Dis good! You like?" asked Manuel. The man moved his head with agreement.

Abby hunkered over the steering wheel and tried to collect herself. Had Rakey left his pile of clothes behind the store? Surely he hadn't walked the mile or more down Main Street in such a state. Ugh. What she really needed was a cup of tea and a piece of quiche at Tea Leaves and Thyme. No such luck or time.

Elizabeth rested back against the seat and silently reviewed all that had happened. Light, invisible traces of cherry, blueberry, and vanilla ice floated in the air as the connoisseurs in the back seat considered each unique sweetness. It was peacefully quiet except when Uncle Rakey asked again, "Where's Ella? Where's Trent?"

"Ella's in heaven with Jesus, and we're on our way to see Trent," Abby answered each time.

For most of Rakey's life, it was his older sister, Ella, who had watched over him. Born with brain impairment, his heart disease developed later in life. Ella was childless. After her husband passed away, she carried on with her duty, living in the little house on Noonday Street until the day she died of a stroke. Then a niece, daughter of Ella's blind, half-deaf sister, roared into town. The old sports car wore a multitude of dents and one cracked-to-pieces brake light held together with wide bands of clear tape. *There will not be a funeral,* she announced first thing, but the townspeople politely got around her declaration in their own way.

Before sunset, the niece settled herself comfortably in Ella's charming home. As the days went on, efforts to befriend the woman, except by the girl at the tanning salon, were rebuffed like junk mail. Occasionally seen in a neighboring county on Saturday nights, wearing down a bar stool, skirt hiking up too far, Ella's niece once demonstrated her ability to drink beer from a western-style boot. Kevin, in the convenience store, remembered how she liked to trumpet that, at thirty, she had four marriages behind her and a passel of kids who called her mom. She stayed through the spring. Then one night, while the community slept, the niece slipped away, hightailing it down the road with Ella's antique piecrust table, her collection of Hummel figurines, and the sterling flatware, all bouncing around, under the tied-down trunk lid.

For the next four months, Uncle Rakey lived alone, and the yard became a mess of weeds. Trent found Rakey dwelling in squalor, his body starved and reeking. The little man had fed himself with canned pickles, peaches and pears from the food cellar. The stove, it was useless. The niece had seen to that with a call to the power company. She figured waiting years for a windfall was better than being under suspicion for arson. She left Rakey with three heavy-duty flashlights and a sub-zero sleeping bag.

The months moved on, and the town's efforts to reach the niece failed. Folks assumed she would return someday to sell the house and lot; however, responsibility for Rakeston Joel Creighton III was nowhere on her list. In farewell parting, she left a couple of long, brassy hairs on the easy chair and a bottle of "Go Go Green" nail polish on the table. On the floor behind the bathroom door, her black halter top and yellow spandex shorts, scrunched in a ball, were forgotten in her haste. Unfortunately, the image of her, fifty pounds too many, wearing that same outfit on her strolls through Dupree Park, lingered in everyone's mind. The state of the kitchen was horrendous, too, but everyone gave her the benefit of the doubt. It couldn't be determined where Rakey took up and she left off.

With profuse tears, Rakey refused each offer to live with Trent and Abby. What if Ella came from Heaven for a visit and couldn't find him?

The town council met, agreeing to let Rakey remain in place, while under Trent's watchful eye. The electricity was turned on, a microwave brought in, and the stove removed. And so it was for the next two years, that Trent, bringing a meal from Abby, came for a daily visit, except on Sunday when Mearabelle, one of the postal ladies, took Rakey to church.

Things continued in this way until the day Trent fell four feet, trying to put up a bird feeder for Abby. "How's it look?" he called, toppling. He landed in a bed of coleus, moaning. For Rakey's supervison, they tried the temporary solution of home healthcare visits. White uniforms and B-12 shots became Rakey's fate. Only a telephone talk with Trent could soothe his crying. But Trent was at the doctor's for a follow-up the morning Rakey barged his way into Summer Day Camp, happily expecting to share the swings with little campers. He wouldn't budge. The new deputy, unfamiliar with the town's inhabitants, insisted on handcuffs. The whimpering transgressor grew wild-eyed and shaky, oblivious to the perfect rows of purple vinca dug up by his heels as he was dragged away.

Abby dropped off her neighbors, then turned around to go down the road and over to the cabin. A quick visit might reassure her fragile passenger.

When she drove up, Trent sat on the front porch. Rakey's head and boney, white shoulders showed from the back seat. Abby lowered the window and relayed the urgent need of a pep talk for their charge.

Trent came over, bringing the right words for the man who was penitent and promised to obey the town rules. Next, he turned to his wife. "Won't hear of it," Trent replied in regard to her assertion she could manage the trip back, just fine. Anyway, he wasn't about to be a slave to the rules and time chart the doctor had given him for leg elevation.

Feeling lighter than air, Abby got out of the vehicle, came around, and helped Trent in. What woman ever imagines chauffeuring a nude man in her car?"

Elizabeth put up the groceries. Earlier, before driving away, Abby issued an invitation for dinner at the cabin, knowing Hank would have to be consulted. Elizabeth opened the petite package of saffron and took a light sniff while chicken quarters browned in olive oil. *Arroz con pollo* would be ready just in case he chose otherwise.

"Fantastic," he later replied concerning Abby's request, "although, it smells like you've been cooking up a storm," he said with a happy face. She looked away. "I'll go shower. Call Abby and let her know. Then I'll want to hear all about your day. Hope things weren't too quiet."

He ruffled Manuel's hair and was gone, which only pleased her more.

They stepped onto the covered porch of the cabin. A dozen baskets, sitting on the tables and floor, overflowed with shell pink impatiens and Japanese silver fern billowing up through the blooms. Rustic seating faced the woods that, except for twelve feet, almost snuggled up to the house. Abby greeted them, and they stepped inside. Elizabeth and Manuel looked all around at the exposed, interior timbers. Off the front hall, on the right, a kitchen led into the dining room. To the left of the entrance hall, a doorway opened to a small master bedroom.

A railing and support beams separated these upper rooms from a sunken living room and two studies, either side of the fireplace. Above the kitchen, the loft area contained two bedrooms and a bath in between, once shared by the children. The remainder of the second story space was open to the informal room below.

They ate at Abby's large table, seated in Windsor chairs. From the front dining room window, they looked onto the porch and the woods just beyond. Another large window on the side wall displayed a berm where purple coneflower, white phlox, and a patch of burgundy daylily bordered by tufts of blue ageratum made a live painting for anyone seated inside. A little apart from the flowerbed, stood a lone, displaced banana tree. Each year, complaining a little, Trent dug up the thing and hauled it to the basement to overwinter. With his newly acquired infirmity, Abby decided to give up any more of her tropical indulgence. The plant would have to hang on by its own the next cold season.

After dinner, the group left the table and moved down to the living room containing a large seating area formed by two love seats and a sofa placed around a low table. The grouping was centered before the massive stone fireplace commanding the room's attention. Its facade of stacked stone traveled from the hearth and through the second story until it reached the angled ceiling formed by rough hewn timbers.

As tall as Abby, a large painting of a black mare, its coat gleaming, honored the fireplace mantel. Twelfth Night had been given to Abby on her birthday of the same number. The animal served her well in the piney woods and palmetto thickets of south Florida where she worked alongside her dad during the thirties. The painting, a gift from her grown children, emerged from an old black-and-white photo.

The rear of the house faced the lake and presented a bank of windows and a set of French doors that led to a sunny deck. Except for Abby's small vegetable garden and a grouping to the right of three Yoshino cherry trees, the back yard, so different from the wooded front, was one long reach of smooth, green grass down to the lake edge.

After dinner, finding cushy places on the sofas, the well-fed guests settled back, and Manuel traveled from lap to lap.

Hank took in the homespun scene. He crossed one leg, then the other. He fluffed the pillow next to him. In his life, he had easily conversed with corporate chiefs, celebrities, even two presidents. So why did the cozy gathering leave him self-conscious? He picked up the newspaper and perused, hoping they wouldn't rely on him to carry the ball. The doorbell rang, and the child ran to see who was there.

"*Hola*," said Manuel.

"Remember me?" asked Lee Wyatt.

"Uh-huh. You crash like cars."

"I'm the one." Some of the brightness came off his high-watt smile.

"Come on in, Lee," called Trent. "But first let me put away Abby's treasured majolica."

"I hope I'm not getting a reputation," he said, walking down into the room.

"How could that be? We know the reason you drove Tim Clarke's tractor into the pond last month must have been a good one."

"Fifty yellow jackets were dive-bombing my head! I had no choice but to let go of the wheel."

Trent smiled. "Anyway, you still have your job at the store. Uh, well, if that doesn't work out, I hear Craig Wilcox is hiring."

"Don't pay attention to him, Lee," said Abby. "If people knew of all the stunts he managed to pull as a teen-ager up in Philly, he couldn't show his face again."

"It's true. I'm not allowed back in that town, and my brothers won't loan me their cars to this day." He paused and gestured toward Hank. "Lee, you know Hank Averill, don't you?"

"No sir," he thrust a hand toward the man, "although I've heard mention of you." They shook. Hank wondered just what the kid had heard.

"You remember Elizabeth and Manuel," said Abby. "They were in the store this morning."

"Nice to see you, again. I hope I can redeem myself after what happened."

"Perhaps I will bring Manuel to see one of your football games."

"Great. I do enjoy an audience; although, my greatest passion isn't sports."

"Have a seat," said Trent. Lee plopped down. Hank could feel himself being studied.

"Hank, you ever play football?" asked Lee.

"I wasn't into sports when I was in school."

"Wow. That's shocking. With your build you'd have been a fearsome lineman, sort of like Harry and Major, the new guys on our team."

"Really?" said Trent. "So, Coach has some good blockers this year?"

"Oh-h-h yeah. He recruited them from some hillbilly shack in the north Georgia mountains. And boy, are they huge. Facing those two hulks during scrimmage is enough to make us want to hide and suck our thumb."

"What would you guess? Two-fifty? Two-seventy-five?" asked Trent.

"Around two-ninety each."

"Wow. And just teenagers," said Trent.

"Well, they may have an advantage in their size, but those guys sure missed out in another department."

"What do you mean?" asked Trent.

"With the few brains they've got, they must be inbred."

Abby's face was a tip-off to her disappointment. "Lee, it's not like you to say such a thing."

"It's true, Mrs. Everson. They made it real apparent."

"How so?" asked Trent.

"They said they were fed up with their last name. You know… weird spelling, mispronunciations. Told us they were going before a judge to get it changed."

"What is it?" Trent asked.

"Ohturghote. German, I think."

"Sounds cumbersome," replied Hank.

"Yeah, can't see the sense in keeping a name a person doesn't like," said Trent.

"I know," said Lee. "It's just that when Harry and Major got back from court, we were all curious, waiting to hear. And guess what? They had a tussle right in the courtroom."

"How come?" asked Trent.

"Those two lugnuts thought the judge was supposed to supply their name. They arrived without the first suggestion. The judge must have felt sorry for them, so he offered a few. But they fussed and argued over every one. Finally, it came to blows. The bailiff broke it up, and the judge gave them thirty seconds. Major and Harry formed a huddle. The judge called time. 'Sir,' said one, 'we've lanced this boil festerin' on our back. We're cuttin' our name in two. So make it legal. From now on… I'm Major Ohtur, and he's Harry Ghote.'"

Laughter all around erased blank faces.

"You rascal!" said Abby. "You led us to Macon and back without our realizing it." Having caught the spirit, Manuel was galvanized with jumping.

Hank discovered himself settling in.

"Abby, bring coffee and cut Lee a piece of pie," said Trent. "If he's come to entertain us, that's great, but if I know him, there's another reason he's here."

The look on Lee's face changed to pleasant surprise. Someone actually realized he had a serious side. For now, he could overlook an aversion to coffee. "Yes, I'll take a cup." Then he mimicked the sound of his dad, "Make mine strong and black."

CHAPTER FIFTEEN

"MRS. EVERSON, I BET your brew is the best," Lee said, receiving the cup from her hand.

"I do take pride in my coffee. I get the gourmet beans through a web site, and I grind them myself." She hovered and waited, watching.

Lee sucked in liquid and immediately occupied himself by cutting his pie into numerous pieces.

Abby turned toward Hank who passed on the after-dinner treats and went straight back to examining ordinary life and the personalities in the room. Manuel sat on a wool rug near the fireplace, trying to win Flossie's favor. The cat had stationed herself just out of reach. Lee, his features vaguely pinched, shoveled pie to his mouth and took impressive gulps of coffee. Trent contentedly stared into space. The teenager's endeavor slowed. The conversing women got up and left the room. They could be seen in the open kitchen fighting with an obstinate cappuccino maker. Manuel gave up on the cat, came over, and sidled next to Hank, making the man grin. The child copied the way Hank sat casually with one leg bent and loosely resting across the other.

"How's your dad?" asked Trent, attentive again. Manuel scooted off the sofa and ran into the kitchen to see if the women had made the strange machine obey.

"Busy as ever," Lee said, patting his sternum and pushing away his cup.

Trent turned to Hank. "Lee's dad is fire chief."

Hank examined the teenager. "Oh. Tom Wyatt?"

"Yes," said Lee.

"That warehouse blaze was a close call," said Hank.

"A firefighter's nightmare," said Lee.

"They should have let the old thing burn down, out in the woods like that" added Trent, "but I understand they thought someone was inside."

"Turned out to be nothing. But, oh man, was it a risky search. Windows boarded *and* dense smoke. Dad had to go in and bring Harmon and Finney out."

"Your father's a brave man," said Hank.

"Thank you."

"Must have been frightening for you," said Trent.

"Didn't know a thing. I was busy downloading music with my headphones on. Maybe I'll live up to his example, someday." He drained his cup. Hank could have sworn the kid's eyes went wavy.

"Oh you're just like him when he was your age," said Trent, appearing to move silently into his memories.

"No way," said Lee, who suddenly looked away. His eyes widened as his stomach produced odd noises.

Hank purposely rattled and re-folded the newspaper and then turned to Trent who still drifted. "Trent. Trent?"

"Uh, what? Sorry."

"Didn't you tell me Lee's father and Kenny were best friends growing up?"

"Yep. Wherever you found one, you'd find the other. And a few times, their play landed them in hot water."

"Really?" said Lee.

Hank detected a hopeful tone.

"It's how I came by a lot of my white hair," said Trent, fingering his beard. "The worst occasion was the day I had to go to the high school after they set off bottle rockets on the roof. Celebrating the principal's birthday. Things were different in those days. Only a month of detention. The Gruesome Twosome was their moniker, but Happy and Go Lucky would have been more correct."

Lee spoke at a slower pace, "Once… I heard my dad say it was really hard when Kenny didn't make it back from Vietnam. Said it took a long time to laugh again."

Hank watched for the effect of such a reference.

"Yes. A sad time," said Trent.

Hank felt heartache in the air. Trent got up and moved about. A soft noise came from the doors to the deck. A furry head then body poked through the cat door. The raccoon ambled a few feet into the room while Flossie fled to the loft to look down, her back stiffening into a curve. Manuel peeked through the kitchen railing.

"Well, hello, Old Boy," said Trent coming closer with the support of his crutches. "My friend comes by this time, every night. Toss me some bread, Abby." She interrupted her cappuccino making and threw a slice, Frisbee-fashion, down into the room.

Hank spied Lee's spinning eyes, which sunk a little as he produced a tiny groan.

Trent handed over the bread, and the ringtail, prize locked in its teeth, went out. At the window, Trent watched the animal waddle across the deck, away from the light of the gas lantern at one corner and into the darkness. "Lee, I wish you'd come by more often," Trent said, still staring outside. "Seeing you, makes me remember what those old days were like."

"I'll visit more often," came out weakly.

Trent came back to the sofa. Hank's sight followed each step. Until now, he had never regarded the compact trimness of the man. Short in stature, there was nothing soft about him. At times powerful determination fueled Trent. His only weakness, if you could call it that, was a susceptibility to the past.

Abby and Elizabeth came back, holding their frothy drinks to savor with the conversation. They took places next to one another on the long sofa, the opposite end from Hank. Manuel begged for a sip of their drinks but was given a cup of warm strawberry milk, instead.

Trent related another memory of Tom Wyatt, captivating Lee. Then, Trent drew away, probably roaming his mind again. Simultaneously, more dark roast rapidly filled Lee's cup. The teenager's head slung around.

"Just like you like it," Abby said in a perky voice, taking the carafe back to the kitchen.

Hank watched the kid take a deep, slow breath. The odor must have hit his head like a brick. Tiny beads of moisture popped on his forehead. He brought the cup to jumpy lips. His eyes accidentally met Hank's. The kid braced and took a swallow. Was that a shiver as he lowered the cup? Lee's hand went to his throat as though he struggled to get words past his grimace.

"Trent?" croaked Lee. The man mentally came back to the room. "The reason I dropped by... was to ask about Uncle Rakey. After the craziness at the store-"

"You mean the mayonnaise jar moving into town legend?"

Lee let out a self-effacing chuckle. "Not tha-a-a-u-u-u-u-u-u-u-u-t." A belch, loud and long, had erupted without warning. "Pardon me! Pardon me!" said Lee. Red-faced, he glanced at Elizabeth and wiped his brow. His shoulders relaxed, and he let out a long sigh while his face drained of too much color. "No, not my mayo slide. I'm talking about the closing act. Someone said they're going to make sure Uncle Rakey is sent to an institution. Could that happen?"

"I don't know, Lee. It seems like Rakey's falling apart since I broke my leg."

"Worse than usual, huh? How about getting some help?"

"I did. Rakey's having fits with the women from the healthcare agency. Doesn't like strangers."

"Something occurred to me," said Lee. "You know how Uncle Rakey knows everyone in town? And the way he memorizes addresses and telephone numbers? Isn't he what you call a solvent or something?"

"Close," said Hank. "The word is *savant*. In Rakey's case, it means a person who exhibits exceptional skill or brilliance in some limited area but has a very low IQ."

"Ella did teach him to read on a beginner level," said Trent, "but I've never caught him poring over the phone book."

Abby came down the steps, returning to the room. "Well, he's got all those street maps he won't part with. They cover the walls of his bedroom."

"It's amazing," said Lee. "He rattles out your information, yet he can't converse in any sensible way for long."

"When I first moved here, I hadn't seen Rakey since he was ten," said Hank. "He came up to me, called me by name like I was a favorite nephew, and recited the address of my grandmother's cottage. Then he disappeared.... Of course, I hadn't forgotten him, either." Smiles broke out in the group.

Hank took in the view of Elizabeth and Abby sitting side by side. Several times he had seen Abby lean into Elizabeth, their upper arms pressing in feminine closeness. After softly voicing a comment, a nod or light laughter emerged between them.

"This may be a lame idea," said Lee, "but out of all the people who make up this town, I figure there's at least two hundred friends of Uncle Rakey, give or take a few, who could pick a couple of days each year to take care of him. We could have a sign-up sheet."

Everyone thought for a moment. Abby focused on seventy-eight-year-old Trent.

"Hm-m-m," mused Trent. "Might be a good idea. Rakeston does much better when he has the companionship of friends. But I don't know if we could pull it off. I'll run it by a few people."

Abby rose from the sofa to move near her husband on one of the love seats. Then Manuel became the entertainment until he wound down and crawled on the sofa to lie between his mother and Hank.

One of the child's sock-covered feet rested against Hank's thigh. Hank considered the smallness of that foot. Then he glanced at his own hand. Rough, tanned skin with veins in relief. Powerful muscles and tendons. A span of twelve inches. The power to take life or give it.

Lee got up to say goodbye.

"Oh Lee, you've let your coffee get cold. How about a fresh cup before you take off?" said Abby, who raced in the direction of the kitchen.

"NO! I mean thanks, but… "

"It can be hard on the kidneys," offered Hank.

"Exactly!" said Lee.

"And your coach," Hank emphatically added.

"Uh-h-h… right! Stimulants. A big no-no."

"Well since you enjoy my blend, I insist you drop by occasionally for a small cup," she said.

"Yes, ma'am. I'll try." He pumped Hank's arm especially well, and everyone wished him a safe trip home.

The fireflies began to dance past the windowpanes. Manuel was asleep, snuggled close to his mother. Taking a deep breath, Hank ran his hands down his jean-clad thighs, pulled himself taller, and rested one long arm along the low top of the sofa back and only a few inches behind the filmy cotton of Elizabeth's shirt.

"Abby and Trent, thank you so much for the evening," he said. "My grandmother wouldn't be proud of my manners; I've never told you how much I appreciate your friendship."

"Thank you," replied Trent.

"We're awfully happy you're next door," said Abby.

"Well," said Hank said, searching for words, "there's one last thing I'd like to say before we leave." Trent and Abby could not commandeer the tired droop of their features, but they mustered their ears. "I woke up this morning… " He shook his head. "It's hard to explain… " He looked over at the child, then the mother. "Elizabeth, if you will allow me, I'd like to pay for Manuel's operation."

Abby and Trent exchanged a bemused look.

Elizabeth's vision centered on Hank. "You are incredibly kind. I would be most grateful to anyone who could help my child. But you are unaware of the cost involved." Her arms were folded, and she lightly touched the scab on her forearm with subconscious meaning.

"I know there are huge fees and follow up care. I'm willing. I've spent very little since coming here, and I'll have nearly fifty thousand in savings." Elizabeth's face showed surprise. "By December, when Dr. Sandholm returns, I estimate that with overtime I could have close to nine thousand more. Any doctor will proceed immediately, once he's informed of a responsible party and some other financial details."

"Details?"

He modulated his voice down as though he was about to speak of some embarrassment. "Next year, when I turn twenty-five, I'll come into funds that should cover the remainder." Abby had a short fit of coughing. Then quiet.

Elizabeth lowered her face and everyone waited. She raised just her eyes, seeking the only other female in the room. Almost imperceptibly, Abby nodded.

After a moment, Elizabeth turned a gaze on Hank as beautiful as a Raphael Madonna.

"Thank you," she said. "I thank you with all my heart."

Exclamations and hugs issued from Abby as the two young people stood to leave. The sleeping child was carried in Hank's safe arms, but the girl's features reflected doubt. Abby whispered not to worry.

They went to the porch. Trent pulled Hank aside and spoke softly. "Abby and I couldn't fall asleep last night wondering what we could do to help. We'd be glad to sponsor Manuel. We were going to talk with our kids, first. Wouldn't it be better if we handled this?"

"No, Trent. For the first time, someone needs me." The two men said nothing else and shook hands. Hank and Elizabeth headed down an ill-defined path, toward the viburnum arch and whatever waited.

CHAPTER SIXTEEN

BENDING LOW OVER HIS father's chest, Javier could hear the shallow breaths between long intervals. Tenderly, he wiped away dirt captured by the damp face of a man too weak to rise from his bed. Javier whispered soft words of encouragement. The old man's eyes flickered open for a moment in recognition then closed again.

The problem with his lungs had been coming on for years. On those days when he felt stronger, he sat in the shade of a brownea tree in front of the hut, smoking and waiting to hear of the latest exploits of his sons. But Carlos, the older of the two, had been dead four months due to the blade of a jealous husband. Brought low by his son's abrupt end, the old man's time drew near.

Javier, the younger son, blessed with a clever mind and the stirring looks of his Spanish ancestry, lived in the shadow of his elder brother. Javier was determined to earn that crown of praise the father had given Carlos, before time ran out.

Carefully unbuttoning his father's shirtfront, he laid each half to the side. He rinsed the washrag in cool water and lathered a section of the cloth with soap. Starting at the neck, Javier used soft, slow strokes, washing the crevices and wrinkles of flaccid skin covering atrophied muscle. Each movement was exact and gentle. At times, Ramiro broke through the fog in his mind but could not help succumbing again to intoxicating rest from his struggles. Javier surveyed the old man's frailness, and he recalled the disrespect his father endured living in Santolo.

Ramiro Gutierrez had been born a dreamer, ideas for success and schemes of money-making filled his mind early on. Vociferous by nature, he often made the mistake of talking of his ventures, a habit begun in the schoolyard and carried on later as a youth in the cantina.

"Ramiro, we hear you have a plan to create new farmland for Mexico."

"I know nothing of what you speak," replied Ramiro.

"Are you not going to transform the Pacific's brine into fresh water and pipe it over the Sierra Madres to the dry plateau?" With that, a glass of water was poured over Ramiro's head.

At the age of twenty, Ramiro began his quest motivated more by taunts than any initiative of his own. He left for Guadalajara to make his fortune. His first attempt was producing Mexican crafts for export, employing a labor force of women anxious to add to their meager family incomes. But obstacles arose, and he regularly sought the cantina. With waning interest, he moved to the next idea—guiding tourists to an ancient Aztec site. It was a small mound of half-buried rubble. For a few weeks, the spot filled with broken shards of reproduction pottery was a money-maker. Gullible tourists worked hard to uncover authentic relics. Then one person, more observant than the others, discovered the words, "made in Mexico," stamped into the little statue of an angry god. Ramiro spent a few seasons in jail.

After twenty years, Ramiro came home to Santolo a defeated man. During his absence, he had been immortalized as a fool in a drinking song, and his shack had been turned into a hut for his neighbor's pigs. He married the only woman who would have him, one who had tired of making her living entertaining men. Then he proceeded to have two sons and drink away the remainder of his days.

At an early age, Javier was made conscious of the stigma under which they lived. He sometimes defended the family honor with his fists. Every slight, real or imagined, increased his mother's animosity toward the villagers. In some strange way, it comforted her to stoke the fire of the boy's shame. She died when he was ten, and he clung to the offenses of long ago. Over time, a root of hatred grew down from Javier's mind into the chambers of his heart.

Javier laid the bowl and rag to the side. He bent near his father's ear to whisper. "I must go away, Father, to take care of a problem, but I will return. When I do, I will have the funds to purchase the old Echevairia home. We will cut back the vines and fix the roof. Those cool walls and the inner courtyard will be peaceful as we drink our Sangria and enjoy the beauty of the *limón* trees I will plant there." He waited in vain to see if there was understanding. He must believe his father heard his words. "I have left a large sum with Pachita. She will care for you, Father." The old man's faith was in the potions and spells the hag could provide. To Javier's way of thinking, the stench from the *curandera* alone was enough to drive away any evil spirit.

Again Javier waited for a response, but he knew the old man lately fell into sleep so deep that he could not be awakened. Javier's mind went to his woman. When I find her, I will make her regret she has caused me to leave him. Kissing his father on the cheek, Javier parted with the words, "Until we are together again and I can lay my fortune in the hands of the man who made me. Then the people of Santolo will honor the family of Gutierrez for many generations." Javier thought he saw a ghost of a smile. The sun was almost down. He walked out of the hut, giving Pachita a painful pinch on her upper arm, accompanied by a warning spurted inches from her baggy eyes and randomly missing teeth. Then he left, walking toward town.

Hours later, Javier waited in the unlit, inner room of the clinic. According to Dulce, Yolanda would be back soon. How opportune, he thought. He told Dulce to put away the mop and go tend her children before he took the youngest and left him in the mountains with the wolves.

Not long after, Yolanda pulled up to her headquarters anxious to know of Elizabeth and Manuel's safe arrival. For almost a week she had been pulled away to Gatolinas to help nurse the children of five families through chicken pox. Searching for the key, she was confident that once inside she would find e-mails from Dr. Weston's office telling of Manuel's diagnosis. Tomorrow, weary but happy, she would return home to Miguel and Puerto Vallarta. She entered the dim waiting room focused more on the extended vacation on which she and her husband were about to embark than the disturbing fact the door was unlocked. She crossed the room then opened the door to the examination area and flipped the light switch. Nothing happened. She blinked, letting her eyes come to terms with the shadows. The contents of her clinic lay on the floor. Her computer and phone, their insides gutted, had been pulled from their couplings.

"*Buenos noches*, Yolanda." It was a masculine voice coming from a dark corner.

She put her bag down and calmly replied, "I suppose you are to account for this."

"How full of insight you are." He stood up from his panther-like form, now a creature of foreboding virility.

She forced herself to speak again. "I knew you would come, but this silly show is unnecessary. All you had to do is ask me where she is."

"I know where she is," he said.

Yolanda hid her surprise. "Then why are you here?"

He slammed Yolanda onto the shiny linoleum, his body above and his enraged face aligned with hers. His fingers dug into the flesh of her shoulders. Shaking her body up and down with each word so that her head was jarred by the floor beneath, he shouted, "I-will-not-be-tricked! Not-by-anyone!"

Blazing violence sparked in his eyes, and Yolanda thought she was about to pay greatly for the crimes he believed her guilty. But some townspeople passed the clinic. Their happy talk traveled on the air as the small group walked back from evening vespers. She screamed for help. Perhaps no one in town was more beloved than she, and Javier knew it. Letting go, he pulled himself up and ran to her desk, climbed on top, and sprang to the row of open windows near the ceiling.

He ran into the mountain vegetation and hid until he regained his composure. By the midnight hour, he was on his way to meet with his boss in Puerto Vallarta. The next day he would fly on business to

Juarez. Eventually, he would use the drug corridors and connections that would bring him into the United States and across a thousand miles to the office of the man who would tell him of his wife's whereabouts—Dr. Weston of Knoxville, Tennessee.

CHAPTER SEVENTEEN

RIGHT AWAY, THE ATMOSPHERE between Hank and Elizabeth changed from agreeable to unsteady and hard to read, that is, when he was lucky enough to see her. An earlier promise to Carl, the offbeat construction supervisor with a love for theater, ate up all of Saturday. Sets required building. Sunday, Elizabeth was gone with the Eversons, and late that same afternoon, he could have sworn she tried to avoid him. Then the workweek began. Hank didn't allow her to get his breakfast and leave Manuel asleep in the shed. Hank's overtime had him arriving home past a conventional social hour, and free Saturdays would be a thing of the past. Right from the start, except for the morning meal, he declared her Sundays off. Aware of what he had effectively done, Hank was ready to buck the trend.

Thursday, the walls were beginning to close in as they usually did during what he thought of as that dull and barren hour before bed. His new schedule brought him home at nine o'clock. Again, a note told him how to heat his meal. He lifted a shirt from the basket of neatly folded clothes and buried his nose in the fresh scent. He put on the shirt and looked at the fireplace cleaned of its overflowing ashes. He walked to the glass doors. The dingy film was gone and his reflection sparkled. He tucked his shirt smoother and neatened his thick hair. His fingers switched off the lamp and he peered out. Light glowed from her window. He placed his heated meal on a TV tray and brought it to the porch. He went to her door and knocked softly.

An opening of a few inches resulted, but hearing Manuel stir, she stepped onto the small covered deck. She was dressed in a white cotton nightgown and cover-up Abby had given her, one in a string of things his neighbor brought, insisting Elizabeth have everything necessary to a woman. In the evening light, the color of her skin reminded him of *café au lait*, making the sweet scent of vanilla rise in his mind. Her brown eyes looked up at him, waiting. Hank swallowed hard and a tense feeling wedged its way in as he spoke.

"Elizabeth, I… uh, was wondering if you would sit with me on the screened porch while I eat my meal? We'll hear Manuel if he should need you." He could see her stiffen.

"No. Do not ever disturb me again at this hour." She turned toward the door.

"*Fine. Sorry I asked.* In Mexico, they must not teach people to be polite." With her watching, he stomped off the wooden stoop, toward the cottage. With the intemperate relish of a child, he made sure the screen door slammed, producing a bang like an M-80 left over from the Fourth of July. Then he sent the small table with dishes and silverware clattering across the hard floor before he entered the dark house.

In bed, her prayers had a hollow ring. She rustled between the sheets again, re-evaluating her decisions. Her direction had seemed clear. Nothing in her spirit led her to believe otherwise. It didn't matter. There would likely be a note in the morning telling her to find help elsewhere.

Manuel breathed softly next to her. She turned onto her back and looked at the white-painted rafters. A golden brown orb spider constructed its web. It had found a pleasant home. Nightly, before twilight turned to dark, she found it enjoyable to watch her guest measure out his silken net. But the evening's turmoil caused the web's beauty to be lost to her. A small moth fluttered wildly along the wall and escaped out the unscreened jalousie window. Manuel made a little sigh. The night was hot, and the sheet clung to her legs. She pushed it away and turned her head on the pillow to study the stars framed in the clear skylight until sleep finally came.

With the clean light of dawn, she found the result of his frustration removed from the porch. If it had not been for food stains on the concrete, it would almost seem the destructive bear passing through had done so only in a dream. On the kitchen table, where she always looked for her daily instructions, she discovered a note.

Please forgive my rudeness last night. It won't happen again. My request was not what it may have seemed, but I will respect your private hours more stringently. Please do not let my temper cause any permanent ramifications.

I know that you and Manuel have no changes of clothing. As your employer, I am requesting that you take the money I placed under the fruit bowl and purchase clothes for you both.

With many regrets,
Hank Averill

P. S. It would please me very much if you each had at least seven new changes of clothing and anything else that you might need.

Elizabeth sat at the kitchen table with her forehead resting in one hand. Seven hundred dollars. She would have to seek Abby's help again. At least the older woman understood her distress over large expenditures of money.

Ever the wise one, Abby took them to the church clothing closet where her friend, Noreen, volunteered. They outfitted Manuel and then turned to the girl. Abby went a little wild with the fun of it all.

"Elizabeth, that dress looks very nice on you." said Noreen.

"Oh my," said Abby. "You'd better not wear that to Sunday service, though. Our young pastor doesn't have a wife, yet, and we don't want him having difficulty remembering his sermon."

One of Elizabeth's eyebrows rose with a hint of irritation. "Since I am a married woman, I don't think Pastor Barton has anything to worry about from me," she replied.

"Of course," said Abby. "Please forgive my foolishness." Noreen handed over more clothes to be tried on.

The point of a husband was an annoyance to Abby like a fat parsley caterpillar in her garden. Her hope had been for Hank, but the knowledge that the young woman was already committed could not be forgotten even if the man, whoever he was, seemed indifferent to his wife and son. Abby sighed and scanned her environment, huge plastic bags full of donations, threatening to trip everyone. She looked at Noreen who nodded. Abby stepped up to the bags. Her arms flew through the items, sorting and folding, straightening any misalignment she could find.

Next, the shoppers traveled to a discount department store for underthings and socks and where Abby argued the necessity, not to mention the value, of end-of-the-season bathing suits. Hadn't she helped them spend only a small fraction of the fund?

Hank left for work that morning, anxious and ill-humored like old times. At break, his calls home were unanswered. He phoned the Eversons, his pretext an unbroken busy signal. "Would Abby mind checking the phone next door to see that all was okay?" he asked.

"She left with Manuel and Elizabeth. Something about clothing," said Trent.

"Oh. Okay, then. Well, thanks, anyway," he said with a lighter tone.

"How about me?"

"Not alone. With your crutches."

"Ouch. Well, I'll tell Elizabeth when she returns to check the phone."

"Oh, no, no. Don't mention it. I'll check it out when I get home. Really, now, don't bother."

"Okay." Trent hung up and absentmindedly pulled at one ear.

For the week, Hank had been transferred to the smaller site in Kennesaw. Under a huge oak the landscape graders had resisted, he unpacked sandwiches Elizabeth prepared. The trunk became his backrest, and he recalled the evening before. The white eyelet around her shoulders had drawn his eyes to her collarbones and the light hollow at the base of her throat. It was enough to make a man want to press his lips there. Frowning, he took a bite of turkey on rye.

As lunch hour ended, he let his head fall back onto the ancient blackjack oak. His eyes drifted across the thoroughfare to the car dealership where colorful flags grabbed attention. Among the vehicles was an older, nondescript car quite unlike his warehoused racing Porsches or the elite, custom BMW now parked who-knows-where. The simple sedan on the other side of the road drew his interest for a different reason. The words, WILL SACRIFICE, emblazoned the windshield. His thoughts stayed there until he heard scrambling sounds in the branches. He glanced upward. Within the leaves, a squirrel stopped moving, poised for action, its tail twitching. Round, black eyes did not blink. Tiny feet remained frozen. Deliberation seemed endless. Finally, with agility and exactness, the squirrel leapt to another branch fifteen feet below, where it clung to the swaying limb and then ran to the solidity of the trunk.

In the coming months, he knew he would have to be just that careful. One stupid assumption, one bad move, and those two would be worse off than before. He rose and returned to work.

CHAPTER EIGHTEEN

SEPTEMBER ARRIVED, BRINGING RELEASE from the tyranny of summer heat. A new flush of color from the petunias planted around the quaint shops, businesses and the 1904 House Restaurant in Olde Towne District refreshed sun-weary eyes. No longer under the burden of soaring temperatures, the townsfolk stood more erect as they strolled down the sidewalks. Even the roses in the courtyards of the cottage came to life again, giving forth ruby-colored blooms.

A routine of work and rest filled Hank and Elizabeth's days like the rhythm of the woodland creatures spending their hours of light in unabated industry and the darkness in restoration of their strength.

Within the cottage, order and cleanliness took over—broken blinds repaired, drapes washed and mended, decades of dust conquered. Then beauty and comfort appeared unexpectedly. The den furniture was rearranged so that at any spot, Hank could take in the view of the lake. With the nutritious meals she prepared, the extra weight he carried most of his young life began to fall away. The fuzzy nightmares that made him wake up panting and in a sweat ceased their visits.

Each night, home from his second shift, Hank looked out through the porch to the sleeping quarters. By nine-thirty, her light was out and darkness settled around the shed. Only Sunday mornings held the promise of reconnection.

By seven, Elizabeth would be in the kitchen, stirring, measuring, and cracking egg shells, producing the efficient sounds that certified, for a morning at least, his house was a home. While she worked, Hank read the Sunday comics to Manuel. The child sat in Hank's lap, giggling at the man's vocal dramatizations. Then the three sat down to plates fit to celebrate the day. It was a menu specified by him and calculated to draw the minutes out.

Elizabeth, speaking in restricted, careful tones, tended to her employer, making sure his every need was met. Invariably by nine, she finished the kitchen cleanup and, with the boy, scooted next door for a ride to church. Afterward, the Everson's habit was dinner out, always including their guests. By two, they returned. Early afternoon was taken up with Manuel's nap while Elizabeth sat on her tiny porch and read the books Hank loaned her. Around four, Hank would see them playing and relaxing on the terraces or dock. He remained inside, numbing himself with hours of televised sports and news commentary.

That first Sunday in September, Trent came to fish off the dock. Abby accompanied him, without letters to write, pecans to shell or garden catalogues to bookmark. Elizabeth, near the shoreline, played in the water with Manuel until he grew tired. Elizabeth threw a big shirt over her suit and came down the dock with the child. She slid into the red chair near Abby. Manuel sat with his mother briefly. He hopped up and pattered back and forth down the length of the dock, enjoying the sounds his feet made until Trent called him over and placed a cane pole in his hands.

"Be very quiet if you want to hook the great catfish," said Trent. "It hides from even the best fishermen."

"*Sí?*"

"Uh huh. Whoever catches that sly animal will win the money prize and their spot in the Fishermen's Hall of Fame." Trent's tone changed to conspiratorial. "You're little, and I don't think he'll see you and your pole, if you're still." Like a bream goes for a cricket, Manuel took in the information thinking of all the red, white, and blue Popsicles he could buy. Forgetting his past lack of success, he stared intently at the water and held the pole tight.

Elizabeth turned to Abby, "It is good that Hank is so generous. Trent is happy fishing off this dock."

"Actually, Hank's grandmother, Kate, gave us fishing rights when we leased our property from her, back in '53. Hank was kind enough to continue the tradition."

"Hank's grandmother must have appreciated her good neighbors, as well."

"Thank you. I think she was glad to have people nearby, freeing her from too much isolation."

"Please tell me about her. Perhaps I will understand her grandson better."

"Uh… Hm. I don't know how much Hank already told you… about the family."

"Nothing."

"Well, I knew Kate many years."

"How would you describe her?"

"Kind. Quiet. She kept herself apart…. Because of her genuine sweetness, people accepted her reserve. She was born into a Baptist minister's family and raised in Virginia. They lived a modest lifestyle, as most everyone did through the Depression years. I imagine her experiences and goals were typical in those days; however, Kate was unusual in one respect. She was one of the most gorgeous women I've ever seen."

Trent turned in his chair and smiled at Abby. "Not as beautiful as someone I know," he said.

Abby chuckled, shaking her head.

"She'll tell you she was a tomboy," Trent continued, "but she was the cutest dance partner within three states. I sure had to work hard to edge out a fellow named Brantley Connors." He turned back to his fishing.

Abby smiled and continued her subject. "Well, Kate Averill really was a beauty. Certainly as breathtaking as Gene Tierney or Hedy Lamarr. She was statuesque and womanly in every way. Dark, curling hair falling around stunning features and creamy skin. Highly intelligent. Serious temperament. She was the type of woman who made men drool on their ties while she was indifferent."

Elizabeth refrained from asking about the references regarding women she had never heard of. Nevertheless, she began to conjure a clearer image of the lady of the lake.

"Kate met Charles Averill just before the war ended. A whirlwind romance, she told me. They married, then Lawrence, Hank's father, was born. Not too many years later, the couple divorced. Lawrence, though young, stayed with his father. They were cut from the same cloth, so to speak. Kate moved here and taught English at the high school in Canton. After a while, we moved to town and rented out the cabin. She and I met for tea each year. Sometimes, that wall like a self-imposed penance came down, and she would reveal her thoughts.

"The last time we met, she was concerned about Hank who was nine or ten at the time. He had stayed with her for the past two summers. It was the first time she was given the opportunity to know her grandson. He was dreadfully unhappy about returning to school, but it was out of her control. I did my best to soften her worries. Then her kidneys began to fail. With her death that autumn, the house was deeded to Hank. He never returned until three years ago."

"What can you tell me of Hank's grandfather?"

"I never met Charles."

"And what did you mean by a self-imposed penance?"

"Did I say that? Oh, Trent... We'd better rush home. Rebecca is supposed to call soon. Excuse us, Elizabeth."

Abby escaped; Elizabeth was just too perceptive, and, in no time, Abby would have spilled everything. As for Hank's grandfather, Charles Averill, the wealthy young man from whom a huge fortune sprang, he was only one subject Abby took care to avoid.

She hadn't lied when she said they had never met, but she knew facts, as everyone did, of the Atlanta family going back generations. With Charles's business acumen, the Averill name would become a combination of old money and fantastic corporate success. The youthful ambitions of the man were detoured for a few years when he was commissioned in the Navy after Pearl Harbor. Near the end of the war, he met Kate in Norfolk, Virginia, not at a USO function but at the library where she worked part-time. Charles, bent on corroborating facts on Gen. Pershing to prove a bet with some buddies, encountered a beauty, instead.

He was intrigued by the disinterested young woman who would rather have her magnificent face over a book than next to his cheek as they swayed across a dance floor. He knew flaunting his family's wealth would only be distasteful to her, so for the next three days he dropped by for scholarly study. On Saturday, sluggish from hours of reading Chaucer at a table near her desk, he sought her opinion of several passages. Her answers returned concise and unwelcoming. Strategizing had been easier in the war room. She was unfazed by every rush, until the next evening.

Three drunken sailors were responsible for raising Charles's good fortune. The sailors had missed the bar by two blocks, taking a left instead of a right. However, they were now quite happy to pass time with the blood-rousing librarian. Warmed with intimate lighting, the deserted rooms were filled, floor to ceiling, with dull colored bindings that made her stand out like a luscious pin-up.

"Man! You sure don't look like ole' Hazel who baby-sits our books down in Swainsboro. Why don't you cuddle up in my lap and read me a story?" said the most deluded of the trio. Ears burning, Charles Averill walked in. He removed them from the premises as easily as a few bugs are tossed outside, and she gratefully accepted his invitation for dinner.

He watched the ramparts around her heart begin to crumble, but he could forget about a quick roll in the hay. She had her standards and he knew it, making him want her all the more. Too many martinis a week later, and he was ready to go to the Justice of the Peace.

A lover of his freedom, Charles woke early the first morning of their honeymoon, frightened by the knowledge rising in his mind, like guns on an enemy battleship. As she slept, he looked at her long lashes fanned out against ivory skin, her cheekbones tinged with rose, and those long, silky legs glowing in the morning light. He would make it work. He knew he could.

As for Kate, it was the only impulsive thing she had done in her life. She woke up in the bridal suite to discover from the newspaper on her breakfast tray that she had become one of the wealthiest young matrons on the eastern seaboard. Lawrence was born nine months later.

Returning from the war, Charles resumed his swinging lifestyle among the scions of the elite, bringing with him a wife unable to relate to lives of dissipation. Trying to please her husband, Kate allowed attendants to care for her child and followed Charles to the rounds of cocktail parties and nightclubs. Seven years later, unable to handle the heartbreak of her husband's female diversions any longer, she filed for divorce, leaving a man who would forever own her heart. For him, loving her was easy, though he knew he could never be the man she needed. He decided there would be no battle over his assets. Already his business ventures exploded with profit. He tried to be more than generous, but she refused the huge settlement he offered, cutting it by eighty percent.

As time passed, Kate's only regret was that she had been unduly influenced by Charles about what was best for their son. Seven-year-old Lawrence lived with his father, attending an exclusive day school. As he grew into a teenager, the boy's attachment to his mother dimmed. In her presence, Lawrence was polite and loving, but he chafed during the few occasions he was forced to spend more than one day at the cottage. His mother's books and a tranquil lake held no attraction.

As time moved on, it was Kate whom Charles called when he was discouraged or stumped by some problem in his ever-growing empire. She listened patiently, the only one he could trust. Every year he visited on her birthday, bringing some carefully selected gift and telling her she was the best thing that ever happened to him. A gentle smile of understanding would appear on her face—she had forgiven him long ago.

At her funeral, Charles stood next to Kate's graveside and beside his third and very young wife. He tried counting the roses in the large spray draped over her coffin but returned to struggle with the fact he would never love anyone as much as he had loved Kate. The angled afternoon sun hit his swollen eyes, making them sting. His lids came down, and he saw her face for one brief moment, reminding him she was gone forever.

During the decades of their friendly estrangement, Kate's financial legacy, with the help of a trusted consultant, grew to an enormous sum. In her will, she left half to the foreign missions of her church and half to her grandson.

Abby, Trent, and Elizabeth got up from where they sat. Manuel handed his cane pole to Trent.

"Come, Manuel," said his mother, "we must go scrub away the beans and corn that are growing in the dirt behind your ears."

He ran up the dock and up the terraces to the house, hopeful he would see Hank one more time before bed.

"*Hola*, Han!" he called, running into the house. "What you doing?"

"Hey, there. Not much. Just cleaning my golf clubs while I watch the tube."

"Me help?"

"Sure. Here's a wood. Wipe it off real good with the rag."

"Wow. This big." Excited, he jumped onto the sofa and stood, making little bounces, wiggling the club back and forth. Then, mimicking what Hank did outside, Manuel swung the club fully above his head, and the light fixture exploded with a bang.

"Manuel! Oh no!" said his mother walking in from the porch at the same moment.

"It's okay. He didn't mean to hurt anything," said Hank gathering the pieces of glass.

"That true, Mama."

"Manuel, you must not stand or play on good furniture," she said. Hank peeped at the old seating and its frayed edges and places where springs were ready to poke through. "Now, put the club down and go to the bathroom." She looked at Hank. "I will replace the light," she said, her cheeks coloring.

"No, no. I'll just get another. It was an accident. You know how it is with kids. Now smile." Her face remained the same and she started to follow the boy. "Oh, by the way... " She paused. "I've been meaning to say that after Manuel's bath... well, it seems that you... what I'm trying to say is it's not necessary to use the old water. It's perfectly all right to draw another tub of hot water for yourself." She thanked him and hurried to the bathroom.

Hank was absent for this ritual the other days of the week, still at work. But on Sunday, Manuel, all clean and in his pajamas, watched TV snuggled next to him on the sofa, while Elizabeth took her bath. Hank's thoughts would drift in her direction, and he would use all his mental self-control not to imagine a picture of her, a half-dozen yards away, the bathwater making her skin glisten. Over time, it was less difficult. He became used to the idea, and the playfulness of Manuel was enough to reclaim the most distracted heart.

She came out wearing a thick terry robe over her night clothes. Manuel scampered to his mother. Hank stood up to tell her about the Fall Festival in October. Chandler Construction had declared that Saturday off. The boy would have a great time, and she might, too.

Without a straight answer, he watched them return to the shed, and a sullen mood claimed him. He faced another span of six lonely days filled with backbreaking work. His gaze moved to the cabinet. Once or twice, during their arrangement, Hank had walked toward the walnut bar that held his whiskey, but a shot or two over ice never seemed to make it into his hand. He turned off the television and went to bed.

CHAPTER NINETEEN

S IX WEEKS WITH A minimum of association plodded by until one morning when Hank stood with Elizabeth at the kitchen table, looking over an assortment of items. Manuel wended around his mother's legs, trying to gain her attention.

"*Rappido, Mama. Rappido, por favor.*"

She held him still for a second. "English, Manuel."

"Why insist on English?" asked Hank.

"Because of something my wise professor once told me."

"Mama. The horses. We go?"

"Oh, look at the time," she said. "I told Abby I would help set up the displays." She glanced down at the boy. "You said your shoes were here. Bring them to me." The child left the room. Hank went outside, taking a loaded box to the truck. Elizabeth checked her list and filled another box.

The boy returned. "Me no have them."

"What? Where are they?"

He said nothing. His mouth parted with worry.

Hank was back, ready to carry the remainder of things. He paused when he saw Elizabeth, hands at her waist and unhappy eyes aimed at her son.

"What's wrong?" he asked.

"Manuel has lost his shoes."

"No, Mama."

"Have him put on another pair," said Hank.

"He does not have another."

"I see. Manuel, where do you think you lost them?"

"No lost. I push them in the lake."

"Manuel!" Elizabeth said. "Please do not laugh, Hank. This is not good."

"Sorry." Hank looked into the boy's eyes. "Last evening, when you were on the dock with Trent, right?" Manuel nodded. "Why?"

"No like shoes."

"Yes, we know. But, remember, your mother left your sandals in Mexico. And it gets cold here. Besides, don't you know that all cowboys wear shoes?"

"Dey wear boots."

"Okay, boots. So how do you think you'll hold onto that horse today without something on your feet?"

Manuel shrugged his shoulders and his eyes filled with water.

"Then, let's go get some new ones," said Hank.

Elizabeth did not argue. She had not seen a single child in the U. S. without clean, colorful footwear.

"But promise you won't throw them in the lake," Hank added.

They jumped in the truck and left for the fall festival with enough anticipation to turn even the two adults into kids, once again. It was a good thing; Elizabeth's heart needed lightening.

Days earlier, among the mail, he found the unopened letter she had sent homeward in August. Return to Sender—stamped in official red ink. He was easily able to determine the meaning of the crimson-colored Spanish. And he felt certain of the sad message handwritten across the envelope.

He had no choice but to knock on her door. He handed her the missive. Her eyes widened as she read. The letter fell from her fingers. She put her face in her hands. Carefully, he put his arms around her. She drew close until her head lay on his chest. He looked down on the top of her head covered with the complexity and softness of her hair.

Her tears flowed. "I'm sorry," he said. Feeling the soft angles of her shoulder blades beneath his fingertips, he gently pulled away.

The festival was larger than usual that year. Cars crawled up and down Arnold Mill Road trying to find somewhere to park. The storefronts left their doors wide open. People selling their wares situated their tables along Main Street and down side alleys. Some of the townsfolk sat inside Dean's Store, talking about former days. At the new park, center of the festival, visitors commented on its beauty and praised its sponsors. In the area behind the nursing home, children waited to bounce around in an inflatable rocket ship or ride the wheel. Caregivers put blankets around the shoulders of the old folks who wanted to sit and watch from the patio.

Hank found a spot to wedge the truck. Elizabeth trotted over to Abby's booth with Manuel in tow. The loose curls of the girl's dark brown hair flowed behind her. Cowboy boots flapped on her son's legs, and new sneakers waited in the truck. Hank followed, a willing beast of burden carrying the cooler, blanket, and cardboard boxes.

They greeted Abby with happy exclamations. She manned the church booth where an array of crafts drew customers. Carl's wife, Diana, soon arrived with her donation of stained glass. Elizabeth made her own contribution. Like many Mexican women, she was an artist with needle and thread. Each head scarf was made by cutting a length of sheer cotton voile into triangles, expertly finishing the edges, attaching ties, and adding colorful embroidered borders. Once the teenage girls discovered the two dozen individual works of art, the collection of scarves flew, and Elizabeth was pressed with special orders.

Word was out that the ponies would not show up until afternoon. Instead, Hank and Trent took Manuel to ride the modest Ferris wheel, a one-time addition to the festival that year. On their last ride, as passengers departed below, they were stopped at the apex, Trent's crutches sticking out the rear like upright, tail feathers. Manuel scanned the tree tops. Pointing to a place in the distance, he exclaimed, "Han, there Mexico. I see *Abuela.*" The two men tried to explain that Mexico was farther away than their eyes could see. They were much more reticent to remind him that his great-grandmother was gone. Energized, the child started to stand on the seat. Hank felt a little arrow of fear and quickly pulled him down, redirecting the three-year-old by counting all the red cars below.

By noon, the festival was jammed with folks from all over the county. Abby's back was aching, and Elizabeth made her sit down. The men brought them barbecue sandwiches and afterward, hurried off as best they could, considering Trent's impairment, to catch the parade. At two, the women were free to join them. Then Carl arrived.

"Hello, Trent. Got somethin' in my truck to make the remainder of the day a little easier," he said in that booming, garrulous manner that was his trademark. Then he turned to Hank, and they discussed the fact that Chandler Construction was pulling back for the slow season, and overtime work would be ending in a week. Hank would gain Saturdays once more, and, weekdays, he would be home by five.

"So, how's it feel to have a full weekend of rest?" asked Carl.

"Wonderful," said Hank.

"Then you're gonna be at church tomorrow?"

"Uh... sure. I hear Brian is an excellent speaker."

"A little wet behind the ears, but he's got my attention." The group talked a while longer and then Carl and Hank went to the truck. Trent's pride flared when he saw them coming back with a wheelchair, but his tired body was boss that day. He slid into the seat with a testy look.

"Trent, you're just so darned serious," said Carl. "You ought to laugh more. Like me."

Trent smirked, threw his head back and responded with an exaggerated laugh like a loud cackle. Carl's attention jerked away. Trent turned to look. A family walked by and stared. The mother pulled the youngest member close to her side.

Carl bent close to Trent's ear. "How 'bout that. They're wondering who your doctor is."

"Huh?"

"They think he messed with your leg when it's your head that needs fixing."

Much to Manuel's disappointment, the ponies had not arrived. Lee Wyatt yelled hello from the other side of the green, waving the second place ribbon for his comedy routine in the talent show. A girl with long, light brown hair and a face like morning sunshine, stood next to him. A first place ribbon for her dance performance fluttered in her hand.

Diana checked her watch and proposed they head over to the wheelbarrow races and the pony ring in the field behind old Woodstock Elementary. Abby agreed, insisting Hank join in the wheelbarrow contest with Manuel as his passenger. They left the park and soon entered the schoolyard through the chain link gate. Carl, still strong as an ox at sixty-three, led the way, pushing Trent over ruts and bumps with ease. They'd been friends for years, one impractical and playful, the other introspective and reserved. Four hauls into the Gulf for deep-sea fishing had forged a permanent bond.

The race field was thoroughly marred from the previous runs and none too welcoming. Hank situated their wheelbarrow at the starting line. Manuel climbed in. They looked to the left and right. Four teams. With a strained smile, Hank looked down at his costume. Each driver wore an elasticized tutu of pink netting and a daisy headband. The whistle blew. They charged down the field. The cockeyed nature of things began to invert itself—to Hank's surprise, he took a commanding lead.

Reaching the fifty-yard mark, Manuel, overcome with excitement, barely held on as they turned back. Carl's lobster-red face yelled encouragement. At the starting line, again, the drivers tore off their tutus and slapped on cowboy hats and toy pistols. Under their noses, a black mustache was planted. The people watching howled with laughter. The competitors raced down again and turned a final time, heading toward the finish.

As Hank and Manuel began the remaining distance, their winning seemed a sure thing until Hank's ten-gallon blew off—winner had to be in full "get-up."

A father and daughter team zipped ahead. The man, ecstatic, lost control of the wheelbarrow, sending his little girl forward and out. Hank, hat now on his head, surged past, hesitated, and turned back, coming to their aid. Manuel, too, forgot about the forfeited prize. His sight fastened on the screaming girl and the red blood making a line down her lips and chin.

Medical volunteers put things right. Compliments were given and received for races well run. Hank's breathing had returned to normal. "I'm ready to make another run," he said. "Abby, let's team up for the next race."

She shook, laughing. "For sure. I bet you want me to do the pushing."

Two short beeps of a truck horn rang out.

"Manuel, do you see what I see?" Hank called. He scooped the boy in his arms and hustled in the truck's direction. The larger gate was open. Jimbo's Ponies pulled into the ring.

CHAPTER TWENTY

ABBY AND DIANA WENT to check on sales at the booth. The rest of the group chose seats near the pony ring. Bright orange leaves on a sugar maple waved like a thousand children's hands calling friends to play. Sumac at the edge of the woods competed with a show of eye-popping red. Sounds from the country music band at the park still reached their ears. Boys and girls ran willy-nilly while mothers and fathers held hands in the cool air. Fair skies let the sun warm each face.

Manuel was led around the oval track on a pony not much bigger than the burros back home. With each circuit, he allowed one hand to release its tight grip of the saddle horn, and he waved to his mother.

After five rides, the child lost his spunk. His mother spread the blanket on the grass and suggested he watch for a while. Carl, guiding Trent's wheelchair, took off for the horseshoe competition in front of the school.

Hank came down from his chair to lounge on the blanket. Within five minutes, Manuel's drooping eyelids won out. Elizabeth sat on the other side of Manuel with her legs curled to the side. She was dressed simply in black jeans and a white cardigan. Her eyes switched back and forth at the variable procession of people while Hank took bites from an apple.

"Elizabeth, you mentioned a professor this morning," he said. She broke from her observations. "I thought I heard you tell Abby your teacher was a young woman, married to the butcher."

"Yes, I was at the village school for my earliest years, and then I was tutored by Señor Hernandez. Except for his fondness for smoking his cigar during math lesson each day, I loved him very much. He is most responsible for my education."

"How were you able to afford a professor?"

"Through the goodness of the Carteña family."

With perfect calculation, Hank tossed the apple core into a trashcan nearby. "Why did they care?"

"I believe they took pity on me. Señor Carteña owns a business in Puerto Vallarta, but he resides in Santolo, his birthplace. I came to work for them after my parents and young brothers were killed in a bus accident."

"I'm so sorry. I had no idea."

Hickory smoke rolled in their direction as the giant barbecue pit roasted chicken quarters. Then a breeze swept the air clean.

"I don't understand," he continued. "It didn't sound like there was much traffic in your region."

"That is true, but the roads connecting the mountain villages are very dark at night unlike American highways, and they wind through the steep slopes as dirt pathways for the most part. It rained for days, making the roads unstable. The bus collided with a truck and went over the embankment. I was asleep at my grandmother's when someone came running to tell us."

"How old were you?"

"Eight."

Hank thought for a moment. "You started working for the Carteñas, then?"

"Yes. My grandmother was not in good health. It was necessary for me to stop attending school and find employment."

"You were just a child."

"You do not understand. There was no family left to depend on. My grandmother worked in the *panadería* making tortillas but earned very little. One morning she walked me to the Carteña home. I was put to work in the kitchen and laundry. I learned of a different way of life."

"Mm-hm, a life of child labor so some fat señor wouldn't have to pay a decent wage."

"No. No. I was magnificently lucky. There are few jobs for little children who all come to their tasks weak and ignorant. Employment ensured that my grandmother and I never went without food. It meant that I was permitted a peek into a world I would have never known but in my imagination."

"Tell me about this place."

"The home is large and gracious. *Hispano-Andaluz* style, adapted to the Mexican climate. Eighteenth century. Many generations." Her line of sight moved to the sky. A subtle change came over her voice. "Señora Carteña kept the home in beautiful order. Each day, she moved about the cool rooms overseeing everything so that Señor Carteña would be pleased when he arrived for the evening meal at eight. Occasionally, he brought guests to enjoy the hospitality planned by his wife.

"I admired everything she did. I loved to dust and straighten her dressing table. Her jewelry sat in a wooden box carved to resemble a large pomegranate. My hands moved slowly. I took special care with the figurine of flamenco dancers that stood beside her comb and brush. Each morning, it was also my assignment to open the casement window and place a vase of fresh flowers on the windowsill. On the way from my grandmother's, I gathered the flowers. Some wild. Some from the garden and wet with dew. Fearing I would drop one, I sometimes squeezed until their stems were bent." Elizabeth paused with a smile. "After Señora read the paper and drank the coffee I brought her, I helped her make the huge bed. How I loved to arrange those sweet-smelling pillows. I longed to snuggle my face in their softness."

"What other work did you do?"

"All manner of household duties. Washing vegetables. Sweeping floors. I prepared her bath in the afternoon. The hot and cold running water were miraculous to me, but I had never seen anything quite so dazzling as all those bubbles. She must have known. Her heart was kind. On my ninth birthday; she told me that her gift was an afternoon in the bath or at least as long as I did not shrivel up like a golden raisin. She prepared the water and left, trusting that I would not break any of her things.

"Lavender oil in the water scented the entire room. A large mirror surrounded with a gilt frame decorated the area above the sink. I brought the footstool from the bedroom, and for some minutes, I made silly faces and studied my features. That glass was something outside my experience.

"I felt like a princess in a palace. Shiny white tiles with cobalt blue designs adorned every inch of the walls and floor. I remember the way the fuchsia bougainvillea growing outside, spilled a branch of its lush blooms into the room, above the tub. Next to one wall, the Señora's crystal perfume bottles sat on a delicate, rosewood table. The angled facets captured the light and sprinkled it over the objects and surfaces of the chamber. Music came to my ears. In the kitchen below, Pablo, the workman, played ancestral melodies on his guitar for the cook and maids as they worked.

"I sat on the edge of the tub and slipped one leg and then the other into the warm bathwater. I pushed off from the edge and let my small body sink into that clear, clean liquid, all the way to my chin, and my skin thrilled at the smooth perfection of that pristine, porcelain tub. At home, I had never bathed in anything but a shallow pan in which I squatted as I washed, then emptied in the yard when I was done.

"When it was time for me to return home that day, the other servants presented a little cake straight from the oven, to share with my grandmother. The night was cool. As I carried that warm gift in my hands and took breaths of the rising, sweet almond scent, I felt happiness again." Elizabeth looked down, smiling, and lightly shook her head. "Please forgive my reverie."

"I like hearing about your life before you came here." Hank had turned on his side, using one of his arms to prop his head. Manuel still slept. "Tell me, when did they begin your studies?"

"Soon. Professor Hernandez came to the house each day to tutor their son. The other sons are grown and married. Eduardo was an unexpected baby when Señora Carteña turned forty-one, so he is very special to them. In the mornings, to have the best light, the professor and Eduardo came into the laundry room where I worked. Eduardo was required to study the great works of literature. He read each sentence aloud and gave its Spanish translation. I was entranced with the stories of Twain, Dickens, Hemingway and Kipling." Elizabeth smoothed her sweater and continued. "At first, I was invited to spend an hour in the schoolroom, but within a week Senor Carteña insisted on increasing the time. Soon, most of my day was spent on my lessons. Eduardo and I were taught together, him being older by only two years."

The professor had, indeed, noticed the quick mind of the servant girl who listened so carefully while she struggled to fold the linens that dwarfed her. She could answer questions, which Eduardo could not. Willing to forgo part of his fee in order to include Elizabeth, the professor made his proposal to the Carteñas. Considering themselves lucky to have the services of Hernandez, the Carteñas would not hear of a discount and agreed to his suggestion if it did not affect Eduardo's studies or the girl's duties. Instead, their son became much more alive to learning with a cheerful companion sharing his schoolroom, and soon the parents grew to love Elizabeth like a daughter. In time, her education took precedence over her tasks.

In the late afternoon while the señora waited for her husband's return, Elizabeth was allowed to sit with her in the main room under the curved *boveda* ceiling as slanted rays of light filtered through the shutters of the west wall onto the red tile floor. The mistress of the house spoke softly to her of the things she must know as she grew into a young woman—posture, etiquette, grooming. The child's status among the household increased, and Elizabeth thought she would never have to leave.

Hank sat up. "I take back what I said. They seem to be very kind people."

"Yes, you understand," she said, smiling. "I wish I could show you the great library, the place that was our schoolroom. It is filled with many books, some of them quite old and exceptional. But Señor

Carteña made sure we also had the latest texts and reference materials for our studies."

"And your professor? What was he like?"

"Portly and dignified. Half blind from a lifetime of intellectual pursuit. He could be a hard taskmaster, though he often had patience with our childish antics. We developed a great affection for him." An amused aspect showed itself in her eyes. "One day when we were older, Eduardo became a little bold under my urging, and he asked our teacher why he had never married. Professor Hernandez looked over the glasses perched midway down his prominent nose and said, 'Why should I have to deal with the nagging of a wife when books have been my pretty mistresses all these years? At least *they* don't talk back.'" Hank and Elizabeth laughed out loud and then remembering the sleeping child, stifled their reaction.

"And what was it he said concerning language?.... Remember? This morning when Manuel spoke to you in Spanish," said Hank.

"Yes, I recall. My professor believed it was important to make an effort to speak the language of the country in which one visits or comes to reside. I used to think it strange he thought I would ever be anywhere but the village in which I was born. Nevertheless, he said that ignoring the language of a country does that nation harm."

"In what way?"

"He held the conviction that different cultures can coexist, but different languages are divisive. Professor Hernandez was not one you would judge pious, but he held the Holy Bible in great regard. One day, he read us the account in Genesis of the great tower. In the very distant past, humanity had grown large and unified in number, able to accomplish amazing feats, yet capable of evil. Wanting to construct a tower that surpassed anything known, they were halted in their effort by God. In a sudden act of power and wisdom, he confused the people by giving them different languages. Afraid of each other, they forgot their project and dispersed across the world, forming separate nations."

"You speak as though the event actually happened. The story does signify there is strength in the coalition of one language, but the Bible is primarily made of myths and quaint morality tales within a frame-work of history. They are not to be taken literally."

She tilted her head, "Perhaps you should ask God to confirm whether they are truth or fiction."

His eyebrows raised, and he did not hold back a grin. "You challenge me. I do admit the book contains insight. You forgot your little Bible in the kitchen one day, and I read the place where you left a marker."

"Yes?"

"Jesus was speaking to a crowd. Some of the phrases would make good slogans for Thornton Concrete."

"Which passage?"

"The one about a good foundation. Building your house on rock instead of sand." He looked away.

"What did you think of the spiritual meaning?"

He returned his focus. "Didn't dwell on that." He watched her look become deep and direct.

"Many consider the Bible strangely set apart from all other books. I tell you, it can be trusted from the very first verse."

"Well, putting our differences of opinion aside, your professor sounds like an intelligent and likeable man." Hank paused for a moment, watching some children with their hands open and waiting to catch winged, brown seeds that whirled down from a tall tree each time the wind blew. He turned back to her. "You know, it's very sad that your parents and siblings died, but it seems your life is working out despite the harshness of your experience."

"Yes, you are right."

Hank thought her soft-spoken assertions could melt the heart of the cruelest despot or even the world's most cynical young man.

Carl and Trent returned, joking about their poor showing with the horseshoes. Manuel sat up, blinking. His sight took in the empty pony ring. The reassembled group left the schoolyard and walked past the historic Dean house. Abby and Diana fell in, delaying the group's progress with perusal at various booths lining the sidewalk all the way to the park. Reaching the ornamental fencing, they stopped their growling stomachs with chicken from the booth sponsored by Wives and Friends of Woodstock Firefighters. The festival crowd thinned. Overwrought children cried. Husbands called a halt to the day, and vehicles pulled out.

Evening came on with dulcet tones like a mother calling her children home. A slight dampness rolled in as the booths were disassembled and packed for storage. The remaining people, who could not bring themselves to leave, headed toward the gazebo and, next to it, a temporary dance floor under a tent pavilion.

Paper lanterns suspended in the gazebo rafters cast their glow in partnership with the curved, luminescent sliver of a moon. Fiddlers heated their bows with music lively enough to make Ginny Taylor tap her feet while one of her great-grandchildren nestled in her lap. The caller's instructions rang out. The tune rushed around the people, urging everyone up. Regardless, those in the group of seven were either way past tired or too shy to dance, not to mention the problem of Trent's leg cast. So they sat on hay bales, like stolid-faced pumpkins and watched the others allemande and slide. Then Carl hopped up and danced a thirty-second jig, transforming the mood in an instant.

Hank had chosen the back row of their group, which left him alone. Two stacked bales gave him a better view and room to stretch his long legs trying to avoid the pots of yellow and rust chrysanthemums sitting everywhere. He stretched his arms and back. The clean smell of hay cleared his head better than a nap in a hammock. The shadowed backs of his friends were in front of him, and he allowed his eyes to roam the group.

In the brisk night air, the boy played among them while their contentment and the music of autumn sent a medley of thoughts twirling through each mind.

CHAPTER TWENTY-ONE

THE NOVEMBER EXECUTIVE SESSION of the city council, under the leadership of its lethargic but charming mayor, John Hoffman, was underway. Only thirty minutes went by before bickering broke out.

Her face stern, council member Marissa Manning rocked a slim gold pen between two of her fingers and stopped. "I don't care what you say, Trent. You're nothing but a washed-up lawyer who doesn't know his hat from his- Oh, nevermind!" Faces registered shock at Marissa's glib rudeness even though she grew more callous each year.

"Watch it, Marissa," Lavon Farrier said, rising from his chair. He turned in her direction and leaned across the table. His muscular arms were supported by spread fingers powerful and sturdy. "You know, if a man speaks that way to another man, he prepares himself for the likelihood of a few blows. So, don't hide behind your femininity someday when things get rough." A few gray hairs glistened throughout the dark ones on the head of the black man who had spent his earlier years as a steel worker on the skyscrapers in Atlanta. Now, at fifty, he owned his own business and was doing well.

"Why, Lavon, how can you speak to me that way? Don't you remember your grandmamma used to work for our family years ago?"

"That's just what I was talking about. Give it a rest, Marissa. And don't act so surprised. We've had just about enough of your attempts to run this city council with your browbeating and manipulation."

"Only trying to help. At Atlanta Accolade, they pay me to do just that."

"Well, here in Woodstock, we try to go with a consensus instead of one person bulldozing their will through every matter."

"I am not trying to bulldoze anything. I'm only trying to point out the fallacy of Trent's argument."

"Gentlemen, gentlemen," interrupted Mayor Hoffman. "Oh, excuse me, Marissa. No one could ever miss your womanliness. It's just that my corns are distracting me. Now, in my opinion, Rakeston is a good enough ol' fellow, but maybe he's one more headache we don't need. Anyway, try to be friendly about this. Let's get back to Trent."

Trent cleared his throat. "As I was saying… I contend we don't have to put Rakey in some unfamiliar place at this time in his life. We *can* work this out. John, look at the list. Over two hundred people care about him and are willing to spend a couple of evenings providing dinner and an hour or two of supervision. We're going to have to turn some of the people away or use them as backup. Lavon is going to hire him as assistant. So most of his days will be occupied."

"Doing what?" asked Marissa.

Lavon, refusing to look at her, spoke to the air. "My company reads thousands of meters a month in this county. I can use some help. Rakey will record my readings in the laptop. You know how numbers are his toys. He's excited, and he'll have funds for repairs on his home."

"Hold on," said Marissa, "I don't know why we are wasting time on this unfortunate man whose heart, the doctors say, could fail at any moment. Only people in a hospital ICU are on more medication. As I've said before, there are state programs to take care of problems like this. Now here you go, Lavon, wanting to give him false hope. He's nothing but a nuisance for this town."

Trent sat up squarely and looked her dead in the eye. "We don't consider Rakeston a problem. We're the ones who are benefited. Most of us need a change of focus from our own, usually petty, concerns."

"Well, I think the answer's clear no matter what you say," she replied. "I'm ready for a vote, but let's hurry. The Haleys are expecting me for cocktails at five."

Two council members, Eric the pharmacist and Dorian the insurance agent, looked at one another, rolling their eyes. "Be careful," whispered Eric. "If her words don't cut us to pieces, her sharp elbows and knees may do the job."

With that said, a vote was taken. Marissa checked her hair and lipstick. Uncle Rakey won, seven to two.

The council members slid back their chairs and drew a few deep breaths now that business had concluded. Conversation drifted to their families and work as they prepared to leave. Marissa arranged her papers, color-coded and alphabetized. She shut her briefcase with authority and pressed her cell phone to her ear as she moved on to the next item of her day. The strain on the men's faces relaxed as the *click-click-click* of her high heels grew fainter.

"Man! After all this time," said Eric, leaning toward Lavon, "she's still got an axe to grind with Trent."

Uncle Rakey spent Saturday afternoon at Abby's, waiting to hear the results of the vote. Antsy, talkative, he acted like a child who'd been told he might be having a different playmate over every day of the year.

Abby checked the names of volunteers one more time and smiled. The persons on the list had the patience to deal with his child-like temperament caged in an aging adult body. They sat in the den waiting for Trent, a happy driver again, minus one Sheetrock Leg Vise, as he referred to it. Abby hated the way the council meetings took their toll on him. While retired at the lake, the Eversons retained ownership of their other residence on Dobbs Road, providing the townsfolk a way around the city charter. They brought him in with a landslide.

Elizabeth and Manuel came to Abby's door to borrow a pencil sharpener. They followed her to her study, a room they previously had no occasion to visit. Uncle Rakey marched ahead of them all to the room that held a particular fascination.

A large desk with a computer filled part of the space. Shelves behind were lined with books. Elizabeth studied the titles. Abby sharpened the pencils.

Elizabeth's fingertips moved across the collection. "Abby, I did not know you had an interest in law enforcement and forensic science.... There is even a book, here, that you authored." She bent closer to see the spine and read out loud. *"Methods of Tracking the Criminal in Wilderness Settings."*

"Yes. When my kids grew up and were on their own, I earned a degree in criminal science. Then, I wrote down what I learned from my father. I used to travel and give a talk or two."

Ten years prior, her book was favorably received by the law enforcement community. The FBI requested an interview, and the elderly grandmother was quite a sensation among her fellow adherents of law and order, but she always insisted the methods she put forth were developed by her father, who acquired much of his tracking knowledge from a Seminole named Samuel Longriver.

Manuel moved close to Uncle Rakey who stared at an object in the glass-covered box on the wall. Manuel pondered the thing. He pointed at the box and snagged his mother with a questioning glance. The item of interest was Abby's snake gun, a Harrington and Richardson manufactured in 1930. The weapon, sixteen inches in length, was designed to fire shot at short range. The display case also held her father's badge and an old black-and-white photo of her holding the gun. In the picture, the badge was pinned to her shirt, and she stood smiling next to her father in the Florida sun. She was ten years old.

Abby told Elizabeth about those early years of helping her father at a time when most of south and central Florida languished as dotted settlements with farmers trying to eke out a living. Orange groves flowed over the hilly upland. Hammocks of cabbage palm, scrub pine and hardwood hid deer, wild turkey, and boar. To the south was that rippling sea of grass known as the Everglades.

"My daddy bought that gun for me in case I surprised a cottonmouth when we followed the creeks on our treks through the woods," said Abby. "That's my last 410 shell propped against the frame."

"Abby catch bad mans," said Uncle Rakey. "Mm-hm, Cagney and Lacey... mm-hm, mm-hm," he added, nodding his head.

Elizabeth turned her puzzled look on Abby.

"A television show. Two female police detectives. He used to watch it back in the eighties with Ella. I've tried to convince him that I wasn't ever a policewoman, but he refuses to accept the idea."

It was then that the two women noticed Manuel tugging at Abby's sweater hem. Bending low to give him her full attention, Abby noticed his face had a look of disquiet. Then he said in a voice she could barely hear, "My papa... he bad man."

CHAPTER TWENTY-TWO

THE STRANGE PRONOUNCEMENT REVERBERATING in Abby's ears squeezed her heart the way she squeezed a kitchen sponge, thoroughly. What the child's judgment was based on, she didn't know. But she was sure of one thing when she had looked into his eyes—he was wildly, deeply afraid of his own father. Elizabeth eased the situation by directing the child to the window. Canada geese flew in to visit the lake, allowing Abby to gracefully avoid making a response. Within minutes, Elizabeth and Manuel left as if the strange words had never been spoken.

Manuel's statement would have made more sense to Abby if she had seen his frightened face the times he witnessed his father hit his mother for the displeasure she caused him. Then one day, the man's cruelty emerged toward the child.

Javier was away the day Elizabeth captured a young iguana warming himself on a sun-blazed rock. The unperturbed animal was the perfect gift for Manuel who turned three that week. The reptile's coloring, an iridescent shade of green, matched the light underside of the leaves above. Manuel grew calm when watching the animal remain still and angle its head with interest toward activity. Lightly tethered, the lizard slept on a small section of tree limb they brought inside and placed near Manuel's bed.

Weeks later, Javier returned to Santolo. Carlos met him on the way, and they approached the house. The child played with his pet inside, near the doorway. Javier entered. He lifted the iguana by its tail, letting the animal hang and its small feet wheel in the air. He looked at his brother and then the child. "Creatures do not belong in my house!" Javier shouted. He swung the reptile back, then quickly forward, slamming its head against the doorframe.

Elizabeth had a direct line of view from the sleeping chamber where she straightened the beds. The child, incognizant of death, looked frozen and confused. The iguana lay limp in the dirt outside. He went to his pet and picked it up. The animal did not move, even in the warm sun. The child collapsed on his bottom, and his wails scattered the birds. Elizabeth came forward. The brothers noticed her look of reproach and smothered it with their disregard. Only Carlos let his head dip a little and his sight avoid her eyes. Then the brothers took something from inside the house and left for their father's place. Elizabeth stepped outside, lifted her son into her arms, and ran to Yolanda. That was the day she decided nothing could convince her to stay with the man.

Yolanda, more knowledgeable than most of the girl's long suffering, was Elizabeth's confidante, during those days. Almost thirty, Yolanda was like an older sister.

"Your decision is fortuitous, Elizabeth. It is time to make arrangements. After Manuel's surgery, you can begin new lives," said Yolanda.

"It is more than I can accomplish."

"I will help you. We will wait until he is gone again."

Two weeks later, Carlos was killed. Then, Javier was forced to go on another extended trip for his employer. The two women began their planning. There would be financial arrangements to be made, a passport and visa to be obtained. Dr. Weston sent confirmation of his availability. Yolanda's savvy mind and work-horse nature took care of the details. Her husband, Miguel, held a position as legal advisor to the Minister of Foreign Affairs. His rank enabled the paperwork to speed through the snail-paced bureaucracy. The sojourners were on their way, two days before Javier returned.

In August, when Javier learned they had gone, he did not like having his revenge delayed. At first, he was thwarted by a mandatory trip to report on his travels to his boss in Puerto Vallarta. Javier further hid his dismay when he learned Julio Santiago put him on loan to the Juarez cartel through February.

Since the early nineties, Mexico had figured heavily in the support of the Colombian cartel that fed America's drug habit. Almost a decade and a half earlier, Florida put on such a fierce campaign to rid itself of narcotics being shipped and flown in, that Mexico rose in importance to South American traffickers. The Mexicans, no longer content to be middlemen only, began to demand one brick of cocaine in return for each one they transported to the U.S. Opportunities arose. Many young men paid with their lives in power struggles between the border cartels, and some of them languished in U.S. and Mexican prisons dreaming of their former days of high living and bloody purges.

Juarez, a desiccated town near the Texas and New Mexico borders, became notorious for the unsavory police who sometimes assisted in kidnappings and murder for the cartel. Corruption was nothing new in Mexico. Bribe taking was seen as benign, almost a matter of tradition. So pervasive was the practice that, in some places, when the clerk in charge of driver's licenses asked, "With test or without?" he was often answered with a handful of pesos.

With so much drug money at stake, the ingenuity of the area's criminals surpassed the ordinary. Border guards were paid off and large tractor-trailers delivered cocaine hidden among Mexican produce headed straight for New York. A different method neutralized the search dogs by placing the illegal substances in well sealed freezers destined for American showrooms. Within the U.S., hubs were established to carry the drugs to their destinations once the supply made it across the border. By the mid-nineties, the Rio Grande Valley was teeming in illegal commerce.

On a ranch in Juarez, Javier again plunged the shovel into the dirt. A stench overriding the smell of dry earth rose to his nostrils. Had someone forgotten to lime the other bodies? He wondered if the step had been omitted as a sensory warning to those who might need it. Within an hour, he created a hole sufficient to receive the canvas wrapped body. The bulging package landed in its grave with a thud. Dark was creeping in and animal cries pierced the landscape. Javier hurried through his task of filling the pit with soil. He needed time to prepare for the after-sundown celebration. In Mexico, it was the Night of the Dead.

A *compañero*, in his twenties also, drove up in a truck as Javier smoothed the ground.

"It does not look like Diego will be trying to skim any more of Torres' profits," said the man getting out of the vehicle.

"Yes," replied Javier, "but he is probably having a good time doing all our favorite pastimes in Hell. I do not understand why he begged for his life as he did." The false concern on his face changed to laughter.

"Now that you're done, do you want a ride to the main house?" said the other man. "I hear much entertainment is to be provided as reward for our hard work."

"Not tonight my friend. I plan to spend the evening in the old way. Drop me at the bunkhouse," said Javier.

"All right, then. But that may mean only one of us will have a hangover tomorrow when we leave for the changing house in Monterrey." His boot kicked at the pebbles and dirt, then he looked up. "Are they the ones who carry the dollars to the U.S. banks?"

"I do not know. I just take care of their people problems." Javier tossed him the shovel and smiled. "The boss says you are learning quickly, but do not try to pass me in this organization."

"How could that happen? I do not have your valuable skills."

"Few do," proclaimed Javier to the arid sky as they got in the truck.

Later, at the bunk house, Javier gathered the things he needed and pulled on a light jacket. He moved into the night where he encountered the ranch pastureland severe and lifeless. A land coated with an irredeemable aura that clung to the stricken place, like mindless maggots. He whistled softly and checked behind, trying to shake the stories he heard as a child. Maybe he would see Carlos tonight. A tingle shot up his spine. It was the second of November and all over Mexico, people were heading to the cemeteries to spend the night in song and feasting in remembrance of their loved ones.

Javier was many miles from his brother's resting place, but Javier would honor him as tradition decreed. A huge piñon pine clung to a rocky prominence. He trod lightly to the specter, its limbs like striated arms reaching in the night air. Perfect, he thought. He laid a line of yellow marigold buds directing his brother's spirit to the spot where Javier would spread gifts of food, cigarettes and alcohol. Sitting down, he unrolled the cotton kerchief that contained delightful sweets—*camote* and *albaricocque* and little cakes in the form of frosted white skulls. Then he lit candles and prepared to stay awake the night. The tequila was rewarding as it warmed his chest and inspired him to sing some of their favorite songs. The exhaustion of long days stupefied his mind, and soon he lay on his side asleep. With no one seeing or caring, the fat candles burned down to nothing and sputtered out as though a commentary on the forgotten lives now in shallow graves on all three ranches owned by Filipo Torres, south of Juarez.

Javier's coworker did not stay for things to heat up red hot at the ranch house. After a meal and two-dozen toasts where he swallowed much less than he made it appear, he performed his most inebriated walk out of the place. As if a joke, the name, House of Peace, graced the doorway lintel.

Inside the deserted bunkhouse, using a cell phone, he made a long-awaited call to headquarters in Dallas with his latest collection of facts, figures, and persons. Javier Gutierrez had become a recent addition to their list.

Afterward, the young man carefully packaged an acrylic picture holder to be mailed to an undercover address. One recent night, the agent handed that same plastic frame to Javier. He admired the Hispanic beauty the man called his "little parrot." They ate greasy *chicharron* and drank *mescal* as Javier noted her merits with joking.

The next day, they rode more than four hundred miles to Monterrey, over dusty roads with a great deal of money concealed in the Jeep. Jackrabbits scrambled for their holes. Desert tortoise contracted into their shells.

"You and I get along well, my friend," said Javier. "Perhaps I will take you with me when I travel to Tennessee to search out my wife. If you are lucky, you will see me squeeze the life out of that loose woman."

The undercover agent, holding onto his hat, nodded and grinned.

The vehicle bounced over rocks. Javier's laughter tumbled out. The sounds rolled over the desert, assaulting brittlebush and desert chicory until seeping into the forsaken earth, and all was quiet again.

CHAPTER TWENTY-THREE

THANKSGIVING WAS A WHOLLY different experience that year. Three times before, Hank had passed on their invitation. When November came again, he accepted. Elderly Harold Barner, across the cove, had always been a guest on the holiday. Sawhorses and plywood formed the long table where twenty-one were fed.

The Everson children and grandchildren congregated each year at the lake. Four girls, ranging in age from seven to fifteen, belonged to Roy and his wife. The two younger girls "oohed" and "aahed" over Manuel, and when he would consent, they made him their little doll inclined to obey their wishes. Dana and her husband flew down from Raleigh. Their son and daughter traveled from college the next day. Rebecca and her husband closed shop in Charleston and brought their three sons.

Abby would never hear of hotel rooms, although her age was starting to give her difficulty. The master bedroom and two loft areas were given to the couples. Trent shared the great room sofa beds with his grandsons. Each year, Abby turned her study into a dorm room for herself and five girls. With all the talk and laughter going on until the wee hours, their grandmother never got enough rest, but she assembled a fuller picture of their lives, pretending to be asleep. At 7:30 in the morning, Trent blew his bosun whistle. Everyone had to be out of bed, returning order to the cabin. Usually, the boys protested. Trent always told them more sleep was fine so long as they were dressed and fed.

Once up, they remembered there was hiking and rock climbing to be done. The ladies were given free rein of the bathrooms while the men, unshaven and rumpled, drank coffee and prepared breakfast.

Daily, Hank wandered in the back door to lend an item or bring Elizabeth's gift of food. After the normal social tidings, he usually lingered, leaning against the old pie safe, slightly apart from the bustle and joking. A question kept returning like a stray dog. How did Abby and Trent handle the change once the extended weekend was over, and the interior of their cabin suddenly rested too calm?

The month was drawing to a close, and the approaching trip to Tennessee came nearer. Fine specialists were available in Atlanta, but Elizabeth insisted on Sandholm. The surgeon's cavalier treatment had not won Hank's regard, but he could put aside dislike for competence. This time, he would be there to correct any rudeness.

The last four weeks of shorter workdays had been filled after dinner with conversation and play on the terraces. Nightfall was coming on earlier, so Hank installed lighting around the perimeter. Elizabeth often sat, wearing a corduroy jacket, watching Hank teach Manuel how to catch a baseball or move a soccer ball from one side of the terrace to the other. When the child grew tired, he sat in Hank's lap, and they played another game. Manuel was required to learn two English words while Hank pressed to acquire ten in Spanish. Elizabeth was their quizmaster handing out milk and a cookie to the winner. Hank customarily lost at the game until one evening when Manuel's laughter came up short, and his eyebrows pulled together with suspicion.

"You know the whole world, Han. But why you no win?"

Hank made a mental note to lose with less consistency.

Each evening, as twilight dimmed further, the lights came on, down the cove in Harold Barner's house. Later, Harold would open the back door and call his shelties in for the night. Without fail, the man, woman, and child turned their heads, listening. Through the cool air and rising mist, Harold's voice was altered into that of a stranger.

With the changes in the woods all around, there was no denying another season gained on the present one. The gray tree trunks were isolated, thick posts without foliage to liven them. A different smell saturated the air, a combination of wood smoke and moist brown leaves fallen layer upon layer on the ground. From their high viewpoint, the color of the lake took on the deeper tone of brackish green. It seemed that all the life beneath the surface was coming to a standstill, waiting for the somnolent winter and the uncertainty it would bring.

On those evenings, Elizabeth would call a halt to their play. Following Manuel and her, up the walk, Hank came lagging behind, taking one last look at the darkening lake before switching off the terrace lighting.

During November, they had gone to a few high school football games. On Saturdays, Elizabeth yielded to some kind of entertainment for the three of them—a park, a movie, or a local tourist attraction. Acquaintances of Hank, who saw him, later debated about the grin always plastered on his face. Yet, nature conspired to make him aware of the coming transition, and his good attitude hadn't lasted. And that's why he found himself seated on a stool in Marietta at Bartram's Grill and Sports Bar.

Another workweek had ended, but he wasn't ready for home. Resentment and yearning were alternating sledgehammers in his head. Four months had slipped by since the last scotch on the rocks, but he was thirsty now. Dressed casually but smart, he had taken the afternoon off to confer with his attorney.

Inside Bartram's, familiarity welcomed him—the varnished wood counter, the shape of the glass sitting comfortably in his hand. A place where, two years prior, he had almost given in to the relentless prowling of a redhead named Suzie, who overlooked his heavyweight frame for his youth. The idea of the soft woman seemed palatable at first, but, unknown to him, he saved himself from a world of trouble. Detracting from the prettiness of her heart-shaped face was a soul as thin as the air of the Rockies where she came from. Somehow, he knew the coming together of a man and a woman was meant to be more—full of satisfaction and ripe with meaning. A week later, she took off with a salesman from Moultrie. A late-model company car wins over a beat-up truck every time.

Hank took in some of the liquid from his glass and looked across the counter at the gargantuan mirror braced to the wall in front of him. Something in the reflection made his thoughts come to a skid. Three college coeds drank wine coolers at a corner table, and they stared in his direction, smiling with approval. The trio of heads came together in discussion, while their smoky-lidded eyes stayed on him, appraising him like they would a coveted dress at one of their trendy stores. His sight averted from the females to the bartender who wiped up moisture that dripped on the counter after beading on the glasses like self-consciousness sweat.

Hank was used to being overlooked, but without effort, forty-five pounds had disappeared exposing an angular jaw line and the cut planes of cheekbones. For the past six weeks, he followed the pattern of an evening run with Brian Barton, relieved the man didn't hasten to talk. Even before their routine, defined muscles in Hank's arms and chest, long hidden under extra flesh, appeared out of nowhere. Now, for the first tenth of a second when he caught sight of his form, there was a delay of recognition, but the pleasant surprise was not enough to make him forget the ill mood that chased him the last week.

The scotch went down easily, and Hank felt his aching neck relax and the dryness in his throat abate. He looked into his drink and took account of the previous seven days. He had thrown an irritating golf club half-way across the cove. For slamming him quickly from behind, he punctured a hole in the back door screen. Flossie, accustomed only to Abby's sweet-soft scolding, received words much too harsh for leaving a maze of powdery paw prints on the warm hood of his truck. And every incompetent driver since Saturday received the man's blaring evaluation and raw recommendation. There was a reason for his crankiness. He had seen someone from the old days.

He was thinking of Ashley Wilshire, one of the girls he had known growing up in the world of debutante balls and lavish parties he was required to attend. She was like so many of them, sired from a long line of blue bloods. Despite the front she put forward with him, she loved the life and relished everything her family's wealth afforded her. That partic-ular Sunday, she came down I-575, headed to Atlanta, after a respite at her rambling mountain lodge in the family's country compound near Jasper, and she stopped for gas at the Towne Lake exit.

"Hank, is that you?"

He turned around at the pump. A stylish young woman stepped up. "Ashley! What a surprise." She looked great as usual—short, black hair and dark, comely, doe eyes. She wore charcoal leather pants and a pale blue angora sweater, making her, as always, a mixture of elegance and sensuality.

"No, the surprise is on me." she said. "I hardly recognized you. You look tremendous. I can see you've lost a lot of weight, and there's no doubt you've been pumping iron."

"Just a lot of work. It's been good for me."

"Now I remember. The word was out that you were holed up in this town. Why are you doing this to yourself?"

"Why not?"

"How can you stand it?" She looked past him, at his old truck. "Hank, you don't have to do this to yourself just because of her."

"Don't be ridiculous, Ashley."

"Oh come on, Hank. You and I used to talk candidly when we were partners in fun at those dull parties, even though I was never your type."

Her recollection elicited a laugh from him. Ashley could easily see through the pretense and artful manners that were put on and worn as carefully as wardrobes. She admired the genuine among the false. However, it was the second part of her words that amused him more.

"We did have some good times," said Hank, "but it's more truthful to say I hardly resembled the male model type you prefer, to be anything but a friend."

"Well that sure has changed. If I could only get you back into some proper clothes," she said, flashing a smile. "But seriously, isn't it about time you gave up the martyrdom? We miss you. Everyone goes through a few bumps in the road."

"Thank you, but I don't believe people are holding their breath until I make the scene again."

"You estimate yourself too lightly, but I sense there's something different about you. I see a confidence that was missing three years ago."

"Perhaps all my life."

"But not now." She kissed his cheek, handed him her card, and walked away.

With her, everything was always out in the open, clear and forthright. He always liked Ashley, but he did not want to be another of her boyfriends, like the most recent addition to her collection of seventeenth century snuffboxes.

Getting into her Jaguar, she took one last look his way. A woman and child came out of the restroom and joined him. One of Ashley's smartly defined brows rose in a pronounced arch as she tried to hold back a smile. Why that sly dog, she thought. Could it be his son? Not likely. But it was evident he recognized an interesting woman even if he thought he had to raid the U.N. to get one. Looking past the absence of make-up and the simple clothes, Ashley could see the loveliness of the unsophisticated girl. Ashley deemed her and would later describe her—natural, exotic, and certainly mysterious. Oh well. Too late, she said to herself in reference to Hank. She always knew there was something special about that man.

The memory of the encounter rubbed on Hank's nerves. Ashley had a good heart, but besides men, she was weak when it came to gossip, and it wouldn't be long before his father heard. Hank avoided the state to the south, the man's current domicile, and Hank built little bonfires of the unread, sure-to-nauseate epistles arriving periodically. He worried little about a visit; Lawrence Averill was somewhat a coward.

Hank knocked back his third drink and put down an empty glass. He slapped a large bill on the counter. Not in the mood to wait for change, he walked out. It was ten o'clock by the time he ripped over the road to the house, frowning.

CHAPTER TWENTY-FOUR

IN THE DEN, MANUEL slept on the sofa. Elizabeth, her small shoulders holding strong, hoped that night she would succeed in buoying the disposition of a quixotic man.

Her head lifted. Keys fumbled at the lock. The uncooperative door rattled. She got up from where she sat and walked into the kitchen. The defeated door opened and slammed shut against its deteriorating frame. He paused, silent. His head hung slightly, and he viewed her with unnerving directness.

"Hank. I am glad you are home. Let me heat your dinner."

"Skip it."

"In that case, Manuel is asleep in the den. Could you and I sit in the living room and go over details of the trip? I made the reservations as you requested."

"Yeah," he answered flatly. They walked past the sleeping child into the seldom-used room decorated with reproductions of Sheraton and Duncan Phyfe. A stately grandfather clock measured the minutes. A small baby grand sat in one corner. The drapes and upholstery were done in a blue and white print that, long ago, had given up its brightness. Having lost their starch, the fabrics drooped like rags.

They sank into the off-white sofa, Elizabeth a few feet apart and turned toward him. Wearing a remote look, he slumped into the cushions, long legs stretched out before him and arms folded across his chest.

"I've written it all down for you." His scowl emerged. She handed over the paper. Their fingers touched. She saw a subtle change in his features. He let go of the unread paper and slowly scanned her length making her want to draw back. Then his sight would not release her eyes. He touched her shoulder, leaned closer, and started to speak, so she turned her body away from away from him and hardened her look. He yanked himself upright and rubbed his face with his hands. His odd look was gone and he grabbed the paper.

She watched him skim the words. He tossed it back with a flick of his wrist. "Hank, I want to thank you again for all you have done for us. We will be grateful to you for the rest of our lives. If I had it in my power to repay you I would be the happiest woman alive. I do know that, even better, you will be in my prayers. May God rain blessings on you always."

His sight rose from the carpet, and he looked at her again. She was taken aback this time by the metamorphosis of his features into lines of deep resentment.

"What is the matter?" she asked.

"God? Raining down blessings? Spare me."

"Why are you upset?" She began to feel alarm at the wrenching bitterness in his voice.

"Just look at me. Look at my existence. I'm sick of all this talk of God's goodness. It's a joke when I sit there in church, watching everyone sing all that baseless sentiment. Guess what? He's not watching us down here like the song says, *because he doesn't care.*"

"What are you saying? You are so fortunate to have this fine home and friends and a way to make a good living. You've been given so much."

Now he broke out with belligerent laughter. Sitting up straighter, he placed his hands on his thighs as he leaned toward her.

"Oh yeah. I'm one lucky guy aren't I? When I visited my grandmother in this house, she used to say the same kind of garbage. You know, like 'God loves you,' and 'Christ died rather than live without you.' Being young, I believed it. And to prove us both wrong, I was called into the headmaster's office, so they could tell me she died. The only person who ever cared about me. I can do without that God kind of love."

"Hank, we live in a fallen world where death still walks. God knows your suffering and will help you if you let Him."

"This is hilarious. If He wants to help me, He'd better get cracking."

"I do not understand."

He stood up, more maniacal laughter escaping at her ignorance. "That's right; you don't understand. There are a lot of things you don't know about me. For one, if I weren't so gutless, there would be a couple of people under six feet of soil, turning into fertilizer and doing this world some good for once." He walked back and forth across the carpet, his face contorted. She watched him, waiting for the surge of the storm. "What, surprised? You're awfully quiet now. God doesn't help people like me, does he? You know, people who would enjoy a little revenge. A rather negative view, I agree. But let me provide some background."

He moved closer, almost standing over her. "Have I ever told you about my mother, Charmaine? No, I guess not. I've been too involved watching what a real mother is like. Do you know how it feels to envy Manuel for the utter devotion he receives? That's pretty sick, isn't it? I should be jubilant for every bit of maternal tenderness he's been blessed with. But you'd have to have known my mother. She was pretty sick herself, and I don't mean the cancer she died from. *Nothing* could tear her away from her symposiums, and Walden retreats, and experiences of the mind," he said in a tone of false reverence. "I don't have memory of her when I was little except the fifteen minutes my nurse allowed me to visit her each morning. Once it was time for meditation and yoga, out I went.

"At boarding school, she came to see me once a year, all the way from England. It was always Thanksgiving. The other boys had gone home to be with their families. I would get word that the limousine was downstairs. Six years old the first time. Dressed in a suit and tie, I descended the steps to enter the waiting limousine. Shyness overcame me every year at the sight of that woman sitting on the back seat.

"It was the same each visit. She would be chatty and full of cheer as we drove into New York City to have lunch. During the ride, she usually allotted ten minutes to conversation about my activities and progress during the year, and then the talk would slowly turn to her thoughts and opinions and latest lecture attendances. I sat still, making sure to listen as we ate our meal in the Russian Tea Room. Then the visit ended with the ride back to Connecticut... she, withdrawn into her private world, and I, lost in the fleeting countryside, wondering what it was that caused me to figure so small in her affections. Each year like clockwork, we arrived at the school by the third hour. My mother would wish me well as the chauffeur opened the door, signaling me to depart. The year I turned fourteen and another Thanksgiving arrived, I was notified by the intercom that her car waited below. My thumb jammed that button, and at the top of my lungs, I sent word back—*I didn't care to go!*

"After that, I received a letter each year until she was dying this past January. Only forty-eight. She begged me to come. I assumed she wanted to tell me she loved me and was sorry for all those years of neglect.

"I could hardly recognize the shrunken woman lying in the hospital bed; the illness had done its work so completely. I stared at her thinning hair draping part of the pillow, trying to feel some emotion for her. She took my hand in hers. A sickening feeling rose in my stomach. She began to tell me how afraid she was of dying. The lacing of her fingers with mine tightened as her eyes got larger, and the fear in her voice accentuated each word. I could see the rapid beat of her pulse in the depression at her temple. Would I stay, she pleaded, because the nights were the worst you know. The doctors were bad and the nurses, ignorant and common, were hurting her. How was she supposed to get well if no one came to see her? On and on she went. Slowly I started to pull apart our interlocking fingers, but her hand went for my wrist. With my other hand, I freed myself from that grasping, needy claw. I couldn't get out of that room quick enough, and I didn't cry a single tear when I got the call that she was gone." He stared at her face. "Well, Elizabeth, no repugnance? Maybe it's not clear I hated my mother."

She ignored the sarcasm that was intended to invoke an onslaught of condemnation.

"Then perhaps you would like to know a little about my father," he said. "A fine sort of chap. Lots of fun to be around. Unfortunately, I only saw him when his conscience gave a little tug or propriety required our appearance together. When I was little, I usually managed to drive away the nannies he hired until he solved that problem by placing me in a prestigious academy, hundreds of miles away. That bought him lots of freedom.

"He's in his late forties now, still very handsome and obsessed with his fitness. He energizes every event he attends. A bit of a rounder too, but when you ooze personality and charm, that's to be expected, isn't it? He makes his amours feel as though they are the ones that make the skyscrapers stand at attention and the avenues bow down at their lovely feet. The women, frivolous and bored, are more than willing to wait in line for Lawrence's magic. To him, the world is a virtual feast, a banquet of all the pleasure his money can buy… or rather could buy.

"There's something else you need to know. This home is a dump compared to the places I used to live. I come from a very wealthy family." Self-inflicted scorn polished ever phrase. "I see you don't comprehend fully. I guess, in your experience, anyone who lives in a house this nice is quite rich. But let me go on."

He dropped onto the sofa. "When I was in my last year at Princeton, my father wanted to introduce me to a woman from England named Leslie Barrett. She and I had so much in common, he said. Inexperienced and unconfident as they come, I didn't date except when some aging society matron needed an escort. Naturally, I was hesitant, sure that any arrangement with a female my age would result in failure, but I was flattered that my father thought differently, especially when I saw how very beautiful she was. Slender as a willow, with light brown hair, and lavender blue eyes. She enjoyed all the cultural events I preferred—the museums, concerts, and plays. It was too good to be true, I told myself. She loved her horses, and so I sat watching her compete in riding competitions that spring. My heart came to life, and she was my all-consuming passion. She was twenty-seven. I was twenty-one. We planned to marry immediately after my graduation. For us, it couldn't be too soon. She asked to make it a stateside affair. Her father was ill, and her mother didn't travel outside England.

"I was thankful she requested a small, private ceremony. But we agreed a few social events should precede our wedding. I must have been deaf to all the jokes made behind my back." He paused, running his hands through his hair and gnawing his lower lip. He took some deep breaths. "We planned to have the ceremony performed in the Manhattan penthouse. The night before, I spent with a few lightweight friends. You know, ponderous in prestige, but absolutely evaporating when it comes to loyalty. But I can't really fault them when what was happening to me wasn't totally out of the ordinary in the world we'd been brought up in. After all, wealth was the absolute center of self-worth, and losing it was to be avoided like disease. However, their assumptions weren't quite right." He shot her a glance. "You don't have the least clue, but that's what sets you apart from the smarmy masses.

"My friends and I spent the evening having dinner at a favorite place on the East side. Afterwards, I was to stay the night at a friend's place, but I begged off and was home by eleven. I entered the foyer, overwhelmed, thinking of the good fortune to be bestowed on me the next day. I came up the elevator and went directly into the study. Words were burning in my heart. I sat down at my desk to write my father, expressing how much his friendship and support meant to me. Another note to Leslie enumerated the aspects of her beauty and detailed my deep devotion. Before the wedding, my penned words would accompany a diamond necklace carried to her by the maid. Leslie was staying with us for the week, to expedite the occasion.

"Earlier in the day, she made me promise not to see her until the ceremony next afternoon. But that night as my hand moved across the paper, I could hear her voice and my father's in the adjoining living room. I smiled. They talked of trivial things as though they had been long-time friends. I was grateful to the core. The three of us had spent the evening hours in that room, playing cards and laughing and growing closer. For the first time in my life I felt connected to my father.

"Then my pen stopped writing mid-word. It was as if my sub-consciousness detected something." He paused. One knee jittered up and down. "Leslie was talking of the personnel changes she planned to make in our ballet company and how the costumes for Coppelia needed artistic adjustment, but it wasn't what she said. It was the sound. On the other side of the closed door, her voice came to me at a low angle. Were they searching for a lost contact lens? Had they been cleaning up some spilled wine? My heart began to pound. I rose from the chair. I took one step after the other. I stood at the door willing myself to pull it open. Finally I did, and there she was, loosely wrapped in a chinchilla throw, lying on her stomach across the Aubusson carpet, a glass of champagne in her hand. The room was barely lit. Her back was to me and my father was opposite her, a shrimp canapé halfway in his mouth and his tanned face gone pale. It's bizarre.... I remember thinking at the time how her peaches and cream skin shone in the light of the candelabra they had set inside the fireplace and how enchanting was the long, lithesome curve of her back that rose to meet her shoulders and hair." A distant, frozen look on his face, Hank leaned over his thighs. "Their relationship preceded my meeting her by two years." His head turned to the floor as he fought primitive emotions rising. His hands hung over his knees, shaking slightly. His face reddened and his eyes sparked. He felt Elizabeth's hand on his back, but he jumped up and walked to the piano where he turned away and braced himself with this arms.

"Now, how fortunate do you think I am? Yeah I've got money. Plenty of it. So much that I don't even care about the three billion in holdings my father lost. Yes, you heard me right. Do you realize how much diversion and dereliction it takes to squander that amount of assets? My father managed to do it all on his own. A decade of irresponsibility, foolish investments, and it can go pretty quick. I knew there had been some big losses, but they were only the tip of the iceberg. The innuendos and off-hand comments of my acquaintances began to make sense. You know, financial ups and downs are the preferred food for the gossip swine." One of his broad hands slapped down on the closed piano lid. "So. My father had tried to marry me off to his former girlfriend. Not to stabilize our failing financial empire as my friends concluded. Her name had great clout, but her parent's coffers were quite empty. She was the one who hatched the plan when their flame was mutually burning out. Don't understand, do you? She gave my father insurance, a signed paper stating her role, to prove she had no plans to back out once she and I divorced. With the birth of a child to secure her position, she would win a large settlement, and according to their agreement, she would be my father's conduit to at least half a portion of my funds. His last years could be as decadent as the previous thirty. Unwisely, I had refused my attorney's appeals for a pre-nuptial agreement."

"A pre-nuptial agreement?"

"A legal device. Used by wealthy people to protect their assets from avaricious women and scheming men. My father insisted it was unnecessary, and I was blinded by love. You see, my grandmother, who lived in this house, left me nearly five hundred million dollars. That sum and a smaller one from my mother are held in trust for my twenty-fifth birthday next August." He stopped and sat down. He shut his eyes and let his forehead rest in his hands. A full minute passed.

She leaned toward him, her eyes earnest. "I am saddened that you had to endure such experiences."

"Are you sad to hear that sometimes, if I had my way, I'd like to crush my father's head beneath my fist like a rotten acorn squash?"

"Yes. You should forgive him."

"I *despise* him," he shouted. "Why should I *ever* forgive him?"

"For yourself."

He thundered on. "I waited all my life to have the acceptance of my father, wishing I could be more like him. Well now I know him, and I'd rather have my arms torn off than forgive that man."

They heard a sound. Manuel stood in the opening between the living room and the den.

The boy rubbed his eyes. "Why you mad, Han?" he asked in a sleepy voice.

Hank said nothing and stormed to his bedroom where he slammed the door.

CHAPTER TWENTY-FIVE

ALL THE LIGHT HAD fled. In an atmosphere as dolorous as a dank, abandoned cellar, he reclined on his bed waiting for the pain to subside. How much time had passed? The only sounds were the intermittent chimes of the grandfather clock and, as the wind picked up during the night, a flapping against the gutter. A warped and crumbling shingle barely held on, thrown around like useless cardboard until the gusts died down. A chill crept into the house, reminding him that death seemed to follow him everywhere. Not the physical form but the kind that decrees vain attempt and isolation.

Now he had even managed to alienate the boy. And she must despise her demented host and his depraved heart. His newly acquired self-knowledge was the flame of a welder's torch, licking his palm. He always thought himself above acting like his father. What went wrong with him in those first moments as they sat on the sofa? Where did that confident urge to use duplicity and seduction come from when he experienced the febrile desire to use her, then and there, to burn up the hatred inside him, no matter the cost to her? He knew where it came from—his own rotting, death-loving will. He was sick of himself. He was sick of the world.

Thoughts flashed back and forth. His eyes roamed the objects in the room as though he would find the answer there. More time passed. Something came to mind. Another world, so dissimilar and somehow peaceful. Brian called it the upside-down kingdom. A place where everything was in reverse from the normal order of things. A place where people lived and acted differently. That Sunday, Brian told them it seemed odd to those who followed the world's system. It seemed odd to Hank. But what happiness had he known operating in the usual way. He wondered how a person could make such a transformation and still feel at peace—asking God to bless those who harmed you, praising God despite catastrophe or injustice, putting others before oneself.

He could never be that good. But Brian said no one could, not without the Son living in and through them. And then there were those words that most intrigued him, something about entering the kingdom with the heart of a child believing in a Father who sustains life. Who is more humble than a child? Who trusts more completely than a child? He froze. Soft sounds came from the kitchen.

She had not left, choosing to remain in the cottage until the crashing cymbals in his chest slowed. Much earlier, Manuel had returned to the simpler world of sleep, and she moved about quietly, turning out the lights. For three hours, Elizabeth sat in the dark. Close to one in the morning, she rose and went to the kitchen to warm some food. On a tray, she placed a steaming bowl of soup with toasted French bread and a large glass of milk. A golden candle sat in an etched glass holder next to the plate, lighting her way through the house. An amber glow fell around her like a gossamer cloak. Two soft raps and she opened the door. She found him sitting up, leaning against the headboard. Placing the tray on the nightstand, she sat down at the edge of the bed.

"I thought you might need to eat," she said.

"You're not afraid of another explosion?"

"I am safe with you."

They grew quiet, and the soup disappeared quickly.

He put down the spoon. "Please forgive me for letting out all that stuff about my past. I've never spoken of it to anyone."

"Would you like my thoughts on the matter?"

"Go ahead. I can't think of anyone from whom I deserve a verbal whipping, more." Her gentle smile welcomed his humor.

"Remember the story Pastor Barton told us about the kingdom where you die to live?" said Elizabeth.

"It has crossed my mind lately."

"Yes?"

"An allegory about heaven, I suppose."

"He referred to our present state in a world that is not fair or gentle. A place where we are all doomed to unhappiness and regret unless we move out of our self-centeredness and self-absorption."

"I'm just a big, egocentric jerk?"

"We all are, in a sense."

"Not you."

"Everyone's heart must be changed."

"Listen, I admit it applies to me, but was it wrong to expect parents who care about their son more than the slimming cut of their jacket or whether Jupiter is aligned with Mars?"

"No. Your hurt is legitimate. But everyone risks being shackled to their losses. Give them to Christ. He bought your freedom. If you receive Him, he will take you into the kingdom because He holds the keys. Each day you will become more like Him as you put your trust in Him and do what He tells you. God is a perfect father. He loves you like no other, and He will never leave. Then you will be able to move away from your hurts. And he will show you that there is always someone in this world who needs your love and mercy."

"So how do you know all this is true? Maybe it's just some spiritual platitudes that have been passed around for two thousand years."

"I know from experience."

"What?"

"I was imprisoned by hatred."

"You?"

"It is true."

"Oh, the bus driver responsible for your family's death."

"No. In my country, death is not a rare thing reserved for the elderly. We are resigned to it. I was older when someone stole my happiness and my future, but God has healed my heart and repaid me with joy many times over."

"What happened?"

"I will tell you another time. Now I must see about Manuel."

"Let me carry him to the shed." They walked into the den where the child slept. Hank looked down at the boy enveloped in a quilt of melon and brown squares and scooped him up.

The child awakened for a moment from a happier dream.

"Han, I caught the big fish," he mumbled before sliding back into sleep.

Hank carried him toward the shed. He could smell soap on the child's skin. They tucked him in the covers, and Hank started to turn on a space heater.

"It is best to leave it off," Elizabeth whispered. "Once we are under our blankets we are fine. I turn it on in the morning as we dress."

"All right. I'll leave you two, then." He began to depart but turned back and moved nearer. "Again, thank you for forgiving my stormy nature. I'll think about what you said. I just want you to know... I'm not sure what would have happened to me if I hadn't met you, friend. I find myself wanting to revolve around you as though you were the sun." He stopped, sensing he might make her uncomfortable and he stepped back.

"Just remember, Hank, only Christ can be the center of our life and happiness. If we place another human being there, eventually they will fail or disappoint or separation comes. Children grow up and leave. Old age and sickness take the ones we love. Never look for the perfect in the imperfect." She moved close and took his large hands, rubbing warmth into them.

"I'm the older, worldly-wise one," he said, "yet, sometimes in your presence, I feel as though I know nothing. Sleep well, Elizabeth." Their hands separated and he left.

Two nights later, he sat in Brian Barton's office. Hank asked more about that extraordinary place and how to enter in. His past came into the open. Wealth, intellect, or earthly relationships made a poor base on which to build a life, he said. He required an enduring foundation, something more substantial than sand. The storms had come early in his life, tearing away his shelter. He would build the rest of his life on something that was permanent, solid like bedrock, or he would have nothing at all.

Brian spoke first about humanity's predicament—man's need to recognize his absolute inability to face a sinless God. Hank understood; even if only for an instant, he had already seen deep inside his own heart, and the awareness of what he was capable of frightened him.

CHAPTER TWENTY-SIX

THE BRIGHT SUN CHASED away any nip in the air that Saturday in early December as Trent and Manuel put their lines in the water.

"Manuel, you remember my friend, Harold Barner, on the other side of the lake? We visited, and you played with the dogs."

"Uh huh."

"Well, Harold saw the Big Catfish last week."

"Yeah?" said the child, eyes opened wide.

"Friends are coming over for lunch, today. Wouldn't they be surprised if we had that rascal of a fish to show them?"

The child shook his head.

"Okay. I want you to use my lucky pole today. It's got special line to haul in big fish and something tells me we're going to hit the jackpot."

"Look, Tren! Bubbles."

"I bet that's him."

Their lines had only been in the water seconds when Manuel felt tugs on his line. "The Catfish!" he squealed.

"I'll help you in case it's that monster," said Trent. They were forced to wrangle with the underwater creature for a moment; then the tension released and the fish flew out of its hiding place. Thud! It landed on the dock like a slab of rock. Manuel ran around the huge catfish, shrieking with excitement. Trent yelled, "You caught him! You caught him!" Fighting to catch his breath, the boy hunched down to get a closer look at his whiskered catch. He didn't seem to notice its filmy eyes or the way it failed to flop and wriggle.

"Looks like the struggle he gave us must've done him in," said Trent.

"Yeah," Manuel responded with awe.

"Let's go show your mama." Up they raced to the house, carrying the smelly trophy.

Down in the murky water, Hank could take the cold no longer and prayed they were gone, because he was coming up, no matter what. He emerged from the lake, his skin revealing a blue undertone. Nonetheless, he was laughing, knowing the feat had been accomplished. Carl Cannon and Phil Arnett, hiding behind a gigantic holly near the shoreline, ran to meet him. They surrounded him with his terry bathrobe that Abby had warmed in the dryer. With great haste, the two men assisted him to the cabin.

They took him to Abby and Trent's bedroom where they peeled off his wet clothes and slapped a wool hat over towel-dried hair. Shivers made it impossible to talk. He slipped on triple layers of clothing topped by a jacket and came out of the bedroom to sit in a chair next to the crackling fire. Diana Cannon and Kristin Arnett put gloves on his hands and covered his legs with an electric blanket. He smiled despite sluggish facial muscles and waves of shaking.

"I'm impressed, Hank," said Diana. "I don't think Carl would have gone to that extent even for his own children." Hank gave a weak nod of acknowledgment.

"Hey now," said Carl. "I got on the roof one freezing December over twenty years ago and stomped around just so our doubting Beth Ann would think it was Santa's reindeer. Not that it worked."

Kristen Arnett gave a surprised smile. "Are you serious?"

Diana nodded vigorously. "Yes, he is. Beth Ann was thirteen. A cranky age. Said she was running away to live at Laney's house because they had Hanukkah and it was real."

Carl politely butted forward. "Didn't I wise up? And then wasn't I the one who got Bethlehem Nights started with the youth group?"

"Yes, and a fine shepherd, innkeeper, and wiseman you've been over the years."

Hank removed his blanket, and the group turned their attention to him. Normal coloring had returned to his face. His brain functioned again. "I could hardly see in that soupy water! I can't believe it worked!"

Phil Arnett added another log to the fire. "Heard you forgot to factor in thawing time. How'd you get a hook into that hunk of icy fish from Harold's freezer?"

Hank took off the hat and rubbed his bright pink ears. "I just looped the line around it half a dozen times. But Manuel's pretty smart."

"Look," said Carl, "if he noticed, we'll just tell him the animal's tangled predicament was a result of fisherman's fight."

"You do have a way with words."

"Yeah. I've had to do my share of ad-libbing."

"Oh, yeah. Your hobby."

"Too many pages of dialogue, overloaded synapses, and a brain vacuum is gonna happen, even when I was a young buck." Carl raised an index finger. "Back in '61, when I played opposite Richard Burton in Hamlet, the mind went blank. Some quick thinking and I salvaged things. Rave reviews all over London." He grinned wide.

"Now, Carl," said Diana. "If anything, it was probably Dick Burt and a dinner theater in Londonville, Alabama."

Abby came from the kitchen, with steaming coffee for Hank. "I can't believe you were willing to risk hypothermia," she said.

"The dive shop doesn't normally stock suits for my height, so I just rented a tank."

"Well, I guess you survived. It helps that the temperature is more like April than December," she added.

"Believe me, the weather report was my green light."

"Think you'll be back to normal in time? They'll be walking over in about five minutes."

"I'm sure of it."

Arnett's two young kids ran around exploring the cabin. Noreen arrived laden down with food. Soon after, Brian Barton joined the party. Swirling streamers in rainbow colors decorated the air above their heads. A sign on the mantle read, "Manuel, good luck on your trip to Tennessee!" A small package covered in shiny gold wrapping paper sat in the middle of the game table.

Finally, the back door opened. Manuel and Elizabeth stood beside one another. Trent came up behind with a closed cardboard box. Before they could step inside, the boy was greeted with clapping and exclamations.

"You did it!"

"You caught the Catfish!"

"Congratulations, fisherman!"

Manuel resisted moving forward. His head leaned to one side. His eyebrows took a questioning stance.

"What's wrong, Manuel?" asked Hank.

The child hesitated for a moment then asked, "How you know?" Everyone's head swiveled around, turning worried looks on Hank.

Harold Barner, having come in the front door, unnoticed, saw and heard everything. He walked to the table as quickly as his eighty-nine-year-old legs could carry him and held up the prize. "I told them, Manuel!" Everyone made another turn to look at the distinguished gentleman who dressed for social gatherings as though it was a night at the opera. "Remember those binoculars I have? Well, I was out there on my dock looking for signs of that lazy old Kingfisher that catches more fish than I do. I thought I might get some tips by watching. Well, what do I see? You. Pulling in the Great Catfish! But I'm not a poor loser, so I got on the phone, and now the whole town knows. Here are your winnings." Satisfied, the child ran to the golden package. Inside was a wad of play money. Manuel skipped over to his mother and handed her the prize. Harold stood a little prouder, having saved the day, though somewhat ashamed at his new ability to prevaricate. In a flash, Carl was over, giving him slaps on the back.

"Manuel," said Elizabeth, "I will save this for you until we get back from seeing the doctor. Then we will use it for whatever you want."

"A dog."

"And what would happen when we returned to Mexico? You know he would run off chasing the forest animals and be lost forever. I think one of those toy bikes you saw at the store would be better."

"Okay. I like that, too."

"Now, friends," said Abby. "Please help yourself to some food."

Happiness gave a boost to everyone's appetite as they crowded around the buffet table. Manuel found Hank talking with Brian Barton. The child took Hank by the hand and led him to the display.

"See my big fish."

"Wow, that's the biggest catfish I've ever seen. It may even be a world's record. Yes sir, you are one strong, brave little boy." Hank reached down and, in one swoop, the child was seated on Hank's shoulders. Like a king, Manuel surveyed the festivities.

The doorbell rang and in walked Lavon Farrier and his wife, Althea. Uncle Rakey was next, along with his driver, Lee Wyatt, and Phoebe, the girl who had stolen Lee's heart with a dance. A voice calling made them look up. Close to the cabin cross beams, Manuel called hello.

Lee stammered once or twice as he introduced his girlfriend around the gathering, and that's when Trent got the idea for some fun. Maybe Carl was right. Trent gestured to Hank. They needed to talk. After some coaxing, Manuel let go of the lock he had around Hank's head and consented to be lowered. Then Trent reached up to put an arm around the man that was almost a foot taller. In hushed tones, Trent tossed out his plan.

CHAPTER TWENTY-SEVEN

CARL ENJOYED A SECOND helping of ham before the men strolled outside to debate the future of an old outboard motor Trent tried to resuscitate since October. Raised during the depression, Trent was shaped into a man who hated to toss a perfectly good item that only needed some work. The men enumerated the pros and cons of his continued efforts as they gathered on the deck.

Hank fought a strong urge to ignore everyone and wrestle with the motor. He looked at Uncle Rakey standing near the deck rail, also seeming out of place. Hank wondered how much verbal interaction the man really understood.

Rakey moved from the rail and took a seat near Phil Arnett. Rakey's focus pounced on Phil. "9482 Mansard Lane."

"Right on target, Rakey. How'd you know about our new house?"

But Rakey withdrew. His attention continued with each face. The man's lips moved silently. Hank exchanged an amused grin with Arnett.

Manuel wandered in and out, trying to make up his mind. Being cuddled by the women inside or having someone to roughhouse with, each option had appeal. Soon the Arnett kids, thinking of the advantage their ages of seven and eight would give them, talked him into hide-and-seek inside the cabin. But they weren't the only ones in a playful mood.

"What is it, Brian? Red flags already?" asked Trent.

Wise beyond his twenty-eight years, he smiled and answered, "These things have a way of backfiring."

"Leave it to me," Trent said, patting the top of Brian's shoulder.

More chairs from inside were added until everyone had a seat. The fire in the built-in grill at the end of the deck roared, keeping them toasty as the temperature began to drop. Lee broke from his girl who was busy scrubbing empty casserole dishes, and he joined the men.

For some time, the talk centered on the current controversy of an interstate arc to replace Highway 20. Then Trent switched the axis of interest.

"So, Lee. Is your heart doing flip-flops over that girl?" asked Trent.

"She's special, if that's what you mean," Lee said with an uncomfortable look.

"Did I hear her tell Abby, you didn't bring her home until one-thirty the other night?"

Lavon Farrier, sat up straight, an indignant look on his normally easy-going face. "Man! If some fellow brought Andrea or Latrelle home that late, I'd kick him in the rear so hard that the soles of his feet would be saying hello to the back of his eyeballs." It was all said in one vehement breath. He looked to the side, hiding his face, and ran a hand across his mouth, suppressing a grin.

"I couldn't help it. I was bringing her home when my car ran out of gas. We had to walk a few miles." Arnett let out a laugh and the other men made asides with smiles on their faces. "Hey, I'm not lying. Anyway, her mom understood."

"Met her dad, yet?" asked Trent with a more serious tone.

"He's been out of town on business."

"I used to know Kip Harding," said Trent.

"Really?"

"Uh-huh. Back when I had my piper cub. He'd be at McCullum taking a lesson. Haven't run into him in a few years, though."

"What's he like?"

"Uh… you know he used to be a Navy Seal, don't you?"

"Phoebe mentioned it."

Carl moved in, cagey as a fox. "Bet she's not aware of just what that means... his training and all. Kip once told me he can use his thumbs to kill a man in five different ways." Lee's head jerked back a few inches.

"I don't doubt it," added Hank. "Behind enemy territory, the only way you know covert forces have been there are the dead bodies lying around."

"Well, all that may be true, but Phoebe really likes her dad." countered Lee.

Everyone eyed each other soberly.

"Oh yeah." said Trent. "He's okay. It's just that he can be impatient and demanding when things don't go his way."

"*Come on*, Trent," said Carl. "Quit putting it lightly. You know he can turn into a madman if something sets him off."

"Hey, Carl," said Hank, "isn't he carrying around a piece of metal in his head since the Gulf War?"

"Too close to an exploding Claymore," said Carl.

"Might be causing the irrational behavior," said Hank.

"Hold on. Let's not give Lee a scare," said Trent.

"Na-a-a-w. It's better to be informed," said Carl. "That way you're not off guard. Let me put it this way, Lee," Carl spoke with a penetrating look, "he may work for Nutra Cereal, now, but he's no Casper Milquetoast. Don't say anything to Phoebe about what I'm gonna tell you. You wouldn't want to make her feel bad, seeing how she's the apple of her dad's eye and all. But one day, over at Morgan's Hardware, he really lost it. There'd been a door buster sale on WD 40. Some mechanic from Kennesaw grabbed the last can, the one Kip was reaching for. Then the guy told Kip he'd better relax before he busted a gut. Do you know, Phoebe's dad was so enraged he followed him outside with a hammer and nails? Before that poor mechanic knew what was happening, the toes of his Nike's were nailed to the walkway. Then, in the next blink of time, Kip landed a right to the jaw, lifting the guy right out of his shoes." Carl sat back and shook his head in serious fashion. He moved in again. "And have you ever wondered why the mailmen hate to have Kip's street on their route?

One unexpected bill and the man's been known to detonate. And how about the time he drove his Oldsmobile into the Miller house cause they—"

"Knock it off, Carl," said Trent. "That's just hearsay. Anybody want to join me in a game of checkers?"

The men acted as if nothing extraordinary had been said, all except Lee, the expression on his face a clear window into his head. Meanwhile, Brian Barton, a silent appeal on his face, leaned against the deck rail.

The sun was past the roof top when Arnett's and then Lavon's wife came outside, ready to drag their husbands home. The outdoor fire had kept them encamped with their stories and their jousting mouths. The men began to rise slowly, stiff from the cool air. After all Manuel's well-wishers trickled away, Hank tried to lengthen the minutes, cleaning up, taking out the trash, and helping Trent replace a burned-out spotlight on the deck. Soon things settled down, at least for the night.

Lee slaved through pre-calculus that evening when the phone rang. He thought it might be Phoebe then remembered she left that morning with her dance troupe for state competition. He dug into the next problem.

"Lee! Answer the phone for goodness sake. I'm peeling boiled eggs," his mother called.

Lee reached for the phone. "Hello."

A deep, masculine voice spoke in return, "Is this Lee Wyatt?"

"Uh-huh."

"This is Kip Harding. I just got back in town. You have some explaining to do." Lee's throat dried up. "Meet me at Charlie's Chili House tomorrow at seven-thirty. Got that?"

"Yes, sir," rasped its way out.

"By the way, make sure you don't say anything to my daughter about this. Clear?"

"Yes sir. I've been looking forward to meeting you, sir."

"I'll be seated in the back, in the very last booth." There was a click and the man was gone. Lee lowered the phone to its resting place, worry setting in like an earache. Blessed or cursed with a good imagination, sometimes it's hard to say; Lee's mind was off and running.

CHAPTER TWENTY-EIGHT

"SEE HOW HE'S CHANGING? No more dark clouds over his head. I knew some male camaraderie would improve things," he said.

"Her female influence hasn't hurt, either," she replied, helping him slip on the oversized jacket. A rolled-up wad of panty hose fell out. They looked at one another and laughed. She retrieved the hose and re-stuffed it with the others around the shoulders. He buttoned up, to hold everything snug. "You'd better hurry," she said and kissed him goodbye.

It was a miserable, wet, Monday night when most people clung to their homes. In the Olde Towne section of Woodstock, Lee drove up and parked in a space near the railroad tracks, across the road from one of the town's landmark churches established long ago. He was glued to the car seat. His erratic emotion obscured the beauty of the park straight ahead. Behind him, on Main Street, an occasional car traveled the drenched pavement, its tires making that familiar swishing sound. But Lee's appointment with a stranger produced a foreign aspect that surrounded everything else. He angled back his seat and continued to stare out. On the streetlight poles, drops of water connected and drizzled down as though the water thought it best to scurry into any shadows and crevices at the base. The thick dampness in the air held most of the illumination at bay until Rope Mill Road and the building fronts along Main Street had been wrapped in impenetrable gauze made of fog. He looked at his watch, yanked himself to upright position and out the car door. Standing in place, he bounced and flexed in new running shoes. Then he ceased. His attention stalled downward; inky puddles lying on the asphalt were dark mirrors revealing the unease in his face. He grimaced and crossed the road to a sidewalk stripped of humankind, where he treaded lightly along the establishments.

He came to the red light at Towne Lake Parkway and passed in front of a single car that was a hard, lifeless machine hunkering and waiting to charge blindly forward. He peered at the windshield. It was impossible to make out the driver's face. Lee made it to the other side. Chilling mist fell relentlessly. Cold air sneaked into his jacket collar and at his wrists. He glanced back at the town's prized mural where warmly portrayed citizens of the county now appeared indifferent and unreal.

The pharmacy, Dean's Store, and all the enterprises, which usually hummed happily, were devoid of life and locked tight. Across the way, the depot, where in decades past many promising goings and comings took place, seemed empty of support. Blank windows. Haunted doorways.

He turned back to the storefronts. A heavy door and tarnished brass handle caught his eye. He stood before Charlie's place, if memory served him right. There had never been a sign, uncovered windows, or indication of service on the other side. Word of mouth brought clientele. Drifting smells of barbecue pork and stick-to-your-bones chili might guide a person if they knew where to look. A long time ago, his dad had taken him there after a visit to the barber shop, nearby, but the pleasant memory was wiped out by a nervous stomach and sweaty palms. His mind stayed on his dad.

Tom Wyatt had been on duty for the last thirty-six hours and would probably pull in the driveway as Lee left for school in the morning—that is, if Lee made it through the night. His dad was ordinarily the kind of man you could talk to, but Lee didn't phone. There had been one thing after another that year.

Lee slipped his fingers around the handle of his destination housed in a 1912 building. He pulled, his strength seeping away. The door edged open and a small bell on the other side jangled the nerves up and down his spine. He entered. The interior of the place was one long, narrow room, dimly lit to give diners a spell of privacy. To some a dive, the place was, in fact, the treasured haunt of old men and weary husbands escaping contentious wives. Old Charlie, looking the same, with his bald head and dirty apron, cleared dishes from the counter.

"Good evenin', son." No one else bothered to look up.

"Hello, sir." Lee surveyed things. Yellowed newspaper clippings still stuck to the wall, chronicling Charlie's contests in the ring. Paunchy and just above short, Charlie looked nothing like the photos of the handsome, young fighter who made a name for himself with a string of wins in New York, long ago. As for the restaurant, nothing had changed during years of operation. Everything was in the same spot—older, greasier, and falling apart with time.

A neon green jukebox, like a monstrous frog in the corner, greeted him with a paroxysm of fiddling known as "The Devil Went Down to Georgia." The few diners, interspersed in the booths along the wall, were transfixed by their thoughts and newspapers. On a television perched high on the wall, a football game played out. Lee's eyes traveled to the last booth. There sat the man. His broad back to Lee, he wore a jacket and brimmed hat in desert camouflage colors. For a second, Lee considered exiting the place, but facing opponents on the football field had given him fortitude. He took a deep breath and pushed his feet forward. Closer, a quiver went through his knees. What kind of face would greet him? Lee stuck his sight to the man's hat and dragged himself onward. He vaguely registered the presence of two people in the booth just before. Maybe they'd come to his aid. Kip Harding sat close to the aisle, hunched over his coffee. Steel probably gripped that mug. Lee's hand lifted involuntarily to his windpipe, but he brought it down again. Gathering a final infilling of air, he came alongside those strong shoulders and that shadowed face.

He bent slightly. "Mr. Harding?"

The man's arm flew up to remove his hat. Lee, panic driven, jumped back, smack into Charlie close behind. "Ugh!" the aged fighter groaned, his belly deflated by Lee's fear-reflexive elbow. Charlie folded at the waist, eyes clenched shut. The tray of tottering, lava-hot chili at the end of his extended arm, tilted. With mesmerizing potential, steaming bowls careened off the platter, landing on Kip Harding and the two men seated in the booth behind. All three jumped up and into the aisle with more alacrity than soldiers being called to attention. Howls blasted from their mouths. Lee's eyes bugged wide. Trent, Hank, and Carl scrambled to divest themselves of their painful consequence. Outside, rolling down the street, a sanitation truck made it to second gear, releasing a bubble of exhaust loud as a bomb.

"Mr. Everson," screeched Lee. "What are you doing here?" He looked at Hank and Carl laughing their heads off and gasping for air.

"It's all a joke. I was the man on the phone," said Trent, shaking off chili.

"What! I'm too young to die of a heart attack." Lee joined in the laughter, helping them pick beans from their clothes and hair.

Charlie wasn't equally entertained and stood there rubbing his shiny dome.

"Sorry, Charlie. We'll get this mess cleaned up," Hank insisted.

"Yeah, you'd better. I'm hurtin'. Last time I took a jab that stiff was during a bout in '58."

"I really apologize for hurting you," said Lee.

"What? Don't be sorry, kid. What's not to admire about a speedy reaction time? Now get to cleaning. Here's some paper towels. I'll fetch the mop from out back."

Lee turned to Trent. "So that was you who called?" The man's answer was an impish grin. "You don't know how scared you had me."

"Oh yes, he does," said Hank scooping goo out of his own collar.

The men got down on hands and knees to swab up two quarts of chili. The other diners returned to whatever forms of escape engrossed them earlier, trying to regain some peace before the usual attacks of indigestion set in.

"Listen, Lee. We made up that stuff about Kip Harding," said Trent as they worked in the middle of the aisle. "He's really a great guy."

Hank piped up. "We deserved compensation after you made fools of us with Harry and Major." Laughter flowed again. They made a pile of paper and slop.

"This is the most fun I've had in a long time," said Carl on all four, looking like a swaybacked mule. "Sorry we were a little rough on you, Lee."

"It's okay," he said, hovering over his own little mountain of mush.

"Hey, look," Trent said. "There's some under the table. Can you reach it, Hank?"

Hank paused. "What's that acrid sme-?"

"Oh, man!" hollered Charlie, returning from the alley, catching his first glimpse.

Their smiles melted as swiftly as the cheddar-jack used to top the chili. A ball of fire roasted the inner edge of the table, next to the wall, in the booth where Hank and Carl had been seated. In their haste to rid their laps of burning chili, Carl's cigar had been bumped from the ashtray next to the napkins. The paper lit into a flame melting the plastic holder. Now, ten feet above, a thin line of fire moved up the dried-out wallpaper seeking areas coated with years of airborne fat.

They dashed around like madmen. Charlie's weak extinguisher could not reach the licking tongues of flame, high above, that climbed just short of decorative tin panels and giant ceiling joists waiting to become burning logs.

Within two minutes of the firemen's arrival, the flames died. Only one section of the interior was damaged. Charlie took it all in stride. "I don't mind a break from my cooking pots and dirty dishes. Been thinking about finally letting go of my lease. Retirement and all that. Who knows? This place could end up a bicycle shop or an antique store." He chuckled and rubbed his stomach. "Anyway, a trip to visit Lola in the Keys would be good this time of year."

Then things grew serious again as the chief walked up, ready to confer. A father and a son. To Hank, the current scene was more fascinating than the fire. He took a gander at Lee and pulled closer into the group, not wanting to miss one word.

A silent Tom Wyatt rubbed his knuckles along his jaw line, pondering. He had directed his men during those tense moments when a blaze either acquiesces or refuses to submit. It was an entirely unpredictable thing in those buildings constructed during the days when America was switching from horse and wagon to pistons under a hood. Now the captain's job was to ascertain the cause of the blaze, but before he did, he had to settle something in his mind. Donning his inquisitiveness like smoke protection goggles, he turned to address his son whose look of dread hinted all the more of Lee's involvement.

Carl wore a worried look. One of his beefy hands gave an "oh well" gesture as he chirped, "Coulda been worse. At least that wasn't Five Alarm Chili we were mopping up." Tom Wyatt's flinty face remained unchanged. Carl shut up.

"All right, Lee," said his father, "how does it happen that you're here?"

"It's a long story, Dad."

"And it's entirely my fault, Tom. His being here *and* the fire," said Trent.

"Right now, I'm anxious to believe anything you say, Trent, but it seems, lately, every disaster in this town has my son's name written on it," he said, alluding to five shoppers who somehow escaped back surgery and one neighbor's tractor that almost ended up providing permanent shelter for crappie in a pond.

Hank watched. Trent began his explanation, but Lee's ears hung down like a dog. It looked as though the kid stared at his father's soot-covered boots and a long scar across the man's hand.

CHAPTER TWENTY-NINE

THEY PUT ON HOPEFUL faces as they loaded two suitcases in the trunk and secured the cottage. The day was frigid but not so hard to bear with crystal blue skies and unstoppable sunshine. Traveling over the miles, in a rented vehicle, they took in the changing scenery whizzing by and listened to children's stories. The tape ended and Elizabeth related a Mexican folk tale with Manuel playing the part of the shy rooster. Hank capped the narrative with an alternate ending that had them laughing. Time flew and the Knoxville skyline came into view.

Hank held the door. Manuel and his mother stepped into the lobby of white marble and polished brass.

"Wow! Do a king live here?" asked Manuel. Hank considered Elizabeth as she tipped her head back, following the atrium ten stories high. When evening came they had dinner in the hotel restaurant, surrounded by Japanese maples and pools filled with koi.

That night, Hank, still pumped with energy, sat on the sofa bed in the sitting room of their suite, caught by a late night talk show with repartee that had never been more entertaining. Even during the commercials, his ear-to-ear grin didn't lessen—dinner had been perfect. The child ate well, already exuding health. And she? He had to admit, in the candlelight, her smile took his breath away. He turned off the television. His grin faded. Just wait until that doctor gave him the first inkling of trouble… .

"This is the building," she said. Hank parked the car. They entered the offices of Cumberland Pediatric Cardiology of Tennessee without an appointment.

They had barely walked in the reception area of Sandholm's office when the mild expression on the middle-aged lady's face transformed with dawning realization. Slowly rising, she studied them and uttered, "You're the one, aren't you? And this must be the child."

Elizabeth remained in puzzled silence.

"We would like to speak with Dr. Sandholm," said Hank, taking the lead. "It's very important. We've come all the way from Georgia. No. Let me correct that and say, they've come all the way from Mexico. We'll be glad to wait."

"Yes. Hold on a minute." She grabbed the phone and dialed. "Lynette. Is he out of surgery yet? Good. Put him on the phone." Seconds passed. "James! You'll never believe this. They're here. Who do you think I mean? That's right. A young man brought them from Georgia. Mm-hm. Let me confirm." She looked at them. "You're Elizabeth Gutierrez, aren't you?"

Mother and child turned to each other with smiles on their faces. "Yes," Elizabeth replied.

"James, it's them. I don't know. Okay." Hanging up the phone, a happy expression erased her lines. "I am so glad to meet you. Please excuse my momentary lack of sense. I'm Sandra Yardley. Everyone has been looking all over for you two. The police. Your friends from Mexico. Have you been in Georgia all this time?" Before Elizabeth could answer, the phone rang, Mrs. Yardley was forced to speak with another doctor and go in search of a patient's files.

At last, she returned, but the door was thrown open and the visitors felt a whoosh of air. A barrel-chested man, about forty-five and all objectivity, stood there evaluating the new arrivals. He walked over to Elizabeth who checked his nametag. Pausing, he looked down at the boy, and their eyes spoke to one another. He looked back at Elizabeth.

"Mrs. Gutierrez, I am so glad you are here. Please forgive my former...
reaction."

"Certainly, Dr. Sandholm. May we talk?"

"Of course. Please come into my office." He turned and reached
down to guide the boy by the hand. "You must be Manuel." Hank
followed behind. Mrs. Yardley sat down at her desk but did not return
to her work until the door closed.

They seated themselves in leather chairs that over the years held
many worried parents. The doctor opened the blinds onto an expansive
view of the rolling mountains in the distance and sat down to search
for a file on his desk. He found the one he wanted and opened it. All
ears, he folded his hands and waited.

"Dr. Sandholm," said Elizabeth, "I would like you to meet a very
dear friend, Hank Averill." The doctor's face logged a flicker of recognition. The two men shook hands. "Hank has taken on the financial
responsibility for Manuel's medical care. And that is why we are here.
With this change of circumstance, would you reconsider my request?
I would still like you to be Manuel's doctor."

He looked at a paper in the file. Finally he spoke. "I do wish to help
you, but the only way I will put Manuel under my care is if you let my
service be without cost. In addition, I will personally cover all hospital
charges. And just as Dr. Weston would have done, I will provide a place
for you to stay during Manuel's recovery."

"Wait a minute, Doctor," returned Hank. "It isn't necessary. I have
whatever funds it should require, and I am very willing to accept this
obligation."

"Let me put it this way," Sandholm replied, ignoring Hank's statement and presenting his case to Elizabeth. "You would be doing something of great importance for me. This may sound strange, but I made a
promise that if we ever found Manuel again, I would take care of him.
You know it is what Dr. Weston would have wanted."

"Thank you, Dr. Sandholm. We accept your kind and generous
offer," said Elizabeth.

"Good. Then we will start right away." Using his intercom he spoke to his secretary. "Sandra, call diagnostics and block off one o'clock until four this afternoon. Tell them I'll need blood work and echo-Doppler."

"Yes, doctor. Right away."

"Now, Manuel, the first thing I want to do is listen to your little ticker to find out what's going on there. That okay with you?" he said with a warm smile.

"I ready."

Beginning to feel like the odd man out, Hank didn't know whether to go or stay for the examination, and a dark mood started to recline on his shoulders.

The doctor got up from his chair. "After Manuel's examination, I would like the three of you to be my guests for lunch. We can walk across the street to Nate's Table for a plate of spaghetti."

"I like. I eat spapetti on the plane," said Manuel.

"You mean *spaghetti*," replied Sandholm.

"Yeah, sp-, uh, *fideos entomatados*. I sorry, Mama."

The grinning doctor turned to Elizabeth. "It'll be a good time to get you caught up with all that's been happening around here. We went on a big search for you two. So come with me and we'll get started." With the doctor's hand on the small of Elizabeth's back and Manuel scooting ahead, the two adults went down the hall to the examination room, in deep conversation.

Hank spoke to that rear view, "I'll wait outside." No one replied.

Hank deflated into a seat in the reception area. He slashed through the pages of a car magazine, but it was doubtful to Mrs. Yardley that even one visual made its way to his brain.

CHAPTER THIRTY

IN THE EXAMINATION ROOM, Sandholm used all his tricks to keep Manuel in a happy frame of mind. Elizabeth was surprised the person she had judged in August to be cold-hearted was, to the contrary, an endearing man. Funny plastic toys stuck to the ceiling, and a mobile of animals served to distract his young patients. She floated into a chair and watched the doctor begin his analysis while building a relationship with her son.

Some time later, talkative and recharged, Manuel was anxious to share everything as they were seated in the restaurant.

"I hear my heart, Han! It make sounds, drum sounds all the time."

"That's right. What did you expect with all the energy you have? Did you tell Dr. Sandholm, you are strong enough to catch the Great Catfish?"

"Is that so, Manuel?" said the doctor.

"Yeah. That fish big. With whiskers like Flossie."

"Whoa, is Flossie a bearded lady?" said Sandholm.

"*No*" said Manuel, giggling. "Abby's cat."

Exaggerated confusion changed the doctor's normal features into those of a buffoon, "Well then, who's Abby?" Manuel laughed more at his new entertainer while an imaginary finger poked Hank in the ribs, letting him know how easily he had been displaced as king of comedy.

The meal arrived and everyone suddenly remembered their empty stomachs as the aroma of oregano, basil, and garlic teased their noses. As they ate, Elizabeth explained their ending up in Georgia and Hank's role.

"You are some survivor," the doctor told her. Without reference to his own dire situation in Japan, Sandholm spoke of being telephoned in New Zealand about Yolanda and Miquel Velez's search. "I was under obligation to give my course of lectures, but I told Mrs. Yardley to do whatever she could to assist in finding you. We notified the police that you and Manuel were missing, and your friends flew to the U.S. Mrs. Yardley said they were very distraught. Being in New Zealand, I was unable to meet with them. They stayed four weeks until their search was cut short by another emergency."

"What is the matter?" said Elizabeth.

"All is well now. Mr. and Mrs. Velez are in Guadalajara at her mother's home. Mrs. Yardley has already notified them that you're here. Yolanda will be calling this evening."

"Was her mother ill?"

"No. Yolanda was four months pregnant when she arrived in Tennessee. She developed complications. Her doctor ordered her to return to Mexico for bed rest. Now she's doing fine and will deliver soon."

"This news makes me exceedingly happy. Yolanda has not been able to carry a child full term."

Elizabeth noticed Hank's plate still full of pasta. "Hank, you are not hungry?"

"No."

"Well, he *sure is thirsty,*" said Sandholm. "I think that's his third glass of tea. Anyway, we'd better finish and get to diagnostics." The doctor looked at Manuel who held a forgotten bread stick in his hand. The child's gaze followed the bustling waiters who sang in Italian—*La Serva Padrona* with a large dash of gusto.

They prepared to leave the restaurant, and Manuel reached for the doctor's hand. They went first, Sandholm's white lab coat flapping in the wind. It was an odd little parade of four that followed the crosswalk in front of stopped cars and marched up the hill.

"Dokker Sanho?" said the child.

"Yes, Manuel."

"Why you walk like a pirate?"

"A pirate?"

"Yeah. Humpy bumpy."

"Oh, I guess I do look like a peg leg. Well, my knee was hurt a while back. Have you ever smashed a finger? Same thing. Just bigger. Actually, much bigger. I'll tell you that story when you're all grown up."

They reached the medical offices. Sandholm dreaded the next part, because it was a rare child that didn't show distress over the blood taking. The doctor always made himself scarce during the procedure, letting the calm, resolute nurses be the bad guys. Manuel's tears flowed and Hank, in an effort to show the child it was survivable, asked them to take a pint of his blood for their bank. Promises of ice cream, a brief prick, and soon it was over thanks to the expertise of the nurses. The echo-Doppler was easy in comparison.

Three hours later, the testing was complete, and the group started to drag, especially Manuel. Dr. Sandholm arrived on the scene, and a meeting was set for Thursday.

"Elizabeth, may I talk with you for a moment before you go? Maybe Hank would watch Manuel while we step outside." Elizabeth looked at Hank.

"Sure," he said plainly.

The doctor held the glass door open for her, and they stepped outside, onto the roof garden. The temperature was beginning to drop. He helped Elizabeth put on her coat. He led her past the seating situated on clipped grass, over to a rail. It was only half past five, but the city lights already shined below.

"Pardon me for holding you up, Elizabeth, but I wanted to make sure you know how grieved I am for the turmoil I caused you and your son."

"You must forget about that. I am so thankful for your help, now."

"It is my pleasure. But there is one thing I would like to ask."

"Yes?"

"There are excellent pediatric cardiologists in Atlanta. After our rough beginning, what made you seek a gruff bear of a doctor, a second time?"

"I remembered what Yolanda said... that Dr. Weston considered you to be an excellent surgeon, innovative, one who never gave up when a case seemed hopeless. And I prayed God could change your heart."

"Amazing. You are very forgiving, and I'm so glad you're here." He took her by the arm and led her back inside. They bumped into Hank's hard stare.

In their hotel room, they ate a light dinner. Afterward, Hank let himself be swallowed by television. Anything to avoid the uncomfortable thoughts wanting to play scrabble in his head. The words that popped up were not very civil.

The boy conked out early. Elizabeth talked long distance with Yolanda.

Hank understood a few phrases as the Spanish from the bedroom reached his ears. He could hear the warm affection in Elizabeth's voice. For a while she became quiet, listening. Then she spoke again. There seemed an undertone of distress in her speech. Hank got up and went down to the lobby for a newspaper. When he returned, she was in the shower.

Returning five floors by the stairway had helped Hank's mood. He lounged with his paper in the sitting room. He thought he heard sobbing. His head came up. Silence, except for the bathroom spray. He put his paper down and phoned Trent and Abby, relating the easy consent of the doctor and that Elizabeth would know more after the Thursday meeting. They expressed their happiness and reminded him they would fly the next morning to Philadelphia for the holidays. Then they would call in two days, eager to hear the doctor's plan.

Hank opened the sleeper sofa, thinking of the sightseeing that could fill the time until their appointment. Shoulders aching from the stresses of the long day, he stretched to rid himself of kinks. Then he made a mental note to ask Elizabeth, if he could avoid blunt intrusion, about her own phone conversation. A certain name had piqued his interest.

CHAPTER THIRTY-ONE

THE DAY FINALLY CAME. Hank sat with Elizabeth in Sandholm's office.

"Manuel," said Dr. Sandholm, "we want to fix that little bass drum in your chest before the holidays, so I'm going to talk to your mom a bit."

Manuel didn't move from his mother's lap.

Sandholm pointed. "See that closet door? Go open it up." A basket held a mountain of toys. The child sifted through the stack. The doctor turned to Elizabeth who had edged slightly forward in her chair. "Yes, I've got good news. His problems can be surgically corrected."

Her dark hair framed a face focused on every word. Hank felt relief filling his chest, pacifying some of his ill feelings toward the doctor.

Sandholm got up from his desk and walked to a large floor stand. "We are living in good times. Until the end of World War II, there was little hope for an adult, much less a child, with a heart defect. With the invention of the heart-lung bypass machine, we could finally operate on the human heart." Elizabeth calmly nodded. Hank absorbed each fact. "But it took another decade for the device to be modified for a much smaller body. These illustrations will help me explain Manuel's situation." He uncovered a drawing on the easel. It portrayed the end result of genetic error beneath ribs and peritoneum, an amalgam of misalignment. A medical illustration next to the drawing showed the correct placement of organs and vessels.

From behind, Sandholm pulled out a visual cross section of the heart. He used his finger to pinpoint an area. "First of all, Manuel has a *ventricular septal defect*. This means that a wall separating the left and right ventricle has a hole that allows some blood flow between the chambers. One ventricle contains blood from the lungs that has been oxygenated. The other holds blood returned from the body and loaded with carbon dioxide that must be removed in the lungs. The hole inside the heart allows the oxygenated and unoxygentated blood to mix, which of course does not promote health. A murmur, the clue we look for, is an additional sound after the heartbeat. Yolanda Velez noted this sound shortly after Manuel's birth. Many children are born with a murmur, and a great deal of these septal defects repair on their own, usually by two years of age. In Manuel's case, it will require open heart surgery." He paused. "Makes sense, so far?"

"I comprehend," said Elizabeth.

"Second, your child also has *pulmonary stenosis*. This condition will need repair but has actually protected his lungs from too much blood. And finally, two of Manuel's veins coming from the right lung enter the right atrium instead of the left where all four are supposed to empty. This is known as *pulmonary venous defect*. We suspected something of this nature because of his *heterotaxy*, usually a partner abnormality, which I will explain in a moment. After surgery and with proper care, your child can expect a normal life." He turned and went to his desk.

Hank put a check on his need to ask questions, remembering—facilitator, benefactor, friend, but not father.

Elizabeth's hand lifted slightly with a question. "Dr. Sandholm-"

"Please, it's James to you both." Hank's face remained blank.

She smiled. "That you are so optimistic about my child's condition eases my anxiety. But you have said nothing about the placement of his organs."

"Hey, we're all a little different, aren't we?" He was grinning. "Seriously, you have nothing to worry about. It is true that Manuel's liver is midline instead of being over to the right, and the stomach should be under his left diaphragm, and he probably has multiple spleens or *polysplenia*. Believe it or not, as long as you and his doctor are aware of Manuel's unusual anatomy, there shouldn't be a problem. This anomaly involving the different organs is the *heterotaxy* I referred to."

Elizabeth glowed. "This is truly wonderful. You are a gift God has sent me."

Hank knew she fought to hold back her emotion. If the doctor had been a man more receptive to the overflow of her gratitude, she would have kissed his cheek a thousand times, Hank felt certain.

"No, I'm no gift. I'm not remotely responsible for the huge advances in the last fifty years. By the way, did you know that Dr. Weston was born with Tetralogy of Fallot?"

Her head angled slightly. "A heart condition, I presume."

"Yes. Dr. Taussig and Dr. Blalock of Tennessee operated on him when he was ten years old. It's sad his life ended at sixty-one, but without that pioneering operation, he would have lived only a few years into his teens."

"Is that why the doctor went into pediatric cardiology?" asked Elizabeth.

"Regrettably, I never thought to ask him." Dr. Sandholm glanced in Hank's direction but was pulled away again.

Elizabeth had taken a pen and paper from her purse. "When is Manuel's operation scheduled?"

"I've set the surgery for next Monday. By the 28th, he should be able to leave the hospital."

"So soon?"

"Yes. That's the typical length of stay. I don't foresee any problems. There will be at least six weeks of observation, perhaps until the second week of February. My wife is a nurse, and we have a guest room in which you can stay. I promise you both will have the best of care."

Elizabeth's face exuded tenderness. "Dr. Sandholm, Manuel and I thank you with all of our hearts," said Elizabeth.

With the sheer force of his will, Hank's eyes were led in a different direction like two lambs herded to safety by a faithful sheepdog, to the distraction of the mountains in the window behind Sandholm's desk.

In doing so, he could avoid any more looks of adoration she cared to bestow on the wondrous doctor.

Elizabeth and Sandholm continued their discussion while Hank listened and scanned the closest ridge. His sight was snagged by one stately hardwood, now absent of all its leaves like the other deciduous specimens mixed in with the varying evergreen hues of pine, spruce, fir, and cedar. The air was clean and clear, allowing sunlight to highlight every detail of the tree frame. It stood taller that all the others. Unlike them, the tree had not been unclothed by the change of season. Lightning had denuded a line of bark with violent transformation, leaving a startling streak of white. Had it been in the spring when mountain fronts had clashed? How many more months before the towering skeleton began to lose limbs and how many seasons would come and go before the dead trunk fell to the forest floor?

He felt the chill of a somber mood. Then he tried to dwell on the fact that the strike itself had loaded nitrogen into the soil, and the open area made by the absence of the tree would allow life-giving sunlight to flood the floor as new seedlings began their fight for permanence. Decomposition of the bark would provide food for lichens, mushrooms, and microorganisms. Eventually, the hollowed and rotting wood would become the hiding place of fox and rabbit, snake and porcupine. Was Hank's existence simply part of the meaningless cycle of life and death, too? He sparred with the doubts wanting to back him into a corner as they used to do.

"Hank?" the doctor called in a friendly tone.

Unconscious of the stony air revealed in his face, Hank turned away from the view. "Yes?"

"You've been awfully quiet. Do you have any questions?"

"I'm only concerned with Elizabeth's confidence and consent."

"Hank," she said, "I think we are both quite certain of Dr. Sandholm's expertise."

"In more ways than you realize," Hank blurted with a blank face.

"All right, then," said the doctor. "The operation is scheduled for Monday morning at eight. Elizabeth, I need you and Manuel to go with Mrs. Yardley to hospital admissions where they will get the paperwork started. Hank can join you in a few minutes. If he doesn't mind, I'd like to ask him about a mutual acquaintance we may have."

The dread of such a conversation broke him out of his speculation, and his eyes locked on the doctor's face.

"Yes, Elizabeth, you go ahead with Manuel. This shouldn't take long." He didn't look at her.

Her movements were tentative, but, finally, the two men sat alone.

"So, what do you want to know?" asked Hank.

"I sense you're offended by my inquiry."

"Just impatient."

"Why?"

"Because I've got better things to do."

"You're part of the family that owned Averill Conglomerate, aren't you?"

"Technically." A smirk slid across his mouth.

"You don't exactly wear it as a badge, do you?"

"Could you get to the point?"

"Are you Lawrence Averill's son?"

"That's me."

"I met your father once, about five years ago. I was in Atlanta for the Swan House Heart Ball.... You don't seem much like him."

"Thanks. That's the best compliment I've received in a while." The moment the words were out of his mouth, he hated himself for the stupidity of the disclosure. "Look doctor, I think I'll be joining Elizabeth now."

"You have deep feelings for her, don't you?"

Hank stood up, his feet unconsciously planted apart, lending firmness to his words. "What are you implying?" Not pausing for the doctor's answer, he went on. "Let me make myself perfectly clear. Yes, I care. I care a lot. And you better remember that. I'm nothing but a friend to her, but if you do one miniscule thing to upset her life or happiness, I promise I'll break your good leg." About to turn and leave, Hank could have sworn he saw a glint of amusement in the doctor's eye, making him want to strangle the man, when the intercom on the desk interrupted.

"Doctor Sandholm, your wife is here."

"Send her in, please."

Hank's mouth fell open.

"Stay for a moment and meet my wife, won't you?"

Hank thought it a ridiculous question when there was no way of escape. Years of training made the automatic mode of gentleman difficult to ignore. Grim, he remained where he was. The door opened and in walked a handsome woman, in her forties, all regal form and striking smile.

From the first moment, it was evident to him by the affection in her face that the doctor was the object of her desire. After the introductions, Hank watched in confusion as the woman, with the innate elegance of a prima ballerina, walked across the room and moved behind the doctor's chair. She encircled his shoulders with her arms, letting her palms and long, slender fingers slide to rest on his chest as she stood behind and graced the side of his face with the caress of her sculpted cheek. Olive skin tones and eyes that were an entrancing shade of green, made it hard to look away from a face that at first appeared ordinary. At her brow a curl of her dark hair beginning to show a few streaks of silver fell forward. The doctor placed his hands on her forearms and lovingly stroked them before she pulled away. Hank wrote off their honeymoon-like tenderness to the doctor's long absence in New Zealand. Introductions were made.

"Hank, you are looking at the best operating room nurse in the Southeast, if not the entire country. Arielle has been our support for the last fifteen years. I witnessed in surgery after surgery that she had more guts and stamina than a soldier in battle, so I told myself I had to have her. Thankfully, she said, yes."

"Now darling, you know it is only my Greek ancestry that enables my outside appearance to cover my fears." Hank listened politely. The doctor continued as if he and Hank were the best of friends.

"You know, Hank, I wouldn't doubt it if she was descended from some noble, Grecian queen who protected the palace with her shield and spear while the king and his men went off to war."

Laughing at her husband's flight of fancy she removed herself as the subject of conversation. "I'm looking forward to meeting Manuel and his mother," she said. "It will be a privilege to take care of them."

"They are fortunate to have your help."

"Thank you. I will be assisting with the prep before surgery next week. I am retired from the operating room, but I like to meet the patients beforehand."

"My loss in the O.R. is my gain at home," said Sandholm. "Now she and I have more time together. The stress of doing open-heart surgery on twelve-year-olds down to infants can be quite draining. For now, we are blessed to be reunited." Hank was amazed at the respect that was evident as the doctor looked upon his wife.

Arielle turned toward Hank. "And we are also excited about our plans. We're beginning a program of medical assistance for indigent children of foreign nations. I will be involved in locating patients and administration."

"It's a wonderful thing you are doing for Manuel," said Hank, beginning to feel shame at the rampant false suspicions he had centered on the doctor.

"We are happy to be of help. Now I must let my husband get his work done."

"All right, Arielle. Don't forget. The concert and Mountain View Restaurant afterward."

"Yes, James, I'll be ready at seven." She moved toward the door. "I'm glad to have met you Hank, especially as my husband told me how important you have been in Manuel's life. We ran up quite a telephone bill while James was in New Zealand, but he was always hopeful we would find the boy again. Last night, he told me how particularly indebted he is to you."

"Thank you, ma'am." She took one of his hands, gently squeezed her appreciation and swept out of the room as she blew her husband a kiss. The door shut. Hank did not race to look at Sandholm. When

Hank did face the man, Sandholm's thumb fanned one corner of the pages of a book on his desk, and he looked out the window as he spoke. "I hope you can see that Arielle means a great deal to me. She has always believed in me, even knowing my faults. My wife is a patient woman, like Penelope waiting for Odysseus to come home."

"Pardon me for acting like a fool," said Hank.

The doctor turned forward again. "Forget it. Just rest easy. The boy and his mother are in good hands."

"After watching over them these months, I've grown attached, and I know how vulnerable they are."

"Yes, they are. That's the other reason I needed to speak with you."

"Hm?"

"Are you aware her husband is a drug trafficker for a cartel near Puerto Vallarta?"

"No way."

"I'm afraid so. I learned from Yolanda that Elizabeth's husband has a great deal of ill will toward his wife and child. It's believed he killed Elizabeth's grandmother in a rage." The shock left Hank speechless until he remembered the phone conversation between Elizabeth and Yolanda.

"Is his name Javier?"

CHAPTER THIRTY-TWO

THE NEXT MORNING, THEY looked out the window of their suite. Large snowflakes drifted down as though poured from a creamware pitcher high above. Landing without a whisper in the waters of the broad Tennessee River, the flakes disappeared instantly. The white dusting covered the banks of the river and the moss-covered soil within woods interspersed with rhododendron.

The day had been set aside for an excursion on the riverboat, *Southern Lady*. Hank, keenly aware of the operation on Monday, grew afraid to take Manuel out in less than perfect weather. Elizabeth persuaded him otherwise. She had packed the child's knit cap, scarf, and gloves. They took him across the street from the hotel to a park, allotting time before the boat's departure.

Crystalline circles fell around the child's head, onto his warm cheeks and into his waiting mouth. Elizabeth took off her gloves and held her hands upturned as flakes came down to adorn her palms for the blink of an eye before they melted. Her delight was expressed in laughter that drifted over the park. A red-suited Santa on the corner swung his bell for donations. The smell of cider wove its way from the stand where a lady sold evergreen and festive bows. Lured pedestrians forgetting their itineraries thought only of the warm comfort of apple and spice. Manuel ran and jumped through the park. From his mouth, puffs of white followed each exclamation. His squeals and laughter drew the attention of jaded adults waiting in their cars at the stoplight. The chime on the clock tower announced the hour. Hank called Manuel, and they hurried to the docks.

The riverboat stood out like a monument, white paint gleaming against a backdrop of overcast skies. Green garland and gold ribbon entwined the railing of her three decks. Victorian fretwork and gingerbread trimmed the passageways and roof railing. Accent molding painted holly berry red gave her distinction. The covered walkways circling the ship were outfitted with chairs for sightseeing. Hank and Elizabeth chose two chaise lounges on the middle level, at the rear of the boat, above the paddlewheel. The moorings were loosened and the boat moved easily into the channel.

Their location protected them from the breeze formed by the vessel sliding her way through the water as she headed down river. Each time the captain blew the loud whistle, Manuel's eyebrows shot up in the direction of his hairline, and the smile on his face was underscored with an intake of air. With their seating close together and Manuel lying back against Hank's chest, they spread blankets across their legs, anchoring themselves in a cozy harbor of their own. The snow stopped falling, and not long afterward, the sun cast its warm light on everything. Their eyes contemplated the scenery that passed before them. Soon Manuel begged for another story about Tennessee just as he had each night before bedtime. Hank had a large supply.

An extraordinary region, Tennessee had birthed presidents and brave men. Manuel had already heard tales of Davy Crockett, Andrew Jackson, and Alvin York.

That day, Hank chose a man who was not a Tennessean but figured heavily in the region. Daniel Boone opened the door for the people of North Carolina, Virginia, and Tennessee to enter the unexplored area south of the Ohio River that later became part of Kentucky.

"Under Daniel Boone's leadership," Hank began, "the Wilderness Trail was carved through the Cumberland Gap and into the valley. They were tough, fearless men. The natural barricades made by dense trees and plants had been cut only by Indian paths. The Gap was a doorway carved by nature into the Appalachian Mountain system, but in those days few men dared to go through. The other side was a hunter's paradise, they'd heard, full of meadows teeming with wild turkey and buffalo."

"Buflo?" Manuel asked, opening his eyes.

"Like a bull but with even larger shoulders and a big head covered in dark, curling fur."

"Oh." Manuel's eyes closed again.

"But buffalo were not what frightened them. Entering that mysterious land meant they became the hunted ones. And so, few dared or had the determination. Until Boone and his men blazed a trail, hacking through vegetation and cutting down huge trees, it was impossible to get a horse-drawn wagon through. It was rough. No maps to go by. No one to call for help."

Hank carried on. Rocked by the cadence of his speech and eased by the warmth of the man's chest, Manuel fell into a late morning nap. Hank slowed his words and then stopped. Elizabeth and he relaxed and let their heads settle back. Minutes passed quietly. They were alone again.

Then she turned her face to him and spoke softly, "Thank you for everything you have done." An edge of sadness sounded in her voice, but it was chased away with a smile.

"I've been glad to help." Hank dove deep into his mind, sifting the information he had gained from Sandholm and formulating questions. Hank was suddenly jolted by a memory. Weeks earlier, Abby spoke of a peculiar comment from Manuel, about his father. At the time, Hank reminded her that children were prone to fantastic expression. Abby must have forgotten the long ago monsters under her own children's beds, because Elizabeth would never have married an evil person. His mind now staunchly corrected, he strained to understand the mystery of such a union.

Hank had also learned that Elizabeth and Manuel planned to return to another part of Mexico and relatives there. Hank could comfort himself that there they would have a measure of safety. And it was unlikely that a man who cared so little would search that large country for them.

"Elizabeth."

"Yes?"

"Dr. Sandholm told me about your husband being implicated in your grandmother's death." Her face lost the brilliance that had been shining there, and silence lasted for seconds before he realized she had nothing to respond.

"Why didn't you tell me?" he said.

"I learned of it only very recently. Even so, I would not."

"Why?"

"Javier is a source of unhappiness."

"How is it that you ever cared enough to marry such a man?"

"I was young."

"Elizabeth, that's quite an understatement. You are only twenty, now. What were you then, fifteen?" He thought he saw the sparkle of a tear. She did not answer. "I know girls are married at an early age in Mexico, but didn't your grandmother or the Carteñas try to stop you?"

"No."

"*Unbelievable.* There you were getting a superior education, almost able to rise above the poverty of your circumstances. I don't understand it."

Strangely, his words seemed to drive away her heavy heart for the flash of an instant as he watched the corners of her mouth turn up.

"So money is not so bad?" she said.

"Well, no." His face softened. Twice, they had debated the misfortunes of his life, which he attributed to his family's great wealth. Daunting lack had given her a clearer eye. Her argument had always been that money was not innately evil; the heart of the owner determined its power for good or bad.

The solace of their bond settled them into quiet again. The child shifted his position, turning his head to the other side and slept on. The boat moved at an unhurried pace. Up ahead, a widening bend could be seen. For a while, their thoughts drifted by like the riverbank.

"Elizabeth, how long had you known your husband when you married him?" he asked, thinking that an overnight romance had fooled a naïve girl into pledging her life.

"I have known Javier as long as I can remember. When I started attending the village school at age five, he was there for the first few months. I looked up to him. He was three years older and the fastest runner. He learned his math lessons very quickly. But the other children did not like him. It was not until I was older that I understood. My heart always ached for him. Soon he stopped coming to school, but each year until he was eleven, he returned for a few weeks of learning. That last year, he stood up and demonstrated to the teacher that he could read quite well. He said he was not coming back again to a class of ignorant ones. Those words only bought him a thrashing from one of the older boys when the day was over. When it was ended, I tried to comfort him. For years after, when I saw him, we seldom spoke, but his eyes followed me like two eagles."

"Was it after he married you that he turned to crime?'

"No."

"You mean you fell in love *knowing* he was a law breaker?"

"I have always known of his misdeeds but, no, to your question." He could not rid himself of the frustration on his face, and she watched him, closely. He locked his eyes on hers as she prepared to speak. "You misunderstand. I never gave myself to Javier…. He took me."

Hank's heart beat fast. He made sure that signs of stress didn't creep into his voice. "What do you mean?"

"Simply, that he took me to be his wife. One evening, as I prepared to walk home from the Carteñas, Javier approached me from the doorway of a shed at the far end of the property. I thought he wanted to talk. Aware of the person he had become, I always avoided him, but I was not so lucky that night. He grabbed me in an embrace. I pushed back gently, telling him that I was to be wed to Eduardo in a few years. I was not alarmed. I quietly explained that plans were already being made by Eduardo's parents. Yet Javier still held me tight. Then we noticed Eduardo standing by the stable, and Javier let out a laugh. Eduardo ran back inside.

"And that is when Javier did what he came to do. I was confused and didn't understand. He pushed me into the wall of the shed, pinning me with his body. He tied a piece of cloth around my open mouth. Just as quickly, he tied my hands and feet with rope and threw me over his shoulder. In the woods, he had a burro waiting. I was slung over the back of the beast, half of my body hanging down each side like saddlebags. My long hair dragged the ground. In my innocence, I thought my greatest danger was that the strands would be pulled out by the hooves of the burro.

"As we moved along, I consoled myself with the thought that Javier was playing a game and would let me go. When we reached his house, he threw me into a small wagon, and he took me to a place deep in the jungle reserved for thieves. It was empty and isolated. He kept me there for many weeks." She fell silent.

So pale she looked ill, Hank still marveled at the lack of emotion he witnessed as she related the event. He didn't know what to say or how to help ease her pain. His head throbbed with each heartbeat. Nausea had hit his stomach like a punch, and indeed, if Manuel had not been on his lap he would have found much relief by standing outside their sheltered area so the cold air could revive him. Then he had one last question, thinking maybe it was not certain.

"And Manuel?" he asked.

"Yes, he is Javier's son."

CHAPTER THIRTY-THREE

SHE THOUGHT SHE MIGHT be dying a little, after her revelation, watching each fluctuation of his features. She stopped the analysis and made herself focus ahead. The blue hull of an overturned boat rested on the snow-covered grounds of a large home on the river. Hank took her hand. The steamboat approached the site, and she watched as two girls in winter clothing came running across the property. They righted the small vessel. Getting inside, they each took an oar and rowed in an imaginary sea, going nowhere. She thought of Yolanda and their disagreement and the fact that her friend would be blessed soon with a baby. Elizabeth let her hand slip from Hank's. She rose to stand at the rail. The *Southern Lady* traveled into the wide arc of the bend where the graceful house and grounds held the river like a mother's open arms. They were adjacent to the home now. She noticed a tall pole planted where the girls played in the yard.

She pointed. "Hank, that object? What is it?"

He resisted his surprise at her distraction and answered plainly. "A flag pole. It's made to resemble the mast and yardarm of an old ship. Supports the sails and keeps the vessel moving." He saw that she smiled as she considered the form. She took a deep breath, and it seemed to him that the tense hold on her body dissipated. Manuel was stirring.

"Mama, me awake." said the child, sliding off Hank's lap, visually gathering his surroundings again.

She looked at her son and came to him.

The loudspeakers announced lunch. The riverboat completed her turn and headed home.

Overnight the weather worsened. Saturday was spent in the hotel. Grim-visaged and speaking little, Hank whipped through a crossword puzzle book, pencil whirring. While Elizabeth finished a novel, Manuel played with paper planes. Hank grumbled, tore out a crossword, and crumpled the page. He saw Elizabeth glance up briefly from her book. He looked away from the safety of their room and out the window into the coming night not yet covered by the drapery. His consciousness darted randomly, running from disturbing images. His head turned back to the room, and he exhaled a long breath. Minutes later he got up from his chair and pulled the fabric panels closed.

"I'll be back in an hour or two."

"Why must you leave?" she asked.

"The stores are open late. When I get back, we're having Christmas early."

The boy and his mother looked at one another. Hank saw her discomfort and paused.

The following morning, the heady smell of incense met them as they left the cold streets and entered the imposing cathedral.

Hank turned to Elizabeth. "I hope this place is a little reminder of home."

"Thank you, but we would have to travel to Puerto Vallarta for something this beautiful," she answered.

Once the large doors swung shut behind them, warmth and soft lighting enveloped them. The silence had the effect of calm and expectancy on all who entered. Elizabeth's fingers dipped into the Holy Water prior to the nave. Manuel began with a flurry of Spanish. His mother answered likewise. For once, she did not correct him.

Their line of sight could not help but follow the crimson carpet to the chancellery with its rows of candles, gleaming brass implements, and representations of the saints. Elizabeth, a new bracelet on her wrist, took Manuel's hand and led the way. Hank followed. They took a seat in a pew near the front. A mood of veneration was hard to resist. Manuel's head swiveled back and forth as his eyes lit on one stained glass window after another.

As they waited, the two adults dwelt on Trent. Abby had called, full of hope concerning Manuel's surgery. As for the Eversons, they would be in Philly much longer than expected. Trent, touchier than a cornered porcupine, recuperated in the hospital—a broken hip, incurred on an icy sidewalk mere hours after arriving. His brothers tried joking—this time he wasn't going to get away with a visit more like a "hello and goodbye."

Hank prayed for his friend. Then his head rose. Robed figures moved toward the front and Mass was begun.

Afterward, people wandered out, but the group of three sat, reluctant to leave such tangible reminders of comfort and security. A sad, pensive look appeared on Elizabeth's face. Hank leaned forward to get her attention, and his eyes questioned.

Putting on her gloves, she whispered, "I am reminded of the past." She stood. Manuel scampered past Hank's legs and into the aisle. They put on jackets and left.

After lunch, with hospital check-in time in the back of their minds, they returned to the crowded park where a choir sang carols. His boundaries designated, Manuel launched into the area, playing and exploring. Hank and Elizabeth sat down on a bench, which had one of its back legs positioned in soft mulch. The bench jerked them off-kilter each time Hank forgot to sit near the edge. Not even a chuckle emerged. He got up and re-positioned their seating. The temperature had risen, so they chose to linger, both their mouths clamped shut. The Lions Club offered Christmas trees in one corner. Next to the tree lot, a manger and petting zoo drew excited children, but the donkey, cow, chickens, and ducks were of no interest to Manuel who had grown up around them. Instead, he was entranced by a dachshund, terrier, and Lhasa apso being walked by their owners through the park. A cosmopolitan gentleman wearing a tweed jacket came along and paused with his friendly, long-haired pet. Manuel stared and the man invited him to approach. Tail waving madly, the golden retriever shook with canine delight at the boy's attention. Shortly, the man went to meet his wife, and Manuel was intercepted by a little girl who insisted on pushing him in a swing. The singers ended their concert and dispersed but not the thoughtful bubble in which Hank and Elizabeth sat. The air seemed denser than water, and the clouds themselves pressed down on their heads. Hank finally roused himself.

"Did you enjoy church today?"

"Oh, yes," she said turning her smiling face toward him.

"Then what was that serious look?"

"I was thinking of something I learned in Santolo."

"What?"

"The people of Mexico are a religious people… but their notions of God have the power to distance them from Him."

"What do you mean?"

"Through time, my people were discouraged from reading the scriptures. So, for some, their belief became saturated with legend and error. Tradition has a strong hold on us. Few know that, in Him, they are a new creation—His child, able to come boldly to the throne."

"Yes. I've been learning about that. How did you gain your understanding?"

"A dream. After my captivity. I needed God but could not find Him."

"Really?"

"It is true."

"What happened?" he said.

"After a period of time, Javier brought me out of the jungle to his house near Santolo, telling me that he would be gone for a while on business. I was to prepare a plot for planting and have everything clean before he returned at the end of the month. As soon as he was gone, I ran to Yolanda. She cleaned and bandaged my wrists. I was covered with insect bites, some infected. As she tended them, she spoke of the villagers who searched for me. Some claimed I went with Javier willingly. Other men she paid to find me gave up quickly. Perhaps they

were afraid, I thought; Javier's name is known all the way to Guadalajara.

"Yolanda told me, 'If I were a man, I would kill him myself.' She
cradled my head on her shoulder and let me cry. But soon, Yolanda
and I began to argue. I told her I would not let her take my unborn
child. She did not understand. She said she would be careful that no
one found out. I never felt so alone. I ran out of the clinic and waited
in the woods... for Eduardo.

"In the low light of dusk, I thought the mourning doves must know
all about me. Their plaintive calls followed me as I made my way
through the woods. My shoes had been lost two months earlier, so
the wet earth pulled the remaining warmth from my feet, and I had
no shawl to wrap around me. Just as I knew he would, Eduardo came
out to bring the horses into the stable. He went about his tasks, and I
watched, hidden among the branches of a Night Syringa. Its fragrance
is overpowering. My head began to ache, and my stomach protested.
I got up from where I crouched. He was walking toward the hacienda
and caught sight of me. I stepped forward. He did not move, staring at
my face. Then his eyes lowered. I was once again aware of my tattered
and stained clothing. In all the time I was away, my hair had not known
a comb, and I was not allowed to wash. He took a step backward and
then another before he turned and ran into the hacienda.

"I told myself it was someone else, not the young man who held
my hand when we had a moment alone, and he talked of our future
together. He was to go away to Mexico City for three years to further
his education. I was to live under the care of his mother and father.
When he returned, we would marry. His family had accorded me great
honor.

"Now, I was plunged down again. Not where I had been before,
with my grandmother and our simple life. That I could accept. As the
wife of Javier, I would be despised."

"Wait," said Hank, his face a picture of confusion. "What made you
return to him?"

"I had no choice. I was his woman."

Hank bent at the waist, emotional pain clearly marked on his face. He let out a sigh.

"Please bear with me, Hank. I am leading to something. I would not trade all my sorrow if it meant missing what I discovered. You see... I had no one. It was then that I thought of the chapel. I went inside. Our priest, old and tired, was seldom there. But the saints would hear my needs, and, most important of all, Our Lady of Guadalupe. She would understand, I told myself.

"I lit candles. Down on my knees I began to pray, controlling my emotions with reverence, but as I waited for those loving words I so needed to hear or a vision of the saints, nothing happened.

"I could hear Enrique working in his forge across the way, making use of the cool evening. For half of a year he fashioned three sets of tall gates. I had seen them. Beautiful and almost complete, the individual iron lengths were twisted into graceful swirls and topped with open finials in the form of overturned hearts. The Carteñas commissioned the gates to secure their courtyard. My hands went to my head. Though I tried, I could not close my ears. Each time the hammer struck, a hard, clanging sound seemed to hit me in the chest. Those sounds vibrated with such authority that I would never again forget those gates were made of strong metal.

"Once more, I appealed to Our Lady. Questions tormented me. I had not slept soundly in weeks and food held no interest for me. I stared at those placid figures, willing them to move, to speak, but nothing happened. Over and over I repeated the words, but no amount of prayer could turn that carved wood into living, caring flesh. I fell to the floor as the night beetles began their climb up the walls. I watched the moonlight recede through the doorway and sleep overcame me."

Hank glanced outward. The boy was on a path toward them.

Manuel ran into his mother's legs. He pressed in, burying his face in her knees, hugging her warmth, and he looked up. "Mama. My shoe." To the side, he extended one foot and the dangling laces.

She pulled him to her lap and tied. Placing him down again, she glanced at Hank's watch. "Oh my. I had forgotten. There is much to do. We must go, Hank."

"But the dream?"

"I will tell you soon."

They returned to the hotel. At five, they left for the hospital. Soon the child was in his hospital bed with his mother's cot nearby.

Later, Hank and Elizabeth tiptoed out to the sitting area. The chairs and sofas were vacant. They chose their places. Hank got comfortable. He was learning to be a patient man.

CHAPTER THIRTY-FOUR

IN THE LOW LIGHTING of the waiting room, Elizabeth leaned against the sofa arm and placed a napkin and two paper plates on the end table. Hank cut the navel orange into sections and handed Elizabeth a wedge. Then Hank selected a slice. They bent back the peel and took their first bites of the sweet flesh, smiling at one another. The lamp near her arm made the bracelet he had given her glimmer. Simple. Discreet. Unlike the exorbitantly priced jewelry his eyes had been trained to appreciate since a child. From where they sat on the faux-leather furniture, they had a direct line of sight into Manuel's room. A nurse silently passed by on her way to a bedside. Most of the visitors had left. The hallway expanded at the corner of the ultra-modern building to form the angular seating area. Floor-to-ceiling glass lined the entire length on the outer side of the hall. The city beyond the glass was still awake and bustling, attired in Christmas frills of a million lights.

Positioned in a club chair at a right angle to Elizabeth, Hank continued to enjoy the way the lamplight played on her face and how the gold charm shot sparks with the movement of her arm. The charm, engraved in tiny script, read, "To a Brown-Eyed Girl." The opposite side declared, "Mangoes Changed My Life - H." He wanted the gift still sparkling when her life was coming to a close on some faraway day. That required real gold. He got around the problem by placing the bracelet in an unremarkable gift box labeled Werner's Drugstore.

On their trip from Georgia, they hadn't suspected things would progress so rapidly and that they would end up celebrating Christmas early, in a Knoxville hotel room. Late on the Saturday afternoon when Hank announced his plan, Elizabeth brought a hand to her cheek. The white dress shirt she had monogrammed in perfect Copperplate script waited in the garden shed. He jiggled her out of dismay with teasing and laughter. He went out and purchased books, crayons and a talking robot. Manuel squealed and clapped as they shot baskets with a foam ball into a net hooked over the hotel room door. When the boy grew tired, they manufactured a make-believe town. Lying on his tummy, Manuel drove his new miniature cars and wrecker truck on missions while Hank laid out roads.

In the hospital, Hank and Elizabeth finished their snack. Hank wrapped the orange peels, got up, and discarded them. Sitting down again, he said, "Elizabeth, you were going to tell me about the dream."

"Yes." She wiped her hands carefully on a paper napkin. Then she hugged her arms lightly and looked away.

"Are you cold?" he asked.

"No. I am fine." Half a minute went by. "I told you of the chapel. I had fallen asleep there. I don't know how long. In my dream I was a little girl again. The other children and I held hands. We spun in a circle faster and faster. We were laughing. Our bodies slanted back as the spinning force pulled. I let my head lean until I saw the twirling clouds. Suddenly our hands broke loose. We fell down. The palm of my hand hit a sharp rock. I got up. Tears and drops of blood fell to the dirt. Some older girls, Anglo, were tending us. One walked over carrying a bowl of water. She knelt down and immersed my hand, washing off the dirt. Then she tenderly wrapped my hand in a length of pure white batiste." Elizabeth paused, looking at Hank. "Once, at a roadside, someone else did the same for my injured arm. And so I knew he had been sent to help me." Hank's mouth parted, but he held back from speaking. Elizabeth continued. "The young woman spoke briefly in English. Then she rose to leave. In the dream I became anxious. I did not know the meaning of her words. Walking away, she took something from her pocket. She laid it down on the lid of a rain barrel and was gone.

"Then I woke up. I was confused. I ran out of the chapel and stumbled my way through the nighttime forest, hoping to avoid everyone as I made my way back to my new home."

She stopped talking and Hank could see that her mind was elsewhere.

"What did the dream signify?" he asked.

"That did not come until later. I reached Javier's place. There was no food. I did not care. My head ached, and I craved more sleep, but first-" She chuckled. "I checked that neglected bed for scorpions. The next morning came and I knew I must go see my grandmother, but there she stood at the door of the house. She held out a present of wedding linens she had been saving for me. A cart holding a wooden chest with my belongings waited behind her. She came inside and heated water. From a cardboard box, she unpacked the items I would need to establish my household. Then she made us a breakfast of hot coffee and beaten eggs wrapped in tortillas. It was the best meal I have ever eaten. With her help I bathed, and she washed my hair. Afterward, we sat in the sun, and she combed out weeks of snarls. We did not say much. I was shamed by her brave acceptance.

"The remainder of the day, we worked side by side, cleaning the small house. She scrubbed the old wooden floor as I hoed the soil, preparing a bed for beans and corn. When our work was finished, we sat on a bench in a narrow strip of shade under the roofline. Her loneliness for me had been great, she said, but I knew she meant her fear. She made me promise to come see her the next day. Then she left. Every day after, I visited her, even if only a few minutes to know again that love she lavished on me."

Hank looked away, wondering what kind of love would let a granddaughter be subject to such a man, but he said nothing.

"I continued to sit outside, letting nature do its healing work. My mind drifted back to the dream. I realized I had known the young woman, as well as the thing she left behind. It was the little Bible I had been given long ago. I was intrigued and thought of the wooden chest my grandmother brought. In the bottom was that forgotten book. Written in English, the book was closed to me at eight years old. For seven years it had lain in the depth of that chest." She paused, fingering the charm. "And as you know, during that time I learned a second language."

"Who was the young woman?"

"The summer after my family died, a group of young people from the U.S. came to our town. They told the mayor their mission was to help build the clinic and to present the gospel. Santolo was one of three towns where they worked. Repairing roofs, painting houses, playing with the children. The townsfolk were puzzled—they knew of Jesus.

"Except for the group's leader, they were not proficient in Spanish. One girl paid special attention to me. Perhaps she had heard of my family's tragedy. The girl must have been frustrated; there was so little she could communicate. Each day she would tell me in the little bit of Spanish she knew, *"Jesús es su amigo."* I thought what she said strange. In the chapel, didn't she see Him nailed to the wood? And his sad, tortured face? Who could lift their head or raise their eyes? But I was wrong. We knew little of the resurrection. Of being raised with Christ… Of our inheritance.

"All these things came back to me over time. Desperate for under-standing, I devoured that little New Testament and my eyes were opened. Ignorance and the traditions of men had kept the gift of abun-dant life far away but not forever. I am still learning. And sometimes I forget… until I align my mind with the truth again."

Hank walked to the hotel in the cold night air. They had talked a long time. He was encouraged. A great sacrifice had enabled mere men to call God, Father… a father who accepted and adored you. Hank shifted his train of thought to Manuel and the knowledge that Hank had helped provide new life for the boy. The error of which Elizabeth spoke would be similar to Manuel, his heart repaired and his mind requiring years of maturation, thinking he must manage in this world, alone, without Hank's guidance, provision, or protection. A hapless child unaware that Hank yearned to give everything.

By the time Hank reached the door of his room, his mood was vanquished with a different thought—a thousand miles and more of separation. He opened the door with the key card and stood before the dresser mirror. Staring at his reflection, he bent the plastic piece with his thumb and index finger into a tense camber. The card shot out of his hand and hit the mirror with a sharp plink. Then he fell into a chair and stewed until his eyes rolled back in his head with sleep.

By six a.m., activity had already begun in the hospital room. Arielle Sandholm moved about, assisting the nurses and guiding surgical preparations. Manuel sat in his bed smiling as though the circus was about to start in his room. He did not fully understand that for him the procedure would be a passive thing.

During the operation, James Sandholm worked on the child's heart and vessels with calm objectivity as the hours passed.

When they brought Manuel from surgery, tubes came from every region of his body. A wire attached to a pacemaker exited the chest wound in case rhythm problems developed within the first forty-eight hours. Elizabeth tied her hair back. She leaned over her child in vigilant watch. Hank, his brow still creased with worry, was assured by the nurses that all was going well. James Sandholm shook him at the shoulders. "Cheer up, Hank. That boy's going to be running the forty meter in four seconds by the time he's sixteen."

For the remainder of the day and the next, they were by his side, amazed at his eagerness to be out of bed. Thursday brought Christmas morning and the hospital Santa to Manuel's door.

Hank chose to remain one more day and drive home to Georgia the next. Then Sandholm would take over and transfer Manuel to his wife and his home.

As Hank walked from the hotel to the hospital one morning, he decided Elizabeth did owe him something. He would extract a promise before he left—when the time came for their return to Mexico, they must say their final goodbye at the place that had sheltered their friend-ship. Then he vowed he would send them out of his life. Even if it killed him.

CHAPTER THIRTY-FIVE

SOMEONE EXTINGUISHED THE LIGHTING. Tittering laughter came from the far side of the auditorium. Probably kids, he thought.

Hank settled back. He could smell the essence she had bathed with. It would have a name like Gingerlily or Aquamarine. Scintillating flower woven with blue ocean and sun, the fragrance was as much an emblem of her nature as those eyes that made him happy to be alive. Now he wouldn't have the advantage of looking into them. But he could breathe her in and hear that pure voice if only for a little while. In the morning he would leave for home.

With smooth deliberation, he had chosen places where the armrest between the two seats was in raised position. He couldn't help it; after all, he was a man, and she had been the one to choose their place of entertainment. Earlier that day, he convinced Manuel his mother must have an afternoon of rest. They studied the city guide. She said she would like to see the constellations in that place the advertisement called a planetarium. Hank hesitated.

She eyed him. "Oh. I am not thinking. An observatory requires the night sky."

"Not this kind."

He felt a little guilty. How was she to know they would be seated together in darkness? And how could she have realized few people would venture out when a new layer of snow made travel difficult. She wouldn't have wanted that, but he would savor this last unforeseen gift. And just as he had done everyday, he would draw that boundary keeping him in line.

Their eyes adjusted to ebony-tinted air. A tinge of excitement tickled their senses as they waited for the show to begin on the domed ceiling. The presentation was titled "Stars in Symphony." In the quiet, semi-darkness, they whispered back and forth.

"Is stargazing a favorite diversion of yours?" he asked, coming close enough to see details of the seabird that held up a tendril of her hair.

She nodded. "When I was a child, my father always knew which evenings would have the best meteor showers. On those nights, my mother, the baby in her arms, came outside. My father brought her chair and wrapped her shoulders with her shawl. We drank cups of chocolate she made frothy with the *molinillo*. As the ground cooled, the fog appeared, filling the ravines. For an hour or so my father told us stories he heard as a child, and soon the night sky was crystal clear. After much patience, the heavenly display began. My young brothers were wakened to help count each streaming light. I was afraid to lower my head and miss a single sighting. My father told me that once the light of a star came near and brushed the tip of my nose, that ball of fire did not want to leave and so transformed itself into a thousand glints living in the falling water where the vanilla orchids grew. He knew I would never forget his words—he had chosen the place I treasured most."

"Your father was a poet."

"His imagination was bountiful, and his family was his life. What about you? Do you enjoy the stars?"

"You know, I don't think I really noticed the night sky much until I moved to the lake."

"Big city life has some grave disadvantages," she said in a teasing tone.

"Yes, but it took a while for me to adjust to country life. A couple of weeks after I moved into the cottage, I woke up in the middle of the night. The bedroom curtains were lit up like a lampshade. I bolted upright. Someone was shining a strong beam on the house, I was sure. Mad as a jackhammer, I grabbed my gun and ran to the front living room. The minute I threw open the door, I knew I was wrong, but I ran to the circular drive, with the gun dangling in my hand. A mind-bending glow filled the entire view. My arms, my chest, everything was painted with moonlight like liquid mother-of-pearl."

"Surely you had seen moonlight before?"

"Of course, but I wasn't prepared for the show it made in a rural setting."

"Yes," she said laughing. "That sounds like you, acting on impulse. Thank goodness you didn't fire at that silver orb. You would have frightened Abby and Trent out of their sleep."

"True, but it was impulse that made me stop that day to help two people without a roof over their heads for the night."

Her head tilted toward her lap. He could not see her eyes, hidden by her lashes. He grew sober and turned back to face the rows of seats in front of them. Their discussion that morning came to his mind, when he told her his calls and cards would help him move gradually out of the boy's life. If she needed him, he would be back in Knoxville within hours.

Before their casual talk could resume, the music began. Where the curved ceiling met the west wall, the border was faintly lit with sunset behind a black silhouette of buildings. As the audience of a few scattered groups waited, the dimness slowly melted into deepest night, and the timeless march across the sky began. Without a sound, the huge machinery turned and positioned itself, adding pinpoints of light. It would carry the audience from dusk to dawn while the great composers added emotion to the precision of the stars. Hank felt her hand take his, but he resisted the urge to look at her.

Orion, Cassiopeia, Pisces, Cygnus, Ursa Major and Perseus began their predetermined paths across the winter sky. The symphonic strains of "Afternoon of the Faun" followed by "Moonlight Sonata" set the universe in motion. Then, weightless and dancing, the first, forward-moving notes of Smetana's "River Moldau" began. Violins created the sprite, staccato sounds of crystal clear water, dripping from rock crevices slowly and consistently, then merging to form rivulets. The musical phrases grew to become a meandering creek and then transformed into a swift, rolling stream. The rippling melody was met and made fuller with the deepening sounds of other instruments. Swirling rushes of music converged like tributaries creating a powerful river. Giving in to the music, Hank and Elizabeth allowed their imaginations to lift them into the night sky, carried between the wings of a snowy egret to fly above the ageless river that was not made of water at all but innumerable, glimmering stars drifting out to eternity. High above, whisked by the flowing air, the two were safe and warm in the bird's soft down and the comfort of their friendship. The cleanest air filled their lungs, and they could see forever. No longer in a building off Clarendon Avenue, they were soaring with their minds as the music held the egret aloft, carrying them along as their ride followed the shimmering dash of luminaries. Just as a river meets the sea, the whirling tempo increased, building in power then breaking free to the vast ocean of celestial bodies beyond our galaxy.

Finally, the music ebbed and their flight brought them back to the solid banks of Earth. Sunrise would be coming soon, and a tiny edge of light broke at the eastern side of the dome.

Waking from their daydream, he turned his head and saw water sparkling in her eyes.

"What's wrong?" he whispered.

"The music is so beautiful… and I am going to miss you very much." The melodic strains slowed to a goodbye as the remaining measures invited closeness.

They leaned in to one another and their lips met in soft, bittersweetness. For a moment they were lost to everything.

Kettle drums boomed, abruptly bringing the composition to an emphatic end and breaking the two people apart. The lights switched on.

The rest of the audience, startled out of their inertia, began to gather their things and rise as the planetarium director came forward to thank his visitors and point them to the exit. Elizabeth and Hank sat stiffly. The director smiled kindly at them and walked away. A door somewhere slammed shut. Finally, they stood. Avoiding each other's eyes, they tried not to stumble, leaving the row and the building. In the car, they said nothing.

When they reached the deserted lobby of the hospital, they stood farther apart than usual, with Hank trying to assess the damage. She appeared tired and faintly worried as she pushed the elevator button. He wandered nearby and without thought, broke an almond-shaped leaf from a potted plant, folded the piece of green, and tore it down the vein. Leaf halves dropped from his fingers.

He returned and cleared his throat. "It's all right, Elizabeth.... I'll be back in the morning to say goodbye to Manuel."

She mutely nodded. A tone announced the elevator arrival, and the metal door slid open.

He quickly said goodnight and took undeviating steps to the exit. Grasping the steel handle, he unconsciously presented the strength of his back.

Once he stepped past the glass portal into the night, he felt drawn to look back. He could see her as the elevator doors came to a close, and he thought he must be mistaken, fooled by the shadows—her face, her look, it was not what he expected.

In the morning, things seemed back to normal, and Hank got her agreement that their final parting would be at the lake. From there a flight would take them home to Mexico. Almost seven weeks would pass until then.

"But *why* you have to go?" The child's yearning to know brought the nurse over, offering a sip of apple juice.

Elizabeth spoke first, then Hank. A few, weak explanations calmed the boy. Then Hank departed as though he had tunnel vision and could only see the exit.

Back at the lake, he was afraid to open the door to an empty house, but he knew what to do. He took everything of theirs that remained and put it into one large cardboard box, which was shoved into the coat closet. After changing into sweats, he trotted down the gravel drive. Where the two drives came together to form the single path leading to the road, he glanced at Trent and Abby's uninhabited cabin. It might be weeks before they could return. A cold wind rustled the pine needles high above. He pulled up his hood and pushed himself forward.

By the time he reached Kellogg Creek Road, his muscles were warm, and his stride lengthened with the rhythm of his arms that pulled like pistons. Two miles later, sweat had formed on his forehead. He yanked back his hood, welcoming the rush of cool air. He ran until he reached the plateau of Woodstock High School and, spurring himself, came the long distance home again. He went straight to the shower. Afterward, a large glass of orange juice revived him enough to go through the accumulated mail. Within the stack was the familiar postmark that guaranteed its place among the garbage. It wasn't his father's customary, light gray, deckle-edge. The envelope had slashes of color in one corner. He opened it. The front of the card proclaimed, "It's a Party!" in the same gyrating colors. Minutes passed as he considered the invitation. Finally, putting all other thoughts behind and resisting fatigue, he pulled his Bible over.

He woke up to a bleak Sunday morning. At church, he sat among the people, and their love made him feel like he was the favorite child of a huge, gregarious family. The following day, he would have Arnett put him back to work.

CHAPTER THIRTY-SIX

JAVIER GAVE UP TRYING to lie on his bunk or sit on the linoleum with his back against the unyielding wall of his cell. Now the only thing that would help him manage the nervous trills spiking in his slim body was to pace back and forth. He paused at the bars, fingers wrapped around those iron will-breakers, waiting for an end to the monotony and interference. He squeezed tightly as if the act would help drain his anger.

"Why don't you relax, my friend? There is no telling how many days before the transport comes to carry us back," said the inmate from Oaxaca, lying in the upper bunk directly across the hallway. Like Javier, he had been caught without documentation.

"You fool," Javier spurted. "Why spend days in a cell like a goat waiting to be made into *birria*?"

The inmate chortled. "Sorry. Maybe your woman is behaving this time while you are away."

"Be careful or I might have to cut out your tongue."

"With what?" He laughed and pulled the blanket over his shoulders and turned toward the wall to sleep.

"May the devil come to take you before your first snore," replied Javier. The blood in the veins traversing his temples seemed to pool there. He put his forehead against one of the cool bars. His anxiety sat like a raving ogre on his bunk, waiting to see what happened next.

With each hour, the chances increased that his jailers would discover his involvement in the operation out of Juarez. Lately he had made a name for himself. The bodies of two DEA agents were found in their burned-out car in the middle of the desert. Javier frowned. At the ranch, why had he received wrath instead of honor?

After the incident, the boss in Juarez suddenly gave in to Javier's request for leave. Javier headed north, and by evening, slept in a new four-dollar flophouse. For those who traveled up from Mexico, crammed together in the unventilated dark of a box van, the luxury of no longer having to be hunched like a ball, smack against everyone else, made their ramshackle beds and attending bug bites a real value. Javier had crossed the border in more comfort than the others, but the necessity of sleep made the men equal in a land with an increasing eye. Most rose before a hint of daylight. Javier merely kicked off his blanket. Texas deputies grabbed him in an early morning raid.

In the jailhouse, as if to mock him, he heard the other inmate resonating with contented snores. The devil hadn't shown, and Javier was driven to look into one of those rooms in his mind, which he did not like to enter. She had never been his woman, and he knew it well. After months of separation, his anger had dissipated, making him think only of bringing her back. Perhaps if he tried to be more refined, gentle, she would love him. Like she had when they were children. He recalled the look on her face when she discovered the beating he took. She came running to where he lay in the dirt. She wore her festival skirt that day. How beautiful it was with three wide bands of color. Yellow ribbons in her braids matched the hem.

The traveling photographer had been at school that morning. It was a long awaited event that came every other year, though none of the children ever had the money to purchase one of those prized pictures of the forty-eight students from grades one through eight. But the teacher always purchased a photo, framed it, and put it up for display, so the children could see how they had grown and changed. Javier stood especially straight and proud for the camera that day. When the photographer returned at the end of the month, Javier paid for a picture, watching the other children. They circled his prize like the native spider monkeys assembled near an unguarded basket of sweet sapodilla. The school teacher sniffed into her handkerchief and eyed Javier. He wondered if she already knew about the Castillo's missing pig.

Later that afternoon, as Elizabeth wiped the grime and blood away from his battered face with the hem of her skirt, Javier was certain she would receive her mother's scolding. The older girls came and pulled her away. He told himself the pummeling had been worth it to have that little angel with the small, white teeth and soft hands minister to him. She did not care who his parents were.

Javier returned to the sandspurs that pricked him. Why hadn't he been able to make her love him? Other than those puffed up Carteñas, he had more money than anyone in the village. With his knife, he could protect her even from *el chupacabra* waiting in the forest for its next meal. But nothing changed her mind. She was respectful and obeyed his wishes, but her heart did not burn for him. When he learned she carried a child, he could not bring himself to be close with her again. The way she had quietly endured their time together made him angry, so he took care of his needs elsewhere. But sometimes his resentment and the tequila became too much for him, and he would berate her to get rid of the demon that taunted him. Javier thrust himself away from the bars and reversed his thoughts, certain he was better off without her.

What about the boy, he asked himself as he walked back and forth in his cell. It was Javier's blood coursing through the child's veins. He smiled, thinking of Ramiro's words when the child was born. "Aha! Look. The infant has the forehead and chin of nobility. They are copies of your own, my son. Together we will show him the way to grow into manhood."

A chime sounded. The electronic clock registered noon. The clerk, on the other side of the metal door, placed the fingerprints on the desk, ready for transmittal. The routine procedure seldom netted anything of import with the ragged men they usually rounded up, while trying to

keep their border town relatively free of the swarm that always threatened.

The clerk gathered her purse and took out her car keys. "Frank, I'm
headed out. My stomach has settled next to my backbone. I'll process
the transmittal when I get back."

"Okay by me. Just drop this file off at the courthouse on your way
back." She nodded and left.

Javier looked up to see the door to the cellblock open. The smell of
turkey and dressing wafted into their quarters. An officer with craggy
skin around his eyes and carrying the weariness of too many predict-
able years, glanced around, slump shouldered. He rolled the cart down
the aisle and the heavy door swung shut behind.

"Be quiet with that cart, man," Javier snipped while pointing at the
inmate across the way. "His stomach is not behaving. He begged only
for sleep. You can bring his lunch later."

"Yeah, think I'll do that," said the man hitching up his pants and
moving to Javier's side of the aisle. "No need for him to eat right now
if he's just gonna lose it all over the floor." The jailer passed the covered
plate through the designated opening to Javier.

"Officer, I am most grateful for this meal, but I may kill myself if
something is not done about the roaches." Javier's eyes popped wide
for emphasis.

"What roaches? They come by and spray once a month."

"With what? Their spittle? I tell you there are four of them playing
Jai Lai under my sheets. See for yourself."

"Can't do that."

"They carry disease. Maybe I will fall ill like him." He nodded
toward the inmate.

"Use your shoe."

"Is this how you take care of your prisoners?" Javier pushed his
animated features as far as he could between two bars. "I should have
a lawyer contact human rights authorities."

The jailer looked toward the ceiling, silently mouthing the words,
"Oh, brother." With a winded breath, the officer placed one of his
heavy feet on the lower cart shelf and removed one of his shoes.

Straightening, again, produced a mild groan. He opened the bars and walked in unarmed. Shoe weapon raised, he slowly pulled back the blanket. Not one to be found. He lifted the top sheet and reached deep with his arms.

Javier snickered in his head. The American jail was like a palace compared to Mexican *juzgados*. Here, a prisoner was fed better than a prize bull waiting for the *picador*. The heating and cooling system, running water, and brilliant lighting made the place easily surpass the simplicity of his *palapa* roofed home.

Javier monitored the cell across the way. Drool slid from the inmate's mouth. His belly moved up and down peacefully.

A snort sounded from the jailer as he lifted the mattress. He let it drop and looked suspiciously at Javier.

"Check inside the pillow case," Javier said with urgency. "And under the bed. They are trying to escape you." The jailer got down on all four to take a look. With some deft work and in a matter of seconds, Javier had the man pinned, gagged, and cuffed to the bed.

Like a *coatamundi* moving through a forest, Javier slipped out the fire exit at the end of the long room and was gone.

Lax maintenance had failed to repair the alarm on the door. By three o'clock, the commotion of discovery was capped with the DEA calling about a certain transmittal. Emitting a few exasperated huffs, they answered the questions and sent the photos. The agency already knew of him. Filipo Torres was trying to take the heat off his ranches in Juarez. He claimed a malcontent named Javier Gutierrez, hired to brand cattle, was responsible for the two charred remains.

By evening, Javier rode to Dallas sitting in the back of a Mexican's truck full of juicy pineapple. Javier used a newly acquired blade to satiate himself on fruit. When they arrived, he paid the driver cash, and wrapped in an old blanket, slept the night in the cab.

CHAPTER THIRTY-SEVEN

LAWRENCE RUBBED HIS MOIST palms together and slid them into the pockets of his finely tailored slacks. It wasn't like him to be thrown off balance in a social context, but this was different. He would soon talk to his son for the first time in three years. The next night would hold a birthday celebration like no other, a tribute to conviviality, but according to his accountant, Lawrence's last hurrah.

The eighty-degree temperature in the middle of January prompted him to open the row of doors off the living room into the walled retreat of his Mediterranean style home. The plants in the courtyard granted a tropical mood to the elegant atmosphere indoors. Nearby, ocean breezes passed down Worth Avenue, circulating among the alee of towering palms and the architecture reminiscent of old Barcelona. But once away from the exclusive shops and gourmet restaurants, the flowing air was slowed to a standstill by story-high hedges surrounding each homeowner's property. On the other side of those faithfully clipped, green walls, sprawled the paradisal winter residences of inventive entrepreneurs, industry CEOs, famous performers and persons buoyed by family legacy, while artful shenanigans had secured the places of some.

Lawrence's home glowed with the peachy color of a sunset, its roof made of barrel-curved tiles in deep coral hue. Built in the twenties, the two-bedroom residence was modest when compared to his former mansion by the sea, but it helped him maintain a tony Palm Beach address. The locale easily lifted it above the aspirations of all but a small fraction of one percent of the national population. Even so, life had pared down dimensions for the man.

The sunlight drew him through the living room doors, down the coquina steps, and into his garden sanctuary. Too anxious to sit, he stood basking in the sun, hoping its rays would infuse him with courage. He noticed the ache in his hands again and studied their shape in the harsh light. For a time, he had ignored the signs, thinking the symptoms would go away, but a minute measure of deformity motivated him to see a doctor.

Lawrence took a deep breath, causing his shirt of Egyptian cotton to emphasize his trim, fit body. He smiled. At least he had not thickened around the middle like so many of his contemporaries. But this would be his fiftieth birthday, and it was time to put away the vanity and illusions of youth. He still had the means to fight indefinitely with the surgeon's scalpel, but he was a realist in some ways and, these days, scathingly honest with himself. Even the young women were losing appeal, their vitality becoming a chore, but at least it made him face the truth. Something was happening inside him—a nagging dissatisfaction, a realization.

Glancing at the fish tail palms in huge teal pots set around the enclosure, he chided himself that he had been remiss by not having them moved to the conservatory. The region could be surprised by a rare frost in the few remaining weeks of a south Florida winter. You can't neglect things and expect them to flourish, he said quietly. Like a relationship.

His marriage had not suffered in that way. His wife preferred her solitude and license to be free of a husband's demands. He liked the idea of her European lineage combining with his money. In the beginning, the marriage between Charmaine and Lawrence had suited them both, but it was never a union capable of nurturing a child.

"Father?"

Lawrence looked up to find Hank standing in one of the doorways where he had been directed by the houseman.

"Hank!" He walked over to his son's outstretched hand, with the socially correct manner they always followed. But he stopped short and taking a deep breath, bypassed the hand and hugged his son. At the same time, Lawrence braced for the rejection of strong words, the words he so richly deserved. Instead, Hank returned his affection. Average in height, Lawrence felt for an instant like a child in the arms of his much larger son.

"I'm so glad you've come. I didn't think you would."

"It's time to let all that go, Father."

"Come sit down, Hank. I have some things to tell you." They walked over to an ornamental table and chairs next to a reflecting pool. "I need to explain my irrational state of mind three years ago."

His palm went up. "Don't, Dad."

"Please. Confession would do me a world of good."

"Then have a go at it." Hank sat down and ran his hands across an exquisite mosaic that formed the surface of the tabletop. Neptune sitting on his throne amid swimming dolphins. It had been executed in numerous shades of color with countless, quarter-inch tiles.

"Hank? Could you look at me? Thanks. I... I know there is nothing in this world that can justify what I did. I simply want you to understand the path that led to such madness."

"It's not necessary. I forgive you."

"Please listen," Lawrence pleaded. Hank's eyes drifted again wanting to avoid the flimsy excuses that were certain to bring up the rear. A liberating ocean breeze floated above the hedge and over the courtyard wall to stir the leaves of a sinuous ficus tree in the corner. Two pairs of eyes met. "Son, I know I'm not much of a man, and I certainly haven't been a trophy of a father. Self-indulgence has been my lifelong mission."

"Castigation isn't necessary," Hank replied without strength.

"The truth is the only thing that will start to bring down this wall I built.... Hank, someone once said the best thing that can happen to a person is not having the means to fulfill every desire. Once I became an adult, there were no restraints for any want I ever had. Instead of freedom, I entered bondage. Ten years ago, when our holdings began to fall apart, I carelessly poured large amounts into wild investments in Sri Lanka, Bangkok, and Belarusk, usually at the urging of my boozing friends. Then ruin started stalking me, but I shut it out. Early in life, I developed resistance for the tedious affairs of commerce." Lawrence exhaled a quick chuckle. "I think it was my father's grandiose endowment that enabled me to graduate from business school. Too much carousing, I'm afraid. Anyway, I often told myself the current crisis would take care of itself. Nothing was going to keep me from chasing the sun."

"Is that why Cliff Duncan kept calling, my last semester at Princeton?"

"Yes. I guess he didn't realize it wasn't likely you would know my location, either. That man was a financial whiz but not a miracle worker. I had fled to Mustique, having the time of my life and avoiding a lot of frantic phone calls. When I tired of island escapades I fled to New Delhi for the polo matches. It wasn't until I arrived in Atlanta that I forced myself to confront the situation."

"Sounds like the time I was fourteen and needed an appendectomy."

"Really? I'm not sure I remember."

"The headmaster put on a frenzied search. Luckily, William Deerfield recalled he had seen you following the Formula One circuit."

Lawrence began to laugh. "Yes, it's coming back to mind. I had to give up a fortune at the Black Jack table that night. The weather wasn't good, but we took off anyway. Seemed like the Grumman moved across the Atlantic at the rate of a frigate bird. Perhaps I'm not the worst of all fathers." Hank smiled. Lawrence stood up and walked to the lotus pool. He remained there, facing away from Hank, resting a hand on the armature of a verdigris lantern that came out from the wall. His head angled toward the dark water. His shoulders flagged. "Son, I'm sorry about her." Hank looked down at the swirls and strange shapes embedded in the coquina at his feet. "I never realized how much you would care for her. I forgot what it was like to be young."

Hank raised his head. "It's all right. It was never meant to be."

Lawrence turned around. "She and I had something that bound us tightly—a desperation for what we thought was life. For her, a thoroughbred farm and championship status. And me? The carnival of spectacle I thought I couldn't part with."

"Dad, let's put it behind us. I'm happier than I've ever been in my life. And in a way, I think our lives are just beginning."

Self-loathing dropped from Lawrence's face, and he smiled. "Perhaps you're right. Anyway, you're looking incredible. If Ashley hadn't already told me so, I wouldn't have known it was you."

"Thanks."

"I'm happy to say it will be the son and not the father who will be sought tomorrow night by the lovely femmes who come to celebrate. Tonight, unfortunately, we're having dinner at the Abercromnie's."

"Sounds fine."

"I couldn't get out of it. It doesn't portend well for the presence of any of our local beauties. George and Eleanor's parties are so staid. But it may be your last chance to see my collection of Venetian furniture. With the funds I garnered from that sale," a wink alluded to his mastery of persuasion and the Abercromnie's weakness for acquisition, "I did manage to keep my favorite settee. I can only economize so far," he added with that sly smile Hank remembered so well.

He felt pity for his dad. If Lawrence's beloved Baroque treasures had been sold, it meant the more valuable artwork, heirloom jewelry, automobiles, yachts, and planes were also gone. After the conglomerate crashed, the personal real estate of three residences and seven vacation homes had been served up until things reached balance again. Lawrence had been lucky. The encroachment ended, and he was left with a respectable standing, though a lifestyle drastically curtailed.

Lawrence put one arm around Hank's shoulders. "I promise to make up for this unavoidable evening over Crown Derby china by giving a party tomorrow night that you'll never forget." Glints of happiness lit his eyes. "For now, how about a round of golf?"

Hank was reminded that fun followed his father as naturally and consistently as the waves of the Atlantic, a few blocks away, propelled gleeful waders into shore. "That would be great."

"I must confess; I have reason for avoiding this pastime with you all these years. It was the powerful drive I knew those shoulders of yours could deliver. And now, looking at you, I bet you've developed the finesse of a pro." Lawrence took a step back, giving one more admiring look before directing him inside.

As they walked up the steps into the house, a final breeze whirled into the garden, disturbing the tiny insect prey of a tree frog not much bigger than a dime. The air current rustled through the bamboo and registered across the water in faint ripples of disquiet.

CHAPTER THIRTY-EIGHT

THEY ESCAPED THE DINNER party with as much grace as possible by ten, pleading their need for a good night's sleep, considering the events of the next day. It was an acceptable excuse, though everyone knew Javonovic Productions would handle the affair. Costly for Lawrence, but their Bulgarian chef was renowned.

Parking the car in its usual spot under the porte cochere, the two of them tumbled from the Ferrari Modena like rowdy school boys. They took a detour away from the house and jogged toward the empty, six-car garage transformed into a half court. With the renovation, the chauffeur's quarters, above, were gone, which raised the height of the garage.

Earlier, Lawrence's medication or his happiness, he wasn't sure which, had allowed eighteen holes of golf without the first twinge. Eager for more play after the Abercromnies, they threw off their dinner jackets and ties, then their starched, white shirts. In bare feet, they pounded the ball over the floor as jazz rolled from the speakers. Rambunctious banter bounced off the walls. For half an hour, they played and perspired until Lawrence begged for rest, sinking to the floor in blithe exhaustion.

Laughter and heavy breathing interspersed Lawrence's words. "Man, what are you trying to do? First you show me that years of golf lessons were a waste, and now you have me chasing the ball around like a pitiful, old fool. Maybe I belong at the Abercromnie's."

"Oh come on. How many baskets did I make once I was ten feet away?"

"I might have made a few more if I'd had an easier time getting the ball. And look at you. You're not even exerted," said Lawrence.

"You still beat me by two points."

"You gave me those out of kindness." They walked outside to the illuminated pool. Stepping out of their slacks and tee shirts down to underwear, they slid into the heated water and swam under waterspouts coming from the mouths of ornamental lion heads decorating the north end. Once the pool had done its refreshing, they were reticent to come back to the cool night air. But ready for a drink, Lawrence went first and grabbed two thick towels from the cabana. They followed the winding path among mature sea grapes and lower growing ice blue plumbago to the house.

Inside, Chen greeted them, suggesting a nightcap. "Thanks, we'll get it ourselves," Lawrence said, standing comfortably without a stitch on, handing over their damp towels and wrinkled clothing. They slipped on matching robes and slippers of tobacco-brown velveteen and went into the library where the houseman already had a fire going. The burning logs and a large aquarium glowing with colorful, iridescent fish provided the only lighting. Father and son savored their cognac, eased by the fine-grained cordovan chairs underneath them, and tranquilized by reflections of the fire playing across the black lacquer of a chinoiserie screen beautifying a dark corner.

Fine woods were on display everywhere, in the furniture marquetry, on the walls polished to a luster, and in the herringbone pattern beneath their feet. A carving, a bold stag within a swag of oak leaves and acorns, adorned the over-mantel of the fireplace. Completed in 1734, it was the one item Lawrence had not included in the sale of the Park Avenue penthouse. The carving was taken down and reinstated in Lawrence's new home. Hank's eyes returned to the familiar object again and again, but it wasn't because of the beauty of composition or the inordinate craftsmanship. He twisted in his seat. The robe became too warm. He brought the back of his head off the leather, but his father spoke first.

"So Hank, this isn't such a bad place to spend my twilight years, is it?"

"No, Dad. I think you'll be happy here."

"And you?"

"What do you mean?"

"You're welcome to live here with me. It's time we made up for those lost years."

"Thanks for the offer, but I wouldn't want to put a crimp on your style." He forced an affectionate smile.

"What? As the years move on, I'll need you to attract the herring." He paused. "All joking aside, Hank, it would mean a lot to me."

"I think my place is in Georgia, now."

"To think is not the same as to know."

"I do know. My life has changed."

"I guess this must have something to do with that woman and child Ashley told me about."

"They're not the only reason."

"So, these persons… what are they? Colombian? Tahitian?" Hank could hear a tiny bit of scorn sneaking through the politeness.

"Mexican. Elizabeth and Manuel come from a mountain village near the Pacific."

"Are you serious? Can she speak English?"

"Of course."

"Frankly, Son, I don't understand. You could have any woman you want."

"I don't want *any* woman…. But regardless, you don't understand the nature of our relationship. We helped one another. Through some problems. We're nothing more than friends." An edge of irritation nudged the back of Hank's neck.

As though he never heard his son, Lawrence continued, "Look, I'm not trying to be rude. I'm sure she's beautiful. At one time, you should have seen the slave I became for a black-haired seductress in Hong Kong. I'd probably still be in trouble, but she said our connection had a bad omen. Or, now that I think about it, I had to leave to watch a certain horse in the Grand Prix de Paris. Oh, I don't remember, but something broke it up." Lawrence grew quiet and let his eyes drift to the ornamental plaster ceiling. Hank figured the man was digging deeper in his satchel of biased reasoning. "Hank, have you thought how your support might be detrimental?"

"How's that?" His look bordered on incredulous.

"To them, the U.S. must be very disorienting, even frightening at times. It would be like pulling one of those exotic fish out of the tank and slapping it down on my desk. How long do you think it would last, gills rising and mouth sputtering? If these persons are from a rural region, how long will their naiveté allow them to survive in unfamiliar society? They'll be eaten up, or they'll change and maybe not for the better. And what about your background? You're well traveled. Your German is good, your French is excellent, and you don't hesitate to read Latin. By twenty-one, you had earned advanced degrees in history and physics. She's probably lucky to have ever owned a book. What communion of the minds could you expect to have? And would she ever feel secure with a man of your wealth? Sounds like a relationship straight from hell."

The color in Hank's face had raised a level. The muscles along his jaw line tensed. "*Look, Dad…* she is wiser, braver than any woman I've ever known. Nevertheless, they're returning to Mexico soon."

"Oh! Why didn't you say so? There's nothing to worry about, then." Lawrence was laughing. "Sorry, I was worried your mother might be spinning in her grave, thinking her Valhalla genes would be mixed with some Indian blood." A feeling of disgust washed over Hank, but he fought anything that might dispel the closeness. Lawrence continued. "Not that it would bother me. And anyway, whenever you do get serious with a female, it's not like you have to marry her. Right?"

"Right, Dad," Hank muttered, turning his gaze back to the fire. So, his father had not changed much, after all. But the man's words created new questions—questions Hank would later feel compelled to examine, one by one.

CHAPTER THIRTY-NINE

F IVE O'CLOCK ON A balmy evening, the celebration began in
a place of enchantment. A beguiling melody beckoned from the
ocean side of the grounds where a grand piano offered its charms.

Hank left his car with the valet and, drawn by the enticing sounds,
followed the path through a sylvan walk of gossamer, green shadow.
Coming out of the woods, he glimpsed the large house named Vizcaya,
a Venetian styled palazzo caressed by the sun. The home, situated amid
a mangrove forest off Biscayne Bay in Miami, was constructed with
architectural genius almost a century earlier, the vision of an artistically
inspired industrialist.

Stopping to adjust his tux as an excuse to linger, Hank appreciated the front facade a while longer. The mansion and its lavish,
parterre-filled gardens had intrigued him since a childhood visit. His
eyes followed the length of the sculptured watercourses on either side
of the entrance drive. The narrow rill emptied into large shell basins
like the scalloped pedestal in Botticelli's *Venus Rising from the Sea*. He
chuckled softly, knowing that in such an alluring place, should the face
and golden tresses of that mythic beauty appear behind a frond or the
other side of a gate, he would not feel surprise.

His line of sight moved again toward the villa. The oval forecourt
contained a central reflecting pool and casual plantings of palms. To
the left and right were imposing, dual gateways leading to the formal

grounds of the estate. Those imperial entrances, composed of pink marble and Istrian stone, had come from Verona. Playful seahorses, accenting the top, had been shaped from Florida limestone. Everywhere he looked—the towers anchoring the corners of the home's symmetrical design, the steps and columns of the entrance loggia, the decorative urns and outdoor balustrades—everything was made of stone. Cut, chiseled to perfection, and laid up at the direction of intelligent minds. But where was the man who conceived and brought forth a masterpiece? A slight frown emerged. For the night at least, Hank vowed, he would lay down weighty issues. With a quickened step, he advanced.

Entering the wide portal of the structure, Hank was reminded the interiors were equally astonishing as the commanding form of the villa. The entry hall, also done in marble and stone, possessed a high ceiling. The airy room ran lengthwise to meet heavy doors at either end leading to the more private interiors. Directly opposite the main entrance, positioned between stately columns, a large sarcophagus-shaped basin sat among potted greenery and lush, royal blue drapery. Figures graced the carved marble, and narrow streams of water from two small fountains emptied into the large container. It was one of two antiquities which had captured his interest long ago.

Home from boarding school one summer and left to his own devices, the eleven-year-old engrossed himself with the glory of ancient Rome. His caregiver, an impatient woman with an East European accent, tired of the dull hours inside the Palm Beach estate. One day she coerced him hanging onto his books, into the car. They took off for Miami and a visit to the famous place. As the boy came upon the water trough inside and learned it dated from the early empire, his growing intelligence was aroused. Yanked along at the elbow, by his high-paid nanny, he looked back, longing to touch that stone vessel and, by some incantation, be transported from his joyless existence and back in time.

Now the grown-up man crossed the vaulted room to study the basin once again. He analyzed the object and his thoughts from the past. Those childhood judgments were formed from naïve perception of

Roman ways. As an adult, he came equipped with a broader awareness of those cruel times. Also, he understood fully, now—whether boy or man, the heart yearned for something representative of power and permanence, something beautiful and awe-inspiring. And, as she had taught him, the heart was often deceived.

Tourists came in the entrance laughing and talking. Pressed for time, he would have to skip the room that held the second piece charging his boyish curiosity back then. The object was a Roman laver, austere on its tall stand. His young mind had envisioned a general, straight from battle to his command tent, at the shallow bowl, cleaning off the rigors of war. Hank moved on, thinking the laver more likely to have been in a Roman household or a butcher shop in Pompeii. Still he could not resist imagining a provincial governor, tossed to the outskirts of Judea, washing his hands there, tired of ruling a troublesome people. He stopped his stroll. Didn't his mind ever cease? He shook his head and went to a large doorway.

Cutting through the middle of the house, whose heart was an expansive courtyard of square dimensions, his head turned upward. The courtyard and the gallery of rooms above had at one time been open to the sky in true villa tradition. A roof now protected the valuable furnishings from humidity, but the fountain and plant-filled space was no less enamoring. His steps led him to the sun-filled East Loggia overlooking the terrace and the bay. He was transfixed by the geometrically patterned, marble floor and its brilliant design. He could have spent some time enjoying its transcendent, three-dimensional effect. But his father was waiting, and the time for rational considerations had fled.

Stepping outside, he saw his father—debonair, charismatic, wearing his tuxedo with the ease of someone comfortable enough to sleep in one, yet able to present himself without a spot. Surrounded by the usual crowd of friends, Lawrence saw Hank and melted through the circle to meet him with a spirited greeting.

"I want you to have a really good time, Son. This party is more about us than my birthday, so imbibe until your head spins." Hank smiled and took a glass from a passing tray as the pianist played the beginning notes of "Rhapsody in Blue." Guests came forward, greeting him as though he had never been gone. They expressed their regard with eyes registering amazement while their manners restrained them from saying how much better he looked. After a while, he was free again.

Following the wide steps, he moved down from the terrace level and looked out to sea where an ornamental breakwater, gently stroked by never-ending waves, grabs your attention as readily as the Atlantic stretching to the horizon. Called the Great Stone Barge, the structure lies planted seventy yards out. Massive in scale, the size of a tiny island, the edifice reflects grandeur. It rests like a Spanish galleon in the harbor formed by Vizcaya's crescent-shaped promenade defining the edge of the ocean. Sculptures embellishing the barge had been aptly described as "the delights and terrors of the sea." Yes, thought Hank, enthralling pearls resting among the barracuda. He laughed and took another taste of champagne. He would simply have to dive in. Maybe the night's pleasures would suffice despite the dangers. He stepped back and walked the length of the sea promenade toward the bridge and teahouse at the south end.

Reaching the point, he reversed his perspective to evaluate the gathering. His eyes were drawn in every direction. He could smell the salt spray that intermingled with the expensive perfumes of the ladies. Greeting one another in small feminine clusters, the women, dressed in jewel-tone gowns, became mesmerizing bouquets of undulating tropical flowers. The shimmering fabrics were surpassed only by the diamonds that glittered around their necks and dangled from their slender wrists and delicate earlobes. The color of the fluid, taut skin of their throats and the soft swells of their plunging décolletages reminded him of the ethereal shade of blush that tints the inner contours of conch shells lying about the ocean floor.

Not left alone for long, Hank was sought by more acquaintances with conversation about old times. He was surprised to find his nerves beginning to decompress. The resplendent views or perhaps the champagne lifted his mood until he was floating. Then, from behind, he felt small, fragrant hands cover his eyes. Turning around, he was heartened to see Ashley in a gown of rich, garnet-red.

"Hello! Am I delighted to see you," he said leading her a few feet from the others. "You look beautiful."

"Now that's just great. You finally show some interest, and I've got the two Deter cousins from Bavaria following my heels like King Charles spaniels." She discreetly indicated their location with a slight nod of her head. The men stood dutifully, a short distance away, watching and waiting for her return.

Laughing, he gathered her two hands in his. "That's okay. What do you want with a Georgia plowboy when you can be queen of the Alps?"

"So true," she said with good-natured teasing. "But I'm so glad you're here. Only you can keep a rein on our pomposity."

"What? Don't tell me you've sold out. We were partners, remember?"

"Yes, but I'm warning you. With time, things can change," she said laughing. "Which reminds me… you and I are not the only ones on whom the seasons have done their work. I saw Leslie. She's in the gardens. Go find her."

Before he could ask the first question, Ashley turned toward her latest conquests and walked away, one on each arm. He bided the minutes by walking aimlessly and, later, spent half-present conversing with an elderly family friend. Finally, he retraced his steps up the terrace, to get the fullness of the view. From that vantage point, the formal gardens on the right spread like a lady's fan from the south side of the house. The word that came to his mind was splendor. Could it be more beautiful than Eden? Then he saw her. She was close, on the ocean perimeter side, near an indolent palm, gazing out to the turquoise sea. Carefully, he went down into the garden.

She did not seem aware of his approach. Tall like a candle, she was seductively sheathed in periwinkle silk. The strapless dress displayed her long, slender arms resting on the horizontal slant of the coconut palm trunk which turned and reached skyward again. He remembered those elegant shoulders and as he came closer, the classic lines of her profile. Quietly, he stepped beside her, his head also facing the water. Behind his back, his hand clenched his other wrist.

"The breeze is coming from the east tonight," he said gently.

"Just like the dolphins swim at dawn," she responded, slowly turning to face him, as lovely as before. "I will always know that voice just as I will never forget your face, no matter how it changes. How are you, Hank?" she said softly.

"Fine, Leslie. It's good to see you again. My father didn't mention that you would be here."

"Of course not. Then it would be certain you wouldn't come." He glanced at the length of her right arm as it lay in startling contrast of smooth, flawless skin, along the rough bark of the trunk. On her right hand, the engagement ring he had given her sparkled. "I wear it as a reminder," she said. "Do you know why?"

Trying to formulate a reply, he noticed a dark man walking up, all suaveness and powerful features, holding two glasses of effervescent, golden liquid. The man handed one to Leslie. Then he looked at Hank with the air of a man used to having control.

Leslie made introductions.

"How do you do?" said Hank to a Middle East royal. The man nodded in cool acknowledgment.

"The prince shares my love of horses," said Leslie. "One of his stallions was sire of last year's Preakness winner."

"Really?" Hank answered, feigning interest.

"Perhaps Allah has smiled on me this year, but I hope to be blessed in other ways as well." The man's dark eyebrows contracted slightly conveying a serious mien.

"May your desires be granted," said Hank with a gracious smile. "Please excuse me. I must see if my father needs my assistance." The couple was left staring as he strode strangely independent and without pretension across the Bermuda grass.

Dinner on the terrace was announced as the sky faded to the intoxicating foreshadows of twilight. Crystal hurricane lanterns glowed across white damask tablecloths. A small gift lay on the plate of each guest. Toasts were made and wonderful aromas filled the air as attendants stepped forward with plates on silver chargers. Promising to dazzle the taste buds and whimsically presented, the food tempted even the most disciplined guests. All the while, the sea smoothed and changed to the fascinating shade of London blue topaz.

After an hour of feasting, the orchestra began to play, and couples flowed to music with the quality of a caprice. Welcoming glances were sent Hank's way by several young ladies, but he rose from the table. Some of the guests already had too much to drink. Boasting and inane talk came from every direction. Still too early to leave, he tried to disappear.

He went back to the gardens ablaze with lanterns except for dark corners where lovers rendezvoused. The fountains sprayed light like stars fallen to earth, and music floated over the air, ravishing the senses. Statuary of human form lined the walkways, as silent observers of the bacchanalia. He passed the quaint travertine fountain brought from the town square of Bassano di Sutri. The lay of the land progressed toward a hill. He reached the summit and the candle-lit Casino. Its curving, stone staircases sheltered couples who talked while others danced and played in the open air under the ceiling frescoes. The painted musicians, above, looked down with animated expressions from the revelry of a Renaissance avenue. Scattered rose petals decorated the azure sky like floating confetti. Hank lowered his gaze. In a dim corner, he thought he glimpsed Alan Thurston speaking in tense whispers with Davis Myers's wife. Hank left quickly, deciding to return through the length of the grounds by a different walk.

He chose to descend the Casino Mount by the Water Stairway. He relaxed again. His hands rested casually in his pockets, and with confidence his legs went down each step. The smell of cut grass and citrus filled his nostrils. From bayside, warm breezes brushed his face and coaxed potted, white camellias to surrender into bloom. Hypnotic sounds of cascading water urged him to take his time. Huge decorative basins marked the way, each draining into the next until they reached the large, central fountain below. Surrounding it on the near side were curved walls lined with Carrara marble busts from the 18th century. There, he encountered the two matching grottos that flank each side at the stairway end.

Moving to the other side of the fountain, he studied the grottos from a distance. Once, he had seen a photo of their construction. Expert artisans carved the alcoves made of half-ton, limestone blocks into sea caves covered in barnacle-clad stalactites. So superior was the result that the hideaways appeared to have been formed by the slow but persistent force of ocean tides across the ages. His eyes wandered over every convincing detail. Embellishing the entrances, larger-than-life sea gods, male and female, braced the openings with their sheer might, and ornate, shell pediments crowned the uppermost point of the mysterious recesses.

It was then that he noticed someone seated inside one of the grottos, wearing a gown the color of tanzanite. Recalling the only person with eyes that same shade, he froze. She called him over.

"What are you doing here?" he asked as she took his hand and gently tugged, making him sit beside her on silken cushions. A copper, cut-work, table lantern in front of them sprinkled dots of light on the table surface and turned the ceiling gold. The candle flame flickered and stood still. He looked at Leslie. Her eyes fastened onto his. She pulled him close, weaving her arm with his, like a supple tendril of mandevilla vine. Her head turned down then rose looking with forlorn beauty into his face. He was stunned, and the walls of their intimate chamber took on luminosity, while the warmth of her, so close, traveled right through his tux. With rare openness, she began to tell him of her need to be away from the others and the pain and sorrow she felt over her loss of him, how stupid she had been, and how her oil-rich prince would settle only for marriage. Even his world-renowned horse farm in Khamis Mushayt could not induce her to live in Arabia with its dust and camel dung, she said. But more importantly, she did not relish marriage to a man within a culture where a wife could be legally dominated like a prize thoroughbred. Her distraught speech, peppered with the expletives that never bothered him before, now seemed disconcerting coming from such perfect, pink lips.

"You wondered about this ring," she continued. "Well, I wear it every day, so never again will I make so tragic a mistake. Hank... if we started over, I could make you happy. I'll never disappoint you again if you give me another chance to have a future with you. We could be on a flight to London tonight. By afternoon, wandering the Victoria and Albert. The next week we'll feast on wine in Provence. Then a month to lie around Naples soaking up the Mediterranean sun. Finally, on to Florence and the Uffizi, to live among those glorious paintings. And when we grow tired, we can come home. Here. To all our friends." She waited expectantly.

"I'm sorry, Leslie... I'm in love with someone else." Without consulting him, his mouth had formed words of which he was absolutely certain.

With something like polar ice hardening every syllable, she spoke. "All right, go back and live in the Third World. Yes, I've heard about her. But don't be surprised when she picks you clean of your last cent and then runs back to her squalor and ignorance."

He didn't hide the reaction on his face as his body drew away. Her hand encircled the lantern. Her muscles clenched and anger made her body jerk. The lantern fell on its side. Hot wax spattered across her gown. Her mouth fell open, and she cursed the world and its maker with all the creativity of her God-given mind.

Without wavering, he pulled loose from her presence. Then he left that den imbued with the power to imprison. He left the gala, too, and the next morning, he left his father, but not before another, more subtle plea was heard.

At the airport, Lawrence waited with Hank. The intercom announced boarding, and Hank got up to leave.

"Son, I'm going to miss you. Thanks for being here."

"I'm glad I came, Dad. I'm going to miss you, too."

Lawrence smoothed the hair at one temple, but couldn't rid himself of a novel turmoil in his chest. "This is strange Hank, but I feel apprehension about your leaving."

"My safety?"

"No, nothing like that." Suddenly, he looked down in embarrassment. "I'm sorry. I meant concern for myself. Won't you stay at least through spring?"

"Dad, you'll be fine. You can come visit me in Georgia. We still have more golf to play, and there are things I need to tell you."

Lawrence set off a dazzling smile and hugged his son goodbye.

Watching the jet climb away, Lawrence lightly rubbed the knuckles of his hands. Locked in his thoughts, forgetting his usual urbane manner, he turned and walked the airport concourse, disinterested in the faces moving past.

CHAPTER FORTY

"ABBY, YOU'RE DRIVING ME nuts today." Trent hoisted himself higher on the pillow. "You've brought me another glass of orange juice for a stomach that's more acidic by the minute. And my sheets are tucked so tight I feel like I'm pinned by a fallen pine."

"I'm sorry. I'll leave you alone."

"Look, there's no use wasting that non-stop energy on me."

"I don't mind."

"*Abby.*"

"All right. I promised the garden club I'd take the landscaping plans for the library over to Marissa for approval... although I'd rather get one of your wrenches and change the oil in my car."

"You don't know how."

"I could learn."

"Abby?"

"What?"

"Try to cut the woman some slack."

"She doesn't like me."

"And she probably knows you don't particularly like her. *Please stop messing with my pillow.*"

"We don't have a thing in common."

"Yes, you do."

"What?"

He raised himself on one elbow. "You're both women."

"What's that got to do with anything?"

"A lot." He rested back. Abby switched on the radio and scurried around the room, straightening and gathering wash. The morning newscasters drove away real discussion with cheery talk.

"Hello!" said someone coming in the front door.

Trent and Abby's ears perked. "Sounds like he's here," she said, switching off the radio. Her face communicated delight as she ran from the room. She enveloped Hank in her love-filled hug. They walked into the bedroom, his protective arm around her. "Come see if you can cheer up my husband." The two men greeted each other with warm regard.

"I wish you had let me know you were coming home," said Hank, taking a chair. "I would've taken the day off to get you settled." Abby sat down on the bed, next to Trent.

"The attendant did fine," said Trent, "but what a bill that's going to be—medical transport all the way from Philadelphia. But how are you doing?"

"Good. It's great to have you home. But I hope the accident doesn't set you back for a while."

"Yeah, I was supposed to be here in January for a city council meeting, but my hip and then pneumonia cost me the entire month."

"I know this is rough on you."

"Unfortunately, I'm making it rough on Abby, too." His eyes switched to her and back again. "But I'm a man, and here they go and tell me I've got a women's disease. Osteo-something-or-other."

"*You didn't drink your milk?*" said Hank laughing.

"Hey, give me a break. Being old isn't a bit of fun."

Abby rested her hand on one of Trent's knees, saying, "He hates to visit the doctor."

"That's right," Trent added. "Before you know it, they're telling you something new is wrong."

"Except for these recent fractures, you're in great health," said Hank.

"Yeah? Well, the hospital doctors thought it was necessary to look at everything while I was there. I've never had so much pricking and prodding. Then I think they're finally taking me back to my room, and I go and make a fool of myself."

"What happened?"

"Nothing. The nurse simply made an odd statement. Landed me on my head like I was shot from a cannon."

"Now, Trent," said Abby, "she made perfect sense."

"Not to me." He turned his weary-looking mug toward Hank. Hank looked at Abby.

She squirmed slightly. "Trent asked the young lady if she was practicing auto repair instead of medicine."

Hank grinned. "Why'd you say *that?*"

Trent fell into disgusted silence. Hank looked again to Abby.

Abby patted Trent's leg once more. "Trent thought the nurse said, 'We need to correct your steering,' rather than, 'We need to check your hearing.'" Hank let loose.

"Go ahead," said Trent. "My brothers had a good time, too."

"Forgive me," Hank returned, rocking back in his chair, still laughing.

"It's okay. It's just hard on my pride. I may have to watch my body fall apart, but I tell you, I'm going to use every last bit of my strength getting something constructive done, even if I have to do it from my bed."

"Trent, you've got more strength of will than any man I know. You'll be up again, soon."

"I hope so. I see my doctor on Friday. Eventually, he'll want me to get those blasted crutches out.... Try to excuse my foul mood."

"Don't give it a thought."

Abby rose, forced to leave for her appointment. On her way out, she made Hank promise to have dinner with them the next evening.

"You know I always show up for your good cooking. And in a few days," he gestured toward the wheelchair in the corner, "if Trent is up to it, I'd like to take you two next door. I've made some changes." They accepted, and Abby left on her mission.

"Tell me, Hank, how is our little man?" said Trent.

"Wonderful. I talk to him almost every night. Everyone up there is marveling at how quickly he's healed."

"Yes, Abby called last weekend," said Trent. "Elizabeth is beside herself that he's gained five pounds."

"And he's more active than ever."

"You miss them, don't you?" said Trent.

"Yes." Hank's gaze lifted from the carpet to his neighbor's face. "I was going to pick them up a week from Friday, but Dr. Sandholm insisted on driving them. The doctor and his wife will be attending a conference in Atlanta. Elizabeth and Manuel's flight leaves on Sunday."

"Oh. I see. That's so soon." The old man's eyes gave away his sympathy.

"I'm awfully glad you're home, Trent."

"Thanks."

I've been talking to Brian about something. I need your input, as well."

"What's up?"

"I called Yolanda Velez last Sunday... "

After Hank was through, they conferred. Then Hank left, insisting Trent rest. For one week they would be flush with time. Work at the site had come to a halt.

Later that day, they spent hours in Trent's bedroom, on the phone, gathering information. Hank manned the word processor, and Abby kept them going with food and encouragement. A fax machine and the internet made distance no problem. It helped tremendously that Trent had moderate proficiency in Spanish and a vast knowledge of the law.

Over the next few days, Hank listened to the man explain, negotiate and accomplish what would normally be impossible from an injured man's bed in a small town in north Georgia. Their efforts were all a gamble. Everything hinged on Hank's interpretation of a stolen glimpse on a winter evening.

CHAPTER FORTY-ONE

THE SCENERY OUTSIDE THE windshield pulled Abby away from her mental to-do list. Taking her eyes off the road, every so often, she reveled in the way the frosty morning had breathed upon nature, leaving a feather-light dusting of glitter. She opened the window halfway, letting the cold air inside. Then her conscience, with chastising authority, drove her back to the day's priorities, and she raised the glass again. Her lips closed like a ziplock bag, and she continued down the road at a steady clip.

The area, near the outskirts of town, down Highway 5, past the library and Enon Cemetery, was swiftly changing. Marissa had already turned down a handful of offers for her acreage tucked way back off the road. Not too far in the future, a developer would come in, naming what had been her piece of land and a much larger expanse Ridge-Walk. Everywhere in the county, spacious, upscale subdivisions and golf courses integrated themselves in the natural beauty of the land overnight. Sometimes, people forgot it was still farm country.

Abby had gotten her wake-up call a few years before, at twilight hour. She rushed out of the band concert at Dean Rusk Middle School where Noreen's grandson played French horn. Afraid they would be late for the Woodstock Centennial Commission meeting, she swerved around a blind curve near Hickory Flat, driving her SUV a little bit like a tank and hit a lovely, on-the-loose Guernsey trying to find its way to the barn. Noreen tried to revive the cow. Heartsick, Abby located the owner. After dropping Noreen at the meeting, she rushed home, grabbed the hose and washed milk off the hood. At 7:45 the next morning, she put the vehicle in the body shop before Trent returned from his trip with Roy.

Abby reached Marissa's home. The gates were open. Abby turned up the long, pea gravel drive five minutes early. The house sat centered within a wide skirt of winter-browned lawn accented by two old magnolias. Their dark green leaves glistened as though dipped in sugar.

The meteorologist had said, "Mid-sixties by early afternoon!" Abby didn't think it likely, although the sun shone brightly. She parked next to one of the spreading magnolias and stepped out of the vehicle. The white frame house was complemented with a wrap-around veranda and a sleeping porch above. How many years had it been since she sat on the veranda drinking lemonade with Marissa's mother?

Christina always insisted they first go to the garden to pick some mint or pluck a strawberry for garnish. Abby's steps shortened as she reminisced. One late spring day, as the two women sat talking, a group of cyclists pedaling down the road turned up the driveway after a fifty-mile ride. Ready for a break, the athletes came to ask about the wonderful smell drifting from the property. Headquartered in Arizona, they had come to Atlanta for a big race. Christina told them the scent came from the wild honeysuckle growing along the fences. She claimed it had the power to make old men cry for their southern homesteads. Next, inside of one minute, Christina had the team of five persuaded to forgo the power drink in their packs. With the ease of a world-class chef, she whipped up a lunch of tender, apple roasted pork shanks over baby greens, and they did not resist her buttermilk chess pie, eating it under the cool eaves of the old home.

Abby walked over to a neglected bed of floribundas in the mid-yard. Christina always had them pruned by Valentine's Day. Abby felt a surge of lamentation. Eight years had passed. A decade younger than Abby, Christina had advanced Alzheimer's now and lived in the nursing home. Reaching the front steps, Abby started to ascend but stopped. She looked to the side, at the separate jumbles of dry sticks pointing up from the ground—the only trace in winter of the lacecap hydrangeas. Beautifully frail, lavender blooms would be perched near the end of each leafed-out branch by late June.

How incongruous, thought Abby. Marissa chose to remain in that pastoral setting when a contemporary loft in midtown Atlanta would seem the woman's first choice. Each workday, she spent an hour traveling to the fast-track firm where she scrambled to prove herself.

Abby rang the doorbell. No one answered. She decided to check the garage situated past a rear corner of the house.

Peering through the window, her eyes found the sports car. Her watch said nine sharp. Her shoulders fell. There was so much to do, and Trent might need her. To him, she was dependable as a school teacher, more task-driven than a postmistress, and scheduled with the efficiency of a nurse's station. Even so, there were many occasions when she relied on her husband. Like the way he helped her remember that, sometimes, the best thing she could do for a person was to stop what she was doing, look them in the eye, and listen. Or the way he could settle her down and help her see what was underneath, not only the obvious. And then there was the way he loved her anyway. Her staunch pragmatism was often tempered by his forbearance.

Abby wrinkled her nose with impatience and stepped away from the window. Marissa had probably gone somewhere to breakfast with Rick Chambers. He'd been around for a while, but things usually progressed only so far. Abby knew he would disappear as the others had, like the pine pollen that colored everything yellow in the spring and washed away with the first rainstorm. In the same way pollen regenerates the forests but sends the susceptible moaning to their allergists, each man made changes in Marissa's world, for good and bad. The last decade had seen a definite downward trend and the outcome—a slow track toward animus and alienation.

Abby decided to wait under the arbor. Located on the back side of the garage, near a knot garden that would be overflowing with herbs by summer, the arbor had benches almost back-to-back. Vine-covered lattice served as divider. One bench faced the house and received most of the blue shade from the arbor's wooden arms. The other bench, in opposite position, welcomed the rays coming from the east and viewed the grove's winter forms. Abby chose the sunny side.

The morning rays warmed her hands and feet, then seeped through the fabric covering her knees, driving away the small ache that visited during winter. A blue jay called nearby. The frost had begun to melt, and vapors rose from the ground. The smell of rich, wet earth reminded her of the way Twelfth Night's hooves used to cut into the damp soil as they traipsed the margins of the Everglades. Before long, her head rested back on the dormant branches of thickly grown Trumpet Vine. Sleep sneaked gently upon her little frame like the chameleon, several inches above her, emerged without making a stir on the gray twigs woven through lattice. On that first mild day in February, all became quiet, and minutes tiptoed by.

Abby's eyes slipped open a minute degree with the awareness of a regular beat, a pleasant, crunching sound that slowly graduated from soft to moderate and louder, then stopped. Still in a dream-like state, her mind had difficulty forming an association. She didn't move, but her consciousness came up another level. A voice repeated the assertions of another.

"For success like a man, I will think like a man. For success like a man, I will talk like a man. For success like a man, I will work like a man."

Eyelids still drawn, Abby wondered where she was as the voices continued.

"I am bold. I am aggressive. I demand what I wa-a-a-a-nt." Jagged sobs came from the opposite side of lattice and vine. Abby jolted thoroughly awake. It was Marissa, back from her power-walk, sitting on the other side, now ignoring the motivational tape at her side and finally clicking the player off.

Abby's head switched back and forth. Was there some way she could get to her car without being seen? Impossible.

The sobs came softer now. Abby made a quick cough. Sheer silence shattered the atmosphere.

"Oh! Is someone there?" Marissa's inner focus, acting like blinders, prevented her from noticing the hunter green vehicle camouflaged by magnolia leaves of the same color. The loud blowing of Marissa's nose followed.

Abby stepped gingerly from the other side, her expression showing sorrow for the intrusion.

"Oh, it's you, Abby." Marissa straightened her jogging suit and tried to smooth her tawny, pulled back hair, in between wiping under her eyes with fingers that still shook from the rare release of emotion, excepting her occasional reliance on acrimony.

"I'm sorry, Marissa. I brought the plans. You said you needed them before the next council meeting. I fell asleep waiting for you."

"Oh, no." She pulled her ever-present agenda out of the pocket of her warm-up jacket to flash through it in dismay. "You're correct. I forgot our appointment. I'm so sorry. This is just terrible. I don't know what's happening to me." It all came out in rapid fire.

"Don't concern yourself. I've been here only a few minutes."

The river of tears seemed to break through Marissa's solid self-sufficiency. "Oh, Abby, it's just that I admire your competence so much… and I'm embarrassed… and not only because you found me crying."

Abby blinked once with astonishment at the words. Marissa looked younger, and her coloring and pert nose reminded Abby of her own daughter, Dana. She sat down beside the lady still trying to clean up from all those waterspouts gone amuck. Completely warmed now, Abby took off her knit gloves. "Marissa, what's wrong?"

The answer came in a voice trembling with despondency. "I don't know what to do, Abby. I've worked so hard. I've given up everything to get where I am. Now, I'm being let go. *Me*, can you believe it? We're… No. *They're* downsizing. My years of dedication are out the window. The question keeps running through my head—what does this say for my goal of being a CEO someday?" Abby's eyes eased into twin orbs of compassion.

"This kind of thing happens all the time. By next month you'll have a job at another corporation."

"No. No, I won't. At least not one I'd be proud of. The last three years, my evaluations have been negative. My bosses don't see things as I do. If only they would give me control. If only they understood my vision. And then there's Rick." She blew her nose. "We finished our collaboration. *A History of Cherokee County Industry* is on its way to the printer, and now Rick's leaving for Greenville and another project." The sniffles were coming again. Marissa raised a hand before her eyes to gather some comfort from the glossy, pink ovals, but one broken nail held limply. She placed her face in her hands.

Abby put an arm around Marissa, giving a gentle squeeze as the tears flowed again.

"And friends? I have none. Then on top of everything... to-to-da-a-a-y is my thirty-fourth b-b-birthday." Her body vibrated with sobs.

Abby patted Marissa's back and waited. The urge to be on her way and the burn of comeuppance words had fully disappeared.

"What is it, Abby? What am I doing wrong?" Abby thought for a moment. Just how brave were the woman's ears? She would have to go easy.

"Hm, let's see, Marissa. You're blessed with talent and determination. Good things. But as I think about it, it may have something to do with... um... attitude."

"Uh-huh?"

Abby took Marissa's hands chilled from the upheaval to hold in Abby's older ones with their parchment-thin skin soft as the velvet pansies at their feet. "Well... sometimes, I don't think you know how very special you are."

"What do you mean?"

"I mean the way you were made or the incredible gifts you've been given as a woman."

"I know I'm reasonably attractive, and I can be entertaining when I need to."

"I'm not referring to those things."

"What, then?"

"Marissa, women are different from men, and it's not a bad thing."

"I'm just as good as a man."

"Of course, but don't underestimate the incredible value your womanhood gives you. I know your father was always respectful toward women."

"Yes. But his own daughter was forever waiting for his attention."

"Marissa, he was doing the best he could under the strain of running Manning Manufacturing. Perhaps you must use new eyes, kinder eyes, to see men fairly. We women also have our flaws, about which, we haven't the faintest. Men can't help the way they're made, and neither can we." Marissa listened intently, and Abby thought her words might be opening a door. "If you think you'll find the perfect man, he doesn't exist."

"When I do find the right man, I'll certainly never depend on him for my self-esteem."

"Who says you should?"

Marissa shrugged her shoulders.

"You will find that special man... if you understand that it is a woman's tenderheartedness, her deeper understanding of the beauty and preeminence of life that is her appeal. That softness draws men to us. Strangely... it makes us strong."

Marissa listened carefully, recognizing her mother in Abby's words.

"And as for your career, the fact that you're not a man isn't why you're failing to get ahead. It may be because you're refusing to honor your true self."

Soon, they got up and walked into the house. They talked and commiserated while drinking coffee and nibbling on Marissa's home-made biscotti. Their laughter tinkled like teaspoons stirring inside porcelain cups.

After Abby left, Marissa sat on the porch, steeping in her thoughts. The last couple of years, there had been times when she longed for the company of her mother. She recalled how they used to sit by the window in the living room during the evening hours and wait for her father to come home when Marissa was high school age. Sitting on the floor curled next to her mother's legs, Marissa read the paper out loud while her mother brushed Marissa's long hair. She could still bring to mind the sound of her mother's voice and smell of Apple Betty coming from the kitchen. John Manning adored his wife. He was a good man and a respected businessman. Growing up, Marissa gravitated toward his dynamism and mistook her mother's calm and selfless nature as weakness. Bit by bit, Marissa was discovering that those qualities, which she discredited as a girl, were the very ones she needed to possess.

Thirty minutes of soul-searching had passed when she heard some crunching on the gravel driveway. A little girl named Hannah came up the lane to the house. The child's mother waved hello from where she waited down at the gate. For a second, Marissa wished she had accepted her neighbor's invitations over the years.

The child was nearing. Marissa considered the sweater that kept the little girl warm. It was the same shade as the strawberries she had placed just for the pleasure of their beauty in a white, Wedgwood bowl in her kitchen. The child's light brown uniform was familiar. A dark brown beret sat upon chestnut colored hair. She couldn't have been much older than seven or eight. She gave her greeting and presented her sales pitch, unafraid, holding a poster illustrating six cookie versions. Darkly fringed, soft blue eyes and pink cheeks were enough to win over every customer. Marissa was no exception, but she couldn't resist giving cogent advice once the sale was complete.

"Now, sweetie, to increase your sales you must have a plan. Your visual aid is excellent, but product samples will put you over the top."

"Yes, ma'am."

"Analyze your market first. Don't waste time going to relatives and friends. And forget the neighborhood. Your quota will rise faster if you limit your territory to apartments and shopping centers where the concentration of potential clients is higher."

"Yes, ma'am."

"And each night, evaluate progress toward your goal. Decide where you can improve your methods and-"

The child's brief, sable eyebrows angled with perplexity.

"Oh, my. Listen to me," Marissa said, shaking her head. "You just have fun today, and enjoy the time with your mom."

Marissa watched the girl walked away. The sun, almost overhead, rested on the child's shoulders and shone on her calves covered in brown tights. A carefree bounce marked her steps. When she reached the gate, the child lifted her face toward her mother. Smiling, they took each other's hand. They went out the gate and followed the white pasture fencing. Marissa's neighbors were still visible to her until passing the other side of three struggling Colorado blue spruce that she had forced to acclimate without much thought concerning their natural qualities. Only by chance had she chosen a spot where they were shaded from the burning afternoon sun.

Her neighbors' voices faded. The veranda grew cold. Marissa turned and entered the house.

CHAPTER FORTY-TWO

"HAN! HAN!" MANUEL RAN toward Hank at full speed. "Catch me!" That was Hank's old cue to scoop the child up and fly him around like a plane. Fearful for the wounds that were only recently healed, Hank fell to one knee, with outstretched arms. The others watched the reuniting, standing by Sandholm's car.

"Only eight weeks, and yet, I see you've grown," said Hank.

"Some day, I be as big as you," said Manuel.

"Well, if you want to keep growing you'd better come eat the great meal Abby made." Manuel ran to Abby and Trent on the porch, swamping them with love. Hank stepped to the car and greeted Elizabeth and the Sandholms. Then he led them to the Eversons and the cabin.

Dinner conversation centered on Trent and Manuel's medical situations. After the meal, the group moved down to the fireplace. In the larger space, Trent moved more freely in his wheelchair. He insisted on bringing out, to Manuel's surprise, a big-wheel bike. The child jumped on his prize and maneuvered around the furniture. His mother admonished him to take care. Like an indulgent grandfather, Trent refused to worry about the heart pine floors.

James Sandholm smiled as his eyes tracked the child around the room. "We're going to miss that little guy, aren't we, Arielle?"

"Yes. For our first 'special needs' patient, we have had the best."

Hank turned toward the doctor and his wife. "And Manuel received superior care. We thank you Dr. and Mrs. Sandholm."

"Please, as I said before, call me James, everyone." His face drew up for a second. "Haven't been able to convince Elizabeth, though."

"Yes. I am often teased about my old-world manners," she replied, smiling.

"So, James, your next pro bono patient?" said Hank.

"In July. A little girl from Honduras. Her problems are more severe than Manuel's, but with a little luck her prognosis should be good. She requires a second operation, so she'll be in Tennessee a while."

"I'd like to ask you about something," Hank began.

"What's that?"

"I've been thinking about forming a foundation for foreign children with medical needs. A place for young patients and their parents. Sort of a transition point, before and after surgery. Could something of that nature serve your needs?" Arielle Sandholm smiled with interest. Hank thought he saw Elizabeth's eyes come to attention.

"That would enable us to handle many more cases than just one or two a year," said Sandholm. "And I wouldn't be forced to worry about them leaving this country too soon. But I may have overestimated the scope you intend."

"It's to be my work. My life. I want to be fully involved. I'd like to partner with you and any other doctors who are interested."

"You could really make a difference," said Sandholm.

"I own twenty acres on the other side of my home. The property follows the perimeter of the lake. I was thinking about separate family cabins, a dining hall. We could manage ten, maybe a dozen patients at a time. There would be recreation facilities, a schoolroom, and a clinic. Of course, all of this is contingent on zoning. The Eversons support the plan. Harold Barner will probably follow when he gets wind of it."

Trent nodded. "I think Harold will be pleased with some activity here at the lake. He's been lonely since Veronica died."

Sandholm finished off his coffee. "Hank, I'll be in Seattle, teaching through March and April. Could we meet in May to discuss this further?"

"Sure. Sorry to spring this on you. I know you have to be in Atlanta by eight."

"It will be great working with you," added Sandholm.

"Yes," said Arielle rising from her seat. "And it helps lighten our hearts over having to say good-bye to Manuel and Elizabeth. We've grown so fond of them." Arielle looked at Elizabeth. The two women struggled to hang on to their emotions. It was harder for Elizabeth who knew that after this first parting there was still a line of beloved people to whom she would be giving her final farewell on Sunday.

The little person at the center of everything shook the man's hand and promised to do all the things that would keep him mending and in good health. "Remember," said James Sandholm, "you are four years old now. So don't fuss when your mother makes you take your medicine. And do what Yolanda says."

"Okay, Dokker Sanho."

Elizabeth kissed the couple goodbye and promised her letters would be finding the way to their mailbox for years to come.

In the kitchen, Abby and Elizabeth put dishes away. Hank helped Trent get undressed and into bed. After whispering something to Hank, Trent pulled the covers up to his chin and wished Manuel and Hank a good night. Hank turned off the light. Manuel pulled close to speak. "Han? My bed. Is it still in the shed?" Hank held off until they trailed out and shut the door.

"It's not there anymore."

Manuel yanked on two of Hank's fingers. "Mama and I, can we sleep with you?" Hank chuckled and shook his head.

"Please. Please. We don't wake up mice."

"Abby wants you and your mother to stay with her. She's made up a bed for the both of you, in the loft. Hey, don't forget. Tomorrow we're going to take that bike of yours on a rally around my driveway."

The sun was back out, shining from the boy's face.

Hank crouched down and gently took the child by the shoulders. "Manuel, in your prayers tonight, ask God to bless you and your mom in a new way."

"Huh? What you mean?" His tan nose crinkled.

It sounded as if the kitchen duties were done. Hank whispered, "Just say, God please do something real good for mama and me."

"Okay."

After settling Manuel in bed, Elizabeth joined Abby and Hank watching the fire. He handed her a glass, and they sipped rosé, which captured the image of waning ribbons of orange and yellow among the embers. Before long, Hank went about making his departure, thanking Abby for the meal. Breakfast would be at his house, he announced. He would come over at eight to get Trent and the wheelchair. Then, careful to control the fire in his eyes, he made the girl central to his speech.

"Elizabeth, Manuel must be asleep. Would you walk with me to the house to see the work I did while you were gone."

Abby broke in, nodding vigorously. "Yes. Go, go. You must see it. I'll be reading. If Manuel needs anything, I'll be right here."

They put on jackets and stepped outside. Over-warm from the cabin's interior, they decided to sit on the front porch until the cold air revived them. Their position hid the gibbous moon rising behind them, on the far side of the lake, but angled bars of light filtered down into the sleeping woods dotted with hackberry and laurel.

"Hank, I am so happy to know of your plans."

"Like you said, there'll always be someone in this world who needs me."

"Yes," she said brightly. "And ever since you told me of the reconciliation with your father, I am even more grateful to God."

"It's amazing... the ways I've changed. When I think back, I don't fully understand that guy. You know... the old one."

She laughed lightly and studied his face. "Yes, you are different."

His focus moved to the right. He whispered, "Look. Visitors." Three deer stepped lightly through the woods, soundlessly treading the mat of leaves in their path. As though they had been convened, the deer approached the cabin, stopping at the wood's very edge, where Trent's narrow swath of formal yard began. The animals stood with serene beauty, black noses testing every whiff of air. Their proud eyes calmly took in the scene. The taupe and snowy white fur of their necks called out to be stroked. In front, the stag, wearing a crown of antlers, gazed with calm directness at the couple. Then turning, it guided its companions back into cover.

Elizabeth let out a little gasp of pleasure.

"Beautiful," said Hank, gazing at the woods. He looked down at her and took her hand. "I'd better get you over to see the house before you freeze." They got up from the bench and walked to the house. Coming into the kitchen, Elizabeth thought she smelled the dried rosemary, mint and basil Abby used to bring. Her chuckles emerged.

"What?" he asked.

"I remember the first time I entered this kitchen, how afraid I was, and how I hoped you would help us."

"You were a brave girl to take a chance on me." He took her hand again. "Let me show you what I've done in the den."

They walked through the kitchen into the other room. Her face radiated surprise. A comfortable sofa, loveseat, and chairs replaced the tattered furniture. Fine side tables and lamps had been added. He walked over to the fireplace that was no longer hidden by the old television. Gas logs instantly turned into a glowing fire with embers. A large cabinet in the corner held the television, and shelves of books were on either side. "It is very nice," she said.

"Soon that ramshackle kitchen will be renovated. I've been busy while you were gone. If it wasn't dark, I could show you the new coat of paint outside *and* the fixed shutter *and* the repaired screen door."

"When did you do all this? You were working everyday."

"At night and weekends. I hired a crew to do some construction. I've added a room. Take a look at the old bedroom, first." He led her, sheltering her eyes from the other end of the hall.

She entered the room redecorated in umber with accents in gold and black. The furniture was elegant yet modern. The small bed had been replaced by a large one layered luxuriously with a thick coverlet and pillows. She grew quiet.

He directed her to the right, but she would only stand at the doorway of the re-modeled bathroom. He sought her opinion of every change. Her words were barely audible when he asked her approval of the deep marble tub and oval sinks with bright, polished appointments. He listened closely. He pointed out the light fixtures and their drops of crystal illuminating the matching mirrors. He studied her face, which looked as if confusion and worry fought to gain control of her features.

"Now, the new addition." He pulled her along. The utility room had been demolished to accommodate the construction of a bedroom. Elizabeth stood at the doorway, taking in the red and blue color scheme. Her sight was drawn to the wallpaper and its border of ships and planes and trains. A shelf along one wall held toys and books. Manuel's blue metal slinky rested over one spindle of the twin size headboard. Her hand went to her heart. She turned and ran back down the hall.

"Elizabeth, wait!"

He reached her in the den and took her lightly by the arms. "Elizabeth, you can take Manuel and leave my life forever, and I will understand. But first, promise to listen." He took the plane tickets from the mantle and handed them to her. "Just hear me out. Whatever you decide, I *will* accept." Tears came down her face. She wiped them with a trembling hand. He pulled her gently to the sofa. "Elizabeth, this has all been a huge gamble, but I love you, and I was glad to take the risk. I believe we were meant to be a family. I want you to be my wife."

"I cannot." She was crying heavily, now.

"Why? If you don't love me, just tell me." He would not demand. He would not call in his debts. He steeled himself for the answer.

"Of course I love you. I will always love you," she said.

Her words infused him with happiness. "Is it Javier, then?"

"Yes."

"Elizabeth, I talked with Yolanda for a long time on the phone. She told me everything…. You are not married. You have never been married to Javier. He stole you and kept you with his threats."

She pulled away and stood up. Her face turned away. "But I am his…. He knew me and I bore his child."

He rose and took her in his arms, letting her tears drench his shirt. After a moment, he lifted her chin.

"Elizabeth, you are not responsible for what happened to you. When fear wasn't imprisoning you, you stayed with Javier, because that is what the village expected of someone in your condition, no matter how cruel…. You told me, once, the traditions of men are sometimes wrong. Everyone and everything conspired against you. You had no family to protect you. So you allowed yourself to be owned by an evil man before you understood the liberty and grace you live under."

Her eyes looked into his with trust.

"Now, do you want to be locked in an unholy bond the rest of your life or will you come with me before God and ask his blessing on a real marriage? One you have entered of your own free will."

She went of her own accord, into his embrace.

CHAPTER FORTY-THREE

ABBY SEARCHED A COOKBOOK for something to keep her imagination from slipping away to next door where her heart had invested so much. Trent slept soundly. She looked to the loft area again, hoping Manuel would not peep over the rail to ask for his mother.

The recipe collection wasn't working. She put it to the side and went to the stairs. Fifteen steps. How had she managed when the children were young and she went up and down a dozen times each day? She didn't remember it being a problem, then. She came to the top and approached Manuel's angelic face. "Child, may your load always be light and your foot sure," she whispered, in the words of her father. Below, the front door opened. Her feet padded swiftly downstairs.

They stood in the entry hall, Hank's arm around Elizabeth, their faces filled with joy.

"Is it, yes?" said Abby.

"Yes!" they answered. The two women met in a hug, but Hank would not let Abby wake Trent. So she was off and running with plans for a wedding.

"Oh," she said, "forgive me. I'll not bother you until you've had some rest, and even then I'll wait until I'm asked." Hank gave Elizabeth a quick kiss and reminded the women they all would be meeting early.

After breakfast, they remained at the Federal style table in his grandmother Kate's dining room. Documents waited for Elizabeth's signature. The day was mild. From the group's vantage point near the open French doors, they could keep watch on Manuel as he charged around the driveway. His mother went to the door several times, calling for him to slow down. Then off he went again leaving Hank to wonder how long the plastic wheels would last.

Trent sifted through the papers and explained the legal affairs that had occupied them. He spoke of Miguel Velez who had been instrumental and who would now guide the paperwork through.

"Elizabeth, please believe me," said Hank. "This was not presumptive action on my part. I had to be certain there were no legal snags hindering us. One way or another, I knew I was going to be the happiest man alive or an embarrassed dolt."

"Yet, I said yes, not knowing how it could be accomplished."

Trent's hands skimmed the arc of the wheels of his chair. "Tell her about Yolanda's testimony."

"She verified to the authorities how you came to be with Javier," said Hank. "That broke right through any legal blocks. And thanks to Miguel's efforts, I can adopt Manuel if you are in agreement."

"It is almost too wonderful to believe," she cried.

"Without Trent, we wouldn't have gotten anywhere from the start. He handled everything with the State Department and immigration authorities." Elizabeth looked at the gentleman, giving him her thanks and a blissful smile. Abby leaned down from where she stood behind his chair and kissed him on the temple. Even so, his normally straight posture was starting to give way.

"Are you needing rest?" Abby asked.

"I'm fine for a while longer. There's that last thing. You'd better tell her."

Abby moved from behind Trent and sat down beside Elizabeth. "I contacted some people I know in law enforcement. Javier escaped from a Texas jail in December. A detainee told authorities Javier is trying to find you."

"Nothing stops him," said Elizabeth.

Hank inhaled and pushed against his chair back, making it creak. "I'd love to be his personal roadblock."

"Don't worry," said Abby, forcing a positive tone. "The man will give up. He has no idea where you are." Elizabeth turned from Abby to look at Hank, his eyes full of confidence, and the grim line of her mouth softened back into fullness.

It was time to call Manuel.

Once inside, he climbed into a chair and peered at the four adults. "Why serious? I not ride my bike fast anymore."

"We are happy," said his mother. "We have something important to ask you. How would you like for us to live with Hank, always?"

"I like."

"Hank and I want to be married?"

"Okay."

"Hank wants to be your papa. He has built you a nice room."

"Show me." he said, jumping down. Then he paused, his small features showing strain. "My papa in Mexico… what he say?"

"It does not matter, Manuel. Some men are not allowed to be a father."

The boy digested her words and turned to Hank. "Where my bed?"

"Climb aboard." Hank bent down and offered his back, and the procession made its way through the house.

Miles away, in a mid-size Mississippi town, a cunning, young man, with eyes like two shards of obsidian, wandered down a street paralleling the Gulf. He sought Madeliene Archambeau, known for her black arts. She claimed she was the one who caused the mayor of Rampley to fall dead with a heart attack.

At ten in the morning, everything was shut tight in the coastal town with the tourist season still two months away. Beach apparel shops and bars painted in garish colors lined the street. In a deserted parking lot, gulls congregated at the top of light poles, rearranging their wings and wiggling their bodies into a comfortable squat until someone drove by and tossed a half-eaten sandwich from their car. A rolling sweeper moved along, cleaning away the accumulation of bottle caps,

Styrofoam cups, and gray sand at the gutter. A woman leaned out of a doorway. Her hair, black as asphalt, billowy and unrestrained, surrounded skin pale as the cigarette butts littering the sidewalk. With her eyes, she called him to come nearer.

His walk became a swagger. They seemed to come out of the woodwork, he mused. Another time, he promised with a grin. His English had improved a great deal over the weeks. He had often tested himself by seducing the American women with his words. Along the way, card games honed his skills and financed his trip. Through Texas and Louisiana felonious diversion and novel pleasures sidetracked him at times, but he never forgot the reason for his mission.

He left the commercial area and entered an enclave of expensive homes. The house, old but polished with money, sat between two others on a quiet cul-de-sac. White fluted columns and stately oaks, at first made him hesitate to turn down the walk and face a gleaming brass doorknocker and kick plate.

Javier avoided the brass and used his knuckles. A gentleman, approaching sixty, graying at the temples, opened the door. Javier studied him. He was neatly dressed in a plaid, button-down shirt, a light brown cardigan and tan slacks. A trace of shaving cream had been missed, near one ear. The eyes held no glint. Expensive leather shoes. A gold watch and wedding band. Not a servant, Javier surmised, although his instincts noted the servile, halting speech. Javier gave the password while his eyes tried to make sense of things. A faded element of cultivation and the faint smell of pipe smoke clung to the older man.

With shoulders rolled forward and feet barely lifting from the floor, he led Javier through the foyer and into an over-decorated room laden with brocade and Victorian furniture. The unforgettable red of the carpet vibrated. Overlapping the shuttered windows, thick fabrics formed enormous swags. Layered panels dripped with finger-size fringe. The complex, weight-laden drapery somehow defied gravity by remaining on the wall. Wooden blinds shunted natural light away from the interior. Javier sat down. He wiped the sweat forming on his palms, against the upholstery.

From a side door, she entered the room. Javier stood. Without acknowledgment, she walked to the liquor cabinet where she poured two drinks into crystal glasses cut like jewels, then handed one to Javier. It sat heavy in his hand.

"Who sent you?" she asked.

"Ricky Quatrain. He told me you have the power to take people out as well as give knowledge."

"Sometimes, I am given the power."

"And wasn't it so for the mayor thirty miles north of here?"

"Yes." Her eyes smiled while her mouth remained immobile. "Mr. Harper was making things difficult for me. My industry, I mean. And then... I don't like anyone telling me what to do. Please, have a seat over here." Their chairs were next to a diminutive table inlaid with malachite and red jasper.

He sat down. He thought the blond woman must have been beautiful, once. A decade or so younger than the man who answered the door, age was making its first appearance, and she was shockingly thin. The bones of her face stood out from her flesh like stark sculpture covered by a layer of beige silk. Under the long-sleeved dress, a cadaver-slim torso sat upon legs like poles. He wondered how she had the strength to stand and walk.

"What kind of business are you in?" he asked.

"*Were* in. You see, the mayor and the backward people of that town waged a personal campaign... even though we provided a good service, taking the discarded material from the regional clinics. From there, we processed the items sending some to research centers or packaging certain elements requested by individuals. What was left was efficiently incinerated."

The door to the room opened.

"I am in session!" she snapped. The man backed out with his suffocated question like a shamed child. "Now, where was I? Oh yes, my business. We are closed now, but it is the mayor who paid the price. So tell me, how can I be of service?"

"I want to know the location of my wife."

"The spirits will not tell me that. They only answer questions with a yes or no." She opened a small box. Inside was a jumble of little sticks.

"Then tell me…. Is she in Tennessee?"

The woman shook the box and poured out the white objects. She studied their arrangement. "No," she answered.

Javier picked up one of the pieces to study. He let it drop. "Is she with a doctor?"

"No."

"Is she with a man named Eduardo?"

"No."

"¡Qué!" yelled Javier, jumping up, making his chair fly backward. He grasped one of the woman's wrists and snarled, "You lie! You are nothing but a fake." He squeezed, hoping to crush the wafer-thin bones.

His breath jammed in his throat. Pressure was on the verge of exploding his brain. He slammed his eyes shut to keep them from bulging from his head. The woman's other hand banded his neck like a choking collar of fencing wire. He let go her wrist. She laughed and cinched tighter. His range of sight grew smaller. His body locked motionless with pain as his feet elevated an inch off the floor. Through his lashes, the image of her serene face bore a hole in his mind. She released him. He fell hard.

"Have a seat," she said gesturing.

Sucking air like a vacuum, he took care getting up from the floor and pulled the chair to the table with a shaking hand. "I am very sorry," he wheezed and panted. "I was mistaken." Coughing shook him. "I did not mean to offend. Let me pay you, and I will be gone," he said, a gurgle underlying his speech as he rubbed his throat.

"Pay me? Didn't Ricky tell you I don't need money? I have enough stashed away for ten lifetimes. I've just retired earlier than planned. Ricky owes me, and he knows the kind of work you've done. I need you to take care of a little problem. Similar to the mayor."

"But I cannot stay. I am searching for my wife and son." His body still oscillated with pain and uncoordinated movement.

"I must apologize. We've gotten off to a bad start," she said in a silky voice. "I can ensure that you reach them. I tell you this with certainty. And with me, you will learn things. In return, you must perform the undertaking I have for you. I promise you will be detained no more than a week or two."

Her eyes seemed to penetrate his thoughts. He tried not to stutter. "I don't know that I can succeed with your request. There are others with more talent."

"You're the one." A smile slid across her lips.

"I must think for a moment," he said as he hunted with disoriented perception for the door. Cautiously, he started to rise.

The woman calmly sat back. "The spirits tell me she wore yellow ribbons in her braids. And she wiped the blood from your face with her hem."

Javier swallowed the last of his liquor in one large gulp, and he lowered himself back onto the chair.

She rubbed his arm softly.

CHAPTER FORTY-FOUR

THE BRITTLE ATMOSPHERE OF winter had fled, replaced by air having a rich, loamy smell that meant the earthworms were stirring. Abby had already deposited seeds—beet, mustard, cauliflower, radish, turnip—in the workable soil of her garden. Hank helped her prune the Nelly Moser clematis clinging to one leg of the deck, and he set up a heating mat near a basement window so she could start the white and rose-veined caladium bulbs that were the signature of her filtered-sun garden.

One Saturday morning, Hank piled scrambled eggs on whole-wheat toast. No matter how he tried, some tumbled off. After taking some bites, he put down his breakfast and walked into the den to look at the lake through the glass doors. The water was untroubled, but the newscasters reminded everyone that tornado season wasn't far off. Ten years ago, during a similar March, a funnel cloud cut through, taking part of Harold Barner's roof.

Hank pulled aside the glass door and stepped onto the porch. Elizabeth was gone for a final fitting. He had been insistent about the wedding date. The sooner the better. He lifted a sweater from the folding chair where she kept the extra garment in reserve for cool evenings when they sat together. He rubbed the soft yarn. He needed her now, to lessen his worries. His eyes and mouth grew serious. He charged out of the house. A walk to the end of the dock would do him some good.

Outside, he heard noises. He looked to the viburnum, each of the plant limbs lined with white blooms. He caught a view through the opening of Trent supported by his walker, making nil progress splitting firewood for a winter all of three seasons away. Hank jogged over. He chastised Trent and took his place.

Thirty minutes later, a split and stacked cord of wood rested neatly against the cabin wall. Hank lowered his body into a seat, having worked himself into a genial mood. Trent was silent, looking at the water.

"Anything up, Trent? You seem a little glum today."

"Yeah? Didn't foresee a walker being part of life." His stare remained forward.

"Don't you know you can depend on me? I'm right next door."

"I know. Thanks." Trent turned a sidelong glance toward Hank. "I got a call this morning. Sonny Wyler died last night in the prison hospital."

"Wyler? The guy who implicated John Manning?"

"Uh-huh."

"I've only heard bits and pieces. Something about taking pay-offs for below standard materials?"

"Mm hm. Three deaths. It's possible there was another, but the wreck damage was so severe that a study of the brakes wasn't conclusive."

"Wyler actually thought there wouldn't be consequences to his actions?"

"Guess so." Trent's index finger fiddled with a wing nut on his walker. Loosen. Tighten. Loosen. Tighten. "Marissa Manning has probably heard the news by now."

"Oh yeah. Now I remember. You represented her father's company."

"I wasn't able to save him from prosecution. Everyone knew he was innocent."

"Didn't Manning refuse to let you put up much of a fight?"

"He said he'd have to shoulder some of the responsibility since he was the one who hired Wyler. Later, Wyler recanted. By then, John had served two years, and there was nothing left of Manning Industries. He died shortly after his release. Some people in this town have never forgiven me... and that includes myself." Hank, a novice at encouraging others, failed to get his tongue to move and shifted uneasily in his chair. "You'll have to excuse this old man and his regrets. When you get to be my age, you look over your life and wonder if you made a difference in this world."

"Believe me, Trent, you have."

"Hey," said Trent with some lightness, "only three weeks until the wedding. Are you ready?"

"I keep vacillating with worry about it never happening and what kind of husband I'll be when it does."

"That's natural. It's a big step."

"How did you and Abby manage to have a great marriage?"

"Actually, adjustments were required."

Hank tossed his head back with a laugh. "With you two, I bet it was nothing but easy."

"It has been wonderful, but in the early years, she paid for my ignorance."

Hank erased a baffled look, regretting his bumbling foray. A sidetrack would smooth things. "How did you and Abby meet?"

"When the war ended, I followed a friend to his home in Gainesville, Florida. Two flyboys who had seen so much death they were ready to jump into life. We went to the competition pool to visit his girl. They talked. I took a walk. My eye caught a beautiful sight twenty yards away. There she was, on the high dive, deep in concentration. She wore a white bathing cap and a sunny yellow bathing suit over slender curves. I said to myself, I'd fight the war all over again, just for her. I approached. She must have sensed my interest. She turned her head and looked directly at me with the most winning smile I've ever seen. It was like a present floating down from heaven, meant for me. Then without hesitation, she took one graceful bounce and threw herself forward in the air. A swan dive of such elegance, I could feel my pulse racing."

"How long before wedding bells?"

"Three months. Then I entered law school. Then children started arriving. From the beginning, she was the playful, fun-loving one. I was the serious force driving ahead, fueled by a childhood in a home where happiness was squashed by the bottle and a dearth of money. My brothers and I bore the brunt. We stayed away, playing ball in the streets. Then came Abby with her strength and optimism. I felt like I could achieve anything."

"I know what you mean," said Hank.

"Two years out of law school, we moved out of our cramped apartment. I went to work for Lockheed, and I bought this acreage from your grandmother. Abby objected to the isolation. That and raising kids near deep water. But I wanted a lake to fish on. Well, career demands eliminated time for that. Fourteen-hour days of labor disputes, contracts, and negotiating. Funny. I had promised myself, as a kid, that someday I'd have a happy family, but my time at home was spent immersed in my work in the basement office."

"Trent, if that's the worst you've done, you're no worse than a million other husbands." Just then the Explorer pulled up, and Abby parked it in its place under the deck.

Trent got up from his chair and nodded in the direction of the dock. "Let's take in some night fishing around eight o'clock."

CHAPTER FORTY-FIVE

HANK READ THE WORDS in Song of Solomon about the mystery of a man and a woman, and the wonder; it was difficult to fathom. A bestowal. She would never have to leave his house again. He finished his reading, left the cottage, and trotted to the cabin where each night they ate together at Abby's table.

Later, Hank stood in the kitchen watching Elizabeth clean the dinner plates in soapy water. She refused help, mindful of his appointment. Her smooth, tan arms moved from dish to dish. The bubbles clung to her skin like little kisses. Musing, he felt a strong urge to wrap her within his arms. Flossie ambled in. He could have sworn the cat looked pointedly at him while letting out a derisive meow.

Elizabeth turned to Hank. "Trent. Is he not waiting?" she asked softly.

"One kiss and I'm gone."

They made the slow trip to the dock in the gray light without mishap, thanks to Hank's sturdy arm. The symphony of sounds coming from the woods signaled that the night creatures were waking with spring. The leaves on the trees had sprouted wearing the peridot color that would later intensify to a deeper green.

As the men situated themselves, the frog chorus moved into full swing. Twilight deepened. Trent cast his line without enthusiasm.

Hank practiced phrases in his mind. He gazed at the surroundings. With the advancement of darkness, land and water were less discernible as things took on fuzzy, confusing shape.

"Trent, thank you for all you've done for Elizabeth and me. You've been more than a friend."

"I just like to feel useful."

"I've been learning a lot from you. About living," said Hank.

"Thanks. You know, looking back, there's only one thing I would change in my life."

"What's that?"

"I would have taken better care of Abby."

"Are you out of your mind? You are everything to her."

"In some ways, I failed her."

Hank looked down through the dark air to stare at the boards of the dock. "Trent, you've just been thrown into a blue funk, hearing about Sonny Wyler again. Believe me—I'm the expert on depression. You can't think clearly. You question everything about yourself."

"I do know that woman loves me…. You should have seen her when we first met, Hank. That girl was bold, unafraid of anything. Did you know Abby was only two when her mom died?"

"No, I didn't."

"Her father's sister lived close by and helped raise Abby while she was little. Her father was a man's man. Wise-faced and lean. Son of a Georgia farmer. And a crack shot. In '22, he was appointed federal marshal over a five counties in southwest Florida. And by the time Abby could read a primer, she was his assistant. Later, he taught her to shoot and hunt. While her friends were playing with dolls, she was learning to find her way through the Everglades.

"When she was a little older, she typed her father's reports on an old Remington. He sometimes took her with him and an old Seminole, to track tricksters and thieves. They might be gone for a week, eating rabbit and wild turkey and sleeping on the ground at night. One time… she was about fifteen… the sheriff was holding a man, in a place called Immokalee. The outlaw had been found with the murder weapon and two mason jars—one full of money, the other, moonshine. He was also wanted for bank hold-ups in Missouri and Arkansas. Well, he broke out one day. Abby's dad was in Tallahassee. Word was, the man on the run was seen in their territory, just south. Everyone went on lookout. Without telling anyone, Abby decided to make a search. She spotted the two-hundred-pound man hiding in an abandoned chicken coop. Sitting on her horse, with her rifle pointed, she forced him out. Then, stout-hearted as a man, she marched the thug a mile back to town."

"Incredible," said Hank.

"Abby's father sent her to college, although she told everyone she planned to work with her dad. Then I showed up to change her plans. It was a big loss for her dad. Hers too, when you consider how much she loved the man.

"Anyway, we married and, at first, things went well until she was inundated with four children in rapid succession. I could see nothing except my career. Knowing my family was there for me, kept me going, and yet how little I thought they needed me. Years of that… and Abby began to change. Her words grew fewer. Her energy plummeted. Meanwhile, I invested in suits for my career, a car to get me to my job, and, later, the dream of a small plane. I invested in everything but Abby. I thought I was the best of husbands." Trent reeled in his line and put the pole to the side. "Things can go wrong even with two people who love each other, Hank. I was impatient. Irritable. All of her confidence dwindled. Repairmen, teachers, salespeople, she would beg me to handle every problem. About that time, Abby's father died. I didn't realize what a crossroad it was for her.

"Everything came to a head one Saturday, a few weeks later. Abby was taking Roy for his swimming lesson. I reluctantly agreed to keep watch over the girls while I worked at my desk. But I barked that she would have to take Kenny, the baby at the time.

"It was Roy's final lesson. He was seven. The other students passed their test and left. Roy's turn came. Abby told me later that on each effort, he made a little headway then turned and grasped the side of the pool. Three respiratory infections the past winter. The teacher used a long pole to push him back, forcing him to continue. Abby said nothing. Just as Roy reached the deep end where it widened out like the top of a T, the instructor heard her doorbell ring. She told Abby to watch Roy. Using the pole like a walking stick, the instructor cut through her side yard.

"Abby said the baby fussed and squirmed in her arms as Roy crossed the expanse where the coping was far away. He faltered and began to sink. Abby ran about looking for something to extend. She could save him in an instant, but only if she put Kenny down. That baby could crawl at the speed of light and wouldn't hesitate to follow her in the water. She raced to find the woman. When they returned, Roy was drifting to the bottom. The teacher dove in and pulled him out."

Just then, Abby's soft voice called from the archway.

"Trent. Come to bed. It's getting late."

"Be there in a minute."

"Well, Trent," whispered Hank as he got up, "I'm not upset because I know Roy's alive, and Abby's doing fine."

"There's more, I'm afraid. I'll save it til later."

High in a tree, the cold eye of a Cooper's hawk watched two heads below, as the men, moved slowly down the dock. The streamlined skull of the raptor rose to scan the tree foliage for winged prey. Sighting its prize, the hawk lifted silently from the branch.

CHAPTER FORTY-SIX

ONE SATURDAY MORNING, ALMOST a week later, Hank was asleep when Manuel ran into the cottage, leaping and crashing down on top of the man who would soon be his father. Elizabeth trailed behind, gathering long branches of flowering viburnum to put in a vase.

Hank sat up in bed. "Who woke the big bad bear?" he bellowed. With mock growls, Hank raised himself onto his knees, his forearms positioned like the paws of a grizzly. Manuel squealed as he scampered off the bed trying to stay out of reach. Hank followed on all fours, and a chase around the house began.

When Elizabeth entered by way of the porch, the wild pursuit was proceeding out of the kitchen, with Manuel laughing and throwing pillows to ward off his predator.

Hank brought his antics to a screeching halt. There his fiancée stood, finding him disheveled, in his boxers, and acting like a kid.

"Manuel, go back to the cabin and eat the breakfast I have there for you," she said. "We must be letting Hank get dressed." Manuel ran out. Hank stood up. She laid down the long stems and walked over. Gently, she pulled his face down and kissed him sweetly on the lips. Like a breeze, she picked up her flowers and left the way she came.

Hank bent over the sink, shaving off his whiskers. He swished the razor in the water to remove the foam and short hairs that clung to the instrument. He opened the drain, watching the dirty water slip away. Never had he known such contentment; never had he felt so good about himself.

Elizabeth and Abby dined at Tea Leaves and Thyme with a gaggle of females. Trent, Hank, and Manuel went for pizza. Once out of the vehicle, they traveled gingerly across the parking lot; Trent had graduated to a cane the day before. Happy enough to break into cartwheels, he insisted the meal was his treat. They ordered Hawaiian pizza at Manuel's urging and made a mental note to pick off any strange toppings.

The boy's face changed from merry to curious. "Han. Why Mama not have her bath at home?"

"What?"

Manuel's hands gestured with his questioning. "Why she leave for a shower?"

Trent and Hank let out a laugh. Manuel smiled, seeing he had been a comic without trying.

"No, Manuel. Our friend, Marissa, is giving a party, over at the tearoom, for your mother. It's called a shower because the gifts are rain drops falling in her lap." Hank sat back, pleased with himself.

"Mama no like her clothes wet."

Trent broke into a grin. "You'd better get used to it," he said to Hank. "You're going to be asked, 'How do flies walk upside down on the ceiling? Where does the sun go at night?' and-"

"Han, how flies walk upside down?" asked Manuel.

Trent chortled until Hank launched into a good, scientific explanation. The waitress brought their large pizza. The two men studied the meal as Manuel wolfed down a slice.

Done in minutes, the child became restless. Manuel followed Hank to a table version of the outdated Pac-Man. The eight-year-old son of the pizzeria owner showed Manuel how the game worked. Hank handed out quarters and walked back to seven uneaten slices of pineapple-loaded pizza.

"Whew. Lucky for me," said Hank. "I've got leftovers Abby sent over."

"Uh-oh. That means I may be facing an empty fridge, but you deserve it. You look a little worn down by parenting."

"Are they always so inquisitive?"

"Uh-huh. And he's only four. Just wait until he's ten, and you're trying to answer his questions about the mystery of life. You'll be feeling like you've been wrapped around an axle, and he'll be more confused than ever, that is, until he asks his friends."

"Hey. Aren't you're supposed to be instilling confidence in me about familial things? Now, finish telling me about Roy. You said there was more."

Their location was a sequestered corner. Most of the diners had drifted out. The afternoon sun flooded through sheers. On a river birch outside, tiny new leaves fluttered with the wind, making shifting patterns of light and shadow on the linoleum.

"Well," his voice was hesitant. "Unfortunately, my blunders rate low on the encouragement scale."

"I'll chalk it up as prevention training," said Hank.

"Roy did live, as you know. Barely. I left work and raced to the hospital. Anguish spilled out with every breath. But when I arrived, I made Abby suffer so much more. I entered the waiting room and stormed up to her. I'm sure there was anger blazing in my eyes. Then I released my frustration. 'How could you let your own son drown?' I yelled. It was a perverse form of relief for me, but it broke something in Abby. I stood there watching the last bit of light go out in her eyes. Once Roy stabilized, Abby and I went home. Later, I woke up about three in the morning. She was gone from our bed. I found her in the woods, near her fern garden. She was lying face down on the ground, cold, alone... crying.

"To this day, a shadow of doubt shows up to jostle me. Did I permanently damage a part of her soul that could have blossomed and rewarded her? Eight lousy words, empty of all compassion. What I'd give to take them back."

Hank swallowed hard to ease the ache in his throat. He thought of all the time he had wasted in his life, believing he was the only one to know misery.

"Trent, you made a mistake. It's obvious how happy she is."

"Over the years, I've prayed it was so. After we brought Roy home from the hospital, the knowledge began registering in my mind that there was a limit to what Abby could handle. Sometimes the self-examination made me sick." Trent massaged the handle of his cane.

Hank didn't know what to say. He couldn't imagine Abby having ever been anything but a whirlwind of confidence and capability. "I'm sorry you both went through such a rough time."

"Thanks. With God's help, I'm a better man now."

"You're the best."

"No. No better or worse than most. But I did make changes. I called my boss and told him I was taking a month's leave of absence. Old Dr. Rundell and I had a long talk. I sent Abby to her aunt for two weeks of rest while I managed the house and the children. I discovered what a loving thing it is for a woman to take care of her family. Anyone can do it for a day. But year after year? I don't know many men who would be willing. All the brains and expertise in the world, but she was content to love and serve us.

"I did a massive overhaul of things. Doc told me to speak words of praise only. But I knew the best intentions can die out. I needed something more than just me. I changed our priorities. Our spiritual lives came first. When Abby's laughter and enthusiasm returned to our house, it was as though the entire world had been made right. We stayed at the cabin six more months. I joined a law firm in Roswell. Then I moved us to our home on Dobbs Street, and we rented out the cabin. The strange thing is, when I retired, Abby wanted to come back to the lake.... So that's what I've learned Hank—cherish her."

"I'm honored you'd share your wisdom, regardless of the pain. I'll be happy if I become half the man you are."

Trent smiled. "You will be, and more." They rose slowly, stiff from sitting, paid the check, and gathered the boy. With Manuel in between, they walked to the car. The child held their hands and filled them in on video game adventures, nonstop. They pretended to listen, but their minds were elsewhere as Hank and Trent came to the same conclusion. To be alive is a holy treasure.

CHAPTER FORTY-SEVEN

O N THE EVE OF her wedding day, Elizabeth had gone to bed with Abby's admonishment to sleep in and remain upstairs. In the morning, Abby climbed the stairs to the loft, with tray in hand.

"Here's your breakfast, child."

"For me? Thank you." Elizabeth stretched then rose from the bed.

Abby placed the tray on the desk. "I'm sorry your mother can't be here today."

"How did you know I have been thinking of her?"

"I wished for mine on my wedding day. And while raising kids, too." Abby finished with a laugh.

Elizabeth's face warmed with affection. "She must know what a good mother you became and not for your children only."

"You bless my heart." Abby's palm lightly touched Elizabeth's cheek. "I'll let you have a spell of quiet. Call me if you need anything."

Elizabeth drank her orange juice and listened to Manuel exclamations downstairs. Carl performed magic tricks using a disappearing piece of paper and an invisible quarter. The boy's awed questions floated up. She stretched again, wondering how she would fill her day in the loft. Everyone had refused her help.

The rehearsal dinner kept her up late the night before. Elizabeth fulfilled a wish. She had thanked her friends by cooking for the group of twenty. With Hank as kitchen assistant, she prepared authentic

Mexican dishes of Chorizo Tamale's and Pozole, satisfying the hunger of twenty who had worked so hard getting ready for the occasion.

With Marissa as wedding coordinator, capable hands took every worry off the bride and groom. When Elizabeth balked at the price of a wedding dress, Noreen offered her services. Using her elegant sense of design, she fashioned a gown. Weighing Elizabeth's request for simplicity, she chose graceful lines and an ivory, bridal satin. Around the shoulder-encircling neckline and at the end of long tapered sleeves, braided satin decorated with hand-sewn pearls lined the edges. Elizabeth's only jewelry would be earrings—each a drop pearl hanging from a discreet diamond cluster, sent by Hank's father.

An hour after breakfast, Elizabeth came out of the bathroom, her wet hair wrapped in a towel.

"Elizabeth, someone is here to see you," called Abby.

Elizabeth ran to the staircase. Yolanda looked up from below and began the climb. When they met, their arms went around one another. Tears wet their faces and spilled onto the baby snuggled between their soft, womanly bodies. Elizabeth led Yolanda to the bed where they placed four-month old Valentina to be admired. As emotion waned, their Spanish flowed like water rippling over smooth stones in a stream.

Yolanda paused, looked down at her child, then brought soulful eyes back to Elizabeth. "I am sorry. I did not know it would be like this," Yolanda said, one finger skimming the baby's tiny hands. Elizabeth assured her those days when they had been at odds were forgotten. Yolanda reached into her bag and handed a gift to Elizabeth. "It is from Señora Carteña."

Elizabeth pulled at the bow of gold cording and lifted away orchid-colored tissue paper. Inside were the porcelain flamenco dancers that had presided over the mistress's dressing table. Elizabeth read the card. "So you will never forget us. For, we will never forget you. With love and best wishes, Senora Carteña."

The Carteña family had not been the same since Elizabeth stopped returning to their home. The old gas lantern above the entryway, inviting life and felicity, malfunctioned and died. The evening meal was no longer anticipated as it had been in those days when Señor and Señora sat at the heads of the table and the professor regaled them with stories of fascinating fact while the two young people peppered his attempts with humor and teasing. Gone was Elizabeth's musical laughter that swirled around the rooms, up the stairwell, and through the open-air tower, like monarch butterflies rising and winging their way to the mountain hillsides.

Yolanda had secretly appealed to the Carteñas after Javier brought Elizabeth out of the jungle. Señor and Señora understood full well what had befallen the girl, and they were deeply saddened, but all ties were broken. Yolanda listened, her heart shriveling in anger. She knew, if Eduardo ever found the courage to fight for Elizabeth, his parents would never allow her re-entry into their world. Pride and custom strongly forbade it. The unborn child required they disavow her in every way.

In the loft, the baby cooed and, with her legs easily pulled inward, grappled with her tiny toes.

"What news have you of Eduardo?" Elizabeth asked, stroking the baby's soft scalp.

"He is well and has found suitable enterprise in his father's business. He also has a wife." They smiled without comment.

Yolanda then related her correspondence with Professor Hernandez who, years earlier, left Santolo abruptly. Now assisting at the University in Mexico City, he was overjoyed to hear about his favorite pupil.

"In his letter, he asked me to give you a message. I memorized it just as he wrote. He said, 'My search is over. The only things of importance in my head have taken residence in my heart,' and 'The only way to truth is through a Person.' " Yolanda looked puzzled. "I did not ascertain his meaning. He hopes you will write to him."

Elizabeth's face lit up. His name had long been in her prayers.

The baby started to fuss and Yolanda took the infant to her breast. Valentina's eyes, open and alert, oriented toward her mother's face, and the women exchanged smiles.

A while later, Abby called from below. Kristin Arnett had come to work on Elizabeth's hair. Yolanda kissed her friend goodbye until the wedding.

Kristin took the stairs like a teenager. Years before, she sold her shop, but her skills were still in demand. Diana Cannon was at the church, turning it into a fantasy of stephanotis and lilies. Brian Barton practiced for his first wedding and then got on the phone to confirm his date with the young woman who liked to cycle through town and who lived for twenty-five second-graders. Harold Barner was pleased. He thought a lot of his granddaughter, too. Trent and Lavon Farrier picked up last minute items and headed to Uncle Rakey's. They sent him to the shower with explicit instructions and, afterward, dressed him in a suit of Trent's, tailored to fit Rakey's small frame.

At the cottage, Hank sat on the screened porch, reading again, the six-week-old letter postmarked Palm Beach. For once, Lawrence had acted out of love and sensitivity for his son.

Dear Hank,

I have been so happy for you ever since your phone call. Your forthcoming marriage is an extraordinary event, and you deserve so much happiness. With regard to my attendance, I must decline. Forgive me that I told you otherwise on the phone. I am honored beyond belief that you would ask me to be your best man, but it is not a place which I have earned. I have firsthand knowledge of your good nature, but I will not take advantage of your forgiveness and taint your day with a shadow from the past. May you live your life better than I have lived mine. I am proud that you call me father.

Love, Lawrence Clark Averill

That afternoon, the church overflowed with people. Except for a few, they were unaware it was a multi-millionaire who married the winsome, unassuming girl from the tropics. Abby, looking lovely as matron of honor, led the way down the aisle. Hank's gift of a silver-handled cane supported Trent, the distinguished best man. Standing with the men, Manuel, his face expectant, his body uncommonly still, held a satin pillow with two rings.

Elizabeth. Hank's sight followed each of her steps as though his powerful love was the thing that drew her.

After the ceremony, the large gathering moved from the church to the terraces at the lake. Arrangements had been made from heaven, declared Abby. Who else but Kate Averill could have decorated the grounds like the gardens of a queen? Lavender clusters of wisteria, later in season than usual, curled halfway up the eighty-foot pines. In the woods, native dogwoods floated airy layers of white bloom. Massed in groupings around the perimeter of the property, azaleas gushed with clouds of color.

Music spun through the air. Photos were taken. Trent guided Manuel to the side and watched Hank and Elizabeth let loose of the world as they were caught up in a waltz.

The cake was cut and dapper Harold Barner declared the food more delicious than the day he and his ravenous squad feasted in a deserted French cafe three days after they breached the shores of Normandy. As the sun dimmed, strings of lights came on, and everyone joined in the dancing.

Mysteriously, Rick Chambers had shown up. He assisted Marissa who carried food to the tables and refilled her grandmother's heirloom bowl with George Washington Catawba Punch. Marissa let Trent pull out a chair for her as he duly noted it was time to enjoy the festivities.

Manuel was the prince of the party, adored by everyone. He had forgotten that his mother would soon leave. Like sympathizing grandparents, Trent and Abby would mollify and coddle, letting him bunk each night on the small sofa in their bedroom. But first, Manuel put his stamp on the reception.

Roaming the party like a little pet pig rooting for treasure, Manuel discovered Lee and Phoebe locked in a kiss behind the musician's stage. He searched out Carl and exploded with his secret. "Well," the man responded, "why don't you go pull that backdrop down? The darn thing hasn't wanted to stay up this whole day. Just give it a good yank." The man mimicked the strong motion with his arm. At first vacillating, Manuel finally ran to do his bidding. The backdrop fell. The string players came to a screeching halt. The flutist cried out, blanketed beneath never-ending cloth. Lee and Phoebe, warned by a speedy sympathizer, grinned on the other side of the terrace.

Once order reasserted itself, the music resumed and Uncle Rakey requested dances of the ladies. He led each partner around for half a minute and moved to the next while pertinent information escaped under his breath. With only an instant of hesitation, even Marissa did a turn on Rakeston's arm.

The white lights rose in brilliance as night drew near. Lee and three recruits, lurking in the shadows, sighted Carl who tested again his power to devise the tall tale. Having found guests ignorant of his reputation, the man related his sighting, at two a.m. the previous spring, of a Sasquatch-like figure coming from some woods off Trickum Road. Cut off mid-sentence, before he could react, the burly jokester was divested of his suit-jacket, shoes, and wallet. With the ease of a freight train carrying one lumpy, overfilled bag of grain, Lee and his contingent transported Carl across the terrace and off the dock. Trent looked on, for once strangely glad of age and infirmity.

The mood of the party mellowed. People congregated in happy groups. Musicians packed their instruments. Voices softened until shouts went out as Hank and Elizabeth emerged from the cottage dressed for departure. Carl, wearing some of Hank's dry clothing, held Manuel high as they all waved goodbye. Then the limousine pulled away into the hush of a velvet night.

Elizabeth slept with her head on his shoulder and one hand on his chest. Hank cradled the curve of her back with his arm. Lying there, holding her close, he considered himself the most fortunate of men. He had never imagined life would have her love in store. But his mind would not relax into sleep. The filmy sheers blew softly in the room, and through the open window, he heard a siren, far below on the city streets. The twinkling lights of lit-up skyscrapers were their stars. He listened to her soft breathing.

Elizabeth had begged him not to take her far away from Manuel, and Hank won a compromise. They would stay three days and nights in

Atlanta if she agreed that, for their honeymoon, no thrift was allowed. She consented and now their lovers' cloister was a luxurious suite downtown.

Later, when summer came, there would be a longer getaway. With Manuel along, they would take Abby and Trent to the shore. Hank had contacted a realtor. At first, aware of his name, she tried to steer him toward exorbitant Sea Island. Instead, he fell in love with pictures of a tabby house on St. Simons. The home overlooked the tidal marsh and a long dock leading to the river and the sea. That would be the place to introduce his father. There Hank would explain the reason for the hope he had.

Hank's mind was brought back to the present with the distant whine of a jet engine, and he noticed the room had grown too cool. Exiled from the day's celebration, a feeling crept back in. It was a little edge of fear that kept returning. Why, he asked himself? What was the thing, the idea concealed in his subconscious and so unwelcome at the pinnacle of their happiness?

He wondered if Manuel missed them already. An unpleasant memory rose in Hank's mind. Trent, Manuel, and he searched for tuxes at the mall. Hank found satisfactory selections. He judged them superior in intrinsic value when compared to his former closet-full of custom-made, black tie options soiled with unpleasant association.

Later, they stopped at the crowded food court. A clown came through the area, advertising a sale at the children's shoe store. Manuel, excited at the red nose and wild orange hair, spoke his exclamations in Spanish while witnessing half a dozen gags. Two little girls sat with their mother at a table close by.

"Oh, look at the brown boy! He talks weird," said the older sibling. Manuel's small head whipped around. The next day, Hank saw temper rise in Manuel for the first time since the day they met. An insignificant discussion between Hank and Elizabeth about America's love for automobiles sparked Manuel to interrupt.

"Me, American."

"You are Mexican," said Hank plainly.

The boy's brows drew together, and his voice rang with insistence, "No! Me American."

How would Hank protect his son from the petty meanness inserting itself into every life? He looked at his wife. Elizabeth murmured softly in her sleep. She pulled closer. Warmed by her silken skin, his nameless fears melted. He figured he would often rely on her quiet assurance. He let his lips barely touch the top of her head. Then, gently, he pulled the thick, down-filled covers over them.

In the morning, Hank's mood was lifted again, seeing her happy face as she lightly kissed his forehead, eyelids, nose, and lips. Their days were spent at historical sites, outdoor cafes, a baseball game, and the botanical garden. Her questions, her pleasure that heretofore were held within, released. She seemed free, aware of his love, taking delight in their time together. And he was captivated by her joy. He told her it was time for some clothes that had not seen other owners. She relented to some purchases, knowing the contentment it gave him. He chose the finest restaurants for dinner, and on the second evening they attended a performance at the grand Fox Theatre. Afterward, they took a carriage ride through the city.

On their final evening, he pulled her onto his lap and pressed his face into the gentle curve of her neck. She melted into him, and his lips moved to tenderly kiss the place where her ear met her cheek. "Elizabeth, would you mind if we stayed in? Let me hold you and pretend we can stay here forever."

They turned off the lights, with the exception of one lit taper, and ate their meal at a table by the window. They talked of their plans for the years ahead. It was time the boy had a dog, he said. A kennel had one waiting for the trip home.

Later, holding each other, they gazed at the city from their bed, a mass of soft pillows as their backrest and roses perfuming the room. Fully in the moment, they shared their hearts and wrapped themselves within each other until they were the wind swirling in tall grass, trees reaching for the sun, light shimmering on water.

CHAPTER FORTY-EIGHT

A T A QUARTER OF eight in the morning, the medical center produced only a minor amount of activity. Since the maintenance people entered at dawn, Javier hid in a restroom on the ground floor. Someone was coming down the hall. He rushed to the sink where he pretended to wash his hands. An old man, heavyset and smelling of pomade, entered the restroom and went into a stall. Javier dried his hands, took a comb from his pocket, and smoothed his hair. He glanced at the stall door. The old man would be out in a minute, washing his hands, praising the morning. Ridiculous chatter, thought Javier. He put away the comb and bolted from the room. The building had come alive. Merging with other people, he studied the lobby directory. He flowed with the group to the elevators.

Alone by the fourth floor, he pressed his back against the rear panel of the elevator and watched the lighted numbers *change*. His mind reiterated a fact—finding her required, secrecy and surprise. The doors opened, and he stepped out and turned left down the corridor. The office was at the end of the hall. A middle-aged lady bent down unlocking the door. She looked up and smiled, catching him off guard. He turned away, went down by the stairs, rapping the iron rail with his fist.

Coming into the lobby again, he noticed the cafe open for business. Coffee would provide the jolt he needed. Was it the modern building or the finely-clothed people stealing his bravado? He thought of the rich American doctor.

Javier sipped the steaming liquid. It didn't matter if he ever made it back to Mexico. His father was dead and Santolo, a place of torment. Javier's own death was guaranteed within a hundred miles of either cartel. Torres and Santiago blamed him for U. S. pressure. Javier's teeth ground against one another. He was going to make her sorry she ever crossed him.

Javier drank again from the cup and studied the lobby, wondering if anyone walking by might be the physician. The tall, silver-haired man speaking confidently, wearing a suit and red tie? Or the blond-haired thirty-something, clad in the green scrubs of the operating room, displaying the build of an action hero? He banged down the cup but remembered he now had forces guiding him, and the emotion waned.

It was a relief to be away from the manipulations of Madeleine. He had done her bidding, but she adhered to him for too many weeks, milking him for venom like a *palanca* for all her evil deeds. A mystery, she held him with her strange compensations. But, no matter now. She was only a *matapalo* tree whose stranglehold could be cut away with a machete. He had finally escaped the unnatural atmosphere. He touched his pocket. Wisely, he had come away with the tinkling pieces that gave her power. They were there, wrapped in a silk scarf that had been hers. The spirits would think it was she who sought them. He snickered into his empty cup. Revitalized, he paid and left.

For the second time, he came out of the elevator on the fourth floor. Before turning down the corridor that led to the offices, he spat on the carpet and squared his shoulders.

Sandra Yardley looked up from her desk. A handsome, Hispanic man entered the reception area.

"Hello. May I help you?" She watched him study the wires around her desk.

"I am looking for Dr. Weston's office. The sign in the lobby sent me to this number, but I see the name of someone else on the door."

"*Oh*. I thought you were maintenance. We had a loose connection but fixed it ourselves. Anyway, Dr. Weston is deceased. I can't believe they haven't removed his name from the directory after all this time." The young man's features showed thunderclouds of distrust. "Sir, I'm quite reliable about this. Maybe Dr. Sandholm could be of service? He'll be in this afternoon." She flavored her words with reassurance.

"Perhaps you can give me the information I need."

"Certainly, if possible."

"I am looking for my sister, Elizabeth Gutierrez. She brought her child here for medical assistance. Can you tell me where they are living? I've come a long way."

"Um... I don't know if... let me see... " The young man fooled with something in his pocket. "Hold on. I'll go check the records." She forced a smile and pushed back her chair.

"Wait." His voice had an edge to it. "That thing." He pointed to the Rolodex.

"Oh... it wouldn't be there. Check and see." She tossed it into his hands as she stood up. She tried to walk, not run, down the hall to the last room where Khari, the nursing intern, made coffee before they started each day. Sandra burst in and pulled the door closed. She strained to slide a filing cabinet in front.

Khari looked up from her book of brain teasers, sitting in a chair. The morning sun shone through the large window onto her gaily-printed uniform. She took a bite of bagel and asked in an even tone, "What are you doing?"

"Help me. *He's* out there!"

Khari hurried over. Using all their strength, they shoved the cabinet until it braced the door from opening.

"Who?" Khari panted and straightened again. Then her eyes went keen. "Manuel Gutierrez's father is here, isn't he?"

"Yes! He wants to know where they are."

Khari raised the phone to her ear. "Dead," she said simply, like a weather report.

Sandra cringed. "And they told us it wasn't likely he'd come here."

"He can't get in," Khari said in her unflappable voice, stacking three boxes of copy paper, alongside the cabinet.

"Maybe not. He's not a big man. But listen. He's destroying the reception area." They froze, trying to decipher the sounds.

Khari patted the filing cabinet. "He doesn't know all the records are kept here."

"He'll keep looking until he finds them," said Sandra.

Khari considered the words of her co-worker then sat her plump frame on a chair. She held her chin with thumb and forefinger.

"Yes, think," said Sandra. "With two kids in college, I have to be around."

"It would help if there'd been time for my first cup of coffee." The stimulating smell drifted from the coffeemaker trickling its contents into the glass holder.

Noises came from the hall. Khari got up. Leaning toward the doorframe, they heard him searching the exam rooms. They looked at one another. The sound of him in the next room, pulling drawers onto the floor, hit their ears. Khari went to the counter.

"What are you doing?" Sandra asked, watching the girl soak white napkins in coffee, one at a time.

"No phone, so I'll make a paper trail." She stopped. Her method was taking too long. She dumped the fruit held in a large wooden bowl. She placed wads of paper napkins inside and poured coffee over them. With the bowl of saturated paper, she ran to the window and scrambled atop the credenza.

The handle of the door turned. Sandra released a tiny squeal of alarm and pushed against the cabinet.

"Hurry, Khari!"

Paper after paper was slapped on the large pane of glass. The driving force on the other side of the door increased. Sandra's eyes grew wide as the hairline crack opened a half an inch.

"Oh no! I need your help," said Sandra, a sheen breaking on her face.

Khari's short arms flew back and forth. Letters, backward facing and almost as tall as her, took form. Spatters of brown liquid glanced onto her face and uniform. "Almost done," she said.

Sandra's face contorted. Her skin flushed deeper. Her squinting eyes opened as a surge of vigor united with hers. Khari was alongside, bulldozing the cabinet. Without relinquishing an ounce of grit, Sandra turned her head to look over her shoulder. The window read—"HELP! CALL POLICE!" A smile came over her face, and she yelled to the man on the other side, "Get away from the door! We've notified the police."

"Ha! You think I am stupid! Give me the information, and I will leave you alone."

"Forget it. You're going to jail where you belong," Sandra called.

The door went shut. His spouts of anger penetrated their thick shield. Silence came. More distant noises began. They analyzed the sounds increasing in quantity and volume. Was he running through the place? Overturning anything he could find? Banging? Crashing? Were those chairs hitting the walls?

Things grew quiet, and the women's faces sagged with relief. Five minutes passed. Their bodies aching, Khari and Sandra relaxed their fortification. Their heads slumped and they waited.

"Ugh!" cried Sandra as the handle started to swivel again, and their hearts shook in their chests. They slammed their perspiring forms once more against the cabinet while a gap opened before their amazed eyes. The space widened to three inches. The view of his snarling lips walloped their emotions. Their knees were about to implode with fear when the pressure at the door ceased and the door shut.

Police sirens. Sandra counted. Two? Three? Still silence on the other side of the door. They reminded themselves to breathe. Then Spanish phrases fired at them through the wood. Another pause. With one horrific slam to the other side, the door vibrated. Moaning rose. Sandra leaned her ear to the door. The sound of staggered tromping exited the office.

With wavering tones, the women gave their report, and the officer inspected the scene. On one side of the portal, the Mexican had left his mark. The perfect veneer wore a distinct crack. Drops of blood dotted the carpet.

The next day, the shop owner of Knoxville's Midtown Florist arranged white cosmos with Queen Anne's lace and pink rose buds. The entrance buzzer sounded. He left his task and came forward. A customer waited at the counter, one arm in a cast and bandages swathing his forehead. A mottled purple bruise covered one third of the man's face.

"Can I help you?"

"Yes, thank you. I recently arrived in this country. I am trying to locate my sister. Would you give your assistance?" In unison, the jittery fingers on the man's good arm tapped rapidly on the counter.

"Certainly, but I don't know what I can do."

"Our mother is gravely ill in Mexico, and I only have twenty-four hours before my return flight. My sister brought her son to the children's hospital across the street for surgery. They are no longer there, and the child's doctor is out of town. If I could discover whether anyone sent the child flowers, they might have knowledge of my sister."

"That's strange. Weren't any of the doctor's staff around?"

"No. The hospital would not help, either."

The florist shrugged and extended a hand in a gesture fraught with apology. "Privacy issues."

Javier shook his head and looked at the floor. "As a boy, I dreamed of coming here, but I have had bad luck in this country. Yesterday, I was hit by a car. My mind is heavy with problems... ." He started to back away toward the door. "A foolish idea. Thank you anyway, my friend."

"Wait. Let me check my records. The child's name?"

"Manuel Gutierrez. Pardon, but I am in a rush." He looked back at the door.

The shop owner began a search on his computer.

"Here's something, but this is from December."

"Yes."

"That must've been pretty rough surgery, it being May and he isn't well enough to return to Mexico."

"Quite serious."

"It looks like several orders for 'get well' balloons from… let's see… Woodstock, Georgia."

He gestured at the cast. "My arm. Would you write that down?"

The florist wrote the location and held it toward the man.

"And the addresses of the senders?" the Mexican asked.

"Can't help you there. The orders were transferred from a florist there. They would have the info."

"I see." He took the paper.

"Look, let me call the shop for you."

"Do not do that." Like a flash, the man was at the exit where he looked up and down the street before rushing out.

The florist's hands dropped from his waist to his sides. How much help is the name of a town, he wondered? "Oh!" he exclaimed, at the half-shut door. He'd forgotten to tell the man—Brenda's House of Flowers. He took off, bowling over an arrangement of delphiniums, but the Mexican was gone. The florist closed the door and picked up the mess on the counter. His hands held still. Maybe he had been unclear; the man's response hadn't made sense. Still, if he notified the shop, someone might reach the woman. What a shame it had to be unwelcome news.

CHAPTER FORTY-NINE

O VER TWO MONTHS PASSED and summer began in earnest. Javier exited the expressway in the stolen Lincoln and turned down an undeveloped road where he found a dirt lane. He stopped the Lincoln and got out. His calculations told him he was near. His nerves twisted, ready to snap—the place was not like Mexico. He threw the keys in the brush. The remaining mile would be on foot.

He stepped carefully at first. The heat of the sun energized the fire ants. One hour of sleep the night before had not recharged him. Sweat glistened on his face. Trudging through briers interwoven like tangles of barbed wire made the going slow as he paralleled the interstate. The plants had grown tall trying to garner every bit of sunlight the trees did not capture first. Thorns pricked his temper. With strange logic he began to run. The sharp points tore small holes in his shirt. Thin lines of blood rose on his forearms. He slapped one tortuous limb away only to have it swing back, slashing his face. The curses blasting out of his mouth were enough to make the saplings shudder. With forceful strides, he carried on in this manner for an hour. He kept his vision aimed ahead. Through the screen of vegetation, he could make out a bridge over the interstate. Smooth, green grass grew under an even greener sign that proclaimed the town's name. He slowed. Everything in him was calmed.

Before long, he reached the sign and a primary road with commercial buildings and parking lots. He halted, looking left, across the bridge, at stores and businesses as far as he could see, and right, where a variety of buildings and new construction rose. The nearest building, a large enterprise, contained a spacious parking lot filled with many vehicles. Bright orange paint accented the store sign and the roofline. While caught in indecision, he heard a siren coming down the interstate. He scrambled down a steep bank into a ditch running with water and muck but full of shadow. In a crouched position, he lowered his head as the siren raced off the exit, turned past his hiding place, and shriveled into quiet.

He unfolded. Turning his head, he saw the circular entrance of a large concrete pipe. He got up and went to the pipe where he seated himself inside. The darkness smelled of rotting weeds and odors he couldn't identify. Looking down the length of the cylinder, he could see where the tube ended and a long patch of sunlight began. Thirty yards away, another pipe, underneath a parking lot entrance, continued the course. Then the elevation of the land rose, and the uncovered hollow did not cut so deep. In the other direction, the ditch turned sharply to follow the way he had come. At its end, another pipe, diving at an angle into the earth, received whatever fell in. The sight of that opening bothered him—light and water swallowed up forever by a deceptive, yawning mouth. He shook off the image and changed his position.

Planting his feet on the other side of the pipe, with his backside braced against the curve, he avoided the narrow flow traveling past. He bent down, cupping his hand to catch some of the cool liquid and rinsed his face. He had forgotten about hunger a long time ago; the proximity of his mission fed his senses well. He massaged the back of his neck. Then he lay back, letting his spine mimic the curve of the concrete as his eyelids lowered. A ripple of laughter rumbled lightly in his chest. He would miss the comforts of that automobile. Smooth, spotless leather. Seats and mirrors that adjusted with the touch of a finger. Music coming out of the speakers, real and clear. Maybe his time was not past. The opportunities here were endless. After he took care of her, he could develop a new plan. One day, he would own such a car having the smell of cleanliness and wealth.

Javier grinned to himself. The old farmer's Lincoln had been easy to confiscate. You could always be certain of their kindness—an old truck to drive, a cot in one of the outbuildings, and plenty of food. Tarrying in Tennessee provided time for his broken arm to heal while he did only enough work to fool the man.

Earlier, at six in the morning, Javier entered the kitchen as the widower sat eating his eggs and yogurt. Javier sauntered to the cabinet that held a small hook next to the plates and bowls. He remembered how protests flew out of the farmer's mouth as Javier took the keys off the hook and the warm sausage biscuit right from the man's hand.

Along the concrete pipe, Javier's tired chuckles echoed. He took a long relaxing breath and fell into the pleasure of sleep, thinking of the meal waiting deep in a pocket of his pants.

An hour passed. Soft, inconsequential sounds of birds whistling, cars driving by, and air streams whirling down the pipe lulled him deeper. He began to dream of a stooped, wrinkle-faced man who held a lit match against Javier's thigh, high and on the outer side. Javier's arms were immovable bars of lead. Although the flame flared with ghastly intensity, his pants did not burn. The pain was unbearable. Javier's arms finally broke free and with wild swipes at the air, he tried to fight off the aged phantom until the physical agony was so horrible he woke with a howl. Bolting upright, his feet fell and splashed into the water traversing the pipe. He looked at his thigh, unbelieving. Near the bottom of the pocket, a large rat clung by its teeth, a portion of sausage biscuit and Javier's flesh clamped in its mouth. Javier locked eyeballs with the determined animal and grabbed for his switchblade. Speared, the rat released and landed outside the pipe.

Javier, his face drawn, huffed in response to the pain. Shaking, he grabbed a kerchief from his back pocket and yanked the cloth around the wound, tying tight. In the flagging stream, he rinsed the blade and dried it on his pants leg. His brain remained crimped with shock; nevertheless, from the sun-riddled banks of the culvert, an object snared his sight.

Among the boulders was a child's toy, the fur matted and dirty, the coloring faded. An open seam exposed stuffing. As though the animal had been stationed between weeds and rock, its iridescent eyes appeared to look at him with warning. He let out a laugh and sent his knife sailing through the air straight for the lion's heart. The pain in Javier's leg already ebbed. He came out of hiding, gathered his blade, and walked into town.

Elizabeth added chicken broth to sautéed celery and onion before looking out the screen door again. Manuel played in the large pen Hank built for the puppy. Her son ran in a circle under the bright, summer rays as Arrow chased the tree branch Manuel trailed behind.

She sat down to work on her mending. Hank was in town, meeting with the architect. In two weeks, they would travel to Tennessee to confer with James Sandholm. She checked the time. Her husband would be home soon, stopping to kiss her hello before playtime with Manuel. Yesterday, it had been a blackberry war, the day before, a survey of Trent's catalpa tree that provided a bounty of fishing worms.

Later, a trail of cooking smells would bring them in for dinner as easily as her calls. But she was reminded of another voice, the one in the back of her head, a voice she had been resisting. She stopped pushing needle through fabric and rested her back against the chair. It was the same refrain. *He will destroy your lives.*

They had learned of Javier's visit to Sandholm's office and his conversation with a Knoxville florist. Hank reassured her; Javier would never find them, hidden in the woods, far beyond the bustle of town and even the suburbs. She glanced out the screen door at her son.

For the length of the afternoon, Javier wandered the area. He kneaded his skull trying to wrest from his brain some method of discovery. His grumbling bounced off the sidewalk. He tightened the kerchief around his upper leg, attempting to bury pain with pressure. A man like himself was about to walk by. They talked. Javier learned of an out-of-the-way place, a back room where he could get meat-filled *empañadas* and *chiles rellenos*.

He went there, hoping the proliferating ache in his head and the vicious throbbing of his thigh would slacken. He took a bite. The smell of pork lard and rich *mole* made his stomach pull inward. He slammed his fork on the table, knocking his glass to the floor. The other men, mesmerized by the look on his face, listened as he threw out his questions. Some thought they had seen her and the boy. Then one man stepped forward.

She was most often with an old woman who employed her as housekeeper, he said. The yellow-haired grandmother lived in a house made of trees. It was next to the big lake. Her millions were hid behind a removable stone in the fireplace. His brother, Gonzalo, had delivered manure for her garden, and she paid him with only one pitiful coin from the mountain of gold that spilled on the floor. But Gonzalo had returned to Tijuana, so there was nothing more the man could tell him.

Javier got up slowly and adjusted his bandage. Every eye marked him as he went out the door. He found a large store where he bought a county map and candy that would help him forget his wound. An hour of watching on a bench yielded nothing. A thousand cars must have passed along the road called 92. The men in the place where he ate said there were hundreds of homes near the lake. Spying on every one would require months. It would make more sense to stay where he was until the day his woman walked by. Javier imagined how her hair would turn white. Who would want her then?

A half an hour slogged by. He'd gotten up and down a dozen times. He walked farther west along the same road. A sign pointed down a different road to a modern post office, and he followed. He came upon the building with a large arch across its front, but, instead of entering, he went to the fence opposite the parking lot, to rest in the grass. He watched the doors. Busy people hurried in and out. Should he risk the brazen move of asking for her address?

A Honda Civic drove up and parked near the glass front. A large black man got out and went inside. The other person stayed in the car. A sticker on the rear bumper cautioned—*Please drive slow. We make frequent stops.* Javier got up and crossed the parking lot. Once close, he looked inside the vehicle. The man's small head sat upon a bony neck having a bend and prominent Adam's apple. He held a clipboard. Javier passed close to the man's open window, noting the rows of addresses in his lap. Once on the sidewalk, he turned back and looked directly into the dull eyes and bland mouth. Javier returned and approached the window. He grabbed the clipboard and flipped through the sheets.

"Mine. Mine," cried the man, like a two-year-old robbed of a toy.

"Be quiet, stupid one!"

The rickety man grew still and quiet.

Javier's nostrils exhaled his irritation as he scanned the list. He could not find her name. Overwhelmed by thousands of entries, he threw the clipboard onto the man's lap, making his narrow shoulders jerk back.

"Listen to me," Javier said roughly. "I must find a woman. Her name is Elizabeth Gutierrez. Tell me where she lives, and I will give you sweets." He pulled jumbled strings of red licorice from a bag.

The man answered with the voice of a robot, "Elizabeth Gutierrez... 102 Haviland Lane." Javier smirked and squashed some of the candy into a limp hand. An intense urge to torment the man slithered through Javier's mind. He grinned. Reaching in, he plucked some of the loose skin on the man's neck and was about to twist. His fingers let loose. A key waited in the ignition. He could travel quickly. How easy it would be to snuff out the life of his passenger, later. The back seat held a laptop. He reached behind the man, grabbed and opened it. No picture, nothing. He tossed it back. His vision went back to the car keys, and he straightened to scope out any observers. Javier squinted, trying to see through the tinted glass of the post office. His eyes were not mistaken; an attractive woman standing within had just noticed him. Javier flashed his sexiest smile. He scanned for the black man. He was busy at a counter. The woman broke from the line to come near the glass. She put her briefcase down. Javier turned forward, proudly displaying his form. Maybe the blond lady in the tangerine-colored dress appreciated his masculine value. His confident grin dissolved. Concern and questioning projected from the woman's face. Javier took a bite of licorice and, backed by his kindest smile, handed the man the remaining treats and quickly left.

Marissa went back to her line.

Uncle Rakey threw his reward out the window. He hated licorice, and he did not like the man. Only one other person gave him the name Stupid. She was the one who made him cry, the one who came to live with him after Ella went to be with Jesus. She was mean to him. She was bad. The man must be her brother. Rakey's eyebrows changed from straight, pulled-down lines to curves of satisfaction. Everything was okay. He sent the man to Abby's house and to the silver badge.

It was a beautiful Friday, so beautiful that Lee Wyatt believed it was impossible for anything dire to happen. Since the age of seven, he had believed that notion. When the sun radiated with strength, but a breeze cooled your skin, and the sky projected a blue vibrant enough to make you hunt for a game of soccer, he used to tell his father houses couldn't catch on fire on a day of that caliber. His father knew better.

Lee had the freedom of a whole afternoon to do what he wanted. He'd earned it after too many summer hours at the grocery store, to help cover college expenses in the fall. His plan was to rent jet skis and meet a friend. The day would be over only when they were thoroughly sunburned and starving, ready to eat a hundred wings at the waterside grill.

A favorite CD in the player swept him along as he drove from an errand at his aunt's home in Roswell, down Highway 92, past Sweat Mountain and across I-575. Remembering a shortcut laced with homes, hardwood sections, and a horse farm where they planned to build an elementary school, he swung right onto Bascomb Carmel Road. After a four-way-stop, he moved into the curve. Then, something more intriguing than the beat took him right out of the music he loved. A man with rude features pushed a woman and little girl through the doorway into their home. Just as quickly, the strange scene was behind. Lee let off the gas, trying to make sense of the sight. An impatient husband or an uncivil neighbor? The look on the woman's face led Lee to believe it was more. His thinking began to flounder. Could be one of those traps he always fell into making his prospects surer as poster boy for humiliation. And Justin was probably waiting at the dock.

He pulled off the road to think. In his mind, he saw his face splashed across the front page of *The Cherokee Tribune*—GREATEST FOOL OF ALL TIME HARASSES PLAYFUL FAMILY. He broke from his visualization, hearing his father's faint words—the enemies of integrity are self-centeredness and pride. Lee moved his car back onto the road and made a quick u-turn.

He was about to pull into the woman's yard when he stopped, seeing the same limping man run out of the house, jump into a burgundy Buick LeSabre and tear out of the yard. The woman followed, screaming. "My baby's in there!" Her upraised arms pleaded with every word. Lee knew the man heard nothing—windows raised, tires grinding and spitting rocks. The car surged west down Bascomb Carmel Road.

Lee charged into the yard. Her story spilled out. She was carrying in groceries when out of nowhere a Mexican appeared, bullying, threatening, demanding keys. Desperate tears flooded her face. Her little girl clung to her skirt. Lee told the woman not to worry.

Chewing the grass with his wheels, he backed around and moved out. A sinking feeling took shape as he raced away—his cell needed charging, and he was real low on gas. He floored his car and came over the hill trying to put in a call. Crackles. Static. Dead air. The Buick crested the next hill at a normal rate. In nothing flat, Lee caught up. He came close behind, waving and yelling out the window, trying to get the driver to stop. The Buick rocketed ahead. Over hills and sliding through curves, Lee followed every move. Along woods and then pasture fencing they zoomed, past ponies whose skittish hooves galloped, led by suggestion. The man and the boy with his teeth squeezed tight, bulleted by Putnam Ford and the old brick church under the trees. Soon the two cars came into the open and reached the road named Bells Ferry. Without stopping, the Buick turned right as though headed on one of the routes to the lake.

Lee followed and exhaled as the man moderated his velocity a mite, negotiating heavy traffic. Several cars separated Lee from the Buick, which picked up speed again. Lee glanced at the pumps where he had planned to fill up, but he went on by. Not a policeman to be found anywhere. Lee sweated, wanting to give up and slam on the brakes. Lines of worry formed between his young brows—he weaved between vehicles filled with families whole and healthy. He drove like every teenager's wildest dream, and it was making him sick with dread. He blinked hard and increased the firmness of his grip.

Traffic evaporated. The Buick returned to light speed. Up ahead, Three Way Grocery attracted the Buick like the store offered free gas, but instead the car turned, tires squealing, onto the road preceding and roared away. Lee refused to be dropped and his car held on, making the turn more carefully. The road was totally clear. He gunned the engine. Down Kellogg Creek Road the two vehicles flew, over Owl Creek, and the long bridge with boats below, then up and down again, making whirlwinds of dust in their wake. By houses they flashed, like Indy cars burning up the road paint and sucking plants from the yards. Lee's engine stuttered. With more noises from under the hood, the tires slowed. He pumped the accelerator but only coasted. The other car pulled away. Lee thought about a baby as his car rolled to a stop. His forehead sank against the steering wheel.

A distant, blaring horn made him look up. A quarter mile away, the Buick idled fitfully, blocked from forward progress by a moving van. Long and loaded, the broken-down truck sat like a potbellied mountain, freezing traffic coming from Galts Ferry Landing.

Lee reached for his practice bag still in the back seat since baseball season and pulled out a bat. He jumped from his car and blazed the distance, reaching the unsuspecting driver of the Buick. He yanked open the back door and swung. The Mexican's eyes rolled up in his head as he flopped against the door. Lee unbuckled the baby from his car seat, grabbed playsuit straps, and snatched the living bundle.

Every vehicle was still rooted to the road. Alarmed drivers got out of their cars. Lee yelled for someone to call the sheriff. The Mexican came to. Holding the side of his face, he threw open his door and fled like a tire-burned squirrel into the cover of the hills.

Sitting in a shallow depression, surrounded by a stand of willow oak and beech, Javier bit hard into a shank of wood and tried to clean the fiery, pus-filled wound. He fell back on the ground, writhing. After the pain subsided, he lightly touched the walnut-size knot on the side of his cheek that would surely turn purple. He craved water for a never-ending thirst, but leaving his hiding spot was out of the question. Darkness worked its way in. It would be another sleepless night.

The next morning contained an excruciating, dogged march down half a mile of Kellogg Creek Road and a short distance up Yacht Club Lane. By afternoon, he stood at the beginning of the gravel drive called Haviland Lane that cut through the formidable trees standing like a garrison on the hill. Two mailboxes, one road. The first set of numbers corresponded to those branded in his memory. He blinked away the blurriness. He ignored the burning in his throat. He was eager.

When he came to the place where the drive branched, he saw glimpses of a cabin to the right. How far the other lane went, he neither knew nor cared. The simpleton had known of what he spoke. The house was built of logs. She would be with the old woman, inside.

CHAPTER FIFTY

A BBY WORKED AT A large bowl in the kitchen when she heard Trent come in the front door.

"Don't forget we have to be at Brian's by six," she called while concentrating on her task. No response. "I'm up to my elbows in elbow macaroni. Could you phone Harold and tell him when we'll pick him up?" Quiet. "Trent?" She looked up from her bowl toward the hall. A ragged young man with a glare that could make pasta go limp stood in the kitchen doorway. Her heart jumped hurdles. "What do you want?" She set down the spoon.

"Where is my wife? I know she works for you." He came closer until she could see the different colors within his bruise and the way his mouth and chin were like Manuel's.

"No one works for me. Would I be laboring in this kitchen if it were otherwise?"

The door off the deck opened. Trent came in from helping Hank with maintenance on the dock. The Mexican grabbed Abby by the arm and propelled her to the railing where they looked down on the stunned face of her husband.

"Let go of her," Trent demanded, leaning heavily on his cane.

The man pulled a handgun from inside his shirt. "Come here!" he roared.

Trent did as he was told, striving to move quickly. Abby and he were prodded through the kitchen and directed to sit in the dining room.

To Abby, the man seemed eager to sit. He chose the head of the table. An odor of putrefaction wafted her way. Sweat stained his shirt. Glassy eyes and dark circles gave away his fatigue.

"There is just one thing I want to know, old ones. Where is my woman?" Swaying, he stood up but eased back down with a painful sigh and rubbed his thigh. He leaned over the table as though he wished to slide his full length on top to rest. One arm, supported by the surface, held the gun. The other hand rubbed the sockets of his sunken eyes. He looked at them again. "My store of patience is empty."

"We don't know this person," said Trent.

"Perhaps you do not, but she knows."

"Abby, do you know the woman he's looking for?"

"No."

"Do not play with me," the man bellowed. "Sharpen her memory, or I will." A quiver traveled over the Mexican.

"I'll discover if what she says is true," said Trent, "but first let me get you some water and a quilt. You must be cold."

"Get the water only, and stay where I can see you."

Trent went to the kitchen. If only he could talk to Abby. He filled the glass. The phone rang.

"Leave it!" the Mexican commanded. Walking with a jagged gait into the kitchen, he kept the gun trained on Abby and ripped the phone cord free. Then he sent Trent back to his seat, and they sat down again. The Mexican reached for the water. Glass clinked against his teeth while shakes rattled his body. Desperate gulps. A groan. He rubbed the top of his leg again. Muted rumblings sounded from his midsection. From his mouth, fluid rushed over the table. The odor engulfed the room. He wiped his mouth with his hand and, with the length of his arm, swept the puddle onto the floor. He sagged more. His breathing came faster and his jaw thrust forward.

When he wasn't squeezing his eyes shut as though he fought for control, the man's gaze drilled them. Abby took short, silent breaths through her open mouth, afraid he would let off rounds to assuage the anger inflaming his face.

"Let me save you more trouble," Trent pleaded. "I will persuade her by making her understand the consequences. Lock us in the pantry. You can stretch out on the floor nearby and rest."

After a few more persuasive arguments, the couple found themselves imprisoned in the dark. A slide lock placed on the pantry, long ago, kept their small children from plundering the shelves between meals. The Mexican's troubled breathing came from where he lay on the floor just outside. The pantry was cramped and dark, but sitting among the smell of tea and spices was a welcome relief. Their arms held one another fast, and they sought God's help. Trent tried to ignore the dull ache coming from his hip. Every once in a while, they heard the moans of a sick man who tossed and lurched in sleep. Their eyes had adjusted, and they could see each other's face by the thin line of light sneaking in at the bottom of the door.

"At least we have some time to think," said Abby.

"It doesn't matter," said Trent. "He's going to kill us if we don't tell him."

Abby's forehead filled with striations. "Nothing in the world could make me."

"I won't either, then. But you run out of the house when I charge him."

"Charge? How? I'm not leaving you.... If we die, we die."

"I can't let him take your life."

"I've had the best of lives, Trent. When we wake up, we'll be at the feast table with our King... and we'll see Kenny again."

"Has your life been everything you desired, Abby?"

"I had you, and that was my greatest blessing."

"Do you know how those words affect me?" His face was haggard with love.

"Yes. I do."

Javier awoke with a violent jerk. He let out a loud string of Spanish meant to drive away the devils excavating the length of his leg with their picks and shovels. The closet door was still locked. Taking his knife, he opened the outer seam of his pant leg. He took great care. During an hour of rest, the limb had swollen like a dense tree trunk refusing to bend. He removed his shoes. If there had been food on his stomach he would have thrown up again as he pulled himself to standing with the help of cabinet doors and countertop. He put his head under the cool water of the kitchen faucet, trying to breach the fever and fog in his head. With distressful steps, he made it down to the great room. He smoothed back the wet strands of his coal black hair and studied the picture of what he determined to be an expensive mare. His eyes moved to the stacked stone fireplace. Having a small portion of his vigor returned, he tried the rocks. They did not move and there were hundreds yet, perched all the way to the ceiling. Eventually, he loosened one at the corner. Behind it was only mortar, not a cavity filled with gold. He threw the stone at the row of windows across the back of the house, shattering the panes. He would not waste any more time. He would kill the old man first. That would make her open her mouth.

Tears ran down the woman's checks as he pointed the gun at her husband. Javier was amazed; they were willing to die. She kept begging him to take her first, but he aimed so the man's death would be slow. His trigger finger started to tense when he heard a high voice calling. "Tren?... Tren?... " Javier's expression froze. He turned his head toward the sound coming through the broken window. He forgot his present occupation and the paralyzing pain as he hobbled into the great room. His view out the broken window, led to tall plants forming a border. A cut archway framed his son changed by the addition of ten months growth. In an instant, Javier had a reason for living.

Elizabeth was about to carry the dieffenbachia outside for a brief dose of sun when Manuel came crashing, wild-eyed and pale, from the side yard into the kitchen. Clinging to his puppy, he headed for the cabinet next to the stove. Clambering in among pots and pans, he slammed the door shut. She put the heavy container on the counter. One hand tightened around the rim, and her eyes glazed over. Remembering. The linen chest where her little one took cover during Javier's storms. She heard a sound at the screen door and looked up. Javier stood on the other side. With a look of triumph he entered.

"You thought you could get away from me?" he asked in Spanish as he moved closer.

"What is it that you want, Javier?"

"I've come to get the money you stole from me," he yelled.

"It is in a bank, in Mexico. Waiting for you."

"You liar. You spent it on this grand home."

"No," she said calmly. "I only borrowed the money so my papers for travel would be approved." She backed into the den, hoping to draw him away.

Javier's eyes went down to slits as he reached for her arm and gave her a shake. "You think I have no brains like the armadillos squashed on the roads of Mexico?" He paused. His grasp loosened, and he moved back. "You think your Eduardo is going to save you? When he comes in, I am going to kill him, too." He threw back his head and laughed.

"Javier, Eduardo does not live here. Let me get you the account number so you can withdraw the funds when you return."

He surged forward and his hand went for her head, intertwining his fingers in her hair until they knotted with the thick strands.

"*No one* betrays Javier Gutierrez."

Her tresses pulled at her scalp as he twisted.

"Where is the boy? I am taking him to his real home."

Elizabeth could feel adrenaline skate through her body. A bright clang of metal came from the cabinet.

Javier released her and turned back to the kitchen, dragging his festering leg. He reached for the handle.

"No!" She ran after him. His forearm blocked her at the waist and swung her around like a rag doll. Her body slammed into a small bookcase where her skull took a strong blow from the point of one corner. She fell in a heap. He bent over her and reached for the band of diamonds circling her finger. Behind him, the glass door to the porch banged open. A force drilled Javier to the floor.

Their size so disparate, Hank knew in an instant he could erase the man's life as easily as you press a bug under your shoe. He fought the enticement, aware the child might be near. Instead, Hank remained above, pinning the aggressor, taking a gun from Javier's pocket and tossing the weapon away. Elizabeth breathed but remained motionless. A cabinet door opened. Manuel and Arrow appeared.

"Manuel, your mother is hurt. Run to the Eversons. Tell them to call the police." The child and his pup darted out the screen door.

After Javier left the Everson's cabin, the couple, frantic to do something, found themselves at a terrible loss. They used their cell phone to call for help, but with their location it could be a while before anyone came. The rifle was packed away, up in the attic, with a safety lock. And the key, who knew? Abby thought of another option.

She reminded him how he'd been reduced to a snail's pace, and that he would have to fire with his left instead of right. She would go. He put his forehead in his hand.

Abby ran to her study and broke the glass on the box. He begged her not to go. She kissed him and said, "Until I see you again." On which side of eternity, neither knew. She left by the front door. Seconds later, Manuel ran in the back.

A frail, tiny woman. Only a single 410 shell in her possession. A gun so old it might explode in her hand. She prayed as she walked through the upper yard.

Chest heaving and muscles twitching, Hank hoisted the man to standing. Anxious to check Elizabeth's injuries, Hank dragged the man along, positioned a kitchen chair in the den near the dividing wall, and flung the man down. The Mexican looked ill and not at all like the striking young man in the picture the authorities sent. The odor coming from him was nauseating. Why had everyone been so afraid? Hank pulled the belt from a robe that lay folded on top in a basket of laundry.

"We've been expecting you," he said as he secured the man's arms behind the chair. "If you would like me to finish what I barely started, just give me the slightest reason."

Javier watched the man as he bent over her, tending her as though she was a delicate thing. Javier uttered in hoarse, ragged stops, "A ha. You must be the one." All the while, Javier's hands worked to free themselves. "You must watch her. When you are at work, she will invite your brother over." The man ignored his needling words. One of Javier's hands wriggled loose. Since the fight, the gun remained in the far corner of the room. His hand crept inside his back pocket.

Hank checked Elizabeth's heart rate for the third time. He called her with soft words. He strained to hear the sound of emergency vehicles. What was he thinking, depending on a preschooler? He must call. He started to rise but froze at the sound of a "click." He looked. The Mexican's upraised arm drew back a blade.

"Stop!"

Their attention flew toward the living room.

Abby stepped from the dimness. "Put the knife down!" Her gun was aimed at Javier. The short barrel rested on one forearm. With unflinching authority, she moved within ten feet. He remained in a state of suspension. "Now!" she screamed and released a blast above his head. Plaster and wood lathe rained down. The knife had fallen at his feet. She raced through the dust cloud and with her foot, slid the weapon to Hank.

An ambulance rushed Elizabeth to the hospital. They hurried the gurney inside. Hank sat at her bedside while surgeons and specialists evaluated her situation. Nearby, doctors amputated a leg, trying to save the life of the Mexican, but, within an hour, systemic blood poisoning ended his days.

Lee was hailed all over town as the baby's hero. Two days later, in the Fourth of July parade, he rode in the cab of a fire engine. In front of the red-tile-roofed depot, near the spot where an actual president once spoke, the fire truck stopped, and they made Lee disembark and stand on the podium for applause. That night he was given the honor of lighting the fuses starting the fireworks show, but in the hospital, there was little to celebrate.

Hank memorized his wife's face as doctors conferred in whispers and drew conclusions from the latest reports. Hank's attention flipped upward. In the ceiling, a dying florescent bulb gave off a high-pitched whine that could easily drive a dog mad. No one else seemed to notice but he did.

CHAPTER FIFTY-ONE

ABOVE THE LAKE, TO the east, the sky exhibited a wash of gray that had not yet reached the black matte of night. In the distant west, heavy moisture-laden clouds shoved their way in and waited, morphing into a strange presence. Those turbulent masses reached high into the atmosphere like looming, black entities, connecting into one force with malice on the mind. At first, the front made itself known with shrewd subtlety, entering the region with light footfalls.

Hank rang the doorbell a second time. Were they both growing deaf? He stopped his grousing long enough to rub the stubble on his face. After a week of sleepless nights, it was a vain effort to draw life into his tired flesh. Manuel and he waited under the covered porch. Water dripped from the eaves. The child, head still, arms straight at his sides, kept mum. The light rain brought the smell of red clay to their noses. Hank looked down and noticed Manuel's damp clothes. Didn't the boy know to put on a raincoat? Hank pushed back his own wet hair. The porch light flipped on, and Abby's empathetic face appeared.

"Hello. Come insi-" A gust whipped by the porch railing and blew a pot of sown zinnia seeds to the floor, ensuring those specks of life would never burgeon from the soil. "Come out of this changeable weather," she said, disregarding the broken container, looking into Hank's red-rimmed eyes.

"Don't have time. Here, Abby." Taking Manuel by the hand, Hank thrust him over the threshold. The boy tripped a little in the transfer, then came close to her side. "Would you keep him? I've got to get out of here."

"Certainly," she said, watching Hank slip away. Her mouth turned down with worry. "When will you be back?" she called.

"Tomorrow, next week, who knows?" his voice trailed off. She glanced down at the child. Manuel's gaze followed his vanishing father. When Abby looked up again, Hank was gone. She leaned out the doorway and heard his truck tear over the gravel and cobblestones. Holding Manuel's hand, they went to the edge of the porch. Just a gentle shower it was, but her ears caught a far rumble.

She led the child inside. Acting as though there was nothing more serious being added to the drama that entered their homes the week before, she bent down to speak. "Now let's get these wet clothes off, and we'll see what we can dig up while your things are in the dryer." His body cooperated as she pulled off shirt, jeans, and shoes. She took Trent's fleece jacket from the hook beside the door and wrapped Manuel in the comfort of the soft fabric and her arms. The jacket dragged across the floor as they went into the kitchen. His face brightened. "I'll fix you and Trent some hot chocolate," she said. "He's already in bed with a book. It will be the perfect thing to help you both sleep." She knew Trent would be overflowing with questions.

Warm drinks were ready. Abby carried the mugs. Manuel ran ahead and jumped on the coverlet to lie in the crook of Trent's arm. Flossie was on the windowsill, grooming. The cat lowered her cleaned paw and watched the child. Abby entered and looked at her husband. Her eyes told him everything.

Hank took another swig from the bottle and tried to find the center line on coal-black roads. The windshield wipers barely slapped back and forth, squashed by the gusher coming down. The country lanes were deserted, and like a strong-willed ox, he plowed on, managing to keep just outside the grasp of the storm coming from the rear. Ten minutes later, still traveling eastward, he reached a two-lane highway nearing Alpharetta.

As it had almost a year ago, the tempting idea of escape came to him. Inwardly, he made his case. *You know what's going to happen to her. Why don't you just head this truck for Maine or New Mexico? If you had only left her alone instead of bringing your cursed life into hers. Did you think you were some kind of savior? And the boy? So he's got a fixed heart. You've only helped him receive a long existence in which to regret the loss of his mother and the fact that he ever knew you. You fool. Once and for all, give up. Without her, you'll crumble. You're weak and afraid.*

The lighted entrance to the golf club showed indistinctly through water streaming across the windshield. He barreled into the parking area of the driving range and stopped the engine. The torrent strengthened, assaulting anything trying to stand. Even so, he exited the truck and stepped into four inches of water that filled his shoes. Grass clippings and debris clung at the waterline above his low-cut socks, annoying his skin. Raindrops bombarded their way through cloth, plastering his shirt and pants to his body. He carelessly reached in the truck for his golf bag. Clubs slipped from the tilted bag into the slough that had been a parking lot. He ranted to the wind, blaming the golf irons as though they were alive and out of sheer meanness had the ability to cost him the effort of retrieval.

Walking to the elevated range, his waterlogged shoes tried to pull away from his feet with sucking power that weighed him down. Using the truck headlights to penetrate the darkness, he teed up the first ball. Bullets of water pelted his head, shoulders, and arms. His sodden lashes stemmed some of the water streaming into his eyes and clouding his vision. He took in a deep breath, drew back his club, and swung. With a sharp crack, the ball took off like a fired missile. It flew farther than ever before, but soon the raw edge of his emotions caused his form to degenerate, and the next drives went askew. The balls that did travel straight were sabotaged by the winds and rain competing to be vilified by his scathing words. With spiteful addition, hail began to fall, bouncing with glee on the ground and off the buildings.

Breathing through his open mouth, choking on water blown in, his anger detonated the way a transformer explodes within a tornado. He walked to the metal light pole and swung his club, shoulder high, with such force the shaft bent ninety degrees around the implacable object. The sound of his laughter ricocheted between the empty golf structures, and he stumbled backward. Then he shouted to the black ceiling the words that blared in his head —"ARE YOU THERE" "DO YOU CARE?" Ear-splitting thunder and a white-hot slash spearing the earth somewhere the other side of the clubhouse seemed to be his answer. He clamped his eyes shut. The light image was still there. Tremors hiked up and down his nerves. A need to run flooded his veins.

There was something inside him, driving him for the last seven days like a familiar, faceless threat. He had only escaped for a time. He might as well be dead. He tore two irons from his bag then threw the rest aside. Raising his face toward the fury in the heavens, he clamored, "COME GET ME, BUT DON'T TAKE HER!" He waved the irons at the electrical sky and sprinted toward the course.

Marbles of ice littering the ground promised a fall and destabilized his mind. He made it past the golf cart shed. Confused, unable to see the path, he tore through a line of pampas grass. Another crash of thunder and searing light etched in his mind the sight of drenched white plumes hanging down in defeat. He came through a clearing to the first tee. Close by, another flash and thunder made him jerk as though he stepped on burning coals. "WHAT KIND OF FATHER ARE YOU?" he screamed and raced down the par five.

He climbed the rise and reached the pen, but overwhelming frustration compelled him to go on. Blocked by a dark maze of tall plantings, he lost the path and reached the second tee by memory. He continued his dash through sheets of wind and rain while oak limbs to his left and right moved up and down like judges' gavels, and long willow branches on the trees by the pond shredded the air. The only thing leading him on the path were the flashes coming more frequently. Past the fairway boundaries where the rough had been allowed to grow wild, the bushes in the undergrowth twisted and thrashed. Leaves blown from their light attachments swirled in the air hitting his clothes and face. Wind sheer blew the rain sideways, stinging his face like needles. And yet he ran on, counting the holes that were symbols of his shame-filled years.

By the eighth hole of his gauntlet, he hadn't tired, though his body went into spasm as each dart riveted the earth so close that light and thunder were one. Still he dashed, making his lungs feel like fire. Ninth... eleventh... fourteenth... seventeenth. He would run and never stop. Until his heart exploded in one final beat, releasing a burst of energy and light so powerful that night would become day. Forever.

He continued as in a dream. Half deaf and blind with exhaustion, he ran down the eighteenth fairway. He hadn't noticed the waning of the storm or the hidden bunker near the green. Taking his last stride, off the lip, unaware, he sailed through the air and fell. Time stopped.

His landing place was the protected, lee side. His body rested in deep sand that had been saving the warmth of afternoon. His eyelids slowly rose. Awareness came. A soft depression cradled him. The thunderclaps had moved into the distance. A few, gentle drops tapped against his back and pattered softly on his cream-colored bed. He fought the sleep trying to drag him down into senselessness, and he brought himself into a sitting position. Lightheaded. Surrendered.

He coughed. The smell of grass and wet pine bark joggled his mind. His run was over; he could go no further. And he was right back where he had been before. The lights of the clubhouse broke through his stupor. The windows revealed the cleaning crew closing for the night. Someone came out with the trash, leaving the door open. Voices floated over. The worker re-entered, and the door slammed shut. Then still-ness again. A few grains of sand chiseled between his teeth. His tongue swept them aside, and he spit them out. It was quiet. Quieter than the den of a sleeping fox curled up with its nose tucked in its fur. Hank looked to the woods. Remnants of rainwater fell from leaf tips to the misty earth. Vapors rose silently. He took a deep breath.

Sore and rubber-legged, he stood and began the walk to the truck, fifty yards on the opposite side of the clubhouse. He came around. The headlights still burned. The sodden bag and clubs waited on the ground. After gathering everything, he climbed in the truck. His hand moved to the key still in the ignition. He held his breath and turned. The truck came to life. The vehicle made a detour to a waste receptacle. He lobbed the fifth into the trash and began the long road home.

Anxiety had roiled inside their stomachs since that violent afternoon one week ago. The hours crawled by as they waited for her to wake. Each passing minute since the trauma, her chances lessened of being with them ever again.

Father and son stumbled through their days. Order and sanity vacated. If it hadn't been for Trent, the pup outside would have been left to dig for grubs. Inside the cottage, it was not a great deal better. Mealtime occurred only after the child's pleas for food broke through. One day, Manuel fed himself solely from the bag of bread he found on the kitchen table. In the evenings, he cried as Hank sent him gruffly to bed. The usual routine of water, story, and prayers was forgotten. After half an hour of tearful entreaties coming from the bedroom down the hall, Hank would relent and allow Manuel to watch long stretches of television while Hank tuned everything out and withdrew into his head.

Abby dropped by one morning. Hank discovered wet sheets on Manuel's bed. She bent to strip the mattress, but Hank barred the way. He lugged the sheets off the bed and tossed them in the trash. Abby stood politely by. Hank mumbled that Manuel could use his blanket for cover. She tried to intervene, offering to bring Manuel to her house, but Hank seemed not to hear.

At the cabin, the shower had passed. Manuel turned on his sleeping couch toward the bed holding Trent and Abby. Flossie had departed the sill preferring her place behind Abby's bent knees. For a time, Manuel's sight wandered the room or watched the periodic turning of their bodies in sleep. Then he went back to driving a miniature truck over the hills and valleys of his coverlet. He stood up in his makeshift bed to look out the window, straining to see any movement on the other side of greenery between the two houses. The porch light at the side entrance of the cottage endeavored to make it through the natural divider.

The southern part of the lake did not experience the brunt of the storm. It had rained softly, on and off. With everything washed clean, the soothing atmosphere was like the beginning of time. Manuel observed the hemlock by the window. The tree sparkled with water droplets hanging from the end of each branchlet like tiny, crystal ornaments reflecting incandescent shine from across the way and the dots of fire in the heavens. Silver moths flitted back and forth among the gleaming white cup-blossoms of a moonflower vine planted between two wispy stands of rosemary tall enough to touch the sill. Each moth drank his fill of nectar in silence then flew off into the night.

Not long after, still standing, Manuel drove one of his toy cars across the broad windowsill and toward a cigar-box service station. His eyes looked up as two beams of light traveled down the opposite side of Leyland cypress. He heard a truck door close.

It was nearly one in the morning when Hank stepped out of the truck. His eyes turned to the sky that had done its best to ravage him. The clouds had fled, and the stars were in their place again. He headed toward the side porch. The screen door springs squeaked. In the kitchen, he took the water pitcher from the fridge and drank it to bottom. He didn't bother to turn on one light. Like a sick man, he collapsed into his bed. He pulled the sheet close to his face and wished he might capture her fleeting fragrance before forever came.

He lay on his stomach. His outstretched arms and legs formed a giant X filling the bed. Weary beyond anything he had ever known, he started to succumb but was brought back just this side of slumber. He thought he heard a sound. He dismissed it. If anyone lurked in the house in the dead of night, he didn't have the strength to care. His eyes closed again. He slept. A minute later he woke. A tiny hand slid into his larger one. Through the blur of tired eyes, he could see the shining black hair of his son. Compassion filled his chest. He turned on his side. Pulling the child close, he sheltered his son from the world, and then they received their first true rest in days.

CHAPTER FIFTY-TWO

THE RINGING PHONE JARRED Hank awake. Sunlight already dribbled along the boxwood and cobblestones. Manuel still slept. Hank rubbed his lower back as he sat up. He reached for the phone and walked out of the bedroom.

Abby was crying. "Hank. We can't find Manuel."

"It's okay. He's-"

"I got up to go to the bathroom at 6:30. He wasn't in his bed."

"Abby, it's all right. He's here with me."

"Thank the Lord," she warbled and sniffed. "Trent wondered if he might have gone looking for you this morning."

"Uh... well, you know how little kids are up and about with the first crow of the rooster."

"You can't imagine how relieved I am."

"I'm sorry he upset you. I'll have a talk with him. Thanks for keeping him, Abby."

"You're welcome. I promise to do a better job next time. By the way, I'm going to the hospital this morning. Why don't I take Manuel?"

"That'd be good. Remember to have him speak to her. Who knows what she can hear." They said good-bye.

Hank returned to the bedroom and docked the phone. He looked down at his child. He did not like to take him to her bedside. Unbearable pain flooded Hank's senses when the boy studied her face and asked when his mother was going to wake up.

Later, Abby fetched Manuel and he left the cottage wearing one of Hank's childhood shirts like a cloak over his clothes. Pale blue with darker pinstripes making a grid, the shirt skimmed the ground and billowed like Superman's cape. Hank didn't mind the boy's request that suddenly came out of nowhere, but Hank wondered what could be the appeal of his old clothing.

He jogged his memory about the garment given him that second liberating summer at the lake. His grandmother ladylike and genteel bought his first bicycle and taught him to ride. It wasn't long before he was jumping mounds of dirt. By then his favorite blue shirt sported black grease from the chain. Next, the pocket began to flop on one side like the tongue of a hound. Hank, the kid who determined to finally master trees, had risked an initiating climb. She waited below in her double knit dress and sturdy navy heels as though she could catch a ten-year-old boy if he fell. He reached for a limb. The pocket snagged and tore. She didn't lose her smile, and he climbed even higher. For his reward, she let him wear the grimy shirt ten days straight. What became of the bike when she died, he didn't know.

Many years later, Hank and Manuel went looking for Kate's collection of board games that she used to keep inside the living room chest. They stumbled upon a sealed box— baseball cards, a remote control car, the folded shirt were all inside.

On the present morning, months later, Manuel donned the shirt for the first time, looked in the mirror, and let his dimples pop. He raised himself on his toes, lifted his arms to the side, and pumped non-existent biceps. Recalling the scene, Hank allowed his own smile to emerge briefly, like a lake turtle coming up for a snatch of air. Then he sank into a porch chair and looked out until the doorbell rang.

Brian Barton blanched inwardly at the sight of his friend. "I've been calling for two days. Don't you answer your phone?"

"Not lately," said Hank, waving him in. Brian put three deli sandwiches in the refrigerator and talked Hank into a swim. In the heat of mid-day, the water soothed his mistreated body. Brian went inside to phone Trent. Coming out again, Brian carried the sandwiches and drinks to the bottom terrace and to the big, wooden cable spool that served as a picnic table.

Trent made it over, and they sat in folding chairs, eating. When finished, no words came, and the three men let the lake breezes truck over them.

Finally, it was Hank who spoke. "Brian... tell me... why has God done this?"

"Hold on," Trent interrupted. "Seems to me God gets blamed for some terrible things."

"Trent's right," said Brian. "This fallen world is never what God intended."

"But Elizabeth and I weren't the ones who gave up paradise."

"If it had been any one of us in that garden, we'd have done the same thing."

"Why do you say that?"

"Because all of us have done it—believe that other voice instead of God's. And action follows belief. Even so, God's heart is for us. His Son made the way. He can turn our circumstances around for our good."

"How could this ever be for Elizabeth's good?" said Hank.

"I know it's hard to comprehend," said Brian.

Trent's heart ached. He thought of Kenny and how much it hurt. He bent his head down and massaged his eyelids to fight the tears that wanted to come.

"Hank," said Brian, "I don't know why God allowed this trial in your life. I'll do everything in my power to help you through it."

Hank barely whispered, "I don't know how I'll make it without her."

Again the group fell under the spell of a contemplative silence.

Trent's eyes wandered the shoreline. He was thinking of something Doc told him years after he lost his sight and then his wife. 'It's true,' he said, 'We never realize that Jesus is all we need until He is all we have.' Trent let his eyelids fall, and he listened to the water being polished by the wind.

Hank took full advantage of any reclining angle he could exact from his chair. With forearms resting along the flat metal supports, he tilted his head back and watched three crows chasing a sparrow hawk across the sky. Must have been invading their nests, he thought.

He caught Brian's attention. "Can God heal her?"

" 'With God all things are possible.' "

Brian and Trent left. Hank estimated he had an hour before Abby and Manuel's return from the hospital and a visit to the playground at Hobgood Park. Hank sat on the screened porch and thought about the earlier conversation on the dock. He thought about his son and how Manuel was leaning on him, trusting him for what he needed. Hank knew that feeling. He could still recall what it had been like as a child, so dependent, so disappointed. And now, if Hank escaped the present situation, he would generate for Manuel the same lonesome misery Hank had known as a child.

The smell of rosemary chicken and roasting vegetables greeted Manuel and Abby when they entered. The table was set and the house straightened. Hank walked to Manuel and picked him up, telling him how proud he was of his son and how much he loved him. Abby slipped out with a quick goodbye. Her eyes shone bright as she went home to Trent.

From that day forward a routine was set, and Hank did everything to bring stability to Manuel's life. As they waited, they carried on. Hank forced himself to run each day. Their schedule was adhered to like a clock. Hank immersed himself daily in the words that gave him strength, and when moments came, ready to shake them, they remained steady on a foundation of rock.

Weeks passed. Each Sunday they joined the congregation to rejoice in Christ's compassion. During a service in mid-September, Hank's mind drifted briefly as Brian's resonating, solid tones held the congregation. Hank sensed calm filling his chest. He took a deep breath. Regardless of the worst possibilities this world could deal him, he would never be alone, even simply walking this earth. He glanced out the window where the crape myrtles rustled in a breeze, creating a psalm with their pale lavender blooms. It was the same soft shade of a dress she wore.

He was no longer so afraid for himself, and he could love her now with a purer love—one that was based more on his giving than his needing. Finally, he was whole.

CHAPTER FIFTY-THREE

HAMMERING VIBRATED ACROSS THE winter lake. A crew layered shingles on the roof of the classroom where Hank would teach. Cabins and a clinic were complete. A large van with seating for eight waited in the new garage. A running course had been cut through the woods, and an outdoor basketball court would be laid in the spring. Lots of interior work remained to be done, but Hank was thankful for jobs scheduled during the dreary winter months ahead. And he wanted to be ready. The first patient was slated to arrive about the time the redbuds came into bloom and the blue herons returned to fish in the shallows.

Abby and Kristin Arnett stood near the classroom and watched Manuel. He held a dog biscuit and coaxed Arrow to perform a new trick. Year-old cowboy boots no longer flopped but fit securely on the child's legs. Hank and Phil had braced themselves on the roof where they discussed a technical problem. They ended their discussion and came down. The crew followed. Once they reached the ground, they heard a ruckus. Everyone looked toward the cottage.

"Lasso me down! Who's that cowboy brave enough to play with a wolf!" bellowed Carl. He and Diana walked to the compound of buildings.

"Arrow's not a wolf!" Manuel shouted back, laughing.

The Cannons, carrying casseroles and a platter, reached the group. "Why sure he is," said Carl. "Look at those clear, sharp eyes and that strong jaw. Besides, that's not Arrow. Last time I saw him, he was still a pup."

"He grew," spurted Manuel with a grin.

With knowing smiles on their faces, Hank and Phil stood to the side, watching.

"You mean, you grew," said Carl. "Now, this wolf here, it looks like you've tamed him real good." The dog approached Carl who took a step back. "He won't fight me for this food, will he?"

"No," Manuel declared, taken over with giggling. He jumped and rolled in the grass, making Arrow wild with excitement.

"Hm-m-m, let me give him a test," said Carl. Manuel got up from the grass. "Abby, you hold the platter. I'll put a finger up to this wolf's nose. I bet he tries to bite off a chunk." Carl bent low, his back to the crowd. Too late, Manuel raced around trying to get a view.

"Ow!" howled Carl. Manuel froze with a worried "o" for a mouth as Carl hunched over crying. Then he looked at Manuel with a grin and a wink. Pandemonium ensued with Manuel trying his best to spank Carl at Diana's urging.

Trent, standing on the deck next door, called his friends and the five man crew with his boson whistle. Be snappy, he was thinking. Fried chicken stacked high as your chin but even more hungry folks could drop by. And as he liked to say—buttered and straight from the oven, a rolling biscuit gathers no moss. Unfortunately, the statement sometimes made people wonder if they might break a tooth. Trent spied everyone coming up the path, and he raced inside to get fig preserves on the table.

As the day closed, it rapidly grew colder. Manuel and Hank left the cabin and trudged back through the leafless viburnum, over to the cottage covered by early evening shadows. Hank could feel himself falling into an emotional slump. He resisted, going on the offensive by recalling the words that renewed his mind. As soon as they got inside, he turned on music and the Christmas tree lights. The fire warmed the room. Arrow bounced between the furniture, still frisky from the weather, but Hank and Manuel moved without hurry.

The music ended as Hank rinsed shampoo from Manuel's hair. Half a dozen plastic boats surged in the bathtub sea. Hank lathered the washcloth and scrubbed the child's legs.

"Sing the song for me, Manuel. In Spanish. Just like you sang for your mother this morning." The week prior, the children's choir performed the song with Manuel's solo in his native language.

"Sure, Daddy." The lyrics came sweetly as Hank washed the child's back. The boy looked at Hank. "Now, you sing."

Hank's fine voice began,

"Who taught the sun where to stand in the morning?
Who told the ocean you can only come this far?
Who showed the moon where to hide 'til evening?
Whose words alone can catch a falling star?
Well I know my redeemer lives.
I know my redeemer lives.
All creation testify,
This life within me cries,
I know my redeemer lives."

Hank looked into his son's face.

"You think Mama liked it?" asked Manuel.

"While you sang, didn't you notice how her skin seemed warmer, and there was a touch of pink at her lips?"

"I notice I sing in Spanish, and she not get mad."

Hank chuckled. He grabbed a towel and lifted Manuel out of the tub. After drying the boy's hair and putting him in flannel pajamas and warm socks, they moved to the den where Hank placed the child on his lap. Arrow settled near their chair. After two stories, Manuel fell asleep. Soon Hank's eyes closed, and his head came to rest on the high back of the chair while, unseen, the lights on the tree capered around the conical form.

Quiet permeated the room. Occasionally, a needle fell from the fir, and with the tiniest "tap," it landed on the tree skirt. Each time a glass ornament expanded in the heat of a bulb close by, a soft "ping" danced in the air. After an initial "click," warm air running through vents created a muted hum. The lamps cast soft light on restful, sleeping faces. Arrow's nose twitched as he sniffed and ran in the wood hollows of his dream. The evening drew late when the phone on the table by their chair, rang. Manuel's eyes opened. Hank picked up. Faint noises and whispering reached his ear.

"Hello," Hank said.

"Go ahead. It's him," a voice said in the background.

"Hello?" he repeated.

"Good evening, Hank."

His hand holding the phone started to shake. He was afraid to make the words come across his lips. "Who is this?" he finally managed, hoping to hear again those feminine tones.

"This is your brown-eyed girl."

He broke down, and Manuel stared at his father.

"It's really you?" he said into the phone and squeezed Manuel tight.

"Yes. I do not understand. They said I have been asleep a long time. Are you weeping?"

"We'll be there as fast as we can." It was all he could sensibly speak.

"Good. I am ready to come home. I will tell you of a beautiful song I heard while sleeping."